Dear Claudia,

Sangre de Toro

Happy reading :)

Rachael x

Copyright

© 2024 Rachael Adam

All rights reserved. This book or any portion thereof may not be reproduced or used in any manner whatsoever without express written permission except for the use of brief quotations in a book review.

The moral rights of the author have been asserted.

This is a work of fiction. Unless otherwise indicated, all the names, characters, businesses, places, events and incidents in this book are either the product of the author's imagination or used in a fictitious manner. Any resemblance to actual persons, living or dead, or actual events are purely coincidental.

Published in Oxford, United Kingdom

Cover art: Nisha P. Sons – nisha.illustrations@gmail.com

ISBN: 9798861419697

Dedication

For Kelly, you were a very good girl. Hope you're having some nice walkies and playing fetch with your sticks wherever you are.

I still miss you.

--

'The corrida, neither an art, nor a culture, but the torture of a designated victim.'

– Emile Zola

Aficion

You sit in the stands and watch

Yeah, you watch the artist at work, you see it all

And you get your money's worth

Just a day's entertainment for you

An elegant dance

Incredible and thrilling!

A great spectacle

Beautiful, words can't describe!

Oh but they can describe you, here's one.

Sadist.

Chapter 1 – Inhuman Amusement

Pepelito could barely bring himself to take another step. With every move, the sharp stabbing pains in his shoulders got worse. With every breath he became dizzier; none of the air seemed to go into his lungs. The sand was getting into his feet. He was so thirsty.

A couple of metres away, someone in a glittery outfit was holding out a red cape. Pepelito took a few steps forward, then stopped. He put his head down between his legs and felt the pain lessen momentarily. He could not hold it up any more. He was feeling faint; all he wanted to do was go back to his field and eat grass. That life had now become a distant memory.

'Don't you want to charge? Why not, huh?' the man with the cape taunted him, waving the material in front of his tired eyes. A trumpet blared a dramatic tune. Maybe if he somehow chased him away, then all the pain would stop. He could not think about anything else.

He took another step forward, kicking up dust, deafened by the noise of the spectators' wild cheering and clapping. It was hot. Blood dripped through his black coat with each ragged, panting breath. And then he glimpsed the metal glinting in the man's hand.

Something was telling Pepelito not to go near him.

With difficulty, he turned around. Every step was an agony. This place had no escape. The door had disappeared. He was trapped.

He twisted his neck as far as the barbs embedded in his back let him, as the man with the cape came close. From his swaggering posture, his impatient, mocking voice, Pepelito knew he was another guy trying to hurt him. There were so many of them. They all came and went from nowhere.

Somehow, he had to get out.

He took a step backwards, panting.

'Come here, toro,' the man said, clicking his tongue. Pepelito ignored him and forced himself to run. The smell of blood was overpowering. Where were the others? What happened to his friend? Something bad! He pushed past the pain on bleeding feet, his neck feeling like it was on fire as he forced himself to jump, throwing himself at the stands.

As he staggered up the stone steps towards the back of the ring, people started screaming. One man grabbed his tail and tugged it hard. He felt a kick in his side. Someone grabbed one of the sticks in his back and pressed down. He was slipping on his own blood. He couldn't breathe. He had to get to the top. Maybe if he got to the top, he could jump out. Yet, with every step he felt fainter. As he climbed higher up the steps, people backed away in fear and disgust.

It was too high for him to jump from the top of the stands to the street. Everything hurt too much. No help was coming. The horrible guy was coming up the stairs with a huge sword in his hand. The sickly aroma of popcorn mingled with the blood in the air. Who was it from? Probably his own. Trembling, he began to walk backwards down the stairs. Towards the man.

No. He couldn't go near him.

'Javier might finish it off here in the stands. Imagine that! What a finale,' someone said, snatching and twisting his tail. Disorientated, Pepelito looked around. He licked a puddle of melted ice cream on the steps. People gasped. It was the first thing he'd had to drink since yesterday.

'Such emotion and beauty in this corrida. So wonderful,' another man replied breathlessly as they gaped at him. Pepelito stared back, exhausted, not knowing where he was. As he approached their row of seats, the two spectators stood up and backed away, terror on their faces.

But what was this?

A flight of stairs led from the stands to the street below.

And the door stood open.

It hurt so much. Each breath was harder to take. With each movement he was growing weaker. But he had to try. Pepelito launched himself down the stairs towards the street, not looking, not caring what was in his way. His feet weren't designed for the hard concrete floors. His aching hooves scraped against the ground. But he had to run, keep moving, find somewhere safe.

Anywhere was better than *there*.

He could hear human footsteps behind him.

Oh no. There were a few of them. They were shouting. One of them threw a bottle at him. A rope brushed his neck. He couldn't let them catch him. He had to run. A child screamed something from a balcony, shock or excitement he couldn't tell. Something caught on his foot, a stone. He stumbled but couldn't stop running. They'd bring him back.

Despite his agony, he forced himself onwards through the blazing heat. Had he lost them? He looked to the side, flinching, his horns getting in the way of his vision. In too much pain to lift his head, he could hardly keep his nose from scraping the ground. But maybe. Maybe there was somewhere quiet he could rest, could try to get these thorns out or whatever they were. Away from the screaming crowds and the sand.

Away from them.

Pepelito turned a corner down a narrow, cobbled street, fighting to stay on his feet as they slid and skidded on the smooth stones. The gradient became gentler as he reached a midway point. His dripping sides heaved as he stood at the foot of the narrow road. A few metres away was an open door and a green mat that looked like grass. Maybe it was. The men's shouts grew louder in the distance; he couldn't run any more. His legs buckled against the hot concrete.

A woman with black hair came out of the door. She began to shut it and hummed to herself. Pepelito's shoulders tensed. Pain sliced through him again; he let out an involuntary squeal of agony.

'What's going on?' She turned towards the noise and stopped dead; the door remained open.

'Oh. *Oh*. You poor, poor creature.'

Exhausted, he stretched out in the road, dimly aware of her creeping towards him. Her voice softened, sounding shocked rather than terrified, speaking half to herself. 'You're bleeding, poor innocent bull…'

'Where'd he go?' he heard a man bark, several hundred metres above him at the top of the street.

'He must be somewhere down there. Let's get him.' Their sharp tones ripped through Pepelito's ears. Every word promised more horror.

Pepelito ignored the woman's gasp. With strength he didn't have, he scrabbled up and pelted towards her open door, taking heavy, choking breaths. He passed inches from her. His feet caught on the mat as he heaved himself inside. The woman gave a cry. She rushed indoors after him. His hooves skidded and his muscles gave out. He collapsed on the floor halfway down the hall; everything hurt too much to try and get up.

After shutting the door the woman took a few careful steps towards him. She knelt down beside him and patted his side very gently. He barely realised with the stinging stabs in his back, the warm blood pulsing down his neck. 'Evil. How could someone enjoy this? I wish I could take out these darts, they're hurting you so much. But I'm scared of trying, pobrecito. I don't want to hurt you even more.'

'Dios mio,' she whispered. 'What am I going to do with you?'

Chapter 2 – Refuge

'It's so hot. Poor animal, you must be so thirsty.' The woman presented Pepelito with a huge bowl of water. The cool liquid made him more alert, less nauseous, but he couldn't lift his head for more than half a minute at a time. The woman retrieved her phone from her trouser pocket. Pepelito fought to keep his head from sinking into the bowl as he drank.

'Good afternoon. Veterinarios Centrales? Alfonso Cadiz speaking?'

'Alfonso Cadiz? A member of…Veterinary Professionals for the Abolition of Bullfighting? That's you, right?' The woman placed a hand on Pepelito's side. He didn't know what to do. They were a few streets away, yelling and shouting and knocking on doors. He trembled at their voices.

'Yes. Why?' Alfonso's voice was wary.

'This is going to sound crazy. A bull just ran into my house and collapsed on the floor. Who knows how he's managed, but he's obviously escaped from a corrida. He's still got the banderillas stuck in him. Could you help?' the woman said breathlessly.

Heavy rain had started outside. A particularly loud thunderbolt struck the ground somewhere not too far; Pepelito tensed up, then gave a cry as the metal barbs dug deeper. Back home he always took shelter when it rained but it was so, so hot. Running in the sand and on the concrete had burned his feet; the cooler air gave him some relief. He wished he could run out and feel the rain on his skin.

Alfonso's voice sounded angry and distressed. 'I think I can hear him. So cruel. I'll do what I can, but his injuries will be so severe, there's a chance I'll have to put him to sleep.'

'No. That's terrible.' The woman sounded so upset. 'But I guess it's better than the plaza de toros…'

'Well, exactly, and thanks for caring,' Alfonso said. 'I'll be with you shortly. Let's see what we can do. Can I take your name?'

'Rita Silvera.'

'OK, Rita. I'll be with you soon. But be prepared for a sad outcome.' Pepelito lowered his muzzle into the bowl again. The barbed darts dug into his back every time he moved. He tried to ignore them, knocking the bowl against his snout as he drank. Water spilled onto the floor. It felt refreshingly cold. But his tongue and throat felt so dry. He had never been so thirsty. He closed his eyes, trying to think of the fields of grass he could hardly even remember.

*

'Buenas tardes,' a male voice said. Pepelito opened his eyes and scrambled to get up, ignoring the stabbing, searing pain as he retreated further inside. Was this guy going to hurt him like the others?

'He's there, as you can see, he's covered in blood,' Rita said, gesturing behind her. Alfonso took a step into the flat. He had unobtrusive glasses and a short beard. Pepelito leant against the wall and forced himself to stand, flinching in agony as the sticks in his back pressed against the hard surface. It hurt so much to move but lying down was even more dangerous. He had to get ready to run again, but could not bear even the thought of another step.

'This poor animal is suffering so much. It's horrific. How can anyone enjoy such a disgusting spectacle?' Alfonso shut the door and walked over to Pepelito, who was just about managing to lean against Rita's blood-smeared wall.

'Let's see what's happening with you, toro. Well, he can still stand up, so that's a good sign.' Alfonso placed a gloved hand on the bull's shoulder. Pepelito was too tired and defeated to react. His tongue was hanging out. Every part of his body hurt. Every small movement worsened the pain.

'You know, I think he could pull through. I'll give him something to stop the bleeding, and some serious painkillers,' Alfonso said, opening his bag of veterinary equipment.

'Come on. Let's see if we can get these banderillas out, stop them hurting you even more.' Pepelito bellowed in pain and fear as the strange human got close to him. He no longer had any energy to resist or fight.

'Poor boy. I know you're scared. I know it hurts. But you won't even feel this.' Alfonso's voice was reassuring and calming. He took out a syringe and a padded bandage, and put a rope round Pepelito's nose so he couldn't easily move. The bull sank to the floor, weak from the effort of standing, the sounds he could hear growing distant.

'Pobrecito. Where will you take him tonight?' Rita said.

Alfonso crouched beside the black bull and slowly, carefully brought the syringe towards his neck. 'Yeah…I need to discuss that with you. He's lost loads of blood; he needs as little stress and excitement as possible. Ideally, we'd take him into the surgery, then get him to a barn or an isolated area on a farm.'

He took a breath. 'It's really, really not ideal. But he's so hurt, I don't think we can move him humanely; it would be extremely cruel and we might be seen. How would you feel about keeping him here for a while?'

'Here? In my flat? I don't have any outside space. It's not big enough for me, let alone *him*…' Rita stared at Pepelito.

'We can go together to the agricultural wholesaler. I'll show you what to do,' Alfonso said, placing a hand under Pepelito's chin and rubbing it gently. The bull braced for agony that didn't come. Against his instincts, the contact calmed him.

Alfonso's face became sombre. 'Look…they had a real big-name matador there today, Javier Castella. I just saw a video of him talking, to hear him you'd think this is the worst event in the history of humanity. It was meant to be his star moment where he killed six bulls.

11

He only killed one, and today's corrida is cancelled. The plaza is closed. So he and his fans are in a bloodthirsty rage.'

Rita's lip tightened. She gave a small nod. She seemed upset. She'd been kind; Pepelito wanted to walk towards her and comfort her. '*Castella* was there? How in the world could my sister have married that scumbag?'

'He's your sister's husband?' Alfonso said, surprised. Pepelito felt the pain lessening where the vet had injected him. His muscles began to relax. The stabbing sensation in his neck and back no longer overpowered and overwhelmed him.

'Sadly, yes. We don't speak. She stopped speaking to me when I became a vegan. She's as bad as he is.'

'Are your parents still around, what do they think about it?'

'My dad…let's say, he made his feelings known, but he's very old. It's him I feel for the most. My mum just reckons we should get on because we're 'family'. I'm dreading when our parents get too old, Maria won't lift a finger to help but she'll control the finances.' Rita sighed, reached over and touched the bull on the nose.

Pepelito was still afraid, but something was different. He didn't know what was happening. They didn't act like other humans. Why were they so calm and gentle?

'I'm sorry,' Rita said, her voice shaking. 'I don't know why I'm telling you this. And of course I'll help this poor creature.'

'You're a kind person. It's a pity your sister and her husband can't see that animals deserve respect,' Alfonso said. There was a huge bloodstain where Pepelito had leant against the wall. He stared, exhausted, as the vet retrieved antibiotic wipes, stitches and a pair of pliers from his bag.

'Aren't you going to knock him out?' Rita's voice was concerned.

'Ideally, yeah. I've given him a sedative, but as he's a ruminant he won't do well with general anaesthetic. After all this, I don't want him choking.' Alfonso patted Pepelito on the side. 'Do I, eh? Aren't you good?'

'Will he be OK?' Rita asked.

'I hope so. It would make me a very happy man if the bull won for a change.'

Chapter 3 – Anniversary Dinner

'So, Castella's second bull, of Don Gregorio Romero. Pepelito, if I remember correctly. What happened there? All the elements of a great afternoon, and we were deprived, just twenty minutes in.' Henry wore a suit and spoke English in an upper-class accent. After slicing his steak, he put a piece to his lips. He spoke coldly to the man seated next to him but loud enough so the 20 other people at the Taurine Club of Kensington's Anniversary Dinner could hear him.

'Yes. I can't say I remember a prior occurrence like this. Not simply did it escape, it ran away and disappeared altogether! The Spanish police seem rather useless, don't they, Henry?' Seated beside Henry, George Stenton rolled his eyes as he spoke.

Behind Henry was the Stubbs portrait of Lord Stedbury, a distant relation of his, seated on his horse. Henry's chair, like all the others in the room, was ornately carved with cherubs and fleurs-de-lis. Hanging above the door, opposite the huge mahogany dining table, was the head of a stag.

'Yes, useless. I'm sceptical these supposed house to house enquiries exist,' Henry said.

'That bull is from one of the larger, more distinguished bloodlines,' said a third club member, Lord Owenstoft, who owned a grouse moor in Northumberland.

'Yes. It beggars belief that nobody has seen it. Although there is, of course, another possibility. The police might simply not want to retrieve the beast. It's often seemed to me that we at the Taurine Club love Spanish culture far more than the Spanish themselves.' Henry speared one of the carrots on his plate. The Cava on the table had cost 500 Euros. As in his Oxford days, Henry had insisted on paying for it in pound coins and having the cashier count them in front of him. Britannia ruled the waves after all.

'Well, one aspect of Spanish culture, anyway. I don't particularly care for the rest of it,' Lord Owenstoft said. They all laughed.

'I can't drink this rot, George, is this all you Winchester College boys could afford,' Henry said, taking a sip from a slightly less expensive bottle and pursing his lips in disgust.

'You'll have to get used to it, if Labour win the next election.' George laughed. He mentioned this unpleasant possibility far too often for Henry's liking.

The huge oak door creaked open. In strode Javier Castella himself, a friend of the Club and the Guest of Honour at this exclusive gathering of English aficionados. Javier's appearance had been scheduled for months. His cancelled corrida in Valladolid had given it an added urgency.

'My apologies for being late, ladies and gentlemen, my jet could not take off on time, because of the air traffic control strike in Madrid, I haven't managed to buy my way out of that yet,' he said. Everyone laughed and nodded in understanding.

'My wife gives her apologies. She is enjoying a spa day at the Armitage Hotel.' Javier smiled as the five-star establishment's proprietor nodded approvingly, two seats down from Henry. Maria Silvera was a councillor for the People's Party in a small town somewhere in Castile and Leon. Henry could never recall the town's name. It was hardly important in any case.

'Any news about the bull, maestro?' George said. Heavens, he could be annoying, Henry thought. He should make allowances; poor fool was getting there, but didn't have half the self confidence that his own, far superior education had instilled.

'Not yet,' Javier said, laughing. His face darkened as he looked round the room and clenched his fist around an imaginary sword.

On the table was a stack of copies of this month's edition of La Salida, the Taurine Club's glossy magazine. Its front page featured Javier, grinning, next to a dying brown bull. Henry picked it up and started flicking through it until he found his own article, 'The Perfect Corrida'. It had been reprinted in the Spectator, and not for the first time, he congratulated himself on his literary prowess. The style recalled his book, 'The Perils of Regulation – How the Nanny State Holds Back Economic Growth.'

'You're remarkably calm, maestro,' George said to Javier in a sycophantic voice.

Javier nodded. 'Yes. Whoever has him should know – that's when I'm at my most dangerous.'

Henry's great pleasure lay in picturing the bulls in La Salida's full colour photographic spreads replaced by particularly worthless humans. Like that gobshite who ran the Rail, Maritime and Transport Union, constantly on strike like some toy town revolutionary. Or the chairman of the Surrey Conservative Association who'd told Henry not to stand back in 2015, so the Tories could change their image from 'posh' and 'nasty' to something cuddlier. That had set his career back decades. The turncoat had only gone and joined the Lib Dems in the end.

Like his bitch of an ex-wife.

Javier surveyed the room and stared at Henry meaningfully. As the president of the club, Henry tapped his glass with a spoon so Javier could make his speech. It wasn't nice to be someone's skivvy, yet, on these occasions, Henry tolerated it. He was in the presence of an artist; for the last three years, Javier had been ranked as Spain's greatest torero. Henry could think of few so deserving of that honour.

'My friends, like fox hunting and so many other traditional gentleman's pursuits, our common passion at the Taurine Club is often derided as cruel. Animals, we are told, have feelings. Some relish the thought of prohibiting the humble steak and kidney pie, should Labour ever grab the keys to Number 10,' Henry sneered.

'Yet, neither the animals nor their defenders give a stuff about us, the beleaguered enthusiasts of an art that defies imagination. Yesterday, Javier's second bull was crueller than anyone in this room could be, even in the antis' wildest imaginations.' He took a breath. The club's members stared at each other.

'Rather than accepting his fate bravely, the toro fled the scene of battle. What to do with such an unworthy opponent? Javier is here to tell us about it.'

As the group clapped, Javier stood up. 'Thank you, as ever, for that warm welcome. Yes, such a despicable act on the bull's part. Such a shame for me and my team. And most of all, the fans who had spent their hard-earned money hoping for a great spectacle.'

Javier gripped his steak knife and held it out as if he was about to stab someone. Rumours had once existed – completely outrageous, naturally! – about Henry himself thrusting a blade into a particularly obnoxious Green Party councillor. Luckily, before things could escalate, he had paid his man in the Met to make the problem go away.

'Finishing my performance is a matter of pride, and the dignity of my profession. It is an outrage that the bull hasn't been returned. So although I don't wish to ask such a favour of you, I'm asking for your help.' Javier's voice was icy. He wasn't a freeloader on benefits, or trying to cross the channel in a dinghy, so the club's members nodded agreeably; they gladly helped the deserving. And who was more deserving than a man who delighted the mundillo with such extraordinary triumphs?

Whatever it took, the bull would be found.

Chapter 4 – Rita's Apartment

Pepelito scraped himself up slowly with his feet, and cautiously began exploring his surroundings. Under the thick bandages, the pain in his back was less overwhelming. This place was like a small barn except the floor was tiled and hard to walk on. Parts were covered with rolls of plastic. Where was the grass? Thinking about each step, he wandered over to one of the buckets of water Rita had placed at the side of the living room for him, and started drinking greedily.

Once he'd finished, he moved onto a small bale of straw her and Alfonso had hurriedly bought with cash last night, from an agricultural wholesalers. It was too dry, but he could eat it. He was getting back his appetite. They'd put something in his food in that place that made him sick and tasted horrible. And then they'd stopped feeding him at all.

As he swished his tail he knocked a photo of Rita's parents from the table. He walked out of the door and wandered towards the bathroom with its narrow doorway. To enter, he had to make the painful effort to move his head to the side.

Unable to see a way out of the flat, he wanted to leave, but then remembered what was outside.

Rita had filled the bath with water for him. He took a few gulps, brushing the grey and white bathroom counter with his horns and knocking some lipstick and a toilet roll to the floor. A foundation bottle now stood precariously on the edge of the bathroom counter above the toilet.

This place was better than *there*.

But it was weird.

He walked into another room with a large double bed in it, a dressing table and two large, freestanding wooden cupboards. He climbed onto the bed and walked around. It was too soft and felt unsteady. As he walked, some of the wooden slats snapped. He lay down for a bit on the dark grey duvet. It was more comfortable than standing up. His neck was starting to hurt again. He rubbed it on the duvet. The painkiller Alfonso had poured onto his neck and back, a bright blue liquid called Finedyne, came off all over the covers.

After a few minutes, he pulled himself to his feet, trying not to move his head so as not to aggravate the cuts. He had drunk so much water. After doing what he needed to do, he jumped off. Now, in the unlikely event anyone else came here, they'd know it was his territory.

Next to the bedroom was another, smaller room. It was shut; he tried to press down on the handle to open it with his horn. Someone had showed him that trick once on the farm. Nobody was there to hit him here. But touching anything with the tips of his horns was painful. He'd got clumsier; he couldn't use them to feel his way round or judge where he was. It took him several slow, careful attempts before the door opened.

This room was small and dark and Pepelito suddenly felt anxious. He backed away, bellowed loudly, scratched the hard ground, although he'd discovered that wouldn't do any good. As he reversed, his hoof stepped on a light switch attached to a floor lamp. He felt slightly better about going in.

The room had a desk and computer at one end, and a filing cabinet. A wall on one side had a notice board covered with pictures. Each one of the pictures had a number and most of them were grouped. Some of them were of houses, some of them of woodlands, or fields.

But mostly, they were of dead humans.

Pepelito backed away, feeling a sudden inexplicable fear. His leg kicked a brown metal filing cabinet, which toppled and crashed to the ground. Papers and documents spilled onto the floor. He walked backwards out of the study, and backed away towards the living room, narrowly avoiding tipping over a bucket of water. The painkillers had worn off. After drinking, he edged himself behind the sofa and lay down, panting but trying to keep quiet.

A key turned in the lock. Rita walked in. She was shouting at someone. She sounded upset. Suddenly terrified, Pepelito kept still, fearing she would hurt him. He pressed his nose to the floor.

'Absolutely not. You haven't spoken to me since before you married him. Now you call, and your husband's 'career', if you can call it that, is what you talk about!' She slammed the door.

'Oh. Really? Let me tell you something, Maria, I deal with death every day. I investigate murders. That's my job, and now you want me to help your husband find animals to kill!'

Pepelito's body tensed as she flung open the door to the living room. 'Think of our parents? Ha! Good one sis, why didn't you think of Dad when you married a man he hates as much as I do!' She threw the phone onto the sofa, it bounced onto the tarpaulin.

'I'm sorry, toro. Buenas tardes. Did I scare you? You've drunk two buckets. You must have been thirsty.' She walked towards him cautiously, not looking him in the eye. He stood up clumsily, his hind legs backed into the corner, unsteady on his feet and weak from loss of blood.

'What's the world coming to, toro? Teenagers killing a guy in broad daylight in the middle of a park?' She sighed, her eyes turning to a large bottle of Finedyne standing by the door.

'Oh! You need your medication. Alfonso said 18:00, it should have been 2 and a half hours ago – but work… I'm so sorry, pobrecito. I'll call him now.' Rita gulped. She snatched up the phone, got up and walked out of the door towards the bedroom. Moments later, she screamed. His whole body tensed in fear of what would happen next.

'Hello? Yeah fine. I don't know, he's obviously wandered about during the day. He's caused quite a lot of damage – he's peed on my bed! Now he's standing in the corner, I think something's scared him. Maybe he hurt himself, I don't know. OK. See you then.'

Rita came back, sighed and sat down on her sofa, squeaking against the plastic sheeting covering it. She turned the TV remote over in her hands, then lay it aside. No, she wasn't about to hurt him. Pepelito came out of the gap between the sofa and the wall, slowly approaching her.

'Pobrecito,' she said, putting her hand out slowly. 'It's OK.'

A knock at the door interrupted. Rita got up. Pepelito retreated behind the sofa. He felt safer there.

'Hey. Sorry. I only just got in. I'm a cop, and today was such a difficult day at work.' She showed Alfonso inside, picking up the Finedyne bottle.

'You're trying your best. That's all you can do.' Alfonso carried a bag containing bandages and medicines.

'His name's Pepelito apparently, it was on the news. Isn't that sweet?' Rita said.

'Nice name. Hola, Pepelito. Aw, you've been a bit destructive, haven't you? But I'm glad you had a little walk. It'll help you get better.' Alfonso's voice was kind and friendly.

Rita pushed her recliner close to where Pepelito was standing, blocking his exit. It squeaked across the floor. He'd been trapped in other places –

It was so hot. He had been there for hours with no water. It was pitch dark. His horns hurt. Were they bleeding? He pushed at the door but it was locked. His friend Ladron was bellowing. Screaming. He could smell blood. The crowd cheered. Horrible things were happening. Someone was laughing. He was so thirsty and hungry. He just wanted water. Excited shouts and applause ripped through his ears. There was a heavy thud –

Pepelito pushed past Rita's recliner, bellowing furiously as she dived out of the way. He trod on her foot. She let out a shout of shock.

'You OK?' Alfonso said.

'Yeah. I'm good. Thank God I'm wearing steel-capped boots. No way am I getting them off,' Rita gasped. Their laughs scared him. Pepelito had to get out of here. Everything hurt and they were trying to hurt him even more.

'Hey, hey, it's OK.' Rita looked at Alfonso helplessly. She lowered her voice. 'Have you seen all the scars on his body?'

'Yeah. He's scared and he's in pain and he doesn't want to let us near him, he's never known humans to be kind,' Alfonso said. Pepelito walked into the bathroom. The bath was still almost completely full. He gulped down the water in the bath, his neck sore when he held his head at that angle.

'You left the water in the bath all day?' He heard Alfonso laughing.

'I ran the bath…in case he ran out of water and got thirsty while I was at work.' There was a pause. The water tasted weird, not like the water on the farm. It tasted soapy.

'What's funny?' Rita sounded annoyed.

'I think it's lovely. Some people have no compassion for animals at all, and you run a bath in case he got thirsty,' Alfonso laughed.

'Look, um. Why don't we both get some tea and try to tidy up some of this damage? Clean your bed, maybe? Then we can see if he comes to us. He's frightened, and us being stressed is stressing him even more.' Their footsteps retreated from the living room. Pepelito did not understand the words but as he lapped up the water his anxiety began to recede. These humans were weird, unpredictable, but they weren't like the ones he'd escaped.

'That's very kind of you to offer. Thank you,' Rita said. 'If you don't mind.'

'No worries. It's always a bit less daunting if there's someone else there.'

As Pepelito drank, the stabbing sensation in his back intensified. He turned away and laid down on the bathroom tiles, his head between his hooves. He closed his eyes and tried to imagine eating fresh grass again, drinking water from a stream.

*

'Hey, you don't have to be scared,' Alfonso said, sitting beside him and stroking his side. From his bag, the vet took out several bottles of medication, and a padded bandage to replace the one from last night. The disinfectant spray Alfonso gave him stung in Pepelito's wounds but he did not move this time.

'Hello?' Rita's voice came from further down the hallway. 'Is there a suspect in the vicinity? OK. Of course. I'll be there as soon as I can.'

'They shaved the ends of your horns too. What a coward. Couldn't take on a bull his minions hadn't tortured beforehand, could he,' Alfonso said quietly as he applied painkillers to the appendages. He patted him gently but the anger in his voice was palpable. Then he pressed the bandage onto his back. The pain subsided slightly. Pepelito shifted towards him, beginning to relax. Maybe he could trust these two.

'Sorry. Could you let yourself out when you're done with him? I have to go back to work,' Rita said briskly.

'Sure, I think we're almost done. Are you OK?'

'Yeah. Someone's just found a body.'

Chapter 5 – Rita

Would Alfonso's belief in animal rights lead him to mistrust the police? Would he think less of Rita, with how some of her fellow officers had treated protesters? Unsuccessfully, she tried to reassure herself. Surely he wouldn't mind; his priority would be treating an animal in such desperate need. And why was she so worried about his opinion anyway?

What she and Alfonso were doing was both dangerous and illegal. She didn't have many people to confide in. Outside work, she didn't have many friends any more. They had dropped away almost without her realising. She had lost touch with many friends due to the frequent late nights and unsociable shifts. Being a cop separated her from other people, in what they talked about, what they did, even when it was off duty.

She hadn't been at the scene of the murder at the park. But she had to break the news to the victim's parents. His name was Juan Stefano Herran and he had been homeless for a long time. He'd recently got a job and been given a new flat, his life was starting to get on track again. His mum collapsed in on herself and his dad just sat and stared. After her sister's phone call, thoughts of the murdered man's devastated family had brought her to tears. Self-indulgent, she knew, but it was hard not to see the contrast.

Coming home to the destruction Pepelito had caused in her flat almost made her feel better. Seeing what humans could do to each other made her love animals and their innocence even more.

In spite of herself, she smiled.

Rita parked up at the murder scene, a luxury hotel. She hadn't been in trouble with the law in her life, she passed the police exams with flying colours. She had never even had a speeding ticket. Her breath caught in her throat. She imagined the sensational tabloid headlines. 'Detective hid escaped fighting bull in her living room, court hears.'

Smothering the walls and floor with cleaning products to get rid of poor Pepelito's blood last night certainly made her feel like a murderer covering up a crime scene. She thought of his obvious fear tonight, the pleading way he had looked at her yesterday with the terrible barbs stuck in his back. Of course she had helped him, humans were cruel enough to each other so why add to all the misery.

She locked the car and headed to join her colleagues at the AC by Marriott, giving the car a quick glance, to ensure there were no bits of straw, sand, animal hair or grass on the seats. She felt like a criminal.

Technically, she was.

*

The scene at Room 306 was cold and clinical. The victim, a woman in her 50s, had been dead just over 24 hours. She lay under crisp white bedsheets, looked almost peaceful. But this was misleading. There were scratches on her arms. She had clearly put up a fight. Rita pulled back the bedsheets and what she saw made her nauseous. The woman had been stabbed several times in the stomach and was covered in bruises. Yet, the sheets and the clothes she was wearing were entirely free of blood.

'Any ID?' Rita asked Jesús Garcia Dominguez. An approachable man with a handlebar moustache, he was her closest friend and a man she'd worked with 15 years.

'Yeah, British national from Edinburgh called Caroline McKenzie. 52 years old. She was the UK director of a retailer specialising in air conditioning units, washing machines, that sort of thing. Had a meeting with her Spanish counterpart her first day here. Aside from that, she was here for a 3-week holiday. She was meant to visit her son in Barcelona, but never turned up, so he rang the hotel. She was meant to check out today, but never did. Had a train ticket but never got on.'

This was different to the murder in the park, whose suspects were currently sat in the cells, telling everything to her colleagues. All murders were unpleasant, sad and squalid in their own ways.

But this scene bothered her. It made no sense.

Unlike Juan Stefano, the woman lying in front of them clearly had money. She was a company director who had flown first class from the UK for a 3 week holiday, and booked an expensive hotel. She had planned to go and travel around and visit her son. After only two days, she was killed.

'We'll need confirmation on this but the time of death looks like it was between 17:00 and 19:00 yesterday. She never checked out, and her son rang the hotel because she was meant to get an early train and meet him at 10 today, and she didn't show up,' Dominguez said. 19:00, Rita thought. She'd found Pepelito around 18:00. A sickening thought emerged, but she pushed it away.

'Either the killer deserves a Nobel Prize for cleaning up the scene, or she wasn't killed here,' Rita said.

'Yeah, doesn't look like it,' Dominguez said, gesturing to the Luminol on the walls, which showed no traces of blood at all. What would her own house look like? To her horror, they'd missed a bit last night; some of the lower part of the wall looked like a butcher's shop. Rita took another look at Caroline. Her other clothes were being bagged up and taken as evidence. Crime scene tape surrounded the door. She had a brief look in the bathroom. It looked pristine.

Rita stepped away from the bedroom and into the corridor. Dominguez followed her. 'Is everything OK? You look like shit if you don't mind me saying.'

'I could say the same thing, Jesús. I'm OK, my life's the usual chaotic mess it always is,' she sighed. Dominguez had been one of the arresting officers on the scene of the Juan Stefano murder today. His usually tanned complexion was pale and his arm was shaking.

'Get some rest, eh. I'll see you tomorrow,' she said.

She walked down to the hotel reception, marched up to the desk and said, 'I need a list of your staff, and everyone who was a guest at the hotel yesterday evening. Plus anyone who may have had access to the area, maintenance companies and so on.'

The woman at the check in desk was clearly in her teens or early 20s but looked as though she was about 12.

'S – sure. Let me get them for you.' From her stiff, shaky demeanour, Rita knew this girl was on the edge of a panic attack. Her first job had been in a hotel; she gave the girl a sympathetic smile, she couldn't imagine how she would be feeling.

After Rita had got the papers and thanked the receptionist she approached Caroline's son Iain. He was sitting on a new and very uncomfortable looking leather chair in the lobby, one of those expensive ones with no back.

'I'm so sorry,' she said in English, holding out her hand.

'Thanks,' he said in a slight Scottish accent. He wasn't crying but he looked stunned. Lost. 'It's just a complete shock really. Mum had been planning this trip for ages. And when I couldn't get hold of her and she didn't turn up – well. It wasn't like her. She's a career woman and always taught us to be punctual. She's a great person. Me and her and my brother, we went to Morocco last year, she was strict when we were kids but now, she's – sorry. She *was…*'

His voice cracked. She laid a hand on his. 'It's OK.'

'Will you find who did this?'

'We'll try.' She took a deep breath. 'Did your mum know anyone else in Spain besides you? Was she meeting anyone else here?'

'My mum spoke Spanish better than me and I've been in Barcelona for 2 years. She had loads of friends here, she said something about meeting people here, yeah.' Iain looked towards the staircase where more police officers were coming down the stairs.

'Would you be able to give us any names?' she said gently. Iain shook his head.

'She said something, but I can't remember. She's just – she's only just died, I…' He was staring into the distance.

'It's OK.' Outside it was now completely dark. She thought momentarily of poor, battered, innocent Pepelito, with his straw bale in front of the TV. Did he still have enough water? Was he OK?

'I do remember something yeah, Mum's animal crazy, especially dogs, her and her partner have got four dogs at home, all rescues, he looks after them when she's away on business. She was going to see about adopting an ex-hunting dog from a rescue somewhere around here, in Villafrechos. She said she'd spoken to some woman about it on Facebook called Raquel or something like that.' A chill went down Rita's spine. She felt a kinship with the dead woman. A fellow animal lover.

'I don't think Mum's even met this woman. She said she was meeting her tomorrow, or trying to, I don't know if she'd arranged it or just wanted to see if she could. I'm sure it's not – I'm sorry I couldn't be any more help…' Iain shook his head.

'You've been fine. Here's my card. Inspectora Rita Silvera Delgado, Policia Nacional. Call me if you think of anything else.' Sometimes Rita felt like an impostor. This was one of these times. His mother might have been a different story, but would he really trust her professionalism if he knew a bull was hidden in her house?

'Rita?' Iain said. 'Can I call you that?'

Rita turned back to him.

'You're going to catch this guy? Aren't you?'

Chapter 6 – Sleepless

Rita returned home around midnight. She unlocked the door slowly and cautiously, before taking off her shoes and trying not to make a sound. Despite his sweet nature, Pepelito was a big and severely traumatised animal.

Coming up to just below shoulder height, he could seriously injure her, especially if he was scared – and earlier, she'd frightened him.

She edged open the door and walked into the low light of her apartment. Pepelito filled the doorway leading to the bathroom, fast asleep after the evening's excitement. Weirdly, having him nearby made her feel safer and less alone. He almost reminded her of her poor old cat Gloria who had died six months ago – another rescued animal.

He was half lying on an old duvet Rita had found as she was getting ready to leave, and thrown on the floor. So instead of getting her makeup off in the bathroom she went straight to her room and took the tarpaulins off the now clean, but mildly damaged bed. She thought about Caroline McKenzie lying undiscovered in the hotel room and felt indescribably sad. To make the situation even more frustrating, the hotel's smart CCTV cameras were downloading an update at the time of the murder, so the police couldn't use any footage.

Rita peeled off her socks. Thank God for waterproof mattress protectors, she thought. Lying on the bed checking her phone, she saw she had several messages, mostly from work. Tomorrow morning, she was going to Villafrechos with Dominguez to interview Raquel Carlos, then visiting the business contact. She questioned whether she'd receive any useful information, but it helped build up a picture of the victim's life. Who her friends were, what she was passionate about.

Scrolling down, she saw she also had a message from her mother. Her heart sank.

'I know you don't like what Javier does for a living, but can you not put that aside for the sake of your sister and take the opportunity for a reconciliation! Soon me and your dad will be gone, and she's the only family you've got – I can't believe how selfish you are!' the message said. Rita clenched her teeth in rage. Her mum didn't have any idea. When was the last time the woman had cared about what was happening in her job, except to moan how 'you could never find a policeman when you needed one these days'?

Like she ever needed one.

'Sorry, I cannot put my differences aside with someone who married such a cruel man. She only got back in touch with me because she wants me to help him find that poor bull. Over my dead body!' Rita wrote. Her finger hovered on the send button. Tears came to her eyes. In the end, she decided not to send it. She deleted both messages, lay back on the bed and tried to stop herself crying.

After several minutes she sat up. Pepelito was still sleeping; he opened one eye then shut it again. Rita crept forward and took a picture of him, knowing it was a bad idea, having it on her phone. She'd have to delete it.

But he looked so sweet.

She had to show someone.

It was past 1am. Why was she doing this? Alfonso would be asleep. He didn't have fucked up sleep and late nights like she did. Besides, it was a crazy thing to do. She was being silly. She'd annoy him. But Rita couldn't stop herself. She texted him the photo as a disappearing message on WhatsApp.

Within a minute he replied. 'Aw. He looks so peaceful after causing such chaos :)'

'He's a sweetheart,' Rita texted back. 'I wasn't expecting you to reply so quickly. Can't you sleep?'

'Not really, if I'm honest.'

'Sorry to hear that. Tonight was absolutely grim. A tourist found murdered in a hotel.' Pepelito had got up. He walked into the room, started sniffing the bed and a wooden table with Rita's makeup on it, knocking an eyeliner pencil to the floor. She'd pick it up tomorrow. He had to pause every so often and had trouble lifting his head. Seeing him struggling filled her with pity and rage.

When Rita joined the police, Dominguez and the others had mocked her mercilessly for being a vegan, but now they kind of got it. The world was brutal enough, and she saw the worst side of human nature in her job. Castella had inflicted such pain. How could she possibly help him?

'How are you, torito?' she said, stretching her hand out to the black bull as he wandered around. He let her pet his nose briefly before retreating, his steps heavy but delicate. As he did so, Rita saw Alfonso had sent her another text. Her eyes were closing. Before the murder, tomorrow had supposedly been her day off. She'd have to leave going anywhere near the bathroom until she was properly awake.

'Can I ask you a question?' Alfonso had written. Rita hated that question. He couldn't be asking *that*. Surely? He didn't seem that kind of guy. She barely knew him. They couldn't have met in weirder circumstances. But part of her wished he would.

'?' she sent.

'The tourist, are you allowed to say what their name was?'

'Not all of the family know, so, no.' Rita wrote back, ready to drift off. The lengthy, agonising pause prevented her.

'OK. I had plans to meet an online friend from Scotland who was in town last night. We had originally planned to meet at 20.30, but after your call, that didn't happen :) I texted her to ask if we could rearrange, and she didn't reply. Usually, she's very prompt in replying but now she isn't at all.' Rita sat up in bed, propped herself up with her pillows. She watched Pepelito standing by the dressing table, swatting a lone fly away with his tail. Stupidly, a tiny part of her felt slightly jealous of this unknown friend.

'It's really odd. We talk a lot and she's not been online at all. It might seem strange but she's happily married and we're just good friends. A couple of her Facebook friends messaged me saying they were worried too.' The air froze in an instant. Rita read Alfonso's latest text and put the phone face down on the bed, not knowing how to respond.

Seeming to sense her distress, Pepelito walked over to the side of the bed, and started licking her arm with his huge tongue. Rita rubbed her hand into his rough coat and he didn't back away. As she gulped back tears, the bull stood beside the bed next to her, and she was grateful for the presence of the animal. She thought of how Gloria would jump on her lap when she was sad, and laughed. Hopefully Pepelito wouldn't attempt anything similar.

'Did someone report her missing?' Rita wrote to Alfonso, already knowing the answer.

'Yeah they did. Her name's Caroline McKenzie. Have you heard anything?'

Chapter 7 – The Breakup

Pepelito was lying in the living room with his head on an old beanbag when someone knocked on Rita's door. One of his horns had pierced the beanbag and a small number of polystyrene balls had spilled onto the floor. Out of curiosity, he started pushing some of them around with his nose to see if they moved on their own. He hauled himself unsteadily to his feet as Rita shut the door to the living room. 'My partner's coming to pick me up. Can you be good and stay here, I'll let you out in a bit?'

He missed the farm's green fields, the fresh grass underneath his feet. The floor was hard to walk on and he often skidded around. Being in a small room alone or with only humans for company was frightening. He missed his friends. What happened to them?

'Morning, Jesús, you're here early,' Rita said. Pepelito smelt that it was raining outside as heavy footsteps walked into the house. This place was a sort of nest for Rita, she ate and even slept here. Knowing this calmed him around her. Her visitors were different.

'What's all this straw on the ground, you keeping rabbits or something, Rita?' Dominguez chuckled with a deep voice. Pepelito was nervous of men; almost every time he saw one he was trying to hurt him. Cigarette smoke drifted into the room, bringing back terrible memories. He walked over to the bucket of water by the TV and lapped at it, hoping Dominguez wouldn't come in.

'Oh dear, yeah sorry, looking after my neighbour's giant rabbit for a week,' Rita laughed from behind the door. 'I'd show you, but he's a rescue and frightened of people.'

'You sure it's just a rabbit there? Nothing bigger, like that bull that's gone walkabout? Me and Flavia were saying, if anyone at work was going to hide it, it would be you,' Dominguez said, laughing.

'A bull? Shut up, I'm not that daft. Do you think I could fit a bull in a flat as small as this?' Rita laughed. Pepelito walked over to the door and scratched at it, pushed down the handle with his horn like he did before. Frustratingly it didn't open. It scared him. Were they going to take him somewhere else?

'What's that stain on the wall? Did you finally murder your brother-in-law?' He heard Rita's shoes spinning round. She gasped in shock.

'No. I hurt myself quite badly a while back on some broken glass, when I dropped that old laptop a few months ago, the glass shattered and I slipped, then I grabbed onto the wall. I cleaned it up but couldn't entirely get the stain out.'

'I don't remember that. If you say so.'

'Well – ' Rita's voice had a note of desperation in it.

'I'm joking. Sounds painful, you OK?' Dominguez said, slurping his coffee.

'Oh yeah, I'm fine.'

'Come, let's find this Raquel or whatever her name is. Whoa, what have you got in there? Must be a big rabbit.'

Their voices became indistinct as the front door closed. Then, from the street, Rita said, 'Wait there. I need to check I turned the stove off.'

Pepelito heard her sprinting back to the house and twisting a key to unlock the living room door.

'Be good, toro.' Then she darted out again, slamming the front door firmly behind her.

****

'You're awfully quiet, Rita.' Dominguez rolled the window of his car down and lit a cigarette. A large cross hung in his car window, saying 'What would Jesus Do?', a souvenir from a trip to America.

Rita leant back in the car seat. 'My sister called me last night. After not being in contact for about 10 years.'

Dominguez snorted. 'I bet that went as well as could be expected. I couldn't get her arsehole husband off the phone yesterday.'

'I told her I had murders to solve and wasn't going to help him find animals to kill, especially not in my spare time,' Rita said, more forcefully than she intended. Glancing down, she realised a bit of manure was stuck to her shoe. Panic rose in her. Could you teach a cow to use a litter tray? How would you do it? Would Alfonso know?

'Sometimes I ask myself, why on earth did you become a cop, Rita?' Dominguez laughed. 'Why didn't you work for, I don't know, a donkey sanctuary?'

'I failed the application to get into vet school,' Rita said as they turned a corner, narrowly missing a red light.

'Know what I could do with right now?' Dominguez said darkly. 'A cold beer and a huge piece of steak.'

'It's 8 in the morning, Jesús,' Rita said in mock reproach, but the edge to his voice told her it wasn't just his usual banter.

'Don't care. I haven't eaten since yesterday. Got home last night to find Luis had changed all the locks and thrown my stuff outside,' Dominguez said, a bitter tone to his voice.

'Don't say anything. It's fine. Think missing our anniversary meal out to interrogate the scum who did Juan Stefano in was the last straw for him.' Dominguez sighed deeply and pressed his foot down on the accelerator, heading for Villafrechos. Rita felt stunned and a little guilty. Dominguez was her best friend. He had put her up during her divorce from her ex when she had nowhere else to go; long before he had moved in with Luis, she had spent several weeks on his sofa. What if he needed her to repay the favour? Her stomach lurched.

'I'm only dating blue on blue from now on,' he growled, as they turned off down a dirt track outside the town, towards a small farmhouse.

*

After about 10 minutes of knocking, Raquel Carlos answered the door, a dressing gown and a bath towel on her head. When she opened the door, two Alsatians, a galgo and a small long-haired terrier came pelting out.

'Are you here about adopting Arabela, you're early, it's not even 8.30, I thought you were coming at 10?' she said. Rita flashed her warrant card.

'Raquel Carlos?' Rita said, watching the woman's eyes go wide with shock. 'Rita Silvera, Policia Nacional.'

'What…do you want,' she mumbled. Rita noticed two or three marijuana plants growing outside, and several more visible in pots in the upstairs window.

'We're not interested in those,' Dominguez said, waving a hand as they entered. The house was huge. The scent of weed mingled with the odour of wet dog. A yellow Labrador bounded towards them and leapt onto Rita. She stroked him and took his paws in her hands to get him down.

'Yes, yes, you're a good boy,' Rita said as the dog licked her hand. Dominguez looked vaguely horrified. The yellow Labrador proceeded to sniff her all over, but left Dominguez alone. Dogs always did this. Surely nobody would think anything of it. But the Labrador's behaviour unnerved her. Was the scent *this* noticeable?

'What's this about? Um – can I get changed? I just came out the shower.' Raquel's face was red.

'Sure, take all the time you need. We'll be in here,' Rita said, walking to the kitchen. She and Dominguez sat down at a white plastic table. The kitchen was large and airy. Inspirational quotes and framed pawprints hung on the walls. At the opposite end to where they were sitting were 10 or 12 food bowls for Raquel's good boys and girls.

'Are you sure you didn't just bring us here to see some dogs?' Dominguez said under his breath.

'I'm saying nothing,' Rita said. She sat in silence and looked around the room. More weed plants were growing in tubs by the sink. Dominguez was eyeing them, almost tempted.

'That's personal use,' Raquel said hurriedly as she walked back in, dressed in tracksuit bottoms.

'As my colleague mentioned, we're not here about that. We're here about Caroline McKenzie. What can you tell us about her?' Rita said.

'Caroline? What about her?' Raquel said in surprise. A huge staffie pushed past and started wolfing down food.

'I know you two were friends, or at least online acquaintances. Her body was found last night, she was murdered two days ago.'

Raquel's mouth dropped open. Alarmed, she looked towards the yellow Labrador for comfort. He trotted towards her, wagging his tail.

'I've never known anyone that's been murdered.' Raquel's face crumpled, as if she was going to cry.

'We're trying to put together a picture of what she was like. What did you two talk about?' Rita said gently. It didn't matter that Raquel only knew her online; the news was profoundly shocking and Rita would have to tread cautiously.

'Talk about? Dogs, mostly, she wanted to adopt one of our rescues, she was going to come here today and meet them all,' Raquel said, blinking back tears, as if the question confused her.

'We know she had friends in Spain, but did she ever mention any exes or anyone she'd been romantically involved with?' Rita said. Dominguez flinched when she asked that question.

'No. I don't know. We didn't talk about that stuff.'

'She was attending business meetings while in Valladolid. Did she ever mention problems at work? Maybe someone was jealous?' Dominguez said. Raquel took a gulp of a glass of water on the table.

'I don't know about anything like that, she didn't talk about it,' Raquel said, shaking her head, looking distressed and pale.

'You said you met on Facebook. Sometimes online arguments can get out of control, had she recently had a disagreement with anyone?' Rita thought of what Alfonso had said about knowing Caroline online, feeling uneasy, almost guilty. Raquel shook her head quickly. Maybe a little too quickly?

'No, no. I don't think she ever argued with anyone. She wasn't that type of person. We just talked about animal rescues.' Raquel put the glass of water to her lips and drank most of it, wiping a tear from her face.

'Is there any reason you can think of why someone might have wanted to harm her?' Rita said. Raquel looked at her, saying nothing, and shuddered. She put the glass down heavily and pushed it away, looking as if she was going to be sick. The staffie stood by her chair with a mournful expression.

'She did get in an argument online, but it was like a year ago. I can't even remember it. I think it was about politics. Fuck. This is awful.'

'Do you remember who it was with?'

'No, sorry,' Raquel said. 'I don't remember the name. There was a scandal with some politician. I think it was that. I don't read the news, I've got no idea. But surely – surely nobody would have followed her here on holiday and killed her just because of that...'

'You'd be surprised,' Dominguez said.

*

'We need to get on the victim's online activities. Raquel's holding something back,' Rita said as they got back into the car. She would know – so was she. She looked at her phone and saw she had a message from Alfonso. She tried to figure out the intention of the message. He'd sent her a photo of a ginger goat with a long brown beard and amber eyes. 'This is Dolores, I'm checking up on her today. How's our patient this morning?'

'How's our patient doing this morning?' the message said.

'He's good,' she quickly replied as Dominguez slumped into the driver's seat. 'Hope you're feeling a bit better.'

'Yeah, just a terrible shock,' he replied. She put her phone away and stared out the window.

'Who's that?' Dominguez said, looking over her shoulder.

'Some guy I know,' Rita said. 'Kind of a long story. I'll tell you over a beer some time.'

As an afterthought she added, 'Jesús? Have you got somewhere to crash tonight?'

'Staying in a hostel tonight and tomorrow. After that, I don't know. Maybe I should try and work it out with Luis.' Rita's heart pounded in her chest. Her shoulders froze as she anticipated his next question.

'Hopefully it won't come to that but I might ask if you can put me up for a while.' He'd more than done the same for her, more than once. Surely he'd have her back; he was no stranger to outright breaking the law to get results. When they finally put Castella inside, it'd be a great story for Dominguez to dine out on. *Remember that bull that ran out of Castella's corrida and disappeared? Rita had him wandering around in her flat! Almost got gored in the arse whenever I took a shower!*

But he was still a cop. They worked together. It was stupid to think telling him was totally risk-free.

Rita took a deep breath. Dominguez would find somewhere to go after the hostel. But they were best mates. She had to offer. 'Sure, you can crash at mine, you know that, Jesús. It's chaotic, though. With the rabbit.'

'Yeah. That might be good, providing you let me cook real meat in your kitchen.'

Chapter 8 – Trolls

Henry's Surrey country mansion, worth over ten million, was owned through a series of complex financial arrangements. He sat at a desk in his study, the walls covered with vintage posters advertising the great corridas of the past. Although electronic wizardry could never replicate the real thing, he often rewatched the most electrifying spectacles from his extensive video collection.

He had not looked at any news since arriving home for the Taurine Club's Anniversary Dinner, but curiosity now seized him. He had to know. He opened the Tor browser on his computer and searched for Caroline McKenzie.

Had they found her yet?

They had.

'Appliances2U director found murdered in Spanish hotel' from the Guardian. He clicked on it, hoping the lefty rag would provide salacious details. None were forthcoming; maybe they thought giving descriptions of the modus operandi would trigger their readers. Just how old she was, a bit about her job and a statement from her family – 'gutted', obviously.

He went down the list of articles. Then he saw one from the BBC. 'Murdered director planned to open dog rescue.' The license fee was working well!

Clicking idly, Henry read on. The woman's sons spoke of her passionate love for man's best friend. With her small fortune, they'd resolved to set up a foundation to look after abandoned dogs; it was what she would have wanted. Dogs! Sometimes it appeared to Henry that he was witnessing the decay of Western civilisation. Doubtless, their friends and family would congratulate them on such a 'lovely thing to do'.

Maybe the Daily Telegraph could give a more balanced perspective. But even here the coverage was strangely biased, with a statement from the CEO of the company she worked for on how she was 'not just a colleague but a friend.' As if the writer was trying to indoctrinate him into thinking this supposed CEO was a model of good business sense.

He closed the tab hastily at his housekeeper's footsteps upstairs. An Englishman's home was his castle. But the authoritarian reach of the nanny state extended everywhere. Many jealous members of 'the lower orders' simply wanted to tear down people like him, and constantly looked for dirt. He didn't want to give the peasants any ammunition. Thus, the Caroline McKenzie searches were erased. Without Javier's opponent, her destiny may have been rather different.

What had become of that bull, anyway? Henry had been inches from the ill-bred creature's face as it barged up the steps, snorting and panting rather than willingly facing its elegant end. He had given it a good shove, grabbed its tail and kicked it hard, to no avail. The bull had fled like a deserter in the war. It was utterly unworthy of Javier's genius and delicate grace. Henry had known that as soon as it emerged.

'Mystery of Spanish bull's disappearance deepens,' said one article. At the top of the page was a photo of the animal, its black shoulders dripping with blood. Someone must have seen where it went. Surely. The Spanish police were even more useless than their reputation suggested. The hot weather obviously made them lazy.

'While the bull's escape is unfortunate, police resources are stretched, with two brutal murders, a break-in at a school and a suspicious fire. As the bull is not loose and there appears no further danger to the public, serious crimes have to take priority,' said Superintendent Gabriel Sanchez of the Policia Nacional. To Gabriel Sanchez, harbouring an escaped fighting bull – from one of Spain's top ranches, no less – obviously wasn't a serious crime!

High time for Henry to do some investigation of his own.

He went onto YouTube and searched for 'Escaped bull in Valladolid full video'. Within seconds he had found it. An inspired aficionado had put the whole thing online. It was 45 minutes long. Henry leaned back and watched the first bull, Ladron, an altogether better-quality beast. How enjoyable that had been! Castella had treated the audience to a fine show. He watched the performance several more times. If only all six could have ended so superbly.

Then there was Pepelito. From the start, the bull had not lived up to expectations. Nonetheless, Henry watched each 'tercio' three or four times, slowing down the video as Pepelito charged at the mounted picador, and as first Castella's assistants, then the man himself placed the banderillas. Such a pleasure to see, as always with this extraordinary talent.

Then everything went wrong.

Unlike Ladron, Pepelito had not approached Castella at all. He stood panting for several minutes, as if he didn't know what was expected of him. When he finally charged, it was in the opposite direction, leaping into the stands. Henry smiled as he watched himself kicking Pepelito in the video. It had felt good to give the cowardly creature some extra punishment. This balanced the scales; typically, it was the army of online harassers from Labour and the SNP who dealt Henry the harshest blows.

Like Caroline McKenzie.

He ground his teeth, replaying that moment when the unthinkable happened. Pepelito reached the top of the stone steps. Javier Castella was now approaching sword in hand. Henry paused the video again and zoomed in on the now wide open door to the bullring, then rewound it to his own appearance. Just as Pepelito dodged him, a security guard strolled up the stairs from the entrance.

Had *he* opened the door?

Henry then watched as Pepelito ran down the stairs, robbing Javier of his triumph. The person shooting the video ran to the top row of seats in the bullring and looked into the street behind him, following for a while before the bloodied bull disappeared from view. Moments later, Pepelito appeared again, but then turned round a corner out of sight, and the video cut off.

Thousands of comments lay beneath. Henry translated the page into English so he could read all the Spanish ones. One translated comment said, 'hahahahahahahaha this is the best thing I've ever seen, pity he didn't take out a few sickos on his way to freedom.'

In the name of kindness to animals, this anonymous keyboard warrior wished him a bloody, painful death!

Just who was the real 'sicko' here?

He looked further down the comments until he found one in English. 'Well done brave Pepelito ♡ so glad you got away from those monsters.'

Monsters? Henry thought indignantly. This lack of cultural appreciation could never be blamed on him; education had never been his brief. In any case, Henry was proud not to have paid any tax for the last 15 years. It was nothing more than theft, and probably socialism.

He continued scrolling down the YouTube comments. Honourable interventions aside, most showed a shocking lack of appreciation for the art of *toreo*. He had several text messages from the Tory WhatsApp group, but ignored those. He bunched his fists with rage as he read further, eyes turning to a penknife on his desk.

'30:56 the guy pulling the bull's tail is a British politician – Henry Dixon.' Outraged, Henry braced himself to read the 106 replies it had gained – many from former constituents. Thank heavens he was in the House of Lords. He'd never have to fight an election again.

'Scumbag. He used to be my MP and he was utterly useless!'

'Omg so cruel ♡ there is something wrong with him.'

'Shame it couldn't of gored him :('

44

Outrageously, this last comment had 501 likes. Henry went to see who had made it – someone called 'angel2004'. A minute on Google revealed the culprit as an 18-year-old near Leeds called Aidan Donnelly, who worked in a gaming shop. Henry wrote the name in a leather-bound notebook given him by the Prime Minister. Where were his parents, hadn't they taught him to respect his betters?

Henry rewound the video until he found the part with the security guard, took a screenshot of his face and saved it. While the Spanish were generally tanned, the guard's skin colour was of an altogether darker hue. *He'd* probably have let a dangerous bull escape deliberately.

Then, he looked at his phone. He had messages from one of the other Tories in his WhatsApp group. 'Hi, Henry, I've just seen a video of you which puts you in a somewhat controversial light. You might want to be prepared when you go on Newsnight tonight.'

Henry laughed. Not if the BBC want to keep their funding, he thought. But then someone rung his mobile.

'Mr Dixon, my name's Robyn, I'm a reporter from the Daily Mirror.' *Mr* Dixon?

'That's *Lord* Dixon,' he snarled. 'Is it so hard to address me by my proper title?'

Where had she – if it was a she, you never knew these days – got his number from anyway?

'Mr Dixon, a video has emerged of you appearing to mistreat an animal while on holiday in Spain, have you got anything to say about that?'

'Nothing at all,' Henry said. 'I was participating in local culture, the way you woke types say we Brits should do when we go to the EU.'

He hung up, then recorded Robyn's name in a separate page in his notebook. It was 11.30 in the morning; too early for calls from liberal snowflakes. He could relax for an hour before the grouse shoot, with some old boys from Eton who'd gone on to enjoy distinguished careers in politics, finance and the arts.

His attention turned back to the YouTube video. Fresh comments had been added since he had viewed the page, many libellous. After wishing further gorings on those with a healthy appreciation of the Spanish bullfight, 'angel2004' had even suggested his hard drive be searched for snuff movies. A shudder passed through Henry at the mere thought, however implausible such fantasies were.

He'd make sure the little scrote wouldn't get away with that.

Chapter 9 – 2,000,000 Euros

'He's recovering well,' Alfonso said to Rita after giving Pepelito his painkillers. Staring warily at him, Pepelito saw the man had brought fresh grass and some carrots, which he placed in front of the television. He edged forward and ate them. Sometimes his muscle injuries made eating hard to face, but he was starting to get his appetite back.

He walked towards the front door, wishing he could leave but scared of what was out there. He missed the outside, the sun warming his back, grass that didn't go dry if he left it a while. This place was too small. Rita was out most of the day and being alone made him sad and scared.

Most of all, he missed the others. He thought of the friend he had met in one of the trucks, and got to know while stuck in the enclosure.

Ladron was big and brown, with huge horns. Pepelito saw one of the ends was bleeding where they'd filed it down. He walked over to Ladron over the bare ground and licked him, standing close as he lay down. Up close, Pepelito could see he was crying. He lay down beside Ladron and licked him around his face. Something hard hit him in the back. He looked around to see where it had come from.

'Stop that.' Pepelito felt a sharp prod in his back.

'This one doesn't know where he is,' the man laughed as Pepelito looked around him, confused. After a moment, he licked at the hair behind Ladron's horns again.

'Look how soft he is. No ferocity at all.'

'Don't do that. Bad.' Something sharp hit him hard in the back again, stinging him. He got up and walked towards the other five bulls. He was nervous of them. One of them had tried to fight with him.

Ladron looked at him imploringly. Pepelito told him he'd be back.

Feeling sad, he thought of how Ladron had given him grateful licks when he came back, sure the men had gone home. They had laid side by side on the bare ground, and calmed each other down.

'I think he wants to go outside,' Rita said sadly. Alfonso sighed.

'He needs to yeah, it's cruel to keep a big animal like a bull in this sort of space for too long. The problem is, he's now famous, and even more valuable than before. These taurinos will be desperate for their 'triumph', Castella especially,' Alfonso said. Pepelito didn't understand how, but somehow, he knew the man was helping him.

'Yeah, I see him looking at the door,' Rita said. 'I think he's sad.'

'Yeah, I think he is, and he needs company,' Alfonso said, holding out a clump of grass in his hand. Pepelito carefully took it and ate it.

'A friend from work might have to sleep in my spare room for a week or so. I know, I know. But I am pretty sure I can trust this guy. I've known him for 15 years.' As Rita spoke Pepelito wandered off into the kitchen. He nudged one of the bread rolls Alfonso had bought himself off the table with his nose and picked it up, before swallowing it whole. There was a bunch of grapes too. He liked grapes, so he ate the entire thing including the stalk.

'It's not like that. He's gay,' Rita said quickly. Pepelito couldn't understand but his hearing was much better than most humans'. He could hear everything through the thin walls.

'It doesn't matter – him staying is not ideal, given the situation, is it,' Alfonso said quietly, and both humans gave forced, nervous laughs. Rita seemed stressed; Pepelito wondered what she was stressed about. He wandered over to a silver fridge in the corner, as tall as the ceiling. He had seen Rita taking things out of there before. He hooked his horn around the handle and pulled as he had watched the policewoman doing, taking several steps back.

The fridge contained a few interesting things. Like oranges and carrots, and a large chocolate cake. Once, the farmer's daughter had given him half an orange. He rolled one off the shelf, pushed it around on the tiles and bit into it. It tasted good, sweet and juicy. The juice sprayed all over the floor.

'Do you have a garden?' Alfonso said. 'Let's take him out there.'

'There's a communal courtyard out the back. My neighbours mind their own business, one of them has parties and gets up to all sorts, my colleagues had to go round a couple times. The whole block used to be four big houses converted into flats. The grumpy old git living at the top does like bullfighting, he's the one that ended up with the roof terrace. But this week he's away staying with his daughter.'

Pepelito sniffed the chocolate cake. It smelt interesting. He licked a bit with his tongue and then chewed into it. It was a bit too sugary, so he grabbed a large carrot from the shelf above and started chomping on that.

'What are you – No! That's Flavia's retirement cake!' Rita screamed, running into the kitchen and clapping her hands. Pepelito swallowed the carrot and felt guilty. 'That stuff's human food, it's not for you, you've eaten half of it!'

Alfonso stood in the doorway. He could barely keep a straight face.

'What? What are you laughing at, it's not funny! That cake is for Friday – it's my colleague's present for her last day, and he's been eating it!' Rita yelled. Pepelito walked over to the vet, who gave him another pat on the back. This only made Rita madder.

'Was your colleague's present,' Alfonso said darkly. 'I don't think it is now. That's another thing I should have mentioned. You should put a lock on your fridge, and perhaps tie it to something and weight it down, so he can't knock it over if he tries to open the door and gets frustrated.'

'A lock on my fridge, Dios mio. It was such an expensive cake too,' Rita muttered.

'Yeah, he's definitely getting bored, aren't you? Why don't we order a takeaway or something, then we can think about taking him outside.'

49

Alfonso rubbed Pepelito's nose and coaxed him through the doorway, laughing to himself. The humans were talking about him. He knew he had done something wrong. But what?

'There's a vegan restaurant called El Pimiento Picante at the bottom of my road, let's get a takeaway from there, it does Mexican food too and some really good burritos,' Rita said.

'OK,' Alfonso said. 'I'll get it, and pay for it if you want. I can get something for Pepelito too, since clearly he wants to try human food.'

'Yeah, clearly he does,' Rita said in an aggravated tone. She was opening and slamming a cupboard. Pepelito smelt strong cleaning products. They irritated his nose so he went back into the living room and lay down, squashing a small plastic object against the floor.

'...And finally. The Fundacion de Toro Bravo is offering a 2 million Euro reward for the return of Pepelito who escaped from the plaza de toros in Valladolid three days ago.' Pepelito got a fright when the TV came on. As he shifted about on the remote control, the volume increased to its highest level.

'I'm very keen for this bull to be returned. Hopefully the 2 million Euros will mean someone comes forward.' Javier Castella's voice was menacing. Frightened, Pepelito stood up, taking quick, shallow breaths, and began to paw the ground, remembering the man's violence. He let out a long, low growl, trying to make him go away.

But he didn't go away.

'As a matador de toros, what would you say to the person who has him?'

Castella looked directly at the camera. 'That person is stupid. A bull is a dangerous animal that cannot be trusted. They might think they have done a good deed, but they're just putting themselves at risk, since he could turn on them at any time. It's a pointless exercise. We will find him. They might as well give themselves up now.'

Pepelito stamped on the ground again, kicking the remote control against the door. He scratched up straw with his hooves and prepared to launch himself at the TV. His muscles stiffened in fear, worsening the pain in his back. His tail swung from side to side. Rita and Alfonso didn't act like other humans. He had to stop this man hurting them too.

'Hijo de puta,' Rita spat as she came in, snatching up the remote. The details of the Fundacion de Toro Bravo flashed onto the screen, with '2 MILLION EURO REWARD' in huge letters below it – then disappeared as the screen went black. Would he come back again?

'2 million Euros? We know where *that's* from. Don't we? Enough to build a hospital.' Rita was raging. Pepelito tensed. Was she going to beat him? But even as he scratched the ground in a threat display, his fear and panic subsided. Castella wasn't going to hurt him. He'd gone.

Creeping back against the wall by the doorway, Rita whispered, 'Hey, torito. Don't be afraid of *him*. Nobody will ever get their hands on his blood money, not if I have anything to do with it.'

Pepelito turned around to see if the matador was back, feeling confused and exhausted. He was thirsty and needed water.

'Hey. You mustn't eat expensive presents. But I'm not angry with you, pobrecito, only *him*.' Rita stretched her hand out.

'Rita?' Alfonso said quietly.

'Cows can recognise people's voices, they remember people who treated them badly, that shithead has probably got him worked up. We should go grab that takeaway, let him calm down, before one of us gets our bum caught on a bull's horn. Then, we should think of taking him outside, even if it's just for five minutes. What you think?' Alfonso spoke in a reassuring, relaxing voice, not angry or scared.

Maybe it would be OK.

'Yeah. I'd like that, but let's take him when it's quieter,' Rita said.

Alfonso nodded. 'Of course.'

'You know something?' Rita said.

'What?'

'This is the closest I've been to a date in years.'

Chapter 10 – Baggage and Burritos

'A date, eh,' Alfonso said as they walked back to the flat with their burritos, plus some drinks and a bag of large carrots and cucumbers.

'Well, yeah,' Rita said; her mood having picked up. She was smiling. Her hand brushed against him as they walked together.

Alfonso couldn't stop thinking about her. At first he had told himself it was because of the Pepelito situation. Rita's desperate phone call had been out of compassion or recklessness or both. After saving the bull's life, Alfonso was invested in his wellbeing, finding somewhere more suitable than Rita's flat where he could have a quiet life free from fear.

But increasingly, his thoughts now turned to Rita herself. At first, he hadn't wanted to admit how much he liked her, for so many reasons. But Pilar would have wanted him to meet someone else after all these years. She'd want him to be happy, wouldn't she? He moved closer to Rita as they walked together up the cobbled road. A shop was still open selling bike accessories, like chains and padlocks.

'Something like this would sort out the fridge. I might have one in the van,' he laughed, pointing out a heavy duty metal padlock. Rita stared at him in horror. She took out her phone. She had smart cameras installed outside and inside, not surprisingly for a cop.

'He's chilling in the living room look,' she said, laughing. Sure enough, Pepelito was lying on the fresh bed of straw, bought with cash, that they had placed in the living room this evening, the old bedding now bagged up and sitting in his van. Alfonso felt a rush of affection for her. They were now standing by the door of the flat. Rita put her key into the lock and they carefully walked inside on the heavy easy-clean plastic sheeting now covering most of the rooms. Alfonso looked down.

'I have another roll of that stuff, it looks like the kitchen needs it,' he said as they walked past the living room.

'Good idea, I don't want him going in the kitchen or my bedroom if I'm not in, I've decided. Started locking my bedroom door again.' Rita shook her head; they went to the kitchen and sat at the small white plastic table. The place was starting to smell like a farmyard. They would have to find somewhere else for Pepelito soon, especially since he was recovering and starting to wander around more frequently. He needed to go outdoors. But taking him round the back of Rita's would be incredibly risky.

Alfonso unwrapped his burrito. There wasn't much point in getting out a nice plate given the current state of the rest of the house. He had to be honest with her, he thought.

'This is weird for me. Since my wife died it's hard for me to think about meeting anyone else.'

Rita's eyes widened. 'I'm sorry.'

'I miss her every day. I know she'd want me to find someone else, that's what she said to me when she was dying. It's been seven years and I still haven't been able to face it.' He had been on a few dates through the apps since she died. But they had left him cold, it felt wrong, and he felt almost guilty. Because there was nobody else like her in the world.

'What did she die of?' Rita said. It was blunt but maybe that was what he needed. He rarely talked about it. He'd carried on with his work caring for animals the way she would have wanted him to, rather than caring for himself.

'She had cancer,' Alfonso said. 'She found out two years after we got married. By then, it was too late. She was 35.'

'I'm so sorry, that's too young, cancer is a bastard,' Rita said.

'Her name was Pilar; she was an animal rights activist and she did all sorts of crazy things. When we met, she had a pet rat she'd rescued from a lab. She'd broken in there in the dead of night, and they'd let them all out.' He laughed and Rita's mouth dropped open, like she wasn't sure whether to be shocked or impressed. Alfonso noticed her black hair falling into her face. He reminded himself she was a cop. Maybe he'd already said too much. In the adjacent room, he could hear Pepelito getting up and sniffing at something.

'She was at university in England, and she dropped out of her course after a year so she could go and save foxes from hunters. She hated police, she was always going on protests and getting arrested,' he said, remembering when he'd had to come and bail her out. Rita looked shocked but said nothing.

'She used to say I was too boring.' He remembered the time Pilar had wanted to jump into the plaza de toros.

'I don't think that's a good idea. The matador's got a sword, for a start. And the bull doesn't know you're trying to save it. It's scared, it's angry and it might gore you. The spectators will try and beat you up, if not worse. You'll definitely be arrested.' She rolled her eyes. It was impossible to argue with her when she was like this.

'I love you, but you're just too sensible. I won't be on my own, a whole bunch of us are going. We need to save them. Who else is going to do it, if we don't?'

'I know. It's an atrocity. But you can't put yourself at such risk for a bull.'

'Animals are at risk for humans every day, look at those dogs who are trained to sniff out bombs —'

'Pilar, it's not the —'

'Well, why not?'

'I didn't know, but she'd been to the doctor that day and they said it was much more aggressive than they thought. She never gave much thought to the risks, but now even less so.' Pilar would have laughed so hard at the thought 'Dr Sensible' had got caught up in all this. Alfonso couldn't help smiling.

55

'Sometimes, I think I should have just let her do it, but instead, I booked us a last-minute holiday in Paris for two weeks, I felt we needed to be far away from here before anything crazy happened. She was furious at first,' Alfonso laughed.

'I'd have been too, if I'd have planned that, and then my husband was like, no you can't, we're going on holiday,' Rita said, taking a sip of beer from out the bottle.

'In the end, we had an amazing time. But she started getting very tired towards the end. And a week after we got back, she started going seriously downhill. Three months later she was in hospital, and she'd never come out.' Rita had tears in her eyes when he looked at her. He wondered if he had let on too much. It was hard to judge when he so seldom talked about it with anyone.

'She sounds…impressive,' she said, and he nodded, still missing Pilar more than words could describe. Rita reached for his hand across the table. He took it cautiously. Her hands were warm. Pilar would want him to be happy, right?

'What about you?' he said.

'I'm divorced. I'm afraid my ex-husband never did anything that worthwhile or interesting. He is an estate agent, which is as boring as it sounds.' She rolled her eyes.

'Work took over my life. He couldn't stand being in second place. I'd walk out of family dinners with his parents to chase down suspects. Christmas, New Year, Easter, all the local fiestas I'd be on call, the busiest times of year, that's when the crime happens. Once I had a call when we were on holiday in Turkey and had to fly back. He didn't understand and I didn't try hard enough to make him,' she said.

She took a deep breath. She looked tired and had some grey hairs, but Alfonso couldn't help noticing how beautiful she looked. 'He used to say I was paranoid and couldn't switch off. That I'd treat everyone like a suspect. That's not paranoid. It's called having a copper's instinct.'

She finished the last of the burrito and took a swig out her beer bottle. 'He had this friend from school, and we would go to their house for dinner. I couldn't help noticing that his wife hardly spoke, and the friend would put her down a lot. One time, I mentioned it to him in the car and he lost it with me. He told me I looked at everyone suspiciously and needed to relax and his friend was a great guy, blah, blah.'

Rita knocked back the beer. Alfonso squeezed her hand gently, feeling sick at what he guessed she was going to say next. 'Six months later, would you believe, my officers arrested this so-called 'great guy' for domestic violence. He'd been knocking her about for years. I knew then, my marriage was over.'

She looked towards the kitchen door nervously, checking something on her phone. 'I thought I heard something but it's OK, he's still sleeping.'

'We separated, and I also discovered once I'd moved out, that he'd been having an affair for three years. So that was that. Finished. Done.' She rolled her eyes.

'Wow,' Alfonso said.

'Yeah.' She sighed heavily. 'Never mind. I'm done with him.'

'I'm curious,' Alfonso said, feeling nervous and not a little intimidated.

'Go on.'

'What does your copper's instinct say about me? Do you see me as a suspect?'

Rita thought for a second. She grinned and looked at him sideways. 'Yeah. Definitely an accomplice.'

Alfonso looked into her eyes across the table. He'd only known her a few days. What was he doing?

'After they found Caroline McKenzie. I got home, I'd been with her son. My mum sent me this horrible text calling me selfish and saying

I should have a reconciliation with my sister. The only family I've got. All that shit. Anyway. Pepelito came into the room.' She took a deep breath. That had been a horrible night. After he sent the text about Caroline, Rita hadn't replied; police protocol obviously. She hadn't needed to. Right after that, Caroline's son posted on Facebook with the news.

Rita's lip trembled. 'I could see the pain he was in from how he was walking. But he came up to me and let me pet him. He could tell I was upset. He stayed with me when I was crying.'

'Quite affectionate at times, isn't he? They couldn't beat that out of him,' Alfonso said.

'No. I can't bear thinking of him like that.' Rita shook her head.

'Animals can be a great comfort,' Alfonso said, thinking of their old rescue dog Lugar, who was so good when Pilar went into hospital.

'I don't know about *comforting!*' Rita laughed. She glanced at the door. 'Can we try and take him outside in a while, just for five minutes? I hate seeing him so sad and bored.'

'We can try. He's better, but still weak and not in much of a state to run anywhere, but we'll need to keep him calm, and make sure he can't go far. Do you have anything heavy we can tie the rope to when we put him in the harness?' Alfonso said. He took one of the carrots out of the takeaway bag, plus the extra burrito they had bought for this purpose.

'The sofa might work,' Rita said. 'That thing is heavy, needs three or four people to lift it.'

'Let's do that,' Alfonso said. 'I better not have any more beer.'

'Say just before 1. That OK, or do you need to go?'

He shook his head; how could it be that late? The lines on her face showed she'd had a tough life. Today, she'd got back from work and changed into old clothes and clearly not made much of an effort. But

Alfonso thought she was beautiful. The fact she cared so much made her even more so. And he hadn't felt this way in such a very long time.

'Rita?' he said as they looked at each other. 'I'd really like to kiss you.'

'Sure,' Rita said, looking into his eyes. She leaned forward across the table and grabbed his shoulders, pulling him in hungrily. His tongue grazed her lips. She was tentative at first but then opened her mouth wider as he explored it. She squeezed both his hands; she felt so warm. Alfonso's heart beat faster. He opened his eyes and the two gazed at each other.

'You're a really good kisser,' he said, and she smiled, stood up and walked over to his side of the narrow table. 'You know that?'

The chair made a creaking noise as he stood up and put his arm around her. They kissed again, less hungry and desperate this time, more relaxed.

'I'm falling for you so hard,' he whispered as a soft thump came from the next room. 'When you called me I never expected this.'

'I thought you'd think I was crazy. I mean, I think I am,' Rita said. Her hair smelt so good.

'If you're crazy I wish the whole world would be as crazy as you,' he said. She looked up at him. She had such beautiful dark eyes, he thought as he kissed her again. There was another, louder thump. Alfonso looked towards the door, then back to Rita.

'Better see what's going on in there.' She gave a soft laugh.

'Yeah,' Alfonso said. 'We can always continue later.'

Chapter 11 – Unexpected Revelations

Someone was making a dreadful racket outside. Weren't the students in the place opposite meant to have gone home, Cristina thought. She looked at the time – 01:05. There had been much more noise recently. The other day, she had heard a heavy thumping from downstairs. There was also a faint smell of manure; who knew where that was from? And that guy living opposite her with his parties and suspicious substances. He rarely greeted her either. Young people had no manners.

She looked out the window and saw that policewoman standing in the shared garden with some guy, holding a rope. What was she up to this late? She hadn't seen her much recently. The police were all useless anyway. In her day people hadn't needed to lock or even shut their doors when they went out.

The policewoman was saying something she couldn't hear. She was facing indoors and holding something in her hand. Cristina watched incredulously as the lights in the courtyard illuminated the scene and a pair of horns emerged.

'Oh, he's very timid, aren't you, toro,' the policewoman said. Cristina listened, stunned. What on earth was she doing, keeping a bull in the middle of a residential street? Couldn't he break her wall down with his horns? He'd cause some serious damage.

'It's OK, come on.' Taking slow, careful steps, the black bull walked out, directly underneath her window. They'd tied him to something in the house. Cristina noticed a large bandage on his back.

Oh.

Everyone had been talking about it in the pharmacy today; it had happened down the road. Cristina didn't care for corridas and the way the matadors strutted round in pink tights and a silly costume. People who liked it said it wasn't a sport, but in Cristina's opinion it was, and she had never understood sports in general. When Spain had won the World Cup that time, she had just gone to bed irritated at all the noise.

But this? What did these two think they were doing? And her a policewoman as well.

She shut the blinds quickly, too stunned to speak.

She had seen something on TV about a 2 million Euro reward for the bull. Cristina couldn't imagine that amount of money. She couldn't think what she would spend it on.

Maybe a nice posh house in the countryside with better neighbours. These days she didn't go out except to do her shopping, there were too many dodgy types on the streets, and she was starting to have trouble getting up and down the stairs. Or go on a cruise round the world, she had always wanted to do that. Maybe if she had that amount of money her grandchildren would visit her more often. This place had gone downhill since she had moved in, it wasn't what it used to be. Maybe that was why they didn't want to come round.

The helpline wouldn't be open until the morning, she guessed. She had a quick peek out the window again, unable to resist confirming what she had seen.

'Dulcito. Come back inside. It's OK,' the policewoman said encouragingly. The bull disappeared indoors.

****

'I can't wait to see you again.' Rita grinned to herself as she read Alfonso's message the next day. Words couldn't describe how she felt. Without Pepelito around, she sensed it could have gone much further than kissing.

After that kiss, they'd gone into the living room and tied one end of the rope tightly round an arm of Rita's heavy sofa. Rita had given Pepelito a carrot while Alfonso put on the halter, then opened the back door. Overjoyed to be outside, Pepelito had tried to give himself a scratch on a tree, partially dislodging his bandage. In obvious discomfort, he hadn't needed much encouragement to go back inside, where Alfonso had checked him over and replaced the dressing. He'd said his goodbyes after that, and kissed her again on the doorstep.

'Likewise,' she wrote.

Within a minute he wrote back. 'I'd love to take you out on a proper date where it's just us two if you know what I mean 😉'

'Can't wait, LOL,' Rita wrote back as she fired up her computer. Smiling to herself, she put the phone in the drawer and turned on her police one. The chocolate cake she had hurriedly bought from the supermarket this morning was already in a fridge in the station's kitchen. Hopefully her own fridge was still in a usable state, now there was an armchair blocking the kitchen door.

'Inspectora Silvera. Here are the files for the Caroline McKenzie case you asked for.' Abdul Mansouri, one of the younger recruits, came and deposited them on her desk.

'Thanks, Abdul,' she said. Dominguez wasn't here yet and it wasn't like him to be late. She sent him a message asking where he was, and waited. There was no response. He'd sent her a couple of drunken WhatsApps last night and she was mildly concerned. Breaking up with Luis had hit him hard; they'd been together six years.

Then she saw her phone was ringing from a withheld number. 'Buenos dias?'

'Am I speaking to Rita Silvera?' came a woman's voice on the other line. Her voice was shaky and quiet. Rita only recognised it because of the cacophony of barks and woofs in the background.

'Raquel?'

'There's something important I need to tell you. It's about Caroline.'

*

'Yeah, so, um, you know when I said Caroline didn't get in arguments online,' Raquel Carlos said as they sat in a small interview room. Her hands were trembling. She looked much younger than she was, with her pale pink tracksuit and pink coat that looked like a dressing gown. Abdul Mansouri sat beside her taking notes. He didn't drink coffee and was usually partial to energy drinks, but as it was Ramadan, he had nothing in front of him.

'I didn't tell you before because I was scared of getting in trouble.' She swallowed almost the whole glass of water and spilt the rest on the table. Rita noticed the dog hairs on the woman's fluffy jumper.

'We were in this group, me and her, that was about exposing people who abused animals. Everywhere in the world, but mostly in the UK and Spain. We'd do things like report them to Facebook and try and find out where they worked, we'd message their Facebook friends and tell them what they were doing. Caroline actually hacked their accounts and posted their messages online. Anonymously, so they didn't know it was her.' Raquel laughed nervously and chewed on her nails like an awkward teenager.

'So, harassment in other words. If you thought any of these people had committed a crime, why didn't you tell the police?' Mansouri asked coolly, bridging his hands on the table. Rita couldn't argue, but she felt more sympathetic to Raquel today, seeing in her a vulnerable, naive woman, who had got mixed up in something she shouldn't. Sounds familiar, she thought with a chill. It sounded like something Alfonso's wife Pilar would have been into. Did he know anything about this group?

'The police? Ha. You lot aren't interested are you, and most of what they do isn't even illegal,' Raquel scoffed. Her statements were more true than Rita wanted to admit. It wasn't like the toreros who had reduced Pepelito to a bloody pincushion were going to spend time inside any time soon.

'I assure you, we would if we had the evidence,' Mansouri said defensively before Rita silenced him with a look. He had only joined six months ago. Not enough time to have the idealism knocked out.

'We weren't just, like, randomly harassing. There was a video of this guy beating his dog in Edinburgh, right. Just down the road from Caroline. He was a teacher, and we got him fired from his school.' This was the first time Raquel had made eye contact. The utter hatred she spoke of this man broke down the shell around her.

'Do you remember his name?' Rita said, filled with unease. Raquel shrugged.

'I don't, sorry. Mac something.'

'Do you think he could have followed her here on holiday?' Rita said. Raquel shook her head decisively.

'No. No, he's in jail, Caroline told me and we were going to celebrate.' Her eyes went wide at the thought of prison.

'Will I go to jail?' Raquel said anxiously.

'Based on what you've told us, no, but I'd advise you to speak to an attorney,' Rita said, knowing there was more to it.

There always was.

'What would happen to all the dogs I look after?' A good question.

'Don't worry about that now. We're not charging you with anything,' Rita said. They might have to; what the victim herself had apparently done carried a sentence of 2 years, possibly up to 6. She didn't feel good about this.

Raquel wouldn't cope inside.

'How can I not worry,' Raquel said looking down, in a miserable voice. 'Do you think – do you think she died because of that?'

'It's certainly a possible motive. Is there anyone else who you can think of who could have wanted to hurt Caroline?' Rita sipped the coffee she'd made in the machine, the first time she had touched it

64

that morning. She wasn't really enjoying it in the face of Raquel's fragility.

'Yeah, yeah there is,' Raquel whispered, twisting a strand of hair around with her fingers. 'But you won't believe me. You lot never do when it's someone famous.'

'Go on,' Rita said. Her phone vibrated with a message from Dominguez, an hour after her partner was meant to be at work. She ignored it and leant forward to listen.

'Like, that matador? You know my sister actually saw that bull run off? She lives opposite and saw it run past with all that stuff sticking out of it.' Raquel's big blue eyes stared like a baby's at the two officers, and despite herself, Rita was flooded with protectiveness. Her thirst was gone; now she didn't trust herself to keep anything down.

He was absolutely capable of murder.

'Castella?' Mansouri said.

Raquel nodded. 'Yeah. Him.'

Chapter 12 – Aidan

Aidan Donnelly was heading to the bus stop after finishing his shift. He was looking forward to doing a stream of the new edition of Assassin's Creed with some mates later. Board and video games were his favourite way to relax, so he felt lucky to have got the job in the shop, at least he was doing something vaguely bearable.

It got him out the house now he'd left college, since his dad died it had all got too grim with his mum quitting her job and going on the sick with depression. Being sat up in his room had done him no good at all. Besides it wasn't like much else was round here. All the good jobs were down south. He walked to the bus stop, the buses were shit out where he lived. He was gonna save for a car and had his license but couldn't afford it. He couldn't afford to move out of his mum's and he was paying for her too. Most of his salary went on helping his mum with rent and electricity bills. If anything was left over he liked to buy games with it or go for a drink now he was old enough, although his anxiety wouldn't always let him do that.

Once at the bus stop, he took out his phone to message his friends about the streaming session later. He also checked YouTube, he had a couple more subscribers and comments on his videos, plus someone had tipped him £20 which was nice. He'd made some comments about that MP or whatever he was, that Tory who'd been torturing animals on holiday. It got something mad like a thousand likes or something like that, it had proper triggered some of them. Too funny. God, he thought. The Tories were all pricks.

He stood at the bus stop. The bus was late as usual. Probably broken down somewhere. He couldn't wait to get a car. Nobody was on the street apart from some drunk guy shouting. He sat down at the bus shelter and put his headphones in, texting his mum to say he was going to be late.

There was someone else coming towards him. From a distance he couldn't make out the face. He was wearing a suit and tie, he must be lost round here, Aidan thought. He put some music on and went back to his phone. Summer from work had messaged him.

'Hey Aidan, you working tomorrow?' He was surprised at her texting him. He fancied her and wanted to ask her out but he didn't have any money and his looks weren't up to much. He wasn't going to uni any time soon. No way she would go for a loser like him, he thought sadly. A couple of his subscribers were girls but barely anyone would look at him in real life.

'Yeah I will be,' he wrote, his heart pounding. 'You wanna grab something at lunch?'

'Sure :)'

'There you are, Aidan. You'll regret your threats,' said a posh voice. What threats? What? A hand gripped his shoulder. He turned around and saw the guy in the suit, now wearing a ski mask and surgical gloves like something out of a horror movie.

Aidan gasped but his scream was stifled. The man pushed him against the bus shelter's perspex wall. He tried to struggle and push the prick away. It was no use. The man's punches winded him. He couldn't breathe; he felt nauseous. A cloth was shoved under his nose. Dimly Aidan saw the man reach into a leather bag he was carrying and pull out a roll of duct tape. He tried to cry out but within seconds he was unconscious.

****

Henry dragged Aidan's limp body three metres to the expensive black car with fake plates and tinted windows he had hired for his visit to the Red Wall. It had almost been too easy. A less daring man than he might have hired someone else to do the deed, but the thrill of the hunt was half the joy of the thing. There were few Henry trusted not to botch at least one of his instructions. One of these failures had almost been catastrophic.

As Aidan's feet hung out the door, Henry picked up a crowbar from the back seat, smashed the security camera on the wall by the bus shelter, and picked up the camera's memory card and battery from the ground. He threw the battery in the drain with a pleasing splash. He couldn't risk being seen; this was a mite more controversial than his previous brushes with the law, expense scandals and Civil Service fraud cases.

'Where to, Dixon?' said George who sat beside him in the drivers' seat as he cut the memory card up with a pair of scissors. He could be a pain in the backside but he could be relied on to be discreet in such matters.

'Be a sport and take us back down to Surrey.' It would be a while before Aidan woke up, Henry thought, looking at him lying across the back seat and taking off the ski mask now they were out of danger. Driving round this dodgy area incognito reminded him of nothing so much as his hunting trips to Africa in search of dangerous beasts.

'Him as well?'

'Of course.' Someone else was driving, so Henry poured himself a dram of 200-year-old whisky as he sat on the soft leather seat, before rolling down the window and throwing the remains of the card outside. This particular bottle had been given to him by Lord Owenstoft, who owned the grouse moor he went shooting on regularly. After a refreshing day in the field, the two Taurine Club members regularly spent many hours discussing the intricacies of the matadors' techniques.

Yes, grouse shooting was another fine day out. There was something so satisfying about watching birds drop out of the sky. Just before his latest short visit to Spain, he had shot a few woodcocks and a wryneck – you didn't see many of those these days! There was some hoo ha from the RSPB about wrynecks being endangered. It was in a freezer in his cellar –not his basement, an American neologism – while he decided what to do with it. If he had it stuffed, it'd be a collector's item.

Of course, the nasty little yob in the back wouldn't appreciate any of this. He wouldn't be able to tell you what a grouse was if it shat on him.

He'd never again show Henry such insolence.

Just as well.

Chapter 13 – A New Arrival

'Here you are, dulcito. Look what we got for you.' Rita and Alfonso tipped the huge sack of food pellets from the agricultural supermarket, too heavy for one person on their own, into the metal trough standing in the living room.

'What's happening about your friend?' Alfonso absent-mindedly arranged carrots and courgettes on top of the pellet pile in an octagonal pattern.

Rita wished she could laugh but her anxiety was rising. 'He's not in a good place. That hostel is dangerous…he was late into work today because one of the other guests recognised and threatened him with a knife. The guy's been charged, but still. I'm his best friend…'

'Look, he's always got my back. We've saved each other's lives. I think he will be OK with…all this,' she added, gesturing to Pepelito. Inwardly, she wasn't sure at all. Two million Euros was a lot of money, and Dominguez was in a tight spot –

No. He wouldn't. She hated herself for even thinking that way.

'Shit. Poor guy. I won't say I'm not worried but if you're absolutely sure.'

'Honestly, I'm not, but I'm not having my best mate stay in that shithole any longer.' She tried to ignore her anxiety as they watched Pepelito eating.

'That'll take him a good half an hour. Enough time for sex.' As soon as the words were out Rita mentally kicked herself. *Really?* The following pause seemed to last a million years. He was still grieving. They'd agreed to take things slow. No way would he –

'Yeah. I'd like that.' Alfonso hugged her. She gasped in shock.

'You sure?'

'I think so. Are you?'

'Yeah.'

Walking with Alfonso into her bedroom and shutting the door, Rita felt anxious, but desperate and hungry for him; a feeling she'd almost forgotten. She suddenly felt young and adventurous again. 'I'll barricade the door with the dresser so he can't come in.'

'Honestly, let's not bother, let's just do it now,' Alfonso said, unbuckling his trousers and reaching under Rita's top to get off her bra. He pulled her onto the bed. It creaked loudly as he kissed her. They explored each other's mouths. Rita's nipples grew firm as Alfonso took them in his fingers. He relaxed onto the bed and she sat on him. Her face flushed as she grew wet with desire. Their breathing got louder and more rhythmic; she leaned forward, kissing him again, pushing down his trousers. He felt hard underneath her touch.

'Where did you get this bed?' he whispered. 'It's so sturdy. Amazing he didn't completely break it.'

Rita burst out laughing. She grabbed him round the shoulders, kissed him so hard she almost bit him.

'Well, I'm worried about my other furniture.'

Alfonso laughed, holding her tight around the hips. 'I'd better stay the night, then.'

****

Pepelito lay in the living room the following day, trying to mentally place himself in a field full of grass. From the street outside, he heard a man saying, 'Guess you're off the case now, Rita?'

'Yeah. Guess I am, now Castella's in the frame.'

'I forgot what an arrogant arsehole that guy is, his big shot lawyer too, saying every question is 'unacceptable'. Though, my gut is he didn't do it. Doubt he could kill her, bring her back and clean up that well in between giving TV interviews and yelling at us on the phone.' The man's voice drew closer. Pepelito had heard it once before.

'He could have hired someone, Jesús.' Pepelito heard Rita turning the key much more slowly than usual, without opening the door. She sounded anxious, although he was glad she was back. Being alone made him so sad and scared. When they weren't there, he worried something terrible had happened to Rita and Alfonso. Humans seemed to live in a world of aggression.

'Nah. Hiring a hitman because an animal rights activist insulted him? That'd be a full-time job.' They were laughing. Pepelito heard the click of a lighter and smelt Dominguez's cigarette. It irritated his nose and reminded him of the men who had hurt him.

'The higher ups already questioned me when the Aguilar stuff came out. Made no difference that Maria cut me off, or that she died to me the day she married him. Hope I'm not about to go through all that again.' Rita sounded tired. Pepelito was tired too. He'd drunk most of the bath water as it was so hot. Rita had bought him some exercise balls to play with. He had chased one of the biggest ones around the living room and caught it on his horn; after a loud bang, it suddenly wasn't there.

'Nah, not this time. Sanchez knows where you stand where Castella's concerned. Oi. You'll love one thing.'

'Oh? What's that?'

'We questioned him for 5 and a half hours, so he missed his corrida!' Pepelito's muscles tensed as Dominguez laughed outside.

'Hopefully the first of many for that hijo de puta,' Rita said under her breath, but loud enough for Pepelito to hear.

'Tell me about it. He was more vexed about that, and that bloody bull disappearing than the fact four of the victim's friends all reckon he did it! Anyway. Look. Thanks for putting me up. You're a good friend. Beats having to sleep in my car.'

'Any time, Jesús. You know that. Right, well…I suppose, we'd best get inside; it's getting dark.' Pepelito listened from the living room as the two police officers walked inside.

'What's all this plastic everywhere? Has this rabbit had babies? The floor needs a clean,' Dominguez chuckled. Rita was silent. Pepelito wondered if he'd done something bad. Dominguez was dragging something heavy behind him and it sounded scary. His feet rustled on the straw and plastic covering the ground. What was this guy up to?

'Why's…your armchair blocking the kitchen door?'

'I'll get us both a drink. There's something I need to tell you, Jesús.' The chair's wheels squeaked loudly and rumpled the plastic sheeting as she moved it away from the kitchen door. Pepelito had little space in the living room. He found the kitchen interesting, although the floor was too slippery and he skidded around too much, like being in that truck with the others. Feeling left out, he got up and ambled down the newly tidied corridor. He stood at the door to the kitchen, pressing down the handle to open it with his horn.

'…so, he's never been aggressive to me but keep your boots and your bullet proof vest on just in case.'

'Shit. OK. That's…' Dominguez's voice trailed off. He stared at Pepelito and moved his chair backwards. The man's eyes were wide and he was shaking with fear. Why was he here, Pepelito wondered. What was he going to do to him?

'Hey, hey, dulcito,' Rita said in a quiet, kind tone, holding out a carrot and encouraging him. 'Aw, he won't hurt you. He's so nice and gentle.'

'What – what the fuck is this shit, Rita? Nice and gentle?' Dominguez remained sitting on his chair and edged it backwards, as far away from Pepelito as he could, his limbs rigid and trembling.

'He wouldn't hurt a soul, would you,' Rita said, putting her hand out.

'What about that picador's horse? Presumably he hurt that?' Dominguez spluttered. Pepelito couldn't work this guy out and it worried him.

'So would you, if you'd been kidnapped, then kept in the dark and tortured. He was only defending himself. Weren't you, hey?' Rita made an encouraging noise. Dominguez's jaw dropped and he paled. He looked into Pepelito's eyes briefly and recoiled.

Frightened humans were dangerous.

Dominguez took a breath. 'Holy shit, woman. You're insane.'

'Well, what would you have done?' Rita snapped.

'I'd have just taken my gun and put him out of his misery. Luis would have hated me, but we're not together any more.' Dominguez scrambled onto the central kitchen table, which was nailed to the floor with two barstools on either side. He sat in the middle, watching Pepelito with a horrified expression. His gun bulged out of his pocket.

'Give it a rest, Mr Tough Guy. You wouldn't have done that. Pepelito's not hard to look after. He's adorable. Look at him.'

Dominguez stared at her, then burst out in fits of laughter. 'Adorable? Listen to yourself, woman. There's mounds of straw everywhere. There's a broken chair in the corner. I don't even wanna think of all the shit he must produce…'

'Can you see any shit or mounds of straw in this room? He's not allowed in here any more when I'm at work.'

'There's a lump of straw stuck to the chair! And why – why is there that huge metal padlock on the fridge?'

'He ate the cake I'd bought for Flavia's retirement do.'

Dominguez snorted. He put his head in his hands, crying laughing. Maybe this guy wouldn't try anything. He hadn't tried to hurt him so far, but Pepelito would have to keep an eye on him.

'Where am I going to sleep? I guess the living room is out of bounds. The bath?' Dominguez carefully descended from the table. His feet touched the tiles in a way that irritated Pepelito's ears. Pepelito backed away as they approached the door. The corridor still made him nervous; he couldn't turn around until he got to the bathroom.

'The bath? I wouldn't do that to you. Besides, given this weather, I've been filling it up for him.' Rita laughed. Dominguez looked dumbfounded.

'You'll sleep in my office, he never goes in here since he kicked the cabinet over when he first arrived,' Rita said, showing Dominguez to the weird room Pepelito hated going into. That room frightened him and he didn't know why. His painkillers were wearing off. Once in the bathroom, he stretched his head towards the bath water; it helped cool him down and distract him from the pain. The bath was now less than half full; the water hard to reach. He put his front feet onto the top of the bath, then into the water, and scrabbled to angle himself so he could get his head down to drink. It was difficult but he managed it – yes!

'You not been tempted to claim the reward, Rita?' Pepelito heard Dominguez yell.

'Never. Didn't your namesake say the love of money is the root of all evil?'

'He never said, 'If a cow is in danger, thou shalt let it trash your home'! What are you going to do with him? You can't keep him here. He needs to be outside in a nice big paddock,' Dominguez said from the box room. Pepelito couldn't work out whether he was an enemy or not. He missed going outdoors. The fresh air and grass outdoors reminded him of happier times. But he had hurt his back under the bandage when he'd scratched himself. He couldn't really itch his back, roll on his side, do so many things he'd once done without thinking without causing himself more pain.

'Another week or so while he recovers a bit more, Alfonso said. He should be able to take the bandage off today, he's round in half an hour. Problem is, Castella is looking for him.' Rita lowered her voice and spoke nervously. This was a sign of fear in humans. What was she scared of? Pepelito lay down on the tiles and ate from the bale of straw Alfonso had placed in the corner.

'How long till he recovers totally?'

'Well, how long is a piece of string? Alfonso said about six weeks for the back injuries if nothing goes wrong. But apparently they've filed down the tips of his horns and plugged them with resin. He can't judge distance well and bumps into stuff. Apparently he might be a bit clumsy for the rest of his life.' Despite Rita's disgusted tone, Pepelito felt safe with her; for some reason she and Alfonso cared about him. Maybe they thought he was human.

'What? That's horrible! Not exactly very brave of the great man, is it?' Dominguez's voice dripped with contempt.

'Yeah, and he still made fools out of them.'

'Rita, look. You've met my uncle. Silvio the ex-farmer. He's a total hermit, out in the sticks with all that nature, he's got two ancient cows so he'd have some buddies too, could have a nice happy life. I can ask – he'd love it, better than here anyway!' Dominguez said. Pepelito stood up and stretched. It was getting easier every day.

At that moment, someone knocked loudly on the door.

'Ooff. It's a bit early for Alfonso to be here,' Rita muttered. 'My phone app isn't working so I can't see who it is.'

'That your boyfriend? I'm telling you, we gotta only date cops,' Dominguez said gruffly as Rita approached the front door. I should go and check him out properly, Pepelito thought, although the strange guy's presence was made less alarming by his friendship with Rita.

From the bathroom doorway, Pepelito watched Rita lift up the blind and recoil, staggering backwards.

'Malditos.'

Her voice was thick with fear and anger. She patted Pepelito on the neck and kissed the top of his head. She was tense; something was very wrong. 'Hey. Hey, toro. Stay there, in the bathroom. Please.'

Pepelito backed into the bathroom as Rita shut the door. The bathroom was small and he couldn't easily fit in here with the door closed, couldn't turn round without bumping into something. His foot crushed a bar of soap he had knocked from the bath earlier. He didn't like it.

'Come on, open up!' A man was banging on the door. Pepelito recognised the voice. Fear gripped his whole body as he remembered the beating the man had given him.

'Open up. He's in here, isn't he!'

Chapter 14 – Lost

'So timid. Don't you know where you are? If you just stand there it'll be a boring show, with such a useless bull. Show some fighting spirit you coward.' The man slammed the heavy stick onto his back three or four times in the same place until he cried out in pain. Pepelito edged out the way, not knowing what to do. Why was he so angry?

'You're supposed to be ferocious. Give me some rage. You'll disgrace your breeder if you act like this, they'll have to give you the black banderillas.' Pepelito looked up and saw the man on a platform above them. He beat, kicked and tormented all the bulls in the enclosure but seemed to particularly enjoy hurting him. What had he done to make the man hate him?

And now he was right outside the front door trying to get in. Pepelito began to tremble with fear and found it hard to breathe.

Rita spoke calmly, not opening the door. 'May I inform you that you're talking to a police officer? Carry on, and me and my partner will take the lot of you down the station and do you for assault.'

'We're from the Fundacion de Toro Bravo. Someone's told us you've got Pepelito. It might be a prank, but we need to come in and see for ourselves.' He hated their voices. Trying unsuccessfully to move backwards between the bath and basin, he scraped some of the plaster off the wall with his foot. Tears dripped down his face.

'Have you got authorisation from a judge?' Rita shouted.

'Well –'

'Well! You can't. It's late, I'm about to have dinner with some guests. I've never heard such rubbish. Next time, leave house searches to the professionals.' Panting, Pepelito climbed backwards into the bath, as close as possible to the wall, and stood with his back legs in the bath and his front legs on the floor, cracking the plastic under his weight.

'One of them's out on license, so dunno what he's playing at, I'll put him straight back inside,' Rita said, loud enough for the men to hear.

One of them spat on the ground outside. 'The boss's sister-in-law is a cop, this is her house. That bitch is something else. She's a fucking crazy vegan.'

'Shit. Yeah. I know her. Rita Silvera, right?' Someone else kicked the door hard. Pepelito's legs shook at their harsh voices.

'Nah, it won't open.'

'Let me try.' The door rattled and shook.

Pepelito was seized by panic as he remembered the things he had seen and heard and smelt them do. Things that happened in confined spaces; at the ring, and much, much earlier, too young and small to resist. He scrabbled out, loosening the basin from the wall, and shoved himself at the bathroom door. It flew open, creaked and came off one of its hinges; as it fell, it tore down part of the blind covering the front door. Rita let out an ear-splitting scream as she dived away and landed in the straw pile in the living room.

'I can't see in there. Reckon that's him?'

'Nah, that door's solid. Let's come back tonight with some more muscle.' He heard the men muttering to themselves, their footsteps retreating.

But he knew them too well.

They'd be back.

They were going to come in. He had to run somewhere far away. He couldn't let them anywhere near him.

He threw himself down the passage and leapt onto the armchair, flinging himself at the kitchen door behind.

It broke and collapsed; he skidded into the kitchen, crashing into the table Dominguez had climbed on earlier. There was a splinter in his hoof. He threw himself at the glass door to the courtyard; it shattered against his horns. A stone statue of an angel that usually sat on Rita's back step fell onto the ground, but did not break. He looked around desperately. The passage leading into the street was too narrow for him. Someone saw him from the other side of the alley and screamed. He turned away, trying to run, he didn't know where.

****

Alfonso pulled up and parked his van around the corner from Rita's. It was dark. Rita hadn't replied to his text. Was she OK? He texted her again but there was no response. Feeling apprehensive, he took his first aid box from the van. He had tried to dissuade her from putting Dominguez up. Could she be sure she could trust him? They'd helped each other out before and the guy was facing homelessness – but he was still a cop.

It was easy for him to forget Rita was a cop too – he had to remind himself. She was stubborn and she'd say she knew this guy better, Alfonso knew that. He couldn't be the dickhead telling her what she could and couldn't do. If his instincts were right, she'd never listen anyway.

That was what he liked about her. Maybe he was crazy.

He'd enjoyed last night all the more because he had not let himself feel this way for so long.

Then there was Pepelito. It brought Alfonso such joy to see a beautiful animal getting stronger, more confident, as he lost his fear of humans and recovered from the violence he'd experienced. Rita's love, care and fierce protectiveness for the sweet-natured bull endeared her to him. It made his admiration for her grow whenever he thought about it. Wouldn't her attitude have got her in trouble with some of the troglodytes she worked with?

He turned a corner and approached her door. He rang the doorbell. Nobody answered, but he heard the sound of a woman crying. His chest tightened. The lights were on. The blind had been pulled down. He couldn't see much but what he could spoke for itself. The bathroom door was halfway off its hinge and blocked the corridor diagonally. He pressed the doorbell again, hearing a male voice swearing.

'There's no bull here, we don't have him, leave her alone,' the man snapped. Rita was sobbing in the background.

'Let him in, Jesús.'

Dominguez fumbled with the lock and opened the door. 'Get in.'

'What happened?' Alfonso guessed what had happened.

Rita stood up and edged the bathroom door to the side; it separated from the other hinge entirely and fell. The kitchen door was lying a metre inside the kitchen, away from the doorway. The armchair she had placed in front of it was upturned. The door to the courtyard was smashed. Tears were running down Rita's face. He held her tightly as they walked to the kitchen together. Behind them, Dominguez slammed the fatally weakened front door shut. Gravity tore it from its hinges, sending it clattering to the ground with a terrible crash.

'Where is he?' Alfonso asked Rita gently as he held her. She shook her head and started crying again.

'Did they take him?'

'I don't know.' Rita swallowed hard. 'They turned up at the door half an hour ago demanding to get in, saying they knew I had him. They got nasty and tried to force their way in – they gave up eventually. But I've never seen him like that, he gets nervous sometimes, but he's pretty calm, you know? And before I knew it? He went for it out into the yard as fast as he could. And now he's broken all my fucking doors – it's gonna cost a fortune to replace…'

'You must have been terrified,' Alfonso said gently, wrapping his arms around her. He kissed her hair. Rita nodded. She was shaking.

'What if they've got him and they're going to hurt him?' she sobbed. Even after the devastation Pepelito had caused, Rita wasn't thinking of herself, just like she hadn't when she'd agreed Dominguez could stay. Alfonso felt his fists clench and a knot of anger in his stomach. How frightened they must both have been. His gloves had become wet with Pepelito's blood as he removed the torture equipment planted in his back. Doing so without injuring the animal further had not been easy. He'd almost cut his own hand on the spikes.

'If they so much as touch him I'll come after them and break their fucking teeth.' He shocked himself at the violence of his reply and the depth of feeling behind it.

Rita nodded, hugging him closer.

Alfonso squeezed her tightly against him. He said gently, 'Come home with me tonight. I'll put your friend up in a hotel.'

'Thanks. I'd like that.' Rita drew a shuddering breath.

'We should go and look for him.' Alfonso and Rita stepped out into the courtyard. The sky was dark. He could hear people on the streets nearby, laughing, chatting as usual. A good sign? It would be a different story if a bull ran loose.

'I'll go look in the streets around here with Jesús, can you stay sort of around here in case he comes back? Or – well – they come back?' Rita said anxiously. Castella's thugs hadn't managed to find him for a week, with thousands, if not millions of others helping. Would the three of them really have better luck?

'Sure.' Alfonso squeezed her hand. She kissed him hard before disappearing back into the house, her shoes crunching on broken glass.

Alfonso walked around the courtyard, glancing at a skip lined up with some bins. The gap behind them was too small for Pepelito. He would need his painkillers and get tired quickly. Maybe he'd hurt himself and was trying to hide in a quiet place. But there weren't many quiet places here for a bull to hide successfully. It was about 9pm, most things were open, lots of people in the street, even if they were some way from the disturbance. Someone would have seen or heard. He looked around at the other floors. Could he have climbed up the stairs?

Alfonso stepped up onto the stone staircase leading to the second and third floors on the opposite side; Rita had told him the owners were away. The stairs were very steep. A dim light came on when he walked onto the first floor landing, but soon turned off again. He continued walking up the stairs to the landing between the second and third floor. He could definitely hear something. He took another step forward and the bulb flickered on.

Pepelito was standing at the bottom of the third floor stairs. He saw Alfonso and did not approach him. He was shivering and panting hard, like he had been that first time. As Alfonso shone the light from his phone, he saw one of the bull's hooves was bleeding. His ears and tail flicked and the whites of his eyes showed, staring at Alfonso in absolute terror.

Alfonso turned away from the bull and edged back across the landing, sitting down at the top of the concrete stairs. Who knew how Pepelito would act when he was cornered and afraid, even to someone who had gone out their way to help him? Carefully looking behind him, he sent a message to Rita. 'Come back. I've got him. But he'll need a bit of encouragement going downstairs.'

Rita replied in seconds. 'Thank God. Coming back now ♡'

He typed a reply. After several minutes, he heard hooves clacking slowly across the hard concrete. Something big and wet nudged the middle of his back. He turned around and saw Pepelito standing behind him sniffing, slightly more relaxed.

'Hey, buddy. It's OK. Haven't you caused a lot of trouble?'

The bull was panting and looked exhausted. Alfonso retrieved a spare bottle of water from his bag and slowly held it out. Pepelito took four or five gulps, then licked his sleeve. His trust felt like an honour; those who raised fighting bulls and arranged corridas saw any lack of aggression as 'cowardice' deserving of brutal punishment.

Alfonso's phone vibrated with Rita's latest text. He read it and snorted with laughter. 'Jesús reckons we can take him down his uncle's farm in a van for taking people to prison – tell him he's wrong please????'

'LOL he'll break the doors down! We'll need a truck!'

Chapter 15 – Uncle Silvio

Rita sat on the sofa between Dominguez and Alfonso, gulping down a glass of water and keeping an eye on Pepelito, who was lying near the television. After coaxing him back in, they'd managed to tie him loosely to the sofa so Alfonso could take a small piece of glass from his foot – and stop him leaving the living room.

'Tempted to ring Castella's helpline. Have some fun with the bastards given we both seem to be homeless as of now.' Dominguez's tone was deceptively light. He spoke through gritted teeth.

'Don't you dare, Jesús, you know what he is,' she said, her stomach clenching at the thought.

'This app's untraceable. Might as well feed them some fake sightings, waste their time before my uncle replies.' He fiddled with something on his phone. Immediately, the speaker began playing loud paso doble music. Pepelito gave him a sorrowful, nervous stare.

'You're scaring him again!'

'Oh, fuck. Fuck.' Dominguez fumbled with the phone. The music stopped. Rita sighed in relief.

'Good news – Silvio says he'll bring his truck and pick us up from the bottom of your road. He's annoyed, and very confused. It'll take him a couple of hours, but he said he'd do it.' Pepelito stared at Dominguez with wary eyes, then went back to gulping water from the large bucket in the corner of the living room. Rita couldn't blame the animal, only those who terrified him. It hadn't been his fault.

'That works, he needs to get vaguely settled before such a journey,' Alfonso said, stroking her hair.

'Is he well enough to go?' she asked.

'It's not ideal but as long as he gets a chance to stop and have a drink. He'll be OK,' Alfonso said.

She glanced at her phone as another message from her mother appeared. 'Why don't you just give Maria one call to ask how she's doing? The police arrested your brother-in-law and kept him 5 hours!'

'That's what happens in murder investigations, suspects get arrested,' she wrote back, feeling nothing but cold stomach-churning fury. This time she sent the message, showing it to Alfonso. She felt safe with him. He didn't judge her. Her ex-husband always felt he had the right to tell her how to behave – and lecture her about her family. He'd always say she was too much. Too opinionated, too blunt and stubborn. When he was in a really bad mood – too fat and ugly.

'You prefer that cat to me,' he'd say when they had adopted Gloria from the rescue centre. Rita could still never forgive her ex-husband for rattling the chair to get her to jump off so he could sit down instead. It had been six months and Rita still missed Gloria more than anything in the world.

Dominguez was now holding out a packet of crisps he had bought earlier and trying to make friends with Pepelito. He clicked his tongue encouragingly. 'Hey, amigo.'

'Yeah, I'd…not do that,' Rita said. Pepelito walked towards him, tail swishing, and snatched the whole packet.

'Hey! Give that back!' Dominguez yanked the half-chewed packet away from the bull's mouth. Pepelito snatched at it again, his horn perilously close to Dominguez's stomach. Dominguez dodged the dangerous horns and lurched into Rita's side, knocking her arm and sloshing her water. He laughed in relief as the bull turned away.

'Damn, sorry, Rita,' Dominguez said, handing her a cloth to wipe up. 'I can't really get used to this arrangement.'

Rita was almost falling asleep between the two men when her phone vibrated again. Knowing who it was, she handed the phone to Alfonso without reading. How could she be 42, in a position of responsibility and still upset by her mum's words? He read it and shook his head.

'Uncaring robot, huh? Imagine saying that about you,' he said, pulling her close beside him. She relaxed into his arms and shut her eyes.

*

'Right, come on, you,' Alfonso said to Pepelito, as the three of them held the rope attached to the harness he was wearing. He was limping despite the dressing the vet had put on his foot, and shuffled nervously out of the doorway, avoiding the now upright but precariously balanced front door. Most of the broken glass and splinters had been swept up, and Rita had placed a tarpaulin to cover their way out.

Her police case files, photos and computer were bagged up by the door, along with her jewellery, some clothes and toiletries, ready to take back to Alfonso's house until her flat was in a fit state to live in again. I'd better take the TV, she thought, but after Castella's unwelcome appearance and Pepelito's agitated reaction, she hadn't felt like turning it on since.

'Get him in first, then we can come back for the rest,' Alfonso said, as they led Pepelito the short distance down the road. She saw a light on in a window. Looking up, she saw a teenage girl who had clearly been crying. When their eyes met the girl mouthed 'Asesinos'. With a jolt to the stomach, Rita knew she thought they were taking Pepelito to Castella. She swallowed hard and carried on walking, taking a small cucumber from the bag of treats and feeding it to him.

'What's all this crap, Jesús?' Silvio said, getting out of his livestock truck. 'I've driven the best part of three hours. Your mum's not far from here. Why didn't you ask her? I'm an old man now. I don't have time for this shit.'

'Silvio,' Rita began as she reached the bottom of the road, feeling a jolt of sympathy for Dominguez. She wasn't the only one with a difficult family.

'Rita, what's going on, what's my nephew done this time,' Silvio said, his tone becoming far friendlier, more affectionate. Dominguez gave an awkward laugh. For some reason Silvio had taken a liking to her when she'd met him before.

'Thanks for coming up, we really need your help.' She clutched the rope tightly as Pepelito came trotting up beside her. He then hung back nervously. A very strange expression on his face, the old man looked at the bull and then back to her.

'We rescued him, he needs somewhere to go, and Jesús says you're a good person,' Rita said, her voice hesitant. She realised she was about to cry.

'Rescued him from where, how could he be rescued here?' Silvio said in confusion. He was right. This place was nowhere near any farms or slaughterhouses.

'He escaped from the plaza de toros,' Rita said, gesturing behind her in the direction of the awful place with her thumb. She looked towards the newly anxious Pepelito – maybe he understood, or was it that car in the distance? Alfonso was feeding him some fruit. Silvio gave her a look of distaste. He looked at Pepelito thoughtfully.

'Oh. Did he? Good for him. I've never liked that stuff. Bit of a rigged contest if you ask me, and the way they strut around so pleased with themselves like they've done something amazing, leaves a bad taste.' He took a cigarette packet out of his shirt pocket. He hadn't mentioned the reward. He probably didn't even know about it.

'I was telling Rita how you know all about cows. He'd be good for your two. She's been hiding him there for a week and he's completely trashed the house and kicked down most of her doors. I'm telling her he needs to be outside in a nice big field like the one at yours, this isn't a place for him.' Dominguez gave his uncle a pleading, despairing look.

'Well, I've only got Maribel now after Beatriz died last month. The old girl is so lonely, she could do with a companion.' Silvio sighed.

He took a drag on his cigarette. Rita looked behind her. The teenage girl was walking towards them with tears in her eyes. She was filming on her phone. With a weird intellectual curiosity, Rita half wondered if she was about to get bombarded with hateful comments from millions of people she didn't know.

'Yeah. I'll take him. I'll get the ramp down so we can get him in.' Rita patted Pepelito's side. Alfonso had taken his bandage off while she was sleeping, revealing several huge, long stitched up scars. She couldn't look at them without wanting to cry.

She really was going to miss him.

'Enjoy your two million, you fucking murderers,' the girl yelled from behind them. Something hit Rita in the back. She turned around and saw a small stone land on the ground.

'He trusts you but you've killed him. I wanted him to live, we all did!' A second pebble fell short, landed on the pavement.

'You're a cop. All cops are bastards!' the girl sobbed, disappearing into the night before Rita could reply. Rita gulped back tears and began walking the hundred metres back to her flat to fetch her valuables. She'd never feared the dark or walking alone. But the shadows seemed menacing tonight, and Caroline McKenzie's murder plagued her thoughts.

Had Castella killed her?

While he lacked the convictions to prove his criminal history, everything she knew about the man told her he was more than capable of taking human life. But Dominguez was right. The timing and choice of victim seemed unlikely.

But if not him – who?

Rita took the bags full of her stuff out of the doorway and pushed Dominguez's suitcase into the street. Most of the plastic and straw was now in the bins outside, but not all of it. She supposed she should tidy it up or try to conceal it but the task was overwhelming. After moving some stuff, her and Alfonso would be back later for her car. That would make it easier.

'We got him in,' Dominguez said as he headed up to grab his suitcase. 'He's got water and some straw, but Silvio reckons we ought to go now so he's not in there too long.'

Rita walked over round the back of Silvio's truck. Pepelito had stuck his nose out the window. He raised his head without much difficulty, but looked confused and sad. She took out the bag of treats and fed him a sweet pepper. Alfonso put his arm round her.

'I've given Silvio the meds he needs to have for the next week, he said he's got some of that stuff at home too, but he might not need much more after a couple of weeks. He's so much more active now, isn't he,' Alfonso said, holding her close as she tried not to cry.

'We'll have to go visit him,' she said, patting Pepelito's nose through the bars. Tearing herself away, she walked over to Silvio and Dominguez.

'You coming with us, Jesús? How you getting to work tomorrow?' she said.

'I'll go back with Silvio; he wants some help getting him in the field. Got the day off tomorrow supposedly, so I could move, although that's now fallen through.' Dominguez rolled his eyes. Good luck. They both knew you could never rely on it being an actual day off. She tried to put thoughts about Caroline at the back of her mind. She was off the case; she had to let it go.

'I'll drive round and pick you up in the afternoon,' Rita said. Turning to Silvio, she said, 'Look after him, he does get scared.'

'Oh, the old girl will calm him down, nothing fazes her. Not much fear in my life, either; nothing's killed me yet, though a rooster came close once,' he said.

Rita smiled. 'He'll be happy there.'

Silvio grinned. 'Safe, too. If anyone comes, I've got some angry geese.'

Chapter 16 – Blood Sports

Aidan woke up in pitch darkness. He tried to stand up and immediately hit his head. He pushed at the metal box holding him inside. He couldn't see any holes. It was hard to breathe in here. He reached in his pocket for his phone, but it had gone. Where was he? He couldn't remember anything! Was this a nightmare?

'Hello,' he yelled, but immediately realised this was a mistake. He felt something hot between his legs. Oh no. He had pissed himself. Whoever it was, was going to leave him here. He should have gone to the gym more often, should have gone for more runs, then maybe he could get out of this situation. He remembered finishing his shift, sitting down at the bus stop; after that, he couldn't remember anything else.

If only he hadn't argued with his mum before he went to work. If only he hadn't taken the piss out of that new guy at work last week. He was such a dick wasn't he. He'd been texting Summer, hadn't he? What if she'd messaged him again and he hadn't replied?

'Hello, Aidan,' said a voice he couldn't see. He felt his blood run cold. Where had he heard that before? Then the metal door slid vertically open with a clank. He tried to pull himself to his feet. The light disorientated him and something was stabbing into the back of his neck. He felt sick. Twisting round, Aidan saw there were seats round one side. The floor was covered with sand. Above the seats was written 'Property of the Taurine Club of Kensington.'

There was a chandelier on the ceiling that looked expensive. The walls were covered with stuffed animal heads. Three bulls, an elephant, a lion, two horses, a giraffe, a moose, a tiger, a leopard – and then a cat. Aidan gasped, sank to his knees, trying to stop himself throwing up. He put his hand round the back of his neck and felt some sort of ribbon attached to a metal object. He gave it a tug and it didn't come out, just drenched his hand in blood. He winced in pain.

'Gonna let me go then, you fucking pervert,' Aidan shouted, panic rising inside him as he tried to stand, disorientated and nauseous. He yanked at the ribbon again, hard. This time it came off in his hand. Warm blood ran down his neck and on his hands. Aidan felt faint and sick. He was looking at a metal dart attached to a green and pink rosette, sticky with blood. He ripped the rosette away and stuffed the dart in his pocket, feeling lightheaded. He took his hoodie off and started tying it around his neck. It hurt too much to tie it tightly, and the fabric became soaked when he pressed hard.

'What's all them animal heads? You gonna add me to your taxidermy collection or summat you weirdo?' Aidan knew he had to keep this nonce talking, he'd seen it on the murder programmes his mum liked watching. He couldn't see an exit. The sand on his hands was stinging him. He was so hungry. He needed to drink something. It was hot in here. There was no way out.

'You said you wished I'd been gored by a bull,' a posh voice spat, he couldn't see him. His voice was full of hate. What? In spite of his fear and agony Aidan started laughing. It was such a mental thing to say.

'You what now?' Aidan gasped. He couldn't see the prick. But he recognised his voice from somewhere. Then out of nowhere, the man strode out from behind a painted wooden board near the animal heads. He had two massive yellow sticks in his hands. He was wearing one of those glittery outfits like in that Spanish video –

Oh. Oh yeah.

'I know who you are, you're that politician. Well, it's true, I wish you had been, cunt, wish it gored you all to death. Game for sick bastards.' Aidan was sweating. His top was becoming loose. He knew he had to fight back. He could hardly breathe. As he attempted shakily to get to his feet, Henry kicked him hard in the stomach. The air was knocked out of him. He felt in his pocket for the dart. His hand clenched around it. He could grab it and stick it in this fucker and then try and run.

Aidan pushed past the pain, forced himself to get up and threw himself at Henry, trying to shove the dart at him. Far too late, he saw the huge blades on the ends of the yellow sticks his attacker was holding. Henry merely smiled as Aidan tried to pull back, then pressed the sticks down into Aidan's back. The dart fell uselessly to the floor and Henry kicked some sand over it.

'One way to truly appreciate something, is to experience it for yourself. It's a great pity there aren't enough of us here to enact the whole performance in its full glory,' Henry laughed as Aidan screamed in agony, an unpleasant smile playing across his lips.

****

After he had finished, Henry got changed out of his 'suit of lights'. Along with the sword he'd used to deal the killing blow, he had won it in an auction at Sotheby's for £350,000. These priceless treasures had belonged to Juan Belmonte, one of the most awe-inspiring matadors of all time; when Henry wore the costume, it felt like he was channelling the spirit of the great man. He washed the blood off his hands in the small sink at the foot of the stairs. He really had to sort out the soundproofing in the cellar. He didn't think the help could hear anything, but one couldn't be sure. No matter how much he paid, shoddy building jobs by lazy workmen remained a perennial headache.

He checked to make sure there were no spots of blood on his clothing, then walked up the stairs and entered the code to leave the cellar. Once out, he padlocked the door and picked up the phone he'd left on a teak dressing table with ivory handles that his great great grandfather had brought back from the colonies. Next to his phone was a bull's ear thrown into the crowd one time, which Henry had picked up and preserved in a jar.

'Am I right in thinking the Club's next Spain visit is next week?' an MP called Eloise Skerrett had written in the Taurine Club's

WhatsApp group chat. Henry didn't care for female politicians other than Margaret Thatcher and, at a push, the Home Secretary and one of the recent Tory Prime Ministers. Women were emotional and couldn't view anything objectively. But Eloise was a rising star in the Tory ranks, who shared his passion for the bulls, making her that rare thing – a female worth his respect.

'Week after,' Henry wrote back. Eloise gave him the thumbs up. A woman after his own heart, he thought. Or she would be, were it not for the tawdry Westminster gossip circulating in the WhatsApp chats Henry checked religiously.

He had to do something else, too. Using his secret account, he went onto the Facebook group Caroline McKenzie had been active in. Henry regularly used this account to keep tabs on his critics, follow their discussions and scour Facebook for posts about himself.

The latest post in the group was a video. There were 40 comments on it. Henry walked into his study and opened the Facebook thread on his computer so he could read properly. Under his computer chair was a snow leopard he had shot on a clandestine hunting trip in Mongolia and turned into a rug. So what if they were endangered? All the more reason to nab one while he could.

One day, he'd be the man to bag the very last one of something.

What a prize that would be.

'I'm heartbroken – they're going to kill him now, I saw them take him away!!! 😭' the thread starter, someone called Lucia Alvarez, had written in translated Spanish. Kill who? What could this be about?

The grainy video showed two men and a woman leading a bull down a narrow street on a rope, bringing to mind some of the festivities Henry enjoyed, where, in time-honoured fashion, crowds of men tugged 'toros ensogados' through the streets on long ropes. Yet this was no festivity. A vein throbbed in Henry's temple as he watched Pepelito eat from the woman's hand. Already one of the worst he'd watched, this soft treatment would surely ruin the bull beyond repair.

95

'Delete this,' an anonymous user had posted. 'I trust one of the people in this video. I'm 100% sure it won't be what it looks like. I'll DM you.'

Incensed, Henry took screenshots of everything and sent them to Javier Castella. He had promised to help, after all, and these fools had deprived Pepelito of the honour of dying in the ring! Genius though Javier was, it smarted a little to discover the Valladolid Policia Nacional had considered giving him credit for Henry's work. Thankfully, his friend had been released without charge, which was better for all concerned.

Henry looked back at his WhatsApps. Eloise Skerrett had sent the club's group chat a message. 'We could sue for defamation here, couldn't we?'

Henry opened the link, instantly recognising the name – Robyn Casey.

'Who are the Taurine Club of Kensington?' the title read – never a good start.

It carried on, 'Last week, Tory House of Lords member Henry Dixon was allegedly filmed violently attacking the bull which attracted worldwide attention with its dramatic escape from a Spanish bullfight. Dixon, a well-known fan of the controversial sport, is president of the Taurine Club of Kensington, a group for devoted aficionados which organises events throughout the year…'

What he read made him sick with fury. Every sentence portrayed the club, its members, and Henry himself in a thoroughly derogatory, unfair and unbalanced light. To be a member was to be snobbish, cruel, corrupt and selfish. Robyn described in detail how the Club's members had recorded their bullfighting and hunting holidays as parliamentary expenses, so the taxpayer picked up the tab. This was inaccurate – as an MP, Henry himself had only done that four or five times, not every time as the article implied.

'Wow. She's just interviewed a group of animal rights fanatics with nothing positive to say,' Henry wrote.

'Think it's 'they' rather than 'she',' Eloise replied.

'Ah. That explains everything.' He would have to do something about Robyn, but maybe it could wait until he got back from Spain, unless he did it in the next week or two. Henry had much to do there. Besides the many corridas he planned to attend, visits to bull farms and hunting excursions, he and his fellow club members would keep the wheels of diplomacy turning, enjoying extensive lunches, dinners and drinks with the great and good of society.

That bloody bull had cheated Henry of a great spectacle that afternoon. It was hard for him not to take the incident as a personal slight; besides Robyn's piece, Henry himself was now the butt of jokes in several cartoons. And what a gift this whole sorry business was for Labour's attacks on the Tories.

Pepelito had to be found; the irresponsible fools and do-gooders who had him would pay.

Henry would ensure it.

Chapter 17 – Setting the Record Straight

'Would you like to explain this?' Gabriel Sanchez yelled at Rita and Dominguez as they stood in front of him. A video was open on his computer.

Rita watched, an awful sinking feeling in her chest. The video showed Pepelito eating something out of her hand in the street. It showed Dominguez and Alfonso coaxing him into Silvio's truck, and the four of them enjoying a cigarette.

'Rita, your brother-in-law is a murder suspect, in fact, Jesús, you spent a whole day questioning him last week! You know how discredited that man is, and how bad it looks for the whole department to assist him in anything right now? To take a side in this stupid culture war? For my officers to hand over, what I'm sure isn't, but appears to be a gentle, sweet natured animal?' Sanchez glared at both of them.

'Señor, you know that I would never, ever assist Castella,' Rita said, saying the matador's name as if it was a swear word. After the scrutiny she'd been placed under three years ago, the endless grillings, the thought of Sanchez believing she'd helped him was unbearable.

'What on earth did you think you were doing, then – you thought you could get some money without consulting me, or the department first, or considering how bad it would look?' Sanchez spat.

'We're all under enough pressure to improve our cleanup rate, the British cops may pitch up here next week over the McKenzie investigation, and I could frankly do without hassle from animal rights extremists!'

Rita could hardly believe what she was hearing. All she could manage was 'Yes, Señor.'

'Actually, we were doing the opposite,' Dominguez mumbled. Rita wasn't sure whether this was a very good or very stupid idea. Sanchez's eyes bulged.

'Doing the opposite? What on earth do you mean, Jesús?'

'Castella sent a group of thugs who work for the local plaza to look for the bull, they chased him into Rita's, obviously terrified out of his mind. You won't believe the damage that beast caused, all her doors are destroyed and there's cow shit everywhere. Most of her house was ruined. Anyway, we managed to catch him and put a rope round him after they'd gone, and rung an animal charity to pick him up.' Dios mio, Rita thought. He didn't drop me in it. Sanchez looked completely unconvinced.

'This is certainly a story that raises more questions than answers. Where are these thugs now?'

'Well, some of them are sitting in the cells downstairs.' It was true, but the arrests were for other incidents.

'What happened to the bull?'

'Oh, I don't know,' Dominguez said. 'Not my problem any more.'

Rita took a deep breath. 'Señor,' she said. She was in enough trouble as it is. And Sanchez clearly didn't believe Dominguez's story.

'Yes?'

'That's not quite what happened.'

Dominguez gave her a horrified look and nudged her hard.

'Just over a week ago, I found Pepelito lying in my street, horrendously injured after escaping from Castella's corrida. I got veterinary advice on how to treat his injuries. I've been looking after him ever since – until the thugs from the ring tried to force their way in. He was petrified so he bolted. At which point, Jesús and I caught him and arranged someone to pick him up, and that's what you see in the video.' Although she wasn't in too much trouble, it was sensible to avoid mentioning Alfonso's name…

'Looking after him where, half the country must have been looking for him at some point?'

'In my flat.'

Sanchez's mouth dropped open and shut and open again like a goldfish. He stared at her as if she was crazy.

Perhaps she was.

'So it was you? You hid Castella's bull in your flat for a week?'

'Yeah.' As she spoke, Sanchez buried his head in his hands.

'Get out of my office,' he yelled.

*

Rita walked out, shaken and stunned. Relief filled her that she wasn't suspended, or worse, charged. Sanchez wasn't much for animal rights. But he was concerned about terrible publicity from his officers handing a docile, affectionate creature, who had unwittingly starred in a viral video seen by millions, to his torturer, a man soaked in animal and almost certainly human blood. The younger generations disliked the police enough as it was.

'How was it yesterday?' she asked Dominguez once they were out of earshot.

'Apart from Pepelito running over my foot and ripping my shirt when we let him in the field, it was fine. Silvio thinks he's great, told you he loves cows. Doesn't think the same about me, couldn't wait to get me gone. He liked Luis, thinks I threw a good thing away.' He sighed, looking sad.

'Probably prefers animals to people. I can relate. But it's unfair. This was Luis's doing, not you.' Rita walked into the kitchen for some coffee.

She missed Pepelito. She had got used to having him around. When she did move back into her flat it would seem strangely empty without him. Instead, she had moved in with a man she hardly knew. Alfonso seemed decent, caring and crazy about her. But the murder and DV statistics suggested this was probably more dangerous than sharing a flat with a bull. She opened her phone and wrote, 'My boss knows. It went better than I thought it would.'

Rita sat down at her computer and opened her emails to find she had one from Caroline McKenzie's son. With a pang of guilt she realised she had forgotten to tell him she was now off the case.

'Inspectora Silvera, I hope you are well? I am just wondering how the case was going. Has there been any progress in finding my Mum's killer?' The truth was, there had been no progress. All the hotel guests had been ruled out, and they were close to ruling out Castella himself.

'Hi Iain, thanks for your email. I've been taken off this case, but I've forwarded it on to Inspector Abdul Mansouri who is now in charge of the investigation.' That email sounded too cold. She put it in drafts until she could think of something better. It was horrible to fob him off like this. As she sipped her cup of coffee, her phone rang.

'Good morning, am I speaking to someone from the Valladolid National Police Corps?' a woman's voice said in English. She had a thick accent and was hard to understand, even though Rita spoke it fluently.

'Yes. Inspectora Rita Silvera speaking.'

'My name's Detective Sergeant Heather Cooper from West Yorkshire Police. I'm calling about a body that was found in the area yesterday; we're hoping you may be able to help.' Heather took a deep breath on the other end of the line.

'The victim's been identified as Aidan Donnelly. He was 18. This was an extremely violent attack against someone young and vulnerable, although he was legally an adult. So you'll understand we're very keen to catch whoever it is.' The woman sounded calm, but couldn't disguise her shock. Rita listened intently.

'An item that was found with the victim suggests a link to your region of Spain and we were hoping you could provide some assistance.' Heather spoke in a businesslike tone, but Rita had to think about her words before understanding the meaning.

'What sort of item?'

'We found a metal dart placed beside the body. We don't think it was the murder weapon, but forensic evidence suggests it was one of the weapons used to attack the victim. There was an engraving on it saying it was manufactured in Valladolid.' Heather's words gave Rita chills as she sipped her coffee.

'Can you send me a picture of this dart? I'll see what I can do,' Rita said. Within seconds, she had it in her inbox. She stared at the gruesome object and disgust and anger coursed through her.

'Malditos. Escoria.' *Scum.*

Just as well he came in here, if he had walked much further, this could have sunk down and pierced his lung,' Alfonso said, patting Pepelito and showing Rita a dart with a bloody ribbon attached. Despite the heat, the bull was shivering and the horror stricken look on his face wrenched her heart. Rita hadn't known cows could cry, with actual tears.

'Bullfighters use such darts. They attach it to a rosette, it's called a divisa, a currency, they stab it into the bull's back just before it runs into the ring. It's to make the bull run out quickly and seem fierce. Sounds like the killer is interested in such activities.' Rita spoke slowly, emphasising each word, not trusting herself not to tear up. There was a horrified silence at the end of the line. She remembered how Caroline's friends had insisted it was Castella who had a motive to kill.

Rita was irritated to hear Heather say, 'So someone from Spain then?'

'It doesn't only happen here. There are fans everywhere, half of them are tourists. You're just as bad with your fox hunting.' Rita replaced her cup heavily, filling the embarrassed silence.

Defensively, she went on to say, 'The killer might not have bought it here, it's likely he didn't. There will be sites on the dark web selling these items. You can probably get them on eBay.'

'Of course. I wasn't suggesting –'

'Doesn't matter.'

'Yes it does. I really do apologise. Would you be able to send us a list of those convicted of murder and sexual offenders registered in the area, so we can cross check if any of them are currently resident in the UK or had recently visited?'

'I'll send you everyone on our system. Was the victim sexually assaulted?' Rita asked, feeling nauseous at the thought.

'No,' Heather said. 'But we're working on the assumption they've killed before; they must be getting some gratification out of it.'

Rita felt something twisting in her stomach. If the killer was from here, nonce cases and violent offenders couldn't just enjoy easy travel in and out of the EU. Did the killer slip through the cracks, or escape a criminal record altogether, like Castella had?

'When was the victim killed?'

'Two days ago.'

Rita took a breath. That ruled him out. Castella couldn't have been released from custody, flown to the UK, killed a random person, got rid of all his DNA and flown back. Could he?

'I'll have a look at our cold cases and send through anything I can find. And we'll get the companies producing such items to provide a list of customers.' Rita copied in Dominguez and Mansouri to the emails she was sending. Sanchez had stuck her on desk duties for the next day or two, which meant she might be able to spend some time helping Heather. More worthwhile than waiting at her desk for someone to walk in and report something.

'Thanks very much,' Heather said.

Rita put down the phone. Once she had rewritten and sent a reply to Iain, she headed to the record storage room.

One file in particular caught her attention as she hunted through cold cases. The victim's name was Sonia Gutiérrez. She had died in 2012 age 32, a few years after Rita had joined the department. She

103

vaguely remembered the case. Not much had been recorded about the victim's life other than having three kids and selling sex for a living. With all her regular clients ruled out and no other murders of those working the streets shortly before or afterwards, her case had gone cold.

But on the day she went missing, Sonia was not working. It had been a Sunday and she had brought the kids to church with her mother, a devoted Catholic. Afterwards she left them with her, before walking to town to do some shopping and meet a friend. She usually hit the streets in the evening, but had never made it to work that night.

Rita looked through the autopsy report feeling like a heavy stone was sitting on her stomach. No DNA was found belonging to a suspect. Sonia was found dressed in clothes that didn't belong to her. There was a gap of four days between the last recorded sighting of Sonia and the discovery of her body.

And her injuries were almost identical to Caroline McKenzie's.

Chapter 18 – Connections

Grabbing the file, Rita navigated the station's passages until she reached the office where Abdul Mansouri was leading the murder investigation. Recently graduated from a criminology postgrad scheme, this would be Abdul's inaugural stint as head of such a case. Rita had a soft spot for him. One of the few officers on the team from an immigrant background, he often worked much harder than the others to prove himself. But maybe not today. Knocking on the door, she heard his shocked laughter.

'Come in? Rita! Jesús was just telling us all how you re-enacted the San Fermines in your living room?' Mansouri stared at her in disbelief.

'I tried to feed him some crisps and he almost gored me! She said, yeah, course you can stay with me, no problem, little did I know!' Dominguez was doubled over with hysterics. Rita felt a little annoyed and singled out, but what had she expected?

'There aren't many people willing to suffer for their principles these days, I'd have done the exact same, good for you Rita, standing up for our bovine friends,' one of the other newer recruits giggled, a 21-year-old woman called Laurentia. She was Flavia's niece who had moved from Romania as a teenager.

'You should have brought him to work. We could have used him to solve crimes,' Mansouri said. Rita imagined Pepelito wandering around the station and her irritation subsided. It *was* funny. What a relief she wasn't facing other consequences except piss taking.

'That's what I said to your amigo when we were getting him into the truck. I said, we missed a trick, can't exactly resist arrest with a bull's horn shoved up their rear end, can they?' Dominguez slapped Rita on the back.

'How's your sister doing, you spoken to her recently? Tell her to send Castella our best wishes, will you!' Mansouri snorted. Everyone laughed, including Rita, grudgingly.

'They never speak, they haven't spoken for about ten years. Can't imagine why, I'd have thought they had lots to talk about, wouldn't you,' Dominguez said darkly.

'Anyway. Let's get back to work,' Mansouri managed to say, looking in no fit state to start at all.

'Abdul,' Rita said.

'Yes?'

'You might be interested in this. A case from eleven years ago, a murdered sex worker called Sonia Gutiérrez. It has similarities to the Caroline McKenzie killing.' Mansouri took the file.

'Thanks, Rita,' he said, turning to the autopsy report. He arranged his face into something a bit more serious.

'Yeah. The injuries found on the victim are similar. But there's a ten year gap between murders. And the victims don't seem to have had anything in common apart from being female. One was a sex worker in her early 30s with young kids at home and the other one was a British businesswoman staying in a posh hotel.' He looked again at the file.

'What was Castella doing back then?' Mansouri asked.

'I think we can rule him out. He was on holiday in Las Vegas for 3 weeks with my sister for their honeymoon,' Rita scowled. Sonia hadn't been her case; that week, she'd had to deal with two armed robberies and a horrific hit and run. When she'd gone to visit her parents, all her mum wanted to do was gush over their holiday snaps. Her father said little and looked defeated. I should visit for his sake, she thought. She just couldn't face it.

Once back at her desk, she copied the information about Sonia to the British policewoman, plus a list of people questioned at the time.

Aidan had lived and died in a different country. But the 18-year-old's murder was disturbing her deeply – and so was the dart found with him. It probably wasn't bought in this area. But it was made here. No doubt taking for granted that it wouldn't be used on humans, someone would have taken pride in its 'craftsmanship'.

Heather replied, 'Thanks very much for sending this over. It's probably not what we're looking for but I'll take a look.'

Flavia had been on that case. Rita sent her a message. 'Hola. Hope you're enjoying a long deserved rest. I'm sorry to bother you. Do you remember anything about an old case, Sonia Gutiérrez?'

'Yeah, I do,' came Flavia's reply. 'That was a weird one. It was near some big conference or other. There were a few VIPs attending who I'm sure knew more than they let on. The old superintendent at the time wanted us to forget it and move on.' Of course he did, Rita thought, dead hookers weren't seen as important, especially when there was only one.

'There are some similarities between her death and Caroline McKenzie,' Rita wrote. Flavia was typing a lot.

Eventually, she wrote, 'Doesn't surprise me. I always thought it wasn't that bastard's first time. By the looks of it, it wasn't his last.'

*

'I told you I was gonna take you out properly,' Alfonso said when they were both home later that night. Rita got changed into a backless dress with sequins. Maybe she was too old to wear it, but fuck it. She put on some heels and they walked to Alfonso's van. He lived a 20 minute ride from the city. His house was much older and bigger than hers, and she did feel like they were rattling around. At some point, she badly needed to sort out her flat. Without Pepelito there, it would feel empty and sanitised.

'How was work?' he said once they were in the van.

'Hey, always a bad idea to ask that question! It was fine. Desk duties until Wednesday. Sanchez is pissed. But not as pissed as he'd be if I'd given Pepelito to Castella.'

Alfonso looked stunned.

'Your boss is an antitaurino?' he asked in surprise. Rita scoffed.

'Of course not. He doesn't give a shit. Just doesn't want the police looking bad, especially him. And our mutual friend is famous,' Rita laughed as they parked up and got out the car. Alfonso had booked a table at a newly opened pizzeria in town that did a vegan menu. They walked inside holding hands and were given a seat by the window.

'How's Dolores?' Rita asked. Alfonso smiled.

'All good, yeah.' Rita glanced at her phone before putting it away for the evening. She had a message from a number she didn't recognise, which simply said, 'Was it you? How could you do this to Javier???'

'Maybe he'll know how poor Pepelito felt now, with everyone ganging up on him,' she texted back before blocking the number. She shuddered, feeling much safer now she was staying with someone else.

'Your sister?' Alfonso said.

'Yeah.' She sighed and shook her head as their drinks came.

'Can I ask something, Rita?'

She shrugged, feeling herself become nervous. Past experience told her men would always ask even if she said no.

'Are there other reasons you hate Castella so much?' Alfonso said. Rita stared at him; given previous terrible first dates, she had been anticipating something like a marriage proposal. Somehow this was worse. She wanted to protect Alfonso, not pollute their relationship by talking about *him*.

But now Castella knew.

He hadn't killed Caroline or Sonia. But he was a dangerous psychopath.

'I don't need other reasons to despise him, but I wondered if there's anything else.'

Rita nodded, taking a deep breath.

'Five years ago, we raided a property maybe about two hours from here, a huge villa owned by a drug baron called Martin Ortiz Aguilar who's now in prison.' She paused and sipped her cocktail.

'Police! Drop your weapons and come out slowly with your hands in the air!' she yelled into the megaphone, standing on the soft red carpet, shaking under her clothes. The ornately decorated walls were now riddled with bullet holes. Was her body armour good enough?

A man with a designer suit and sunglasses strode towards them. He pointed a gun at her chest. She leapt over to the side, knowing it was too late –

'Oh, go fuck yourself, bitch.'

'I was shot during the raid and spent three weeks in hospital. We lost two of our best officers that day.' Rita sighed. Her eyes were filling with tears. She remembered walking the opulent rooms, the champagne worth thousands, the ostentatious decor, gold plated furniture and diamond encrusted chandeliers Aguilar had bought with his stolen fortune just because he could.

'We found documents showing Castella owned a share in this villa and several other properties linked to Aguilar, through shell companies and offshore accounts. He wasn't the only one, there were other famous people and politicians. Judges too, even a bishop! Aguilar was – is – one of the most notorious gangsters in Spain. Not just Spain, he was involved with the mafia and the South American cartels. He's scum.' She took a deep breath. Her pizza came, but she scarcely noticed.

'We had witnesses. We were going to throw the book at Castella for involvement in Aguilar's businesses and benefiting from the proceeds of crime. But the prosecutor's office wouldn't help us and the case was never filed. So he walked. Of course he claims his innocence.' Rita spat the words out. She dug out a photo on her phone she had found back then, of Castella, Aguilar and another drug dealer at a party in Monaco, and showed it to him. He stared in disgust.

'There's worse. Much worse.' She lowered her voice. You never knew who was listening.

'Castella was directly running Aguilar's businesses. He was 2nd or 3rd in command. After Aguilar was jailed, he took over. But we've never been able to get anything solid. He's got friends high up. Something always happens. Evidence goes missing. Charges get dropped.'

'I always thought, that the justice system, the prosecutors and judges, had the forces of right and good on their side, and they'd work with us in putting together a case. I thought if officers died they'd move heaven and earth to get every last one of those who could be the slightest bit implicated,' she said, her voice hardening.

'Did I get a wake-up call. I was suicidal for months. I almost left the police over it, and I joke around but being a cop is all I ever really wanted to do.' She shut her eyes.

'Why did you stay?' Alfonso asked gently. It was a good question. Rita thought about it for a few moments.

She held his gaze, feeling herself flush. 'I stayed for my colleagues at first, and then because if I left, I knew the criminals would win. Including the ones who wear a badge or sit on the judge's bench. And you know what the worst part was?'

Alfonso took her hand across the table.

'After I came out of hospital I tried again with Maria. I turned up at her party offices with the evidence we'd collected that he was in business with Aguilar. She started shouting. Called me psychotic. Got security to kick me out.' Rita picked up a slice of pizza and bit into it.

'Because I was related to her, some of my colleagues said I was corrupt. Not just an animal killer. A drug dealer who's destroyed thousands of human lives. Imagine. I'd rather starve to death than take his money.' Alfonso held her hand in a warm grip. She didn't want him to get hurt.

'He's completely charmed my mum. She doesn't want to know. She's one of these people who puts 'family' above everything, so according to her, I'm the unreasonable one.' Rita swallowed hard. Sometimes she forgot how much it hurt.

'Remember all those crime scene photos and documents in my filing cabinet?' she said quietly.

'The one Pepelito knocked over that day?'

Rita nodded.

'Most of the photos were from a case of two murdered drug dealers who'd fallen out with Castella. One of them wrote about it on his Instagram. We're pretty sure they died on his orders. The actual murderers are in jail, but they won't talk. I don't know if we'll ever have enough to convict him.' She exhaled. Did Silvio appreciate who – and *what* – Castella was? Dominguez said he'd raised the possibility of the matador trying to find 'his' missing bull; true to form, the old man was dismissive.

'Ugh. Caroline hated Castella. She hated matadors in general. She was a great researcher. Maybe she found out something she shouldn't…' He took a sip of his beer out the bottle. She shook her head.

'We've ruled him out,' she said quickly, not wanting to expose him to the awful thing swimming around in her mind. She hated herself for even asking, let alone bringing his wife into it.

But she had to know.

'Alfonso, did you or Pilar ever used to know someone called Sonia Gutiérrez?'

'Sonia?' he said. 'I've not heard her name in years. Pilar knew her from animal rights stuff, they used to go on protests together. But they lost touch. Sonia was… troubled, and Pilar used to feel guilty for not keeping in touch or making an effort. They hadn't spoken in about a year, then one day we read on Facebook she'd been murdered. They never found the killer, did they?'

She took a breath, looking Alfonso straight in the eye. Her heart jolted in her chest. 'I know this is a lot. But whoever killed her also killed Caroline – the day Pepelito escaped. Before you wonder, I know it wasn't you. At the time she died, you were helping him.'

She couldn't think what could have connected these two women.

Now she did.

Chapter 19 – High On His Own Supply

Lying next to Maribel under a tree, Pepelito found it hot but pleasant. She was the first member of his species he'd seen since the plaza workers had driven him from the enclosure into that tiny room. Far away from the arena, he was trying to put its horror and violence out of his mind. The fresh air had eased the pain in his back and in his heart.

He hadn't seen a cow for even longer, not since he last saw his mum. He'd been so young. Sometimes he still remembered her comforting presence. Maribel was different; bigger than he was, without question the dominant one. She was 15, too old to be interested, but that did not matter; with her, he could be sociable and felt loved. She was calm and accepting. Perhaps here, he could start to heal both his mind and his body.

But he sensed the terrible sadness in her. She had recently lost someone too. She had been a dairy cow and before Silvio retired she'd had calves taken away, seen other cows sold. They had a lot of space and Silvio was a kind, if irritable man who left them alone. He wasn't cruel or violent. But there were things he didn't want to or couldn't understand.

'Maribel,' Silvio said; she got up and strolled towards him. She adored the farmer. Pepelito still didn't know if he truly trusted any humans. He knew he had done something bad a few weeks ago. He'd made Rita afraid. Maybe she was angry with him. Maybe that was why Silvio took him. He was happy to be here but the journey had exhausted him; it was disorientating being somewhere so different.

He didn't miss Rita's flat or the street noises and the walls and the lack of grass, but he missed her and Alfonso, they had been kind to him and protected him. He got up and walked to the water trough. A group of geese hissed at him as they hung around it. Yesterday one had bit his leg, so he'd chased them. He'd have to do it again.

He turned round slowly and walked towards Maribel as another farmer chatted to Silvio by the fence. 'That's a nice-looking bull. Where did he come from?'

'My nephew won him in a bet with some guy, and I just lost poor old Beatriz so he gave him to me.' Silvio took a drag on his cigarette. Pepelito picked up on his anxiety and irritation.

'How much is he?' the other farmer was asking, looking towards Pepelito.

'He's not for sale.'

The other farmer looked disappointed. 'He looks like the bull in that YouTube video I saw.'

Silvio shook his head in confusion.

'On the internet.'

'No idea what you're on about, son. Don't ask me about the internet. Never even sent an email.' After a few minutes the other farmer left, followed by several geese who snapped at his legs. Silvio looked confused and annoyed.

'What was that about, Maribel? That guy only talks to me when he wants something.' Maribel walked forward to be stroked. Silvio didn't like other humans, Pepelito thought, watching the geese and chickens scratching around in front of the dilapidated farmhouse.

'How you doing, Pepelito? Your back any better than yesterday?' Silvio said cheerfully as if he was chatting to a neighbour and expecting a reply.

'Lovely weather today, isn't it? Not too hot. Nice day for sitting outside and having a smoke.' Was he supposed to do anything in response? Pepelito wasn't sure. Sometimes he found the kind way people now treated him difficult to navigate. There were things he had learned not to do, to hide in front of humans. Pain and fear had been constant companions during his previous encounters, but now he seemed to have no reason to fear anything. When he dropped his guard, his new protectors even rewarded him with treats and affection. He found their reactions disconcerting; they were so different to what he knew he had to expect.

'Ladron is it? He'll be my first,' the man smirked, pointing out the brown bull who merely looked at him sadly and then lowered his head into the trough in the corner. The food pellets tasted weird and they'd all felt tired and sick afterwards. But there was nothing else to eat.

'Then this one second.' The man pointed at him. What was this about?

Curiously, he approached the barrier where the men were standing, craning his neck over the high, whitewashed side. When he was little, sometimes the farmer's daughter had stroked him and fed him treats. But instead, the man swung a fist at his nose, punching him hard. 'What's this? Huh? Think you're a dog? Think you're my friend? Don't you know who the fuck I am?'

Pepelito hastily retreated, reeling, before the man could hit him again. Turning back to the enclosure keepers, Castella said, 'Make sure you knock that out of him before I see him next.'

Pepelito took a few more gulps of water and gazed at Silvio, who smiled indulgently at him and reached to pet him over the wooden fence. He let the man touch him, then backed away, needing his space.

As he ambled towards the barn, he heard Silvio answer his mobile. 'What do *you* want, now?'

'Of course not, don't be ridiculous, son.'

'Who told you that? People say anything these days don't they. How'd you get this damned number?' Silvio waited for a few seconds, then hung up. Pepelito tore at some grass. Why was he so bad tempered sometimes, had someone hurt him too?

'You're popular aren't you,' the old man said conversationally, lighting another cigarette. Pepelito stared at him, wondering what that was about.

115

'Ah well. Sent him packing, didn't I.'

****

Javier Castella grinned and bowed extravagantly to his fans at Madrid's world-renowned Las Ventas Arena. He lifted up the bull's ear awarded him for tonight's breathtaking, passionate display of bravery, and tossed it to someone in the audience, before parading around smirking as the dead beast was dragged away. He walked to the ringside barriers to kiss some of his female fans' cheeks, before striding back to the changing room to thunderous applause.

In front of the full-length mirror, he gazed upon his reflection and congratulated himself on his triumph, ruffling the chest hair which he kept meticulously groomed, like one of the prize winning poodles Maria bred for competitions. Despite everything, tonight Javier had outshone himself before Las Ventas's famously discerning audience, with acts of artistic genius worthy of Mozart or Beethoven.

Once out of his costume Javier stared at the unlock screen on his phone, a topless picture of himself with his red cape covering everything below his waist. Before tonight's corrida, he'd had a message from Eloise Skerrett of the Taurine Club of Kensington, one of his many bits on the side. He had not replied yet; he liked to keep women waiting and remind them he was important. He posed for himself in the mirror in his smart white shirt and black trousers, basking in the fact he had so many admirers, women fell at his feet and his talents were recognised throughout the world.

'I can't wait to see you next Saturday,' Eloise's text said. As he finally replied, he grinned to himself. Maria was away that weekend for one of her party conferences. He'd had enough. She was losing her looks and she never stopped whining. It did his head in. He would have ignored her problems and pretended to be interested like he usually did, were it not for what Rita had done to him.

He knew that crazy bitch had purely done it to spite him. With no ferocity, that bull was only fit to be a hamburger. He'd be found and punished for his cowardice. Javier Castella would not be defeated by a mere animal. Fury overtook him when he thought about that day's humiliation. Let himself think about it too long and he'd set fire to something.

Gritting his teeth, he fixed his hair with mousse, before heading to the stretch limo waiting outside. Once ensconced on his luxurious leather seat, he said to the driver, 'Four Seasons Hotel.'

'Right away, boss.' The limo driver set his GPS for the most expensive hotel in Madrid, where Javier was meeting his latest fling. He liked to keep three or four on the go at once. This one, Anastasia, was 22; she'd gone to school with the Russian president's granddaughter in St Petersburg, adding an extra layer of prestige. Tomorrow, he was meeting Lola, a model he'd met on holiday with his wife in Venice two weeks ago.

Javier checked himself out in the mirror before viewing his stock portfolio. Business was another of his many talents, and today, everything was up several percent. Then he entered the code to the luxury bar in the back of the limo, and took out an intricately carved box, given to him as a gift from a bull rancher near Bogota. Inside the box were a tiny gold spoon, a mirrored tray and eight vials of white powder.

Tonight's standing ovation echoed in Javier's mind as he opened one of the vials and brought a small spoonful to his nostril. Telling himself as he always did that he was in control, this was nothing, he wasn't anything so pathetic as a drug addict. No, this was a reward for another outstanding performance. He wasn't lying in some alley shooting himself up with heroin. Everyone did it – it was barely even a drug!

He sniffed, breathing in deeply, proud of the fact he could stop any time he liked. He wasn't some junkie craving a fix. Addiction was for the weak, for those stupid enough to get themselves hooked on his products. Feeling Colombia's finest go to his system, he leaned back with a relaxed sigh, and another text popped into his inbox. His life was perfect. He was perfect – brave, manly and successful. He had the looks of a Greek god. People only said the things they did because they envied him.

He read the text and smiled to himself.

Today had turned out well.

The message said, 'We've found him, boss.'

'Excellent,' Javier replied.

Chapter 20 – Party From Hell

'There's something so beautiful, so electrifying about man going on foot against beast, and completely dominating his opponent, isn't there,' Henry smiled, sitting on a plush red banquette near the corner of Lord Owenstoft's drawing room.

Henry had issued Robyn Casey an impromptu invitation to attend the Taurine Club's last social before their group trip to Spain. The journalist had readily accepted. Going to this event, they were told, would unveil the Club's true nature – an association for connoisseurs of fine art, rather than wealthy, privileged sadists. So far, they were unconvinced, sitting in the dimly lit, oak panelled room and staring at a copy of La Salida, open at a grisly double page photo spread.

'I find it a great metaphor for man's mastery of nature. It's no surprise those who wish to outlaw it in Spain are such killjoys regarding the British countryside,' Lord Owenstoft said, enjoying a glass of his 200-year-old whisky.

'Ah, you see, I'm more of a horsy person, I enjoy when the entire performance is done by one person on horseback,' Eloise Skerrett said.

'I'm sorry, by the entire performance, what do you mean,' Robyn said, as the reporter wrote notes for a follow up to their initial unflattering piece.

'I mean – when all the stages are done by one person on a horse, including the finish. I bet you think that's cruel, don't you,' Eloise grinned, a ghoulish look in her eye. Robyn had eaten a big dinner with colleagues from the newsdesk right before they came. The sensations in their stomach told them this had been a serious mistake.

'Well, it depends,' Robyn said.

'Depends on what?' Eloise said, getting too close to them. Robyn could smell the sweat underneath her overpowering perfume.

'On, um, whether they hurt it.'

'Of course they *hurt it*. So what? It's just a bull. There's no difference between enjoying a corrida and eating hamburgers and steaks. I bet you eat those all the time.' Eloise smirked.

'Well, I have some food intolerances and can't eat meat, there's a long list of things I can't eat, if I don't want to end up in hospital,' Robyn said in a light-hearted tone. Eloise's face was shocked and disapproving, as if Robyn had just confessed to a sin.

'None of that stuff's real, you know, it's like Covid. I'll tell you what is real though. Vaccine poisoning, maybe that's why you think you can't eat meat.' Robyn stared at her with interest, but not exactly surprise. The conversation had certainly taken an unexpected turn. This would have to go in the article too. Did the Prime Minister know a member of his cabinet believed this stuff – or, for that matter, agree with her?

'Maybe,' Robyn said politely. Henry glanced at them, giving them an odd look.

'You seem a nice guy. Do you have a girlfriend, Robyn?' Eloise said, putting her arm around Robyn's chair.

'I'm not a guy,' Robyn said. The aficionados had misgendered them about 20 times this evening. That didn't bother Robyn; they'd heard it all before and had a skin like an elephant. They had interviewed neo-Nazis in prison before. This lot were nowhere as threatening – posh weirdos with disturbing hobbies. Nothing Robyn couldn't handle.

'But do you have a girlfriend? Or are you *gay*?' Eloise insisted as she brushed the back of Robyn's neck, sounding disturbed at the last word. She was 30 but, in that moment, reminded them of someone much older, namely their ex-girlfriend's permanently drunk, lecherous, horse-racing obsessed aunt.

'I do,' Robyn lied, shifting away from her, glad they were up to date with all their boosters.

'Well, whoever she is, is very lucky,' Eloise breathed, pouring yet another glass. 'I'm seeing a man myself at the moment.'

'Oh, yeah?' Now Robyn was interested. Eloise would already have to resign after her statements this evening. No harm in a few more clicks.

'Yeah,' Eloise said, smiling blissfully. 'Javier Castella.'

'I haven't heard of him,' Robyn said.

'He's a matador, he's so talented. When he uses his sword, it's so beautiful, like a painting, or a poem,' Eloise gushed, downing another glass of wine. Wasn't she meant to make a statement about some high-speed rail project tomorrow?

'But he can't see me all the time, he's got such a busy schedule, going to Mexico and Peru and exotic places like that. The bulls are so dangerous, and his wife sounds like a bitch. I feel so sorry for him. He says he'll leave her soon and we'll be together,' Eloise said in a miserable tone. Robyn tried to disguise how enthralled they were.

What a scoop.

They couldn't believe the material they had managed to gather. Incredible. This would cause the Tories endless controversy – no bad thing – and drive up sales considerably. Surely they'd get a pay rise. Maybe they'd be able to apply for jobs at more prestigious outlets. Overseas maybe, they liked the look of New Zealand. Get out of Terf Island, although it was several months since they'd faced anything seriously nasty.

Robyn excused themselves and got up to go to the bathroom, where they texted the editor of the Daily Mirror with the audio file of Eloise's comments about vaccines. The editor texted back, 'Wow. That is mental. Um, get this written up ASAP. Let's put it online tonight.'

'She's having an affair with a matador, who happens to be married to a Spanish politician, can't make this shit up lmfao.' Robyn sent him the second file. The editor reacted with a shocked emoji. Hopefully the aficionados wouldn't notice how long they were taking. But Robyn knew these people would probably blame it on 'a confused snowflake who can't decide on a toilet.'

'Holy shit Robyn you've got a gift – she knows you're a tabloid journo and told you anyway!!!!' he texted back.

'She's fucked off her face, like taking candy from a baby 😂'

'See if you can find out if they do illegal bullfights in the UK! I bet Dixon organises them, he seems really bloodthirsty haha. Maybe one of them's into something *really* bad, like dog fighting.' Robyn gave him a thumbs up and finished up in the toilet, before returning to sit next to Eloise, who was on her fourth glass of Spanish wine.

Eloise gave them an embarrassed stare and staggered to the bathroom. Robyn was left talking to Henry Dixon. They smiled at him. 'Thanks for inviting me along. I'm having a very interesting evening.'

'I'm glad you're finding us interesting. It's nice to meet you too, Robyn. I do hope you're not about to write another hit piece, or I will have you stuffed and mounted on my wall.' The two both laughed at the poor-taste joke, Robyn a bit more awkwardly.

'I wouldn't, no,' Robyn said.

'Are you going to have any of the beef entrecote?' Henry said. These people probably had beef at every meal, Robyn thought.

'I can't eat meat. I'd go into anaphylactic shock.'

Henry regarded the journalist with distaste.

'As long as you're not a vegan,' he said with a sneer. 'I cannot abide vegans.'

'No. Why not?' Robyn said, hoping for another salacious headline.

'Genesis 1:26 states God gave Man mastery over the beasts, if you know your bible. And yet, vegans are so nauseatingly, unreasonably self-righteous.' He spoke wistfully, a faraway look in his eyes. Was he drunk?

'Are you religious?' Robyn asked. The article already had a quote from a Spanish priest at a Catholic Church in Birmingham, condemning cruelty to animals; whatever Henry said would be put to Padre Marcos for a reply.

'Not especially, but regarding vegans, I do believe the Good Book is correct.' This was a strange lesson for a non-believer like Henry to take. Robyn pictured a headline saying, 'Lord Dixon: Vegans condemned by bible'.

'What's funny?' Henry said in a genteel but cold tone.

'Veganism,' Robyn said coolly, sipping from the water on the table. It tasted funny; they decided not to have any more.

Henry looked unconvinced.

'After this evening, would you be tempted to go to a corrida yourself?' he asked.

'I actually saw one on holiday in the South of France once, as a child.' Robyn prepared to make another escape to the bathroom to transfer the latest files. Where was their phone, anyway? They'd put it on the table next to Henry's port bottle. Hadn't they? It couldn't be in their rucksack, the waiter had taken that when they entered. Oh, they'd find it…

'What did you think, there are some fabulous toreros in the South of France?' Henry said, his face lit up.

'I can't say I enjoyed it, to tell you the truth, I felt a bit sorry for the bull. Sorry, I think I've lost something,' Robyn said, distracted looking for their phone. They peeked under the antique table at the fabulously expensive carpet. It wasn't there.

Robyn went into the toilet, maybe they'd left it there by mistake. They were annoyed, they never lost things, they prided themselves on being organised. They were just getting started on this freak show and losing anything put them off their stride. After checking all the cubicles of the men's and women's toilets they came back into the room where Henry was waiting.

'Were you looking for this?' he said, holding up Robyn's phone.

'Oh, brilliant, thanks.' They hoped to make their bathroom run and head off in a half hour, not longer than that. They didn't want to discuss the merits of differing capework styles much longer. Tonight couldn't have gone any better. Time to head off, open up the laptop and turn this into something passable.

'One second please, I have to make a phone call to my partner,' Robyn said pointedly. Half this lot had been thirstily eyeing them up all night.

They headed to the men's bathroom, shut themselves in one of the cubicles and looked for the files to send to the editor. Robyn couldn't find any of them. The recordings had all gone! Had they pressed delete by accident? These files had to be in the memory card; maybe some weird folder in the cloud. The phone had no signal either; turning it off and on didn't help. They walked out of the cubicle. What was the matter with them? That feature they'd worked on, about that poor lad with early onset dementia. He was 25 like Robyn. If *he* could get it that young –

'I should go, it's obviously a bit late for me,' Robyn said, apologetic.

Oh shit. Where were their car keys? Robyn told themselves not to panic. Surely the keys would be in that compartment at the bottom of their bag where they always were.

Surely?

'I'll show you out,' Henry said.

'No, it's –' Robyn started.

'No, it's fine, allow me,' Henry said and followed them out into the night. As he walked close, terror seized Robyn as they realised their keys were gone and heard the sound of their own Volkswagen unlocking.

'I know what you're doing,' Henry hissed, grabbing them from behind, knocking all the air out of them so they gasped for breath. He twisted their hands behind their back and marched them towards the car and its wide open boot.

'No,' Robyn started to yell. But Henry clapped a hand over their mouth as he pushed them towards the boot of the car. They hit their nose on a plastic box they were meant to be taking to the dump and felt blood trickle over the wet tissue he held over their face. They'd seen him! They knew what his name was!

He'll have to kill me, they thought groggily as they slipped into sleep.

Chapter 21 – Peckish

Every night, Pepelito had learned, Maribel went into the barn and stayed there until morning. Beatriz had been gone a month; she missed her lifelong companion desperately, and in the barn, her scent was strongest. Pepelito didn't enjoy the barn. He preferred night-time grazing in the open field he had missed for so long; he'd had enough of confinement. Maribel tried to stop him exiting, not because she feared punishment. She simply needed a comforting presence.

She nudged and licked him as he lay next to her. He'd been so happy to find her, but now he wondered if they'd broken something inside him when they cut the tips of his horns. It wasn't just humans who he didn't understand any more. Sad things had happened on this farm, years ago other cows had been taken away and not come back, but Maribel had never known the viciousness he'd experienced. If he told her everything, would she even understand?

Pepelito got up and walked slowly out of the barn. He walked around a bit in the field and grazed. He got his teeth into a big tuft of grass. It was dark. This area was quiet at night, with a forest behind the farmhouse, and more fields down the hill. But at the bottom of the hill there was a heavy truck coming; he listened to see if he could recognise the sound.

The noise filled him with unstoppable feelings and thoughts as it got closer. Shivering, he walked back into the barn and buried his face in some straw, while Maribel watched him with concern. The vehicle was getting louder; another car followed. Maribel sat up; with a growing sense of fright, they listened together as the truck parked on the track, too close for him.

Then the occupants got out.

He remembered them.

The old girl was outright alarmed; she stood up with a start and stared around the barn, before bolting out of the door, feet skittering on the ground. Her manner unsettled him but he followed her, not wanting to be alone. She started mooing loudly as the men approached the grassy hillside she now shared with Pepelito. Maybe he could run, hide somewhere in the long grass, leap over the fence.

'…yeah. That's him, isn't it, just like on the YouTube video.' The torch light shone in Pepelito's eyes and he backed away, cringing at the brightness.

'Yeah. It is. Look at his brand, that's a fighting bull.'

'I thought so. I'll help you catch him.'

Pepelito watched in terror as about 12 of Castella's assistants marched into the field, straight towards him. He drew himself up, hating their scent, hating their voices, hating what they'd done. He didn't feel like the big, threatening bull he was desperately trying to make himself seem.

He scratched the ground with his hooves and sent a lump of dry soil flying into a tree behind him. In the dark they couldn't see his fear as he walked backwards. Voices yelled behind him. They threw a rope around his horns, tugging him backwards. When the men pulled it hurt his back again. He ran forward, trying to shake himself free.

He couldn't.

Someone was grabbing his tail and twisting it hard. Two people had him in a choke hold. He couldn't breathe. One of them punched him.

Pepelito kicked the man pulling his tail. His hand fell away and the bull ran forward into the group of men who seemed to be everywhere, catching someone's t-shirt on his horn. The man shoved at him, then shrieked in fear and rolled onto the ground. Pepelito slipped and trod onto the man's hairy stomach. The man wriggled and writhed, gasping for air as he crawled away.

He had to get out. Five or six people were holding the rope round his horns; more were pulling the other end from the truck. They yanked so hard he couldn't run any more without hurting his back. He mooed out in pain but no help came. Stones and twigs scratched his hooves as the men tugged him past his gate, across the gravel driveway.

'Get him in quickly. That crazy bastard in there's probably got a gun.' Someone took hold of Pepelito's tail and pulled so hard he thought it would come off. His struggling didn't make any difference. Trusting humans had been stupid. Someone else kicked him hard in the side as he stood in front of the truck, trying to resist being forced in.

He dug his feet into the ground and kicked out with his back legs, knowing his life depended on it. From behind, someone hit him hard with a stick and he staggered halfway up the ramp, feeling blood on his feet.

He knew who that was.

He ran at the knackered out horse across the sand. The crowd screamed with delight. Maybe that would stop all these problems, all this pain, maybe the horse had something to do with it? He never liked horses, so unfriendly. Then, too late, he saw the spear in the rider's hand –

'Fuck is wrong with you?' the man spat at Pepelito as the bull kicked out at him. But as his tormentor waved the stick again, hooves slammed against the ground and heavy breathing grew louder. Maribel powered fast towards the truck, running straight for him, headbutting him so hard he fell into the fence and landed in a clump of stinging nettles. He swore, then let out a screech as the retired dairy cow stood on his groin.

One of the others kicked her. She pivoted towards her attacker, slamming her hind foot into the head of the man sitting in the nettles. He groaned, hit his head on a water trough and slumped into the plants. The rope slackened as Maribel scattered them. Pepelito heard them smacking her. She gave a frightened moo as one of the men grabbed her tail.

He couldn't let them do that.

As the rope loosened he reversed off the ramp towards Maribel's attackers. Pepelito tossed his head and caught one of them in the stomach. The scent of blood was powerful as it ran down his horn. The man shrieked and staggered backwards, clutching the wound. Maribel headbutted him in the back as he fell.

But moving his head so fast brought the pain from Pepelito's injuries back savagely. He tried to shuffle away backwards, thirsty and tired, as his feet stuck to patches of mud.

'Let's go, and run that cow over so we don't have trouble leaving,' one of them spat, the enclosure keeper who had beaten him for comforting Ladron.

The man Pepelito had caught with his horn scraped himself off the ground, gasping and grunting. The bull tried to walk after Maribel, trembling with fear. As he followed her the rope jerked hard, pulling his head back, dragging him away from his field, towards the truck, up the metal ramp. The cold, hard flooring hurt his feet. Unlike in Silvio's truck, there was no bedding or water. His head slammed into the side of the truck furthest from the door.

'That's what you get for escaping,' another man said, wrenching at his tail as the rope was tied behind him. Was it the one he'd stood on earlier? He couldn't tell. He shut his eyes, crying silently.

'Let's just do the cow in and go. Come on, get in.' The enclosure keeper walked round to the front and got in, slamming the door hard. The door to the back of the truck crashed down and shook when it shut.

Pepelito couldn't see anything. He hated not being able to move. He tried to free himself. It was no use, everything he did restricted his movements even more. Ladron had known not to expect anything else. He'd given up in the end, he'd just acted how they wanted. Pepelito wondered if he should do the same.

'Andres?' Pepelito heard another guy shout, somewhere in front of the truck as the engine started. There was a soft hiss somewhere behind him.

'Andres? Wake up. Oh – fuck! Wake up! Wake up, will you?'

'We need an ambulance!'

'Don't be stupid, Tomas. Let's just go, we've got what we came for,' the enclosure keeper shouted, as a chorus of honking and squawking grew louder.

'There's no pulse! He's dead!' Tomas shouted from outside. Pepelito's whole body tensed up at the noise. Forced to keep his neck in one place, the still healing muscles were in agony. Something slammed against the door of the truck, startling him. As he struggled unsuccessfully to free himself, a clattering of wings, honking and hissing, drowned out the men's voices.

'Stupid bird. Get away from me!' Something hard and heavy thumped the side of the truck again. There was a loud squawk, a tremendous hiss as clothes tore and feathers flapped. Something clattered deep inside the farmhouse.

'Someone help! Get them away!' As the men shouted, there was a heavy thud, followed by two smaller ones and the sound of ripping fabric. One of the men yelled incoherently. The closest one to where Pepelito was trapped collapsed to the ground, sobbing.

The man Pepelito had gored groaned in pain from the truck's passenger seat. 'Hospital,' he wailed.

'It's 5 in the morning, what's this crap, boys?' Silvio was shouting. The truck's back door slid open a crack and Pepelito took a deep breath, filling his lungs with the fresh air.

'What are you doing to my prize winning bull, son?' Silvio snarled. He marched up to the truck and tugged the door fully open. Pepelito saw two of his tormentors sobbing like babies, shielding themselves from the geese and their vicious, jagged beaks.

Their clothing was cut to ribbons. There were gashes on their faces. A third lay on his side in the mud, not moving, as two geese with bloody bills sat on him and pecked at his throat.

'He's a rescue, how dare you treat him like that?' Silvio said in a cold voice, jabbing one of the men with a stick. The man got to his feet, slowly and painfully, his eyes wild as they stared at the lifeless corpse.

'Who sent you, son?'

'Castella,' came the mumbled reply.

'Castella? What's the matter with him, man, can't he come himself?' Silvio gave him a withering look. He walked round to the front compartment of the truck, opened the door and reached past the back seat to the end of the rope. It tightened, then slackened, becoming looser. The skin on the top of Pepelito's head was rubbed raw and he flinched as the farmer freed him.

'Dear, oh dear,' Silvio shook his head, turning towards the body of Pepelito's other torturer as it lay in the stinging nettles. As the sun appeared on the horizon Maribel watched triumphantly from some distance away. With Castella's minions looking on miserably, covered in blood, mud and goose poo, Pepelito trotted over and nuzzled her. The old girl mooed softly and headed back through the gate.

Perhaps he'd misjudged her.

'Police and ambulance. There's been an attempted livestock theft,' Pepelito heard Silvio say as he and Maribel ambled back into the field together, a single goose trailing behind them.

He could be happy here.

Chapter 22 – Sonia

'You won't believe it, Rita. About 10 of Castella's thugs broke into my uncle's farm last night, tried to take your bull, got him into the back of the truck before Silvio stopped them,' Dominguez said, pulling up his chair the following day. He looked shaken up. Rita took in her breath sharply. Most of Castella's associates had convictions for violence, some had spent significant stretches inside and all were sadistic and brutal. It made her sick to picture how they'd have rewarded Pepelito's affectionate and inquisitive nature.

'Dios mio. How is Silvio?'

'Fine, supposedly, but I think he's pretty shaken up by it. I did find a room but I'll stay at his tonight. He's pretty lucky if you ask me. That prick really scraped the barrel, hiring these morons,' Dominguez said, taking a ham panini out of his bag.

'I told him, he needs a good lawyer. I know Castella's going to try and take him to court to get the bull back if he can't steal him, and he'll probably get some bought judge to go along with it. Silvio's so stubborn, who knows if he'll listen. I've been telling him for years he needs to get a proper home security system, he's got quite a valuable tractor he's not sold as he 'hasn't found the right buyer'. You cannot believe the amount of burglaries in that village, stuff needs to be nailed down.'

'I can't see the police round there being much help.' Rita felt shock and not a little responsibility. She doubted Silvio appreciated what he was up against when he took Pepelito on. She hadn't either.

Dominguez shook his head. 'Nah. The village cops showed up, remember we worked with them on that double murder two years ago. Nice but useless, even with something like this, supposedly their specialty.'

'I can picture it,' Rita sighed. It was true. They were undertrained, understaffed, had outdated equipment and were completely unprepared to deal with someone like Castella.

'Not sure they'll try again in a hurry. 2 of them died! Though Silvio only mentioned it at the end of the conversation as an 'Oh by the way'. One of them was Andres Mecano, Castella's picador.'

Rita let out a laugh of shock, unable to summon any sympathy. 'That guy was a piece of work. Didn't he just get out of prison?'

'Yep, just did 3 years inside for racially aggravated assault. That old girl of Silvio's. Maribel. Seems to have developed a vicious temper in her old age. She trampled him, or Pepelito did, or both, then she kicked him in the head, right into a water trough. As for the other one – fuck knows, it could just be another of my uncle's stories.' Dominguez shook his head, trying and failing to keep a straight face.

'Remember Jose Enrique de Ruiz? We did him for pimping a few years back, remember. Real scumbag. Silvio says – get this – two of his geese pecked the bastard to death.' Rita stared at him. It wasn't unbelievable. She remembered being at her colleague's uncle's once and getting on the wrong side of the gaggle, who strutted around the farm like mafia bosses and had names like 'Diablo' and 'Bruta'.

'Pepelito's fine by the way, I thought you might want to know. Silvio adores him by the way, thinks he's great and won't stop going on about what a lovely temperament he's got. He did gore one of them, though, mind.' Dominguez scoffed.

'Pobrecito, he must have been scared out of his mind.' Rita remembered his terror at the men's voices. De Ruiz had been in trouble for pimping. Was it possible Sonia had got on his bad side?

'He's OK. Apparently quite bruised and knocked about. Silvio said your fella's coming to take a look later?'

'Yeah, he is, I'd like to come too, after the grim first day back on I've got. No doubt apologising to Bonita Gutiérrez for not having found her daughter's killer after 11 years.' She'd never worked on the case, but the thought filled her with anxiety – and shame that until now, nobody had paid attention.

'Ugh. Thought you might, me I've got an extra day stuck on the desks. See you after work then. Can see you've missed him, and it'd do Silvio good to see some official faces around that aren't from the village cop shop. I might get him to listen about the alarms.'

*

Bonita Gutiérrez opened the door to her sparsely decorated home. She looked at Rita and Mansouri with sad eyes as the two officers stood on the doorstep. She clasped her rosary beads and clutched the fabric of the black dress she was wearing tightly, as if it was a security blanket.

'Señora Gutiérrez, we are so sorry,' Rita said.

'Well, don't just stand there. Come in. What's this about.'

'I'm so sorry for what happened to your daughter. I can't imagine how difficult it is, losing a child in these circumstances,' Rita said as they walked into the house and Bonita shoved them into the living room. The floor was rough and wooden, and the walls were bare except for a crucifix above the door; it was as if the home itself was in mourning. Bonita sat down heavily on an uncomfortable leather sofa in the corner of the room, took a cigarette out the packet. The house stank heavily of smoke.

'What's happened, then? Have you got him yet?' Her voice was resigned, but tinged with contempt.

'Señora Gutiérrez, serious mistakes were made in the original investigation of your daughter's murder, and we apologise on behalf of the entire department,' Mansouri said. Bonita gulped and took a puff on her cigarette.

'Of course there were! 11 years ago, I tried to tell you people that. But you lot didn't want to listen to me, what could the mother of a prostitute tell you.' Bonita swallowed hard. Rita saw she was shaking with rage.

'We are reopening your daughter's case, and this time, we will do everything we can to catch whoever killed her,' she said. The woman had been so badly let down. Rita's heart was breaking for her.

'That's what you said when it happened. What's this about, why now,' Bonita said suspiciously.

'We have evidence that the person who killed your daughter has killed one other person, and possibly more,' Rita said. Bonita's face hardened and she turned pale. She gripped the side of the hard sofa she was sitting on.

'You didn't care when it was just her. My little girl wasn't important to you, just some dead hooker, that's what you saw, it's what everyone saw.' She spoke through gritted teeth.

'And now he's killed again, has he. I told you he would if he wasn't caught.' Bonita brushed a strand of greying hair away from her face.

She breathed out heavily. At that moment the door unlocked and a girl of about 14 with long highlighted blonde and red hair walked in. 'Hi, Abuela.'

The teenage girl stared at the cops and did not acknowledge them at all as she went to sit next to Bonita. She put her arm round her and said in a quiet voice, 'Is this about my mum?'

Bonita nodded, clasping her hands together. 'It is, Lucia.'

Her stomach plunging, Rita realised she'd seen the teenager before. Lucia was staring at her with a frightened, guilty expression. She had seen her the night they'd given Pepelito to Silvio; the girl had chucked a stone and shouted at her. Their eyes met and the girl quickly looked away.

'I understand this is difficult for both of you. I want to find out what Sonia was like as a person, what her life was like,' Rita said, trying not to show a reaction. Bonita's face froze.

'I was 3,' Lucia said, her lip trembling. 'I don't remember much. I remember she used to play with us, she used to tell us stories.'

'I told you, your mum was the kindest person, she'd do anything for anyone,' Bonita said, her voice cracking as she lit another cigarette on the sofa. She spluttered a little and Lucia rubbed her back. Bonita wiped her eyes with the fabric of the loose-fitting dress she was wearing.

'I'm sorry to ask this, but did Sonia ever talk about work, any violent or difficult clients, people who didn't want to pay up, people who had disturbing requests?' Mansouri said. Rita's heart sank. The question had to be asked. But the initial inquiry focused only on Sonia's sex work, not on other ways she could have encountered her killer. One of her clients, a man called Jorge, had even been charged with murder, although the charges were dropped before any trial could happen.

'What do you think! I've been through all this before, millions of times, it was all you lot were interested in asking me about, you never asked about anything else, if you had seen her as a bit more than a fucking prostitute, maybe you'd not be sitting here with me today!' Bonita howled. Lucia looked deeply uncomfortable. She hugged her grandmother as the older woman let out several choking sobs.

'You should go,' Lucia said in a voice too grown up for any child. Rita got to her feet. Mansouri awkwardly followed.

'I really am sorry,' Rita said to them both. Lucia squeezed her grandmother's hand and walked them to the door in the bare room, not speaking.

'I'm sorry too,' the teenager said in an undertone. For a second, she looked like she was going to say something, but didn't speak.

'That went well, didn't it,' Rita muttered once they were in the car.

'I know I could have phrased it better. But most sex workers are killed by clients or pimps, let's be honest.' Mansouri looked troubled. It was a reasonable assumption. But the previous investigation had

136

focused on it to the exclusion of absolutely everything else. Unsurprisingly, Bonita was furious.

'Caroline McKenzie wasn't a sex worker, was she, she had money. She couldn't be more removed from Sonia in background and lifestyle.' It came out more annoyed than Rita intended.

'Maybe this guy just hates women, no other reason behind it. And sex workers are an easy target for serial killers,' Mansouri said.

Rita shook her head. 'These victims had something in common. Caroline liked going online and trolling all sorts of people who treated animals badly. And we know Sonia attended animal rights protests with hardcore activists like Pilar Cadiz.' A shudder passed through her. She was dating Pilar's widower. Castella would fit Alfonso up for murder if he could. He'd get her fired – or worse. Like Aguilar, he had friends in high places and readily used the law to get what he wanted. And if that didn't work –

'It's worth looking at, but we've ruled out Castella, and I don't know if this is more than a coincidence.' Mansouri's tone was defensive. Rita tried to shake off her rising irritation. She regarded him sceptically.

'I just think – sometimes it is just a coincidence, you know?'

'Maybe. But we can't just look at one line of inquiry.'

Mansouri nodded, looking doubtful. 'Well, no. To be honest, I've been feeling a bit out of my depth on this one. I don't know why the boss put me in charge – pissed off with Jesús, probably, but sometimes I think he wants me to fail at something.'

'Don't think like that. You should have phrased it more sensitively but it's not the wrong question. Everything is worth looking into.' Rita said, surprised at his rare criticism. He seldom joined in when others vented their frustration.

'We shouldn't completely rule it out, though,' Mansouri said, a lot less confidently, sounding younger than his 24 years. She felt for him. What had Sanchez been thinking?

'No. Let's see what light Jorge Ramirez can shed, then.' Rita's anger crystallised towards the officers who had so badly botched the previous investigation.

She had to make things right.

*

Jorge lived on the sixth floor of a run down tower block. The building looked as though it was rarely if ever cleaned or maintained. The floor stank of piss and the lift had broken down. Dim lighting illuminated the graffiti on the walls, which included nothing artistic, just tags, scrawled phone numbers, pictures of cocks.

'What do you want?' he said nervously, opening the door. Peeking in, Rita noticed that he couldn't open it fully because of all the piles of newspapers and books inside.

'I'm sorry to bother you. We want to speak to you about Sonia Gutiérrez,' Rita said. Instantly the man's expression changed. His face was frightened. He had washed and showered but had an untidy beard and his tracksuit top had stains on it.

'I didn't do it, I'd never hurt any of the girls,' he said, in a shaky voice.

'I know,' Rita said. 'We're hoping we can catch the person who did.'

'I liked her, she was nice,' the man said miserably, opening the door. Mansouri and Rita stepped into the tiny bit of floor space.

'We're here because you knew Sonia. Would you be able to tell me anything about her?' A heavy feeling settled in Rita's gut. Had his life gone downhill to this level after he became a suspect, or was it always like this?

'Sonia was nice, I used to see her every week, sometimes twice a week if I had extra money, it was like she was my girlfriend,' Jorge said sadly. He had difficulty speaking, and stammered and sucked his teeth.

Swallowing, he moved half of a pile of newspapers balanced on an old chair onto the floor, so he could sit down. 'I went to her funeral.'

'Tell me about her, you said she acted like your girlfriend, did she tell you much about her life outside seeing you,' Rita said. Mansouri looked uneasy, embarrassed.

'She told me she had three kids. She told me…' He thought for a moment, looking down. He obviously didn't get to talk to people often. 'She told me about a rich Italian guy who paid for her to go on holiday to Venice with him. I'd have liked to take her to Venice.'

'What was his name?'

'Marco something,' Jorge said. Rita looked at her notes. The Italian had been questioned at the time but had a solid alibi. He had since died.

'Did Sonia ever mention a woman called Caroline McKenzie? A businesswoman from Scotland?' It was a long shot. Jorge shrugged.

'I don't know. No. Who was she?'

'She was murdered about ten days ago, and the reason we're speaking to you today is because we believe she was killed by the same person who killed Sonia,' Rita said. Jorge looked shocked. His mouth dropped open.

'I didn't do it, you don't think I did it, do you,' he stuttered, looking as if he was about to cry. Rita shook her head.

'No we don't, but just for our records, we'd like you to confirm where you were between 17:00 and 19:00 on Saturday the 16th of April,' Mansouri said. Caroline's estimated time of death.

'Two weeks ago? I – I was with one of the girls, a Nigerian lady, she said her name was Serena, it was the first time I've been able to pay in months but my benefit money came through on time and my mum gave me some extra so I thought – thought I'd have, you know, a

139

treat,' Jorge said, looking embarrassed and sad. He couldn't be a serious suspect in Caroline's murder; he would have stood out like a sore thumb in the expensive hotel where she was found.

'Am I in trouble?' he gulped. Mansouri shook his head.

'This is very important, Jorge. Did Sonia ever mention any enemies, anyone who might have wanted to hurt her?' Rita said gently, looking into his eyes. Clearly, nobody had asked him this before.

After a minute of thinking, he said, 'That stuff she used to tell me about, that's dangerous, all that. I wanted her to stop doing it.'

'What stuff?' Rita said.

'Protests. She used to go on protests a lot. She said she wanted to make a better world for her kids than what she'd grown up in. I told you she was nice. But it's dangerous. You can get in trouble, you can get arrested.' Rita felt a pang as he spoke. Sonia had been at the bottom of society but she had cared, cared so much.

Maybe she'd lost her life for it.

'Did she mention anything in particular?' The sex workers he saw were providing more than just their physical service. She doubted he had friends that he didn't have to pay for. The thought was so desperately sad. It was lucky for him that Sonia had been there.

'Yeah, she told me someone beat her up.' Jorge hesitated.

'Go on.'

'She used to go and stand outside the plaza de toros with a poster of a dead bull. But why would she want to do that, it sounds so horrible?' Jorge stared around, lost and confused. Rita's chest tightened; she recalled her phone calls with Heather.

That sick bastard with his darts.

'It wasn't horrible. Sounds like she wanted to wake up people's conscience.' Rita spoke firmly.

'What happened?' Mansouri said.

'She said someone going in grabbed her and threw her against a wall and started punching her, then some guy got him off her. One of her kids was there, the youngest, that's what made her the most upset,' Jorge swallowed, looking disturbed and frightened by his story.

'Did she report it to the police?' Mansouri said. What do you think, Rita thought, flipping through her file. This hadn't come up when Jorge was questioned previously. The police had only seen him as a suspect, not a witness – a weirdo with mental health problems who found companionship with sex workers like Sonia.

In reality, he was another victim.

'No, she said they wouldn't care. It was, like, three weeks before she died, and when she told me about it, that was the last time I saw her, I had to pay a huge bill. I didn't have the money.' Jorge picked up a filthy mug of coffee from under a pile of magazines and turned it over in his hands, staring at the police officers anxiously.

'Did she say anything about what this man looked like, or anything like that?' Jorge thought for a few moments after Mansouri asked the question.

'She told me, he'd said if he saw her there again, he'd kill her.' Jorge gulped. The way Sonia had been uncared for in death, the contempt with which police had treated the family, made her murder even more horrific.

'I'm sorry, I'm so sorry. I don't remember any more. It was a long while ago. I liked Sonia. I wished she really was my girlfriend.' Rita put a hand on Jorge's back.

'You've been very helpful,' she said.

'Are you going to get him?' Jorge said.

'I hope so.'

*

As soon as Rita was out of the tower block, she composed an email to Heather on her phone.

'Hi, Heather. Please call me ASAP. We're looking for the same killer.'

Chapter 23 – Hello Again

By the time Rita and Dominguez finally got to Silvio the sun was retreating from the sky. Pepelito began sidling happily up towards the fence. Maribel stood chewing the cud from a distance. It felt strangely beautiful. Nothing from Heather, but Rita was about ready to forget about work for today.

'Just there, Dios mio, he wasn't in a great way,' Silvio grunted, pointing to a thick, partly crushed patch of thistles and stinging nettles. The thick tracks of the gangsters' truck as it had reversed and re-reversed were still visible. Several goose feathers were trodden into the ground. Next time might not be so lucky, Rita thought with a jolt to the stomach, wishing she lived closer.

'Wasn't in a great way? You said he was dead!' Dominguez said, recoiling as Silvio's killer geese waddled towards him.

'Yes, that's right, he was.' Silvio sniffed and lit a cigarette. Rita grinned as Pepelito came right up to the fence and licked her. His coat looked much healthier and sleeker, and he was clearly so pleased to see her. Alfonso was coming soon, and after spending some time with their four-legged friend, they'd go home together.

'Hola dulcito, yes, yes, you're so good, toro, am I pleased to see you,' she grinned.

'How is he doing?' she said, rubbing his nose.

'He's great, being outside with Maribel has done him the world of good. He's got much more energy,' Silvio said, adding, 'Wouldn't you say so, my boy?'

Dominguez backed right away from the fence, towards the farmhouse door. Heather still hadn't emailed back, and Rita was both impatient for a reply and glad not to be bothered while she spent time with the animals.

'And hello, Maribel,' she said as the elderly cow walked towards them.

'My uncle's killer cow herself,' Dominguez said nervously. Maribel's horns were sharp stumps protruding from her light brown coat. She was bigger than Pepelito and strode up to the fence looking tough, her huge udders swinging, then stretched her neck over the fence.

'Hello,' Rita said cautiously.

'Don't be ridiculous, boy. My old girl just sent some good for nothing where he belonged,' Silvio snapped.

'She killed someone, Silvio.'

Yes, looking at her posture and size, it was easy to imagine Maribel had killed. Rita picked some grass from behind the fence and offered it to her cautiously as the two men sat on the bench together talking.

Rita took some water out of her bag and drank. Alfonso texted her to say he was on his way. *You take your job home with you*, her ex-husband always said. She'd felt oddly ashamed of asking Alfonso about Sonia Gutiérrez on their date. He wasn't a suspect. But he was entangled regardless because of his beliefs, the people he knew, the choices he made. While Alfonso treated Pepelito's wounds, *someone* was abducting and murdering Caroline McKenzie.

He – it was almost certainly a he – would have watched the corrida.

To aficionados, not fighting, being cowardly, a toro manso, was the worst 'crime' a bull could commit. Seeing Pepelito escape would have enraged this perpetrator.

He liked pain, he liked torture.

Denied his pleasure, he'd got it another way.

Rita watched as Pepelito and Maribel excitedly toyed with an old tyre from Silvio's truck, rolling it towards each other and chasing each other around the field. Watching them playful and happy reminded her of a younger Gloria. Even Silvio's geese added to the beauty, floating in the lake, or resting at the shaded end keeping cool in the heat. Animals were what gave her life. They were what kept her going.

Watching the deadly gaggle strut past like a football gang, Rita felt her phone vibrate in her pocket. Her mother was calling her. This time, she couldn't really avoid her. It was her dad she wanted to speak to; it was difficult to face, but she'd have to visit in person at some point to catch him in private.

'Yes?' she said.

'Finally. I've been trying to call you for two days. You never answer your phone!'

'I've only just finished work. I'm working on a serial killer investigation. I've not got time for much else.' After the day she'd had, she was exhausted. Tomorrow, she was going to the plaza de toros. Maybe one of them knew the killer. Maybe one of them *was* the killer. The thought of being anywhere nearby left her feeling contaminated.

'It's Maria's birthday at the weekend. Just give her one call. One call, please. Make your old mum happy.' She ignored what Rita said completely.

'We've been through this, Mum. I can't have anyone in my life who's OK with *him* as a husband.' Pepelito walked back towards her, obviously wanting to play. A cow from a neighbouring farm mooed loudly – loudly enough for her mother to hear.

'So was it you? Are you a farmer now? Why on earth did you do it?' her mum snapped.

'Do what?' A butterfly flitted past.

'The bull, Rita. What possessed you to keep that bull indoors?' Rita could hear Alfonso's van coming up the hill and just wanted to get off the line. Then she was torn up with a sudden guilt for feeling this way about the woman who raised her.

'Mum, he collapsed in my road, looking like one of those dolls the bad guys stick pins into in horror movies. There was so much blood.

145

So I rang a vet. How could I bring him back to this torture?' Her voice was tense. She couldn't tell her mum about Alfonso. Anyone she dated would never be as good as her ex-husband with his estate agent's salary, and her mum would shoot off endless questions and uncalled-for advice.

'He's not fierce. As soon as he was shown love, when people were gentle and kind, he was just like a big dog.' Rita's mother sniffed dismissively.

'Your perfect son in law's sent thugs from the ring after him twice, first time I had to move out because of pobrecito getting so scared he kicked down my doors to get away from them. The second time they broke into the farm and tried to steal him!' Rita spat.

'I see,' her mother said at last, sighing loudly, after not speaking for two minutes. Her voice softened a bit as she said, 'And how is he doing now?'

'Who?' Rita said.

'What's the bull's name?'

'Pepelito,' Rita said, confused.

'Well, is he OK? Pepelito? Maybe you can send me a picture?'

'What? Mum, what is all this?'

'I've just got off the phone to your sister. He didn't have the decency to tell her himself, she read it on some celebrity gossip website. She's spent the whole day in tears. Javier's been having an affair!' Her mother sounded on the edge of tears herself.

'Just one?' Rita said under her breath.

'I beg your pardon?'

'Nothing. What do you want me to do about it?' Rita snapped. Her sister knew who Castella was when she married him. And now she expected sympathy?

'Just call her.'

'I'll think about it,' Rita said.

'You've always liked animals, it's one of the good things about you,' her mother said grudgingly. There was a long pause.

'Well, I'd better go,' she finally said. 'Look after yourself. Love you lots.'

'You too, Mum,' Rita said, not knowing how to respond to this sudden display of affection at all.

As Rita stood by the fence with the animals, she heard Silvio messing around in his tool shed, scoffing 'Oh, don't be stupid, son!' into his phone. Dominguez laughed, giving her an amused glance.

'You'd never think anyone died here last night, would you?' he mouthed.

'Tell your boss to come here and fetch him himself, if that's what he wants!' Silvio snapped as he came out of the shed.

'That isn't nice, is it,' he sighed, sitting down next to Dominguez on his wooden bench. 'Nobody important, just some sinvergüenza, one of Castella's boys. I've got to give him back, they say, or they'll kill me. I'd like to see them try!'

Dominguez opened his mouth but the farmer silenced him, jabbing his finger in his face as Alfonso's car pulled up outside the farmhouse. That wasn't an empty threat, Rita thought, feeling herself shudder.

'Of course I won't, before you ask! Why would I do a thing like that?'

****

'He's so much better than he was, aren't you, toro? When I saw him first he was bleeding so much and in so much pain, I was worried I'd have to put him to sleep.' After checking Pepelito over, Alfonso walked back out of the gate, taking a cautious glance behind him at Maribel.

'Dios mio, he's been in the wars! And this ludicrous clown in a sequin jacket has the damned cheek to demand him back with menaces?' Silvio's voice was indignant. Pepelito knew he wasn't angry with him. He just spoke like this sometimes.

'Tell me about it. But good news is, you've already reduced the dosage to 50%, you can bring it to 25% for 7 days, then stop. Any signs of discomfort or illness, call me straight away.' Alfonso patted him from over the fence and fed him some grass.

What a happy day he'd had.

'And his tail? Damned fools, twisting it this way and that.'

'A bit swollen and bruised, but there doesn't seem to be anything broken, just keep an eye on him over the next week,' Alfonso said, touching Pepelito on the nose. Every day it was easier to raise his head, to crane it over the fence, to rub on things, give himself a scratch. He liked watching the cows in the field below his, especially one with brown and white splodges.

The cows liked watching him, too.

'Well, I'm glad he's on the mend.' Silvio seemed the happiest Pepelito had heard him around humans.

'This is one very well-loved bull. I think that's half of it, don't you?' Alfonso said.

'You should start locking the barn door at night, Silvio,' Rita said.

'It's a damn shame. But yes. I already have. Don't you worry about me.'

After the humans had gone Pepelito followed Maribel back to the barn. He had lots of space – it was just him and Maribel. He rolled in some straw and chased an old football around for a bit, but she was old and didn't like that sort of fun for long.

He'd been wrong about her. Humans seemed to speak her name with a kind of awed respect. She'd seen enough in her life to understand exactly who those men were.

'Got enough of everything, do you? If you need anything, you know where I am,' Silvio said as he locked the barn door, speaking to him and Maribel as if he was the owner of a guest house. Maribel put her front foot over his as they rested.

*

'…thinking of telling the boss I'm done. Nearly had my eye out. I'm not about to get pecked to death to feed his ego.'

'Think of the money, though, Hector.'

'Yeah. We'll need guns, if we come back. Not doing that in a hurry, just for a bull.' Pepelito sat up and listened with his excellent hearing, safe behind the barn walls. The voices were coming from down the hill, several hundred metres away. He nudged Maribel hard as she slept. She stirred, sat up and pushed him away with her nose, giving an irritated grunt.

The men's tone of voice alarmed him. 'Yes. We'll need guns. We'll need to shoot that mad bastard, and that other cow he's got. She's vicious.'

'Yeah. But then there's the geese. I can't cope, I can't…'

'Maybe poison?'

Maribel got to her feet. She made a loud, very long moo and prowled around the barn. After a few seconds Pepelito did the same, and their neighbours picked the call up. The cows' bellows echoed around the hillside as the men approached, and then came the raucous sound of honking.

'Oh, Jesus. We better go.'

Chapter 24 – Heather

Rita had given up waiting for a phone call during the long drive. Curled up on the sofa with Alfonso, she was watching a Netflix documentary about penguins. By the time Heather finally called she knew she'd stayed up too late, and felt herself dropping off.

'Sorry for calling you so late, I hope this isn't a bad time. Only just this second got off the phone to TVP,' the British policewoman said as Rita dragged herself off the sofa.

'TVP?'

'Oh, sorry. Thames Valley Police.'

'I'm sorry to do this, can you pause it,' she whispered to Alfonso, before walking out of the room, into the office they were both using. He was a good guy. Maybe the best she'd ever had. It had to be too good to be true. He'd get pissed off and have enough at some point. Surely.

'If this is a bad time –' Heather said.

'It's not. Just – a long day. Visiting a friend.' Rita yawned, shutting the door to the office and sitting on the swivel chair.

'Lucky you. I lost touch with all my friends when I joined the force,' Heather sighed.

'This is one on four legs. The best kind.' Rita pinched herself to keep from shutting her eyes. Now she had to speak English to this woman late at night.

'Ah. Like, a sanctuary? My son helps out at one of them,' Heather laughed.

'Something like that.' There was a pause. Rita turned on her computer and opened the now repaired cabinet, taking out the files she had for Sonia Gutiérrez and Caroline McKenzie. With Castella ruled out, Rita was back heading up the case alongside Mansouri. He needed moral support; his confidence had been shaken after their meeting with Bonita.

'So, tell me why you think it's the same killer, then,' Heather sad, her voice now tense and serious. Rita swallowed and drank a glass of water.

'Heather, I've read the postmortem report for Aidan Donnelly's killing. From my observations, the injuries found on the body are similar to those found on bulls during a fight, and appear to be made with similar weapons, like that dart,' Rita said calmly. Pepelito's suffering, exhaustion and helplessness in the face of such violence had been unbearable to watch. To even think of killing a person like that...

'Caroline McKenzie wasn't killed like that, though, was she? I haven't had time to go through the report properly, but...' Heather asked.

'No, although the cause of death was, again, multiple stab wounds. And Caroline had strong opinions on animal rights. She had a history of harassing people she believed were responsible for cruelty. As I said, this perpetrator has an unnatural interest in such activities. I believe he targeted her deliberately. We have since linked her case to another victim, Sonia Gutiérrez, who often protested against bullfights. The last time she did, shortly before her murder, she was violently attacked.' Heather listened, saying nothing.

'We've not found any history of protests or anything like that with Aidan. The kid had just turned 18! Is there any way it could be a coincidence?'

'It could be, yes. But there's a similar lack of DNA found on his body. In all cases, he's abducting them, killing them, removing forensic evidence and dumping the bodies near where they were originally abducted.' There was a long silence. Caroline hadn't been killed at the hotel. And Sonia was found near a busy church, in an area many people walked.

Heather said shakily, 'Other police forces have been reviewing cold cases on our request. TVP found two, found a guy aged 55 who they said *might* be possible. But the only problem is, his ex-wife is already serving life in prison for his murder, although she always said she was innocent. That's why it took so long to call back, because they've not managed to track down the information…'

'Do you have any information about the victim's life?' Rita said.

'Nah, that's all I've got, I'm afraid. Police bureaucracy, you know what it's like,' Heather sighed.

'Who was the other possible victim?' Rita said.

'Her name was Samantha Berger, she was 30, got murdered a year ago. No animal rights protests, but she had a criminal record for direct action to do with other things, environmental issues, war. I think that's more likely, she was killed in quite a similar way to Aidan.' Looking at the postmortem report on her screen, Rita winced as she read the details of Samantha's now horribly familiar injuries.

'So if I am right, this sick fuck has killed at least four people.'

'What's confusing me though Rita, is if it *is* all the same person, is there's a gap of 10 or 11 years and then two within weeks of each other. A killer like this doesn't just stop.'

'Yes. It's possible he's been in prison or had a serious illness and couldn't continue for a while. But it's likely there are more victims out there, who we don't know about.' Rita's calm voice gave away little emotion. The last time she'd dealt with a serial killer was over five years ago, a killer nurse in a local hospital. While the woman's crimes had been horrifying, this case hit far closer to home; Rita felt a connection with the victims.

'My God. Why do you think the UK murders are so much more elaborate and violent than the ones in Spain if it's the same guy? Surely he could get that – that *equipment* he's using more easily there?' Heather spoke in an agonised tone.

'Maybe he feels more confident, maybe he has more time. He might feel more comfortable there,' Rita said.

'Rita, you said your victims had a history of animal rights activism. If he's choosing them that way, he's really doing his research, isn't he? He's researching them for weeks. Aidan looked to be a random victim, but maybe he's not,' Heather said, as Alfonso opened the door to the study and then swiftly closed it. At least *he* had an alibi.

A sickening thought came to her, one she'd been trying to swallow down.

What if helping Pepelito made her – or Alfonso – a target?

'Yes. This is someone who chooses his victims. I don't think it's random – even with Aidan, if you dig deeper you'll find a reason.'

'How do you suppose he's getting rid of forensic evidence, or is he just not leaving any in the first place?' Viewing Aidan's body and attending the crime scene was clearly taking a toll on Heather. Rita sat, sickened by her question, and its likely answer.

'I think this is someone who has money, and lots of time to dispose of evidence. He clearly travels a lot between at least two different countries.' Rita swallowed, not wanting to voice the other thought.

'So someone like a long distance lorry driver, maybe?' Heather said.

'Yes. Although this is someone well educated with detailed knowledge of forensic techniques. I also…' She took a deep breath and drank some water.

Saying it out loud made it more real.

'These cleanup jobs are too perfect for one person. I think he's had help.'

'Jesus Christ. You think that's likely?' Heather inhaled sharply. It was a terrible line, but Rita could hear how shaken she sounded.

'I'd say it's more likely than not.'

'And a question for you,' Rita said, she had her opinion but it helped to confirm it with someone. 'Why do you think he's doing this?'

'Um, probably tells himself they've wronged him somehow, that they deserve it. But I think the real reason is, he loves to kill.' A dog barked in the background as Heather spoke, her voice thoughtful.

'Yeah, I think so too.'

'Has there been any progress on finding a customer list for those darts?' Heather sounded exhausted too.

'Yeah, we've got a list for the last six months for a company called Divisas Taurinas Laguna de Duero, but they also do rosettes for cattle competitions, so you'll have to check what was actually bought. I'll send it over now.' Hadn't she done it earlier? Today had been so long. Even if the killer had bought it directly from the company within six months, the order would be difficult to trace; most such orders were made through associations.

'Cattle competitions? My wife's dad's a farmer, he loves those, he has a herd of prize winning Herefords!' Both women laughed. But the site made her nauseous, even the innocuous pages. And how innocuous could these competitions be for cows whose ultimate destination was dinner?

'Look. Thanks so much. I'll let you go. There will be a press conference tomorrow at 2pm and we'd obviously like it if one or more of you attended via video.' Hearing these words, Rita was filled with dread.

'Yeah, we'll be there, one of us anyway. Take care, Heather.'

Rita hung up and walked back into the living room. 'Sorry about that.'

'No worries,' Alfonso said, putting an arm around her and turning the TV back to the documentary. As the penguins walked across the Antarctic ice Rita shut her eyes, feeling so comfortable with him. She needed to get her flat sorted, but it could wait.

*

'Has it finished?' Rita said blearily. The credits had just come on; she sat up slowly and rubbed her eyes.

'Yeah, you slept through three episodes, I didn't want to wake you because it seemed like you needed it,' Alfonso said, holding her foot gently.

'Oh, crap, I was enjoying it. I guess it's time to go to bed again. I need an early night. We're going to the plaza de toros tomorrow. Speaking to some possible suspects. Can't say I'm looking forward. I feel kind of sick.'

'Ugh. That's gonna be hard.'

'Yeah. It just feels personal now,' she said, picking up her phone.

'Speaking of which. Look at this, Alfonso. Mum was calling me selfish for not wanting to have anything to do with *him* a few weeks ago, now he's cheated on my sister it's like she's joined some militant group.' Not wanting to send her mother anything more recent, Rita had fired over a grainy screenshot of her and Pepelito from the video of him walking down the street. Her mum had just given it a love heart reaction.

'Aw ♡ I love Pepelito, what a sweetie, so proud of you for saving him darling daughter! Love you lots!'

Alfonso shook his head. 'I don't even know what to say. Better late than never I suppose.'

'Who knows if it'll last, I never know with her. She's pissed off at him. Guess I'll take that.' Rita shrugged, checking her police phone in case Heather had sent her anything else. She hadn't, but someone else was calling.

'Sorry to call so late, is that Inspectora Silvera?' The girl on the other end sounded very young. Her voice was pleading yet oddly formal.

'Speaking.'

'It's Lucia Gutiérrez. I need to tell you something to do with my mum.' Rita froze. She got up and mouthed 'Sorry' at Alfonso as she walked out the door.

'Can you meet me on Saturday?' Lucia said, taking a very quiet breath. Rita didn't have the heart to tell her to call back.

'I can. Can you come to the station?'

'Um, could we, like, meet somewhere else, there's a cafe in the park? And – can you not wear a uniform when we meet?'

'I can do that,' Rita said, wanting to collapse in bed.

'Can you, like, come on your own?' Lucia's voice was anxious and insistent.

'I can't –' she started; this was a 14-year-old child. And apart from the safeguarding issue, Lucia had thrown stones at her. Her mind flashed to the teenagers and the dead man in the park. Lucia didn't give her those vibes, but Rita needed backup regardless.

'Please. Now I know the truth, you're the only cop I trust.'

Chapter 25 – Scheming On It

This is a textbook example of sabotaging a reputation, Henry thought, reading the subtitles on a silent Prime Minister's Questions from a bar in the House of Lords. Rather than informing the Commons about a new high speed rail proposal, Eloise was being interrogated on whether she believed food allergies were a result of vaccine poisoning and her affair with Javier Castella. Journalists could truly destroy one's career!

Luckily, Henry had intervened before Robyn could significantly damage his own.

One particularly gobby Labour MP stood up in fury. 'I've got an email here from a constituent whose son died of a peanut allergy, several years before Covid existed. Is the right honourable member going to resign for her comments?'

'No, I won't – I find this suggestion from my right honourable friend outrageous! Plenty of doctors agree with what I'm saying. And it's not just Covid. I don't put any of that poison in my bloodstream, and that's that,' Eloise interrupted. Henry felt a sneaking admiration, despite his scepticism about her medical ideas. Good for her! The Labour MPs in the chamber shouted, outraged and stunned.

"And that's that?' Are you serious?'

'Britain rightly had one of the most successful vaccine programmes in the world, doesn't her stance undermine that, Prime Minister?' one Tory MP who was far too wet for Henry's liking said. Why was he sticking the boot in?

'Not at all. She's a Transport Minister, not a Health Minister, her opinions are her own business,' the Prime Minister said. But Henry knew Eloise would no doubt be resigning at some point today. A shame, but sometimes cells had to be sacrificed to keep any organism healthy, and the Conservative Party was no exception.

Besides, she'd be back, he thought with a smile – unlike Robyn.

Henry leaned back on his expensive leather seat and poured a glass from the subsidised bottle of champagne a waiter had just brought him. He wouldn't have time to deal with Robyn properly before going to Spain, but the journalist was at least unable to do any more damage. Robyn deserved a real punishment for such effrontery.

He thought of Belmonte's costume, hanging up in pride of place by the bottom of the stairs to his cellar; he'd pack it tonight. There were others in his circles who would enjoy such delicacies. Perhaps he could assemble a real audience if he handled the matter with discretion. He'd have to remember to leave enough food in the cellar until his return to the UK.

He took out Robyn's phone from his pocket. He had unlocked it using an app on his own, which was useful for replying to their contacts.

'Hello, Robyn, hope you're feeling better, any more gossip – anything on Dixon?' the Mirror editor had written, setting Henry's teeth on edge.

'Nothing on Dixon yet, the slippery character avoided me the whole evening,' Henry replied. There was also a message from Robyn's mum.

'Hi darling, are you OK? Are you coming to Nanna's birthday tomorrow?'

'I don't think so. I've not been feeling well, I did a test and it said I had Covid,' Henry replied. He had installed a location disguising app when he took it from Robyn, but he would have to dispose of it sooner or later, probably in the Thames overlooking the Houses of Parliament. It was a pity he had missed the Cotswold Foxhounds' last outing of the season, or he'd have got one of the terrier men to throw it into the woods for him on the day.

158

Then, he turned Robyn's phone off and checked his own, careful not to have them on at the same time despite their substantial security features.

'Hello, Henry! Looking forward to welcoming you and the Club to Spain – you have the use of my private airfield! Tell me, is Eloise coming?' Javier had written.

'At the moment, I assume so, I've not heard anything different,' Henry texted back.

'I don't want to risk being seen with her at the moment, given the situation. Perhaps you could gently dissuade her from going?' Javier replied.

'I'll see what I can do, but I might not be able to,' Henry replied. A crucial Commons vote was looming, concerning tax evasion – a vote which threatened to affect *him*. Eloise could always be relied on to follow the Conservative line when she actually went to the debates, as opposed to wining and dining with party donors. Her credentials weren't in doubt. But Henry had to make sure she was motivated to attend. He wouldn't do that by talking her into a hasty cancellation of her well-deserved holiday.

After all, he knew how *he* would react.

'Thank you, sir!' Javier replied, and this honorific from the famous Spaniard gladdened Henry's heart. From this quarter at least, he received the respect his title and birth entitled him to, even if others behaved with less deference.

'How goes the hunt for the wayward bull?' Henry wrote in his next WhatsApp.

'I've located Pepelito, although getting him back is proving a challenge. But nothing I cannot handle.' Henry brought the glass of champagne to his lips as he forwarded the matador's message to the Taurine Club group chat. They'd soon have a real celebration. The electrifying dance between man and beast would reach its stunning finale. He'd make sure he got the best seat, right in the front row.

There'd be no escape this time.

'You're here for two weeks, right? I'll have him back before the end of your trip. I'll finally be able to put on the show we all deserve.'

'I'm sure that won't disappoint.' Henry looked up from WhatsApp. Someone had got bored, and rather than select committee meetings on BBC Parliament, the television was now showing the news.

'Good afternoon, welcome to the three o'clock news with me, Paul Bournville. Our top story this hour – police in both the UK and Spain have stated at a press conference that they believe the murders of Caroline McKenzie and Aidan Donnelly are connected, and have warned that a serial killer is responsible for the deaths of as many as five victims over an 11-year period. We take you live to the conference now.' Only five? Henry thought, wondering who they'd unearthed. Who were these keystone cops?

He'd had many more than that.

'We are doing everything we can to catch this suspect,' said a policewoman with short, dyed blonde hair, round glasses and, no doubt, a heavy northern accent. Not exactly Sherlock Holmes. Almost certainly a lesbian, she had that look about her. Who put her in charge of anything?

What 'suspect', anyway?

They hadn't arrested anyone.

'This is an extremely dangerous man; if you have any information or see something suspicious, even if you don't think it's important, please contact police immediately. We believe this perpetrator is an extremely dangerous man who should not be approached under any circumstances.' Heather had repeated herself many times, and seemed anxious; hardly what Henry called a communications professional. The investigation would run far more smoothly with a man in charge, but not even the police were immune from wokery.

Then the Spanish policewoman appeared on the screen via Zoom. Her background was the Policia Nacional logo. She had long untidy black hair, a bit awkward like that girl at that party at Balliol College. Tegan. He'd had a jolly good time with her, they all had; sometimes he liked to think about her over a glass of wine. She'd rung the police afterwards, naturally, but they had seen sense. Unlike Tegan – who let her into Oxford? – the well brought up Old Etonians had brilliant prospects, and all went on to excellent careers.

And why not? It was only a bit of fun.

He'd killed two birds with one stone when, years later, he'd spotted her ex-husband, walking home alone from an election hustings at Guildford Town Hall. Who would believe a woman unbalanced enough to stab someone 76 times?

'Thank you, Heather,' the subtitles said. Rita Silvera reiterated how keen she was to catch the killer. How sorry she was for previous police failings and how she was doing everything she could. She wasn't going to let anyone down. How nice of her.

Rita cleared her throat as she spoke in instantly translated Spanish. 'We have found many similarities between the cases. We believe the killer is travelling regularly between the UK, Spain, and probably other countries. Ourselves and our British colleagues are doing everything we can to catch this killer. The public should be vigilant but should not be alarmed and should go about their business as usual.'

Where did he know that name?

'Those involved in protests or discussions on animal welfare and similar topics should take care, as the killer has deliberately targeted these groups, he has a grudge against such people,' Rita said, trying to look authoritative, and Henry was sure *she* wouldn't be attacked with sniffy comments in the Guardian. Police officers telling people to be careful what they wrote about politics only set the civil liberties lobby off when the Tories were responsible.

'If you've got any information, no matter how trivial it seems or how long ago, please tell us. Please do not worry about getting in trouble if you speak to us. Our priority is finding him before he kills again,' Rita implored, looking worn out. She reminded Henry of a bull whose strength was fading and needed a few darts to liven it up again.

'Any questions?' Heather said to the journalists seated in front of her. As thrilling as it would be to have his questions answered on air, Henry resisted the temptation. Rather than flamboyantly taunting the media, he would retain an aura of mystique.

Ah yes.

Rita Silvera was Javier's sister-in-law.

She had helped Pepelito escape. Rumours even existed that she had hidden him in her home. The latest video he'd seen showed the bull walking down the road with his doting rescuers, eating out of Rita's hand like a spoiled pet rather than a ferocious fighting machine to be dominated and conquered with a sword. And this animal rights extremist deigned to call him dangerous?

Henry imagined sitting in the stands, watching Pepelito meeting his fate. The president of the bullring – a role Henry aspired to – waving his red handkerchief, signifying the double-spiked, heavier black banderillas that meant disgrace and dishonour, a fitting punishment for a timid bull too spineless to charge. Then, a satisfyingly well-placed thrust with a sword, before Pepelito was dragged unceremoniously away to the boos of the crowd.

Rita would be watching too, in tears. Maybe she'd even jump in and try to save that pathetic creature as it tried to look up, bleeding, with a sad, doleful expression like the unworthy coward it was, rather than the fearsome Iberian warrior he expected and tradition demanded. And, after her four-legged friend, she'd be next.

He imagined her howls of devastation and terror, relishing how much the thought excited him.

Would Rita yell insults like Aidan had, or was she more of a screamer?

One way or another, Henry would find out.

Chapter 26 – Gotcha

Rita had only talked for ten minutes, but she had stayed on the gruelling video call for over two hours. Unlike Heather, who had led the conference, she hadn't taken any questions. But leaving the chat, she wondered if she'd just put a target on her back. Serial killers often followed police investigations into their crimes closely. Some, like BTK and the Zodiac even tried to involve themselves and 'help'.

Had *he* been watching?

Something told her he had.

'Can anyone confirm they can give me backup this weekend when I meet Lucia? Just in case of any safeguarding issues, she's 14.' Rita felt increasingly anxious at the meeting, and any guests the teenager could invite. She wondered if agreeing to see her was a mistake.

'Yeah, I'll come along and sit at the back somewhere. I don't think people assume I'm a cop,' Laurentia said, speaking Spanish with a strong Romanian accent. Only 7 years older than Lucia, she could be mistaken for a teenager depending how she dressed.

'Thanks, Laurentia.'

'As in… that Lucia? Wonder what she wants to talk to you about?' Mansouri was confused and spoke nervously as he rose from his black office swivel chair. Since their ill-fated visit to Bonita Gutiérrez, he'd been awkward with her.

'Yeah, says she has some information about her mum she wants to tell me now she knows the truth.' Because of how she'd helped Pepelito, Rita guessed. Maybe Lucia thought she wasn't some typical uncaring cop.

Perhaps Lucia felt she could trust her.

'Considering her mum's feelings on all this, yeah, that'd make sense.'

'Yeah. Right, Jesús, Abdul, you coming to the plaza?' she said, getting up; hating the prospect of stepping foot there. She wouldn't be in the stands long, if at all, but she'd see and hear enough. The fury she felt, picturing the spectators paying for their tickets, was now tinged with fear.

Would the killer be there, watching?

'Yeah, let's get on it. Just gotta remember not to murder anyone ourselves,' Dominguez muttered.

'Sanchez wants to see me, see you there in a bit,' Mansouri said. Rita was glad of Jesús's presence as they walked out the door of the police station, heading down a narrow street in the direction of the ring.

'I hope my uncle's going to be all right. I told him to consider giving him to a sanctuary, if that prick harasses him again. The village cops won't take the threats seriously, they think it's a joke. Too bad it isn't anywhere near our jurisdiction.' Dominguez sighed. Rita felt horrific. Silvio was an old man. He'd willingly taken Pepelito, and adored him, she reminded herself. But he didn't ask for any of this.

'Probably wouldn't do him much good to move again but yeah, maybe they'd be more experienced with dealing with this intimidation,' Rita said quietly, feeling for her gun in her pocket.

'Maybe. I heard Castella bragging about his kills on the radio this morning. What did he say? "I've got an unbroken record of killing every bull I've ever faced, and I'm not about to lose that record." As Dominguez spoke, Rita could picture it.

'Ugh. Pepelito just wants to live.'

'Yep. Going after him is a can of worms those guys don't wanna open.' Walking past her road, Rita gave a brief glance in the direction of her flat. She couldn't face going in and sorting it out. A cleaning company and some builders had given her a quote. The amount was eye watering, so she'd have to do most of it herself instead. She had another message from Heather.

'Just had an email about that 55-year-old victim in the UK,' she said, looking at the British policewoman's latest message.

'Oh yeah?'

'Guy called Graham Ferry. His ex's been inside for 8 years. They've just received the paperwork to let her out.'

'8 years for something you didn't do. Dios mio.'

'Yeah. Apparently there was a police corruption scandal, and the guy who was in charge resigned last year, so now they're looking into old convictions.' The narrow, paved streets gave way to wider roads again. It wasn't far now; the nausea in Rita's stomach intensified.

'Sounds familiar,' Dominguez muttered, rolling his eyes.

*

'Right, here we are,' Dominguez said as they arrived at the plaza de toros. A group of German tourists were buying tickets to the next corrida, which started in an hour. They looked excited and happy – to watch 6 bulls get slowly stabbed to death. Rita felt physically sick.

'If it starts in an hour, they'll have been in the dark for hours already with no food or water,' Rita gulped, thinking about how Pepelito had reacted to being locked in the bathroom. It was such a hot day. Dominguez gave her a look.

'Yeah, but this is our national tradition isn't it, for better or worse. There's not much you or I can do to help them except catching the killer, and any of this lot who are helping him,' Dominguez said under his breath as they approached the ticket kiosk. He was right. They didn't have many suspects. A witness had come forward saying she'd seen the enclosure keeper, Valero, attacking Sonia shortly before she died, but after eleven years, there was no guarantee this was reliable.

'Police, we're here to ask you some questions,' Rita said to the girl at the desk, putting a foot inside the doorway.

'Is this about that bull, I thought they'd found him?' the girl said, looking confused. She looked barely out of high school.

'No, it's about a murder. Several murders, actually,' Rita said, taking several deep breaths as she looked around. The ticket kiosk was full of bullfighting posters of varying sizes. One, from several weeks ago, advertised Castella's unfinished solo corrida on the 16th of April. Pepelito's name was listed along with Ladron and four other bulls in small print on the bottom.

'Oh,' the girl said, looking shocked.

'Where were you on the 16th of April after 17:00?' Rita asked, nauseous.

The girl glanced at the poster. 'That's when that bull escaped, right? I was here. Then they shut the whole thing and sent us home so they could go and look for it. I went home and then went out with some friends.'

Rita gulped back her overwhelming rage. Selling tickets to corridas was a terrible thing to do but this girl was just trying to earn some money.

'Can anyone confirm this?' she said.

'Sure,' the girl said nervously, writing something down on a notepad. 'My mum and my best friend. I'll give you their numbers.'

Rita took the piece of paper with the numbers on it. The kiosk was also selling tourist guides, fridge magnets and keyrings with bulls and matadors on them. Swallowing hard, she showed the girl the picture of Caroline McKenzie. 'Have you ever seen this woman?'

The girl looked at the photo. Something clicked. 'I dunno. Maybe. I think I saw someone who looked like her. She was having a conversation with some guy, I recognised him because he'd bought a ticket. It was a bit weird. They were arguing. But I don't speak English. So I didn't understand it.'

'Did you see what he looked like?' Rita said, her stomach lurching. If that had been Caroline, it would be one of the last times, if not the last, anyone had seen her alive. 'You said he bought a ticket? Was that the first time you'd seen him there?'

'No, he's bought tickets a few times,' the girl said. 'He's English. He dresses in posh clothes. I don't know. I'm bad with ages. In his 40s, or maybe 50s?'

'Anything else you remember?' Rita asked. The girl shook her head.

'Thank you,' Rita said, her heart racing. 'Can you come to the station later and make a statement?'

'Uh, sure,' the girl said. 'Is it OK if I come later? After work.'

'Work, huh.' Rita's heart pounded in her throat. The blood rushed to her head as she stepped out of the kiosk. She gasped for breath and tears came to her eyes. 'I don't know what your name is but you seem nice. Take my advice. Get another job. These people are evil.'

The girl looked at her dubiously.

She walked a few paces away from the kiosk towards the entrance, then her foot caught on a crack in the pavement outside. She didn't feel the pain first, didn't even realise she'd fallen. When she did, the tears came out of embarrassment. The German tourists were eyeing them warily. Couldn't you find anything to do in our city? I hope the rest of your holiday is shit, she thought. By their faces she realised she'd said it aloud. Or had she? Maybe she hadn't…

'Go home and get some rest, eh, Rita, Abdul will be here in a sec,' Dominguez was saying as he helped her up. Her breath caught in her throat as she stood, blinking back tears and hyperventilating. A group of people were watching her. Were they going to the ring or just passing by? She imagined them gawping like that in the stands, imagined them enjoying the bulls die. Imagined one was the killer.

'I'm fine,' she said to Dominguez as they passed through the side entrance to the arena. She wasn't; she hated everyone and everything she'd see here.

'You sure?' he said.

'Yeah. Let's do this.'

*

They found the bulls' enclosure half an hour later. It had high walls with steps and benches on one side. At one end was a locked door leading to the cells and the maze of dark one-way passages towards the arena. One bull was left; they always kept two as replacements in case something went wrong with the others. The bull, which was a light grey colour, was standing in the corner, looking up fearfully at Rita and Dominguez as they stood above him on a metal platform. Today was so hot; there was no real shade and no water in the bull's trough.

'I'll handle this cruel bastard, Rita.' Dominguez spoke quietly.

'Those village cops let you out fast. Pity you weren't gored, Valero,' he whispered, shaking his head, as the enclosure keeper climbed the stairs leading to the platform. Dominguez smiled, said 'Buenas tardes' and held out his hand. Rita stared at the man without speaking, her legs trembling under her trousers.

'Can I help you?' Valero didn't look worried to see the police.

'We're working on a serial killer investigation. Some information we've received leads us to think the killer frequents this place.' Dominguez spoke in a calm voice, hiding his dislike.

'Really? What information?' Valero said warily.

'I need you to answer some questions, if that's not too much trouble,' Dominguez said. The corrida had started, the band was playing its sinister music. The remaining bull appeared incredibly distressed, walking around in circles and trying to jump at the wall.

'Don't you dare try anything! I'm not having another one get out after what happened two weeks ago, I knew there was something wrong with that one.' Valero grabbed a long metal pole lying on the platform. The bull backed away from the wall and retreated to the corner, shaking. Rita felt nauseous.

Before Valero could beat the animal, Dominguez handed him Caroline McKenzie's photo. Politely but firmly, he asked, 'Tell me, have you ever seen this woman before?'

Valero shook his head, barely pretending to look.

'Where were you on Saturday 16th April after 17:00?'

The man shrugged. He completely ignored Rita, only speaking to Dominguez. On this occasion she wasn't complaining.

'That's when that bull got out! I was here, then around 17:30, I went to look with the others,' he said confidently. The grey bull gazed miserably up at them.

'I went to a bar around 8, when we couldn't find him. I was there most of the evening.' This Rita found easy to believe. She could smell the booze on him.

'What about this young man?' Dominguez showed Valero a picture of Aidan. Again, he barely looked. Out of sight, the crowd cheered with happiness. Their sick enjoyment made Rita want to throw up. The lone bull gave a sad cry from his muddy prison. Valero stared at the animal in fury.

'Shut up, you're pathetic, no wonder you're just a replacement,' he spat at the frightened creature. Rita stared at the bull, hoping against everything she could save him.

'Excuse me, señor. Could you look again at the photo, please?' Dominguez said. This time Valero looked properly.

'No. Never seen him.'

'What about this woman?' Dominguez said, showing the enclosure keeper the photo of Sonia. Valero stared at the picture.

Suddenly his entire demeanour changed.

His eyes widened with fear. He shakily put the pole down. Rita kicked it and it rolled over the side, crashing onto the soil below, away from his prisoner. Valero swallowed hard, his whole body shaking as he clung to the metal railing like a life raft.

'Excuse me, señor,' Dominguez said coldly.

'No comment,' he gulped.

Chapter 27 – Perfect Symmetry

A night in the cells hadn't done Valero any good; he was sweating and having trouble composing himself. His lawyer Antonio sat beside him, as nervous as a rabbit caught in headlights. They weren't the only ones. Rita's night had been sleepless; embarrassed and ashamed of letting everything get too much. She attempted to keep her face looking hard, not anxious, glaring at Valero like shit on her shoe.

Sonia's clothing from the day she went missing had finally been found, ripped and covered in blood, in a plastic bag hidden in a cardboard box at a storage unit Valero rented. He had access to bullfighting equipment through work, and kept various darts and knives at his home. It was his job to jab the darts into the bulls' necks as they went into the ring. He had a criminal record, mostly for petty crime, but had spent time in jail for domestic violence.

But he couldn't be the main killer.

Various bars had provided receipts from the day Caroline McKenzie was murdered, showing he started drinking much earlier than when he claimed to stop looking for Pepelito. The hotel's server was hacked shortly before the murder; Valero had no computer at home. His racist Facebook comments and frequent visits to fascist websites didn't make him a killer.

And he'd never been to the UK.

'Let's ask again. What was your relationship with this woman?' Rita showed him the photo of Sonia; he physically recoiled, his lips tight. His skin had turned grey, he looked ill. His lawyer Antonio looked towards them, almost pleading for help, until Valero finally said, 'No comment' in a shaky whisper.

'You knew her, didn't you?' Rita said.

'I didn't do it,' he stuttered.

'Nobody's accusing you of that,' Rita said, leaning towards him.

'We know there's someone else. You couldn't have done all five,' Mansouri said, taking out the bloodstained bag with Sonia's cut off leggings, crop top and underwear.

'So go on. Why were these items in your storage unit?'

'I've never seen them before,' Valero said, gaping at the clothes with a terrified expression on his face, not looking at his questioner.

'But you knew Sonia, didn't you?' Mansouri said in an unemotional voice.

'I didn't –' Valero started, as Mansouri gave him a cold stare.

'Oh, we know you did,' Rita said. Valero glanced back and forth between the two officers, disorientated, before finally pointing his finger at her.

'I know who you are – you're that bitch who took the bull! You should be in jail for theft!'

'Theft? This is a bit more than that,' Rita snapped.

'You knew Sonia,' Mansouri said. Valero shook his head.

'Yes you did. You knew her, and you hated her. You hated her because she hated what you did, and she had the temerity to say so.' He gave a cold stare across the table. Valero opened his mouth in outrage, clenching his fists.

'You. If you don't like our traditions, get the fuck out of our country! Go back to – to – the Taliban! Don't call me a murderer because I told that bitch where to go!'

'It was a bit more than telling her where to go, wasn't it, Valero?' Mansouri rolled his eyes, ignored his racist insults and drank a glass of water.

'Why do you care? She was just some hooker. Getting involved in things she knew nothing about.'

Rita inhaled sharply. That statement said everything.

'I think you saw Sonia outside the arena regularly, every week, every few weeks, whatever. She'd scare tourists off with her gory placards. She probably yelled at you. And in the evening she'd start work, she'd walk up and down the streets, flaunting her body, looking for customers. It made you even more mad. She was a whore. You don't like whores, do you? Especially not a whore who got paid to sleep with weird, dirty old men, give them the girlfriend experience, but would refuse to take your money, because she hated the very sight of you. She made you sick. Didn't she?'

Valero stared at Rita dumbfounded.

'It wasn't just me. We all hated her,' he mumbled.

'You threatened her, you beat her up to get her to stop coming – in front of her daughter. But that didn't work, did it? So someone you knew, someone even more psychopathic than you, suggested a plan to shut her up once and for all. The police wouldn't bother about a prostitute, you thought. But he didn't stop there, and he didn't start there either. Did he?'

'No. No. That's not how it happened, it wasn't like that,' he gasped, shaking his head.

'Tell me.'

Valero took a deep breath. 'When I hit that bitch, I was trying to scare her, I was teaching her a lesson, that was it.'

'What sort of lesson could throwing her against a wall teach her?' she asked.

'I was trying to get it in her head, you can't mess with tradition. If you don't like it, get out.' Valero's lawyer had barely spoken, and looked as though he wanted to leave and go far away.

'You can't mess with tradition, but you can hide evidence in an unsolved murder for 11 years?' Rita sneered.

'A guy gave it to me to get rid of for 10000 euros! He – he said it was some jewellery he'd stolen, I kept it in case it was valuable!' Valero shouted, his face bright red.

'Really?' Mansouri said, raising an eyebrow. Valero glanced at the ceiling, around the room and toward the door, his hands shaking. Maybe he wasn't lying; people did far more stupid things than this every day, Rita thought.

'I didn't know what to do. Someone would find it, if I threw it somewhere. You can't burn clothes, people will ask why, if I threw it in a river then someone would see me, they always do in the movies. So I just hid it, where only I could go. Until you lot found it.' The last sentence was spoken resentfully.

'Changing your story doesn't make it any more believable, Valero. I don't just think you disposed of evidence. He paid you a lot of money. You helped clean up the scene, and the body, didn't you?' He didn't deny it. Rita could almost taste it, she knew he was going to crack.

'Is that right, Valero?' Mansouri said. The suspect sat, his face impassive. Eventually he nodded imperceptibly.

'He killed her in the ring, didn't he? That's what the sand's for, to soak up the blood. If there was any left, nobody would think it was human. They wouldn't bother testing it.' Rita leaned forward, looked him in the face.

'Did you watch his 'performance', or just hand over the keys so he could bring her in?'

'Just the keys, they wanted me to watch but I got out of there until he was done,' Valero whispered. Rita's stomach tightened.

'Did you supply him the weapons he uses to torture his victims?' Valero did not reply to her question, staring at something far in the distance as his world collapsed. The enclosure keeper who had beaten and tortured countless bulls was now a caged animal himself. He'd spend at least the next 25 years locked up with paedophiles and terrorists.

They both knew it.

'Only for her.' It came out in a strangled whisper.

'What's his name, Valero?' The man shook his head.

'Tell us now, and you might have a chance of parole before the 25 years is up.' Mansouri was being the good cop. Rita doubted it.

'I don't know,' he said, evasive and frightened. His eyes darted around the room for help, like Chicero, the grey bull he'd been tormenting the previous day. She couldn't bring back the woman who'd lost her life for caring about the bulls, but they'd shut the arena, rescuing Chicero and four others locked in tiny ringside cells.

'You don't know? Or you don't want to tell us?'

Valero looked petrified, staring ahead as if at some unknown presence. Finally, his lawyer spoke for the first time since the interrogation started. 'My client doesn't have to answer this question.'

'I never learned his name, it was never, actually, him I saw. Only the guys working for him,' he insisted.

'What guys?' she said quietly.

'They're all rich. Upper class British guys. They come here on holiday to watch bullfighting.' Valero breathed out harshly.

Rita thought of Flavia's VIPs, who 'knew more than they were letting on.'

'Give us some names.'

He shook his head. Rita wanted to punch him into the wall. 'I don't remember. Maybe one of them was called George.'

****

Tegan sat on her bed in her cell. At first the shock of being inside had devastated her. But she'd settled into a routine, the other lifers said the first 5 years were the hardest and it was true. She had the support of her loving daughter Chloe, although she could only see her once every two weeks for a one-hour visit. She had learned to draw while in prison, and had some of her exhibits displayed on the walls. She worked a few hours a week in the shop selling cigarettes and phone cards. Her good behaviour meant she could now get longer, more frequent phone calls, which made her happy.

Her last appeal, three years ago, had failed. Despite her daughter's endless campaign for her innocence, she'd long since accepted it wasn't happening. When the news about Caroline broke, the charity who had taken up Tegan's case sent letters to the Court of Appeal and the police force who had investigated originally. But nobody expected anything from it. She was in her 50s, what would she do if she got out anyway? Being inside had got comfortable. She knew what she had to do and where she had to be each day. She never had to worry about a roof over her head.

Tegan just wished she was allowed to see her kids more often, that was what really hurt. Her daughter was always telling her she had to fight harder.

These days she didn't have it in her. It wasn't going to happen.

She heard keys jangling, a pair of hard prison officer's boots tramping the floor. The screw gave the door a sharp knock. What could this be about? Her cellmate was working in the canteen; she was the one that usually kicked off over something.

'Ferry.' Ah, she liked this one, Ashley his name was. He was Black with short cropped hair and a short beard, about the same age as her daughter. Some of the screws were dickheads, but he was all right, she had to get on with one or two given she was never getting out. He sometimes gave her cigarettes and talked to her about his kids. He seemed like a nice guy doing a shitty job.

'Yeah?'

'Get your stuff. You're free to go, conviction's overturned. Your daughter's picking you up, we've just told her.'

'What do you mean?' Tegan said, disorientated and uncomprehending.

'You heard what I said. We should have been told three days ago but as usual we were the last to know, they didn't bother telling us until today. The Court of Appeal has ordered your immediate release pending a retrial.' Tegan's mouth was wide with shock. What was she going to come back to? This place was her home, it had got so familiar.

She'd almost come to like it.

She opened her mouth and couldn't speak, overwhelmed with emotions. Ashley unlocked the door as she scraped together her bag of toiletries, photos and other bits and pieces. 'I can't believe this is happening.'

'Nor can I, but that's what the judge said. Here's his letter.'

Dazed, she only looked at it briefly. She took her bag and walked with him towards the prison exit. It was 8pm and she was tired; not long until lights out.

'Is it true? You're getting out, Tegs?' one of the other women shouted. After what she was convicted of, this was deemed very unlikely.

'So it seems, yeah,' the screw said, and she followed him towards the prison reception. There, they gave her some paperwork to sign, and she filled it out, feeling like a zombie. The thought of the outside world she'd never expected to see again both terrified and excited her.

The gates were open, apart from the exercise yard she hadn't seen the open sky in 8 years. Unlike her cell, the outside was raining and cold.

As Tegan walked out of the huge iron gates and Chloe got out of her car, journalists surrounded her, taking pictures and shouting for her attention. 'Have you got anything to say? How do you feel?'

'Who's the real killer? Any ideas?'

'I don't know,' Tegan said as she stumbled towards her daughter. What about money, she thought stupidly? What was she going to do about getting a job?

Once the two were on the road, Chloe's car phone rang. It was strange for it to be so easy; phone calls were such a precious commodity in prison.

'Hello? Is that Chloe? It's Heather. Is your mum there, how's she doing.'

'It's the police, Mum. Yeah, she's good, just shellshocked,' Chloe told the officer.

'Sorry to ask, when she's this minute got out, but I'd like to see her today.'

*

'I know this is difficult, so take your time. Did Graham ever mention having any enemies?' Heather asked Tegan as they sat in Chloe's small living room. The grandchildren she'd never met were in bed upstairs but Lego still remained on the floor.

She shook her head. But recollections she'd numbed over the years flooded her. Memories she knew played their part in ruining her relationship with Chloe's dad, then her marriage to Graham – making her eventual conviction plausible. She gripped her daughter's hand tightly, swallowing hard.

The police hadn't believed her then. But now, everything had changed.

'Enemies? If they – no. It was me they were really after.' The words were out before she'd decided whether to say them.

'Who's *they*?' Heather inquired gently.

'Posh boys at Balliol. But why, after all that time? I don't even know what their names were. I blocked it out.' Fear and shame crawled over her. With all that time to think inside, she'd rarely thought about *this*.

'Mum, what?' Chloe's fingers dug into her arm. 'What is this?'

Steeling herself, Tegan drew a breath, and began to tell her story.

Chapter 28 – Fiesta de Dementes

'Wow. According to some Spanish website, someone has been arrested from the Valladolid bullring, just near where we are supposed to be staying. They're claiming it's regarding this supposed serial killer,' Eloise said, sat next to Henry in his Gulfstream jet as the club members waited for the plane to take off.

'They surely can't imagine they've already found the serial killer,' Henry said, irritated. He seemed stressed today, Eloise thought.

'Apparently, the investigation isn't over – they just say he helped the killer. All corridas have been cancelled there for the next two weeks. Probably so they can plant evidence,' Eloise replied, rolling her eyes. Even worse, it was supposed to rain on their third day. If severe enough, that would spoil the hunting excursion they had planned.

Wasn't Spain supposed to be suffering from a drought?

Clearly not a very bad one.

'I hope they refund our tickets, that being the case,' Henry sniffed, before adding reassuringly, 'Ah. It's Spain, plenty of bullrings we can attend without an interfering police presence.'

Eloise nodded, half listening as she composed a series of tweets. One said, 'I'm being silenced and persecuted by the deep state – freedom of speech anyone? I won't resign!!'

Another said, 'My grandparents would be ashamed by what this country's become. Britain fought a war for freedom, only to surrender to Covid tyranny! #VaccineGate'

'There's no serial killer. The left are looking for excuses to ban it,' she muttered once she'd finished tweeting. The video she'd seen on Facebook earlier had been very persuasive.

'What makes you say that?' Henry appeared a little flustered.

'Well, for a start, Spain's new policing minister is a vegetarian,' Eloise said.

'I see. I have to say, I believe there is a serial killer, but the police are rather making a meal of it,' Henry said, an odd expression on his face.

But today, Eloise's mind was not on Soros, the Rothschilds, the World Economic Forum or the Great Reset. A more immediate preoccupation was bothering her, one which threatened to spoil her entire visit.

What, if anything, had she done wrong? Why was Javier avoiding her? Her comments had been spoken in a moment of weakness, but since they were reported, he'd been avoiding her. He had been stressed recently. Perhaps his mind was on his next encounter with el toro. But another, worse possibility was unsettling her thoughts.

Maybe he was patching things up with Maria.

She leaned back in her seat as they prepared for take off, checking her messages again. Nothing.

She bit her lip, eyes brimming with tears, trying, but failing, to resist the temptation to text Javier again. He had made her feel so special. He could have any woman he wanted and he chose her. Surely he wasn't going to stay with his wife after all this?

As the plane took off and began to soar through the clouds, she took out a copy of La Salida, and flicked through it to cheer herself up. But so many of the gory photographs within its pages were of Javier Castella. On one knee in the sand, waiting for his next victim. Prancing around with a pair of banderillas. Standing with his sword, looking determined. She wanted to cry.

Eloise loved the thrill of following her passion; touring the prestigious bull farms, possibly even having a go herself with a young calf. Years ago, she'd done just that on an intensive course in Mexico and long dreamed of repeating the experience. Yet without Javier's flirtatious texts, Eloise's mood soured. Her paranoia alighted on its new target.

She'd been nothing but patient. What had she done wrong?

Did he find her embarrassing?

She put the magazine aside. Henry had taken out a packet of luxury cigars.

'Where did you get those?' Eloise said.

'A gift from a friend at the San Isidro Festival. No health and safety mandarins here to wag their fingers. These are the same brand smoked by Papa Hemingway himself,' he scoffed as he lit up. Indeed, the packet, custom made with the warnings removed, had a black and white picture of Ernest, with one hanging out of his mouth.

'May I?' she said, feeling a frisson of excitement at smoking on a plane. Few were so daring in today's times. How dare Big Pharma tell her what to do with her health? Only she had the right to make those decisions.

'I'll make an exception for my general dislike of women smoking, and there is something elegant about a woman smoking a cigar,' Henry said, handing her one and sparking it up with his antique lighter. What a gentleman! The only problem was, she didn't like him that way.

She only wanted Javier.

Thinking about him was driving her insane. Why was he ghosting her like this? Her last two messages had been delivered, but he hadn't read them and it kept showing him as online!

How could this be fair?

*

Sitting in the stands at Salamanca with the Taurine Club the following day, Eloise leaned forward to get the best view, trying to focus on the spectacle in the arena, rather than the one surrounding her. Last night, the aficionados had sat in an expensive restaurant opposite Valladolid's now closed plaza de toros – where some spiteful tourist had taken pictures and sent them to a tabloid. The restaurant was a dream target for an enraged animal lover, with bullfighting posters littering the walls, and a huge bull's head overhanging the table.

'Disgraced anti-vaxxer MP takes bull by horns on cruel corrida holiday – with YOUR money' said the headline, illustrated with a picture of Eloise, a syringe marked 'COVID-19' and a worried looking cow. Henry was only mentioned once in the article, whose fire was directed solely at her. The media only ever seemed to go after her – they'd been like this when she wouldn't wear a face nappy.

This was just like fascism – in fact, it was worse.

When their immune systems were ruined, and hers was healthy and intact, maybe they'd think twice about calling her 'disgraced'.

Feeling twitchy, Eloise gazed at the opening procession of the matadors and their assistants, trying to put her worries out of her mind. Javier was only on at the end; the feared rain hadn't materialised.

'This bull should have gone to Javier Castella a few weeks ago, now Rosario is taking him,' Lord Owenstoft said, smiling, as the unfortunate creature entered the arena. She caught a glimpse of Javier talking to another matador and felt as if she'd been stabbed. Usually so prompt, he hadn't replied to her texts.

He hadn't even looked at her.

She watched the first bull, looked at the way it ran. It kept looking for an exit. At least someone was about to have an even worse day than she was. She didn't feel a moment's pity – after all, this was what it was bred for. It was hot and the Spanish weather took a bit of adjustment for the already preoccupied Eloise. Every few seconds, she looked away from the drama, checking her phone to see if Javier had replied.

20 minutes in, after killing the bull with a perfectly placed swordthrust, Rosario bowed deeply to the crowd. Some of them threw flowers at him. Lord Owenstoft smiled. 'What a wonderful performance!'

'Yes! Magnificent!' Eloise had only half been watching, hooked on waiting for a text from Javier, a message receipt, anything – and what people were saying about her on the internet. The journalist who had reported her comments had since been reported missing – obviously emotionally unstable. The media hired anyone these days for their fake news.

'Personally, I found it rather boring. The bull was something of a mediocrity,' Henry said.

Then it was the turn of the next victim, a bull transferred here from Valladolid after Pepelito escaped. This one was a bit more energetic. It actually did what it was supposed to. Rosario did look sexy in his costume. As Eloise craned her neck to get a better look she almost – *almost* – forgot about Javier.

This was such a beautiful art, Eloise thought, better than football or anything like that. Watching Rosario's exquisite taurine ballet reminded Eloise why she'd become hooked as a 15-year-old, during that exchange trip to the South of France with her 8K a term private school. Recently, she'd started getting angry emails from know-it-all doctors, saying her education was wasted. Why couldn't they shut their mouths if they couldn't be kind? She'd got to government. They hadn't, so whose education was wasted again?

In his flawless, inimitable style, Rosario used his sword masterfully on the second bull. How wonderful, Eloise thought! While it was dragged away, she got up and strolled to the small ice cream stand a few rows above hers, a bit more able to enjoy the afternoon's entertainment. There weren't many people in the queue. Supposedly, many Spanish people hated bullfighting.

They were missing out.

She sat back down as the third bull entered the ring, with a different matador she didn't know the name of. This one was annoying her with its constant mooing. As Eloise began enjoying her ice cream, her phone vibrated. She'd forgotten the pink bullring cushion she always took to corridas back at Henry's villa. Her back hurt from sitting on the plane too long. The uncomfortable stone benches were giving her backache. She took out her phone, half watching as the bull was stabbed with a spear.

The message was from Javier.

But it was in Spanish.

It was clearly not meant for her.

It said, 'Hola Lola como estas? 😙 sí, me encantaría verte esta noche después de que termine mi corrida. Te tengo una sorpresa 🙂 Besos, Javier. ♡'

It took all Eloise's effort not to smash her phone on the concrete step and run out of the bullring in tears. She swallowed hard, wiping her eyes with the white handkerchief the spectators used to indicate that someone had killed the bull so wonderfully he deserved one or both ears – after a particularly outstanding performance, maybe even its tail.

The fourth bull entered; she hardly noticed. Before anyone could assume she felt sorry for it, she looked down, her tearful eyes glued to her phone.

'Looks like this one might try and escape. That's always exciting,' one of the other club members sneered, a horse trainer who worked on the Grand National. Eloise's lip trembled. She wished someone would ask if she was OK. Didn't they care?

'Entertaining, yes, but we don't want another Pepelito,' Henry laughed tersely.

Then it was Javier's turn.

Eloise couldn't bear to look at him. But she couldn't tear herself away. Maybe the message she'd received was some terrible misunderstanding. He stared straight at her as he waited for the fifth bull to come out and she thought she saw him smile. Her heart raced – and then she turned round and saw the good-looking pair of young women sitting a few rows above.

It was all too much. She picked up her stuff. Henry gave her a concerned glance as she walked towards the exit, the hot sun beating down on her back.

Maybe she'd be better off with him.

As Eloise walked to her waiting taxi, clutching her key in her fist, her sadness dissipated. Rage filled her deep inside, consumed her, burned her up. How dare that little Spanish shit treat her like this? How dare he act like she was nothing? They'd had such a great time. She'd thought he was in love with her. He'd told her as much.

The whole time, it had been a lie.

Javier wouldn't get away with this. The whole world would know what a cheat he was. Like so many men, he was a liar and a bastard. He had promised her the world – and broken her heart. And now he wouldn't even look at her. How dare he hurt her like that?

She was going to make him pay.

If she couldn't have him, why should anyone else?

Chapter 29 – Moment of Truth

Rita ordered two cokes at the place Lucia had suggested and sat just outside the door, in a small, shaded courtyard. Laurentia sat inside, out of sight. She hadn't slept and kept replaying the events at the plaza de toros, her collapse, the claustrophobia, the way she saw people looking at her. She had to stay in control or she'd lose everything.

Lucia turned up about 20 past 5, just as Rita was thinking about going. A denim bag slung over her shoulder, she was wearing lip gloss and a lot of blue eyeliner. She sat down, looking breathless.

'Hey,' the teenager said nervously. 'Sorry I'm late.'

'That's OK,' Rita said. 'How are you?'

'OK, I guess,' Lucia shrugged, drinking her coke out the bottle. She took a packet of cigarettes from her bag and offered one to Rita.

'You're far too young to smoke.' She shook her head. The girl shrugged.

'What are you gonna do about it. Put me in jail?' Lucia said, lighting up, but she didn't seem annoyed, just resigned as she flicked ash into the tray.

'I started smoking at your age, I only managed to stop five years ago. It's a bad habit to get into, expensive too.' The teenager rolled her eyes but looked self-conscious.

Then, Lucia looked at the table. She was silent for a while and when she spoke next she was close to tears. 'I'm really sorry, Rita. I hope my video didn't get you in trouble. The bull, he just seemed so loving and trusting. When you gave him away, I thought you were killing him. I didn't know Alfonso was an activist. I assumed the worst. I'm so sorry. I wanted you to know that.'

'Nah, slap on the wrist and that's it. My boss thought the exact same as you. He said it made the police look uncaring.' Rita kept her voice light and jokey.

Lucia gave an embarrassed smile. 'You'll think this is cringe, but I found him relatable, because – I don't belong in this world and I just want to run away.'

'What do you mean?'

'That first video of him. It just reminded me of, like, being beaten up at school, or the other girls having a go about my mum, with everyone stood around watching. When I'm at school, I just want to escape, like the bull did. A lot of times I just don't go.'

A rush of sympathy hit Rita. Lucia needed protection and care. Finding the killer might help her and her family find peace.

'That must be really difficult.'

Lucia nodded and sipped her drink, shuddering. She took a drag on her cigarette and quickly changed the subject back. 'But yeah. He's a peach. Super brave and adorable.'

'Yeah, when he knows you're a friend, he's super affectionate and full of love.'

Lucia nodded, finishing the cigarette and drawing out another one. Teenagers were always rebellious, but it was worrying how much this 14-year-old was smoking. 'Aw. What a legend. I love animals.'

Rita held the girl's gaze. 'Were you going to tell me something? Because I can chat about this all day, but...'

Lucia took a deep, nervous breath. She tapped the cigarette over the ashtray.

'Yeah, sorry. I was…it's my anxiety. Abuela said you arrested someone, is that the killer?' The girl's voice was a mixture of fascinated, sad and hopeful. Watching her, Rita couldn't imagine what it would have been like growing up in this situation, the shadow of her mum's murder hanging over everything. Lucia was both childlike and far too grown up for her age – nowhere near as tough or worldly as she was trying to seem.

'I don't want to say too many details, without other members of your family present,' Rita said.

Lucia looked crushed.

'You don't have to treat me like a child, I'm strong enough to hear it.'

'Legally, I do,' Rita said. The girl rolled her eyes and took another puff, reminding her a lot of herself when she was that age – weird, edgy posturing mixed with childish vulnerability.

'I dunno if this is important but. A few years ago, Abuela was going through my mum's things and she found this. She can't bear to throw anything out that belonged to her. Anyway, this was from a conference or something, it's from the weekend my mum died. I think maybe she picked it up from a hotel when she saw a customer.' Lucia said it so matter of factly. She passed a battered leaflet across the table.

Inspecting it, Rita saw it was in English.

'Standing for Freedom and Building Growth: Preserving national traditions and building a conservative movement across Europe.' Rita had a look at the list of speakers, who were from a range of different countries. Their mayor was on the list, a man she hated. He didn't do much work and was constantly on holiday – and was the president of the city's bullring.

These had to be the VIPs.

'Henry Dixon: Lessons from Margaret Thatcher on prospects for a sound economy.' She'd heard that name before. But where? A conservative UK politician. What had he been doing here, she thought, irritated. The leaflet also mentioned another MP called George Stenton.

Valero had mentioned a wealthy British guy called George.

'What made you think this might be important, Lucia?' she said, more sharply than she intended.

'It wasn't me. It was Abuela. She's always going on about what was on at the time and how none of the guests at the events were looked into. I love her, but...it gets too much sometimes, like, she's always sad, especially when it's my mum's birthday and things like that. That doesn't make me a bad person, does it?' Lucia gulped.

'Not at all. Families are difficult,' Rita said. The girl was visibly relieved.

'So, a few weeks ago, like, that guy, Henry Dixon, it went viral that he was at that corrida. He hurt the bull, he tried to stop him getting away! It was horrible. Like, I just remembered that leaflet. So creepy that it was for the day before Mum dying.' Lucia's voice rose. She spoke passionately.

Ah yeah.

That was where she'd heard it.

To Rita, this sick spectacle was the national shame. And these pompous, privileged men came from overseas just so they could watch it.

'Maldito. He's not the only powerful man who enjoys this sort of thing,' Rita said. She went onto Google and searched for his name. The top result in English said, 'Lord Henry Dixon accused of mistreating escaped Spanish bull'.

'Pobrecitos,' Rita whispered. As well as Pepelito, the article had pictures of Castella's first bull Ladron bleeding, his tongue hanging out, hardly able to walk as he stood waiting to die. Trapped in the dark, driven mad with fear, Pepelito would have heard and smelt everything.

'This guy loves his corridas, doesn't he.' Henry was president of something called the Taurine Club of Kensington, an association for British bullfighting lovers. To view anything on its website, you had to pay and then fill out a form to become a member. No way was she doing that.

A chill came over her.

'Upper class British guys. They come here on holiday to watch bullfighting.'

'Did you watch that video? The one of him escaping? It just made me so happy. I know it would have made my mum happy too.' Lucia's face lit up. Rita shook her head.

'I should. I'm being a wimp. It just broke my heart to find him like that.'

'I think you should see it, not the horrible parts, just the end. There are some funny comments as well.' Lucia was keen for her to see the bull's amazing escape. But the idea of watching the vile, preening Castella and his assistants torture Pepelito made her want to throw up. The video would send her into a spiral of rage.

She'd have to watch it now.

Henry Dixon had been at the corrida.

He'd been in the vicinity of at least two murders.

He fit their profile.

'I suppose I should,' Rita said. The surrounding tables in the cafe were empty. Lucia's eyes darted around the street. In silence, the girl drank the last of her coke. Then she spoke.

'Abuela would kill me, but I want to be a cop when I'm older, so I can catch people like the guy who killed my mum,' she said nervously, fiddling with the lid of the coke bottle.

Rita stared her in the eye. She wanted to hug her, but tried not to display these maternal, protective feelings. 'Keep your eye on that goal, then, and try not to skip any more classes. I think you'd be amazing.'

'You're gonna think this is dumb.' Lucia's lip trembled. Rita shook her head; the information given her so far had been anything but dumb.

'But sometimes. Always in summer. Sometimes, when Abuela used to fetch me, before I started getting the bus, I used to think I'd seen someone watching me, looking at me when I came out of school. I've known my whole life my mum was murdered. So maybe that's why. My mind playing tricks. Everyone told me not to be stupid, so I don't talk about it usually.' Lucia's cigarette had gone out. She lit it again.

'But you know that Henry guy? When Abuela found that leaflet, I couldn't believe it. Because the guy I used to imagine sometimes looked exactly like him.'

'Like, I'm sure it's nothing,' Lucia said nervously. Neither of them spoke. Rita felt sick. Kids felt they were invincible at that age, and especially with girls, few listened to them.

'It doesn't sound like nothing.' Rita had a nauseous feeling twisting up her stomach. Lucia looked doubtful.

He'd get a kick out of it, wouldn't he?

Watching the daughter of his victim.

Staring at her from a distance.

'Hmm, I suppose.'

'Lucia.' Rita's heart was pounding. 'If you see this man following you again, you must call 091 immediately.'

****

After eating dinner with the other club members, Henry retired to his bedroom at the villa, where he saw he had an email from one of his old Eton chums. The chilling subject line said, 'Tegan'. A name Henry and his friends never uttered after that party and their unspoken gentleman's agreement. What did this fool think he was doing with such a message?

'You may want to be aware of this, Dickers, in case there is future legal trouble down the line,' the email said. Below was a link to an article.

Seeing its title, Henry felt numb.

'I am innocent, says released ex-wife of stabbing victim.'

Reading on, he began to feel tingly, light-headed and nauseous.

'Tegan Ferry, whose conviction for the murder of her ex-husband has been overturned, claims crucial evidence has been missed in the case.

Speaking today upon her release, she said, 'Graham and I certainly had our differences. But, I never, ever wished him dead. I have spent 8 years in prison for a crime I didn't commit, while, it appears, his murderer has walked free to kill again and again. I'd like to thank my family and friends for their support.'

Tegan's daughter Chloe said, 'I'm grateful for all those that steadfastly believed in my mum's innocence. Now, our focus must turn towards seeking justice for my stepdad and catching the real killer."

She didn't say 'identifying', did she, he noticed, with a sinking, falling feeling in his chest.

Just 'catching'.

Catching the real killer.

Wealth wouldn't deter people like Rita or Heather. They couldn't be bought, either. He composed a hasty reply to his old chum, requesting information on Tegan's whereabouts. No answer came, and after ten, fifteen, thirty minutes, he sensed it never would.

They were onto him.

If they weren't, they soon would be.

Chapter 30 – Found You

'I see you arrested Valero Cotillion again. Prison's the best place for that cutthroat,' Silvio said to Dominguez, who'd found somewhere permanent to rent and was dropping by to fetch his stuff.

'He grew up in Colmenar, right?' Dominguez patted Pepelito over the fence and fed him a huge carrot. Pepelito didn't understand any of what they were on about. But they were relaxed, so, so was he. He craned his neck to eat the carrot; the pain was now a dull ache and only really bothered him when he was sad, stressed or hungry.

Swishing his tail, he looked over at the bottom of the field. The brown splodged cow he liked had wandered up to the fence. Out of all the cows in that field, she was his favourite. It was driving him crazy with frustration. He liked the way she interacted with him, the way she smelt.

He had to figure out his way in.

'That's one way to put it. He's a bad lot. His father was a brute without shame, and the son is worse,' Silvio said disdainfully.

'He's not gonna see the outside for a long time after what he's admitted to,' Dominguez said, as Pepelito gulped back the last of the carrot. For once, Maribel wanted to play with him. She nudged him with her nose, kicking Silvio's old tractor tyre towards him.

'I've put in some new alarms and I've had no more trouble, you'll be happy to know. Think Valero getting done has put the frighteners up our mutual acquaintance.' Silvio laughed.

'Just be careful, won't you. Don't underestimate Castella. Though I'm surprised he finds the time with all those women after him.'

'Women? What do they want with someone who stabs a poor bull whilst dressed up like an idiot?'

'You're asking the wrong guy.' Dominguez always brought nice vegetables. Pepelito grabbed the cucumber he was being offered.

Patting him, Dominguez went on, 'Hope Rita's gonna be OK. I'm kinda worried. Sanchez told her to have some time off, but yesterday she was still working. She won't want any time off but I think the bastard's right. She had some sort of panic attack right before we arrested Valero.'

'All you and Rita do is work these days. Much too hard. I'll be glad when you've caught this scoundrel.' Silvio's voice was disapproving.

'Me too,' Dominguez said through gritted teeth.

'What do you think, Pepelito? You agree.' At first, Pepelito had found it disconcerting when Silvio spoke to him like a human, but now he knew the old man was showing his love.

'This one knows about the value of work, don't you, amigo,' Dominguez laughed, stroking Pepelito under his neck. The bull turned away and went to join Maribel, pushing the tyre towards her with his snout. Near the fence, the splodged cow stood watching.

Playing with Maribel reminded him of happy memories, playing with other young bulls on the farm he grew up on. While he'd been one of the lucky ones, kept back for the ring until he was 5, violence was never far away. But he'd had fun with his friends in their spacious field. He missed them.

When bad things came into Pepelito's mind he reminded himself where he was. He had food, and plenty of space and freedom. Maribel and his human protectors loved him, and he loved them back.

But Silvio was an old man, and the others were often stressed and sad. While they believed they were keeping him safe from cruel, evil people, Pepelito increasingly saw it the other way round. They weren't made for the violent world of humans, the world people like Castella and Valero had forced him to live in.

He was the one who had to protect them.

*

That night, Pepelito and Maribel slept in the barn together as usual. Pepelito shifted around in the straw until he was comfortable. It was easy to keep cool here.

Maribel knew about Ladron now. She made it known that he couldn't have prevented what happened to the big brown bull whose calm demeanour soothed his nerves, who'd helped him feel less afraid of the others trapped alongside them.

He wasn't bad.

He'd done nothing wrong.

She blamed herself for things, too. Not looking after her calves well enough. Fighting with particular cows, who then disappeared. Being so irritable with Beatriz during her illness, not realising how sick her best friend was.

He snuggled up beside her. The pain was minimal now, but he often felt awkward and clumsy. Sometimes he scratched Maribel with his horns by mistake, and she'd kick him, not hard, but enough to let him know she was annoyed. It never happened before he'd come *there*, and it upset him. Would he ever get less ungainly?

The air was silent apart from an owl hooting somewhere, cars far in the distance. Through the barn walls, he didn't really notice the man creeping around just outside the range of the sensor, scattering seeds on the ground near where the geese slept.

****

Rita couldn't sleep that night.

She tiptoed out of bed, turned on the computer, logged onto Facebook and replied to some messages, many of which were weeks old. Most of these people, she rarely spoke to. She'd forgotten who some of them were. Her mum had shared a petition about banning bullfighting, which annoyed Rita. This new-found conviction was, she assumed, solely due to Castella's treatment of her sister. Meanwhile, Maria herself hadn't reached out at all.

Loads of people had shared that video of Pepelito. An ex from school had written to her the day it happened. 'Hey, Rita! Don't you live there these days? Did you see this?'

It wouldn't help her sleep, but she had to stop being a wimp.

She went onto YouTube, found the video, and pressed play at the point he leapt into the stands. Her breath caught in her throat as she watched the bull run up the steps, bleeding, confused and in so much pain; reduced to licking melted ice cream from a step as the spectators unleashed their violence.

Spectators like Henry Dixon.

The aficionados tried forcing Pepelito back into the arena, their bloodlust unsatisfied. Their faces contorted with shock, rage and hatred. Castella strode up with a sword towards the wounded, panting bull, his mind on his 'unbroken record'.

'Dios mio,' she whispered as Pepelito dodged them, escaped down the stairs to safety, in obvious agony but finally, finally free. Out of sight, someone had opened the door that saved the bull's life. Rita wondered if she'd ever learn who this angel was, if she could ever thank them.

As Lucia suggested, she scrolled down to look at some comments; apart from a handful of taurinos they were all supportive.

'The best corrida ever – OLE! Enjoyed seeing this dim-witted, hapless beast outsmarted at every turn!'

'Bravery, charisma and talent – what else needs to be said? Hope the artist is enjoying a well-deserved rest in his meadow 😊'

She read further down the list until she found the oldest comments, posted shortly after the video was uploaded.

'30.56: The guy pulling the bull's tail is a British politician – Henry Dixon.' This was in Spanish, but almost all its hundreds of replies were in English.

'Shame it couldn't of gored him :(' someone called angel2004 had written, along with several further humorous replies.

'Anyone checked his hard drive? Prob got 100TB of snuff movies lol.'

'@ vivalostorosespana wtf u srsly callin me racist cos I dissed ur 'sport'?? 😂😂hahaha fuck off, hope u get a horn in ur arse lmao'

Rita clicked onto the profile – then stopped dead, her stomach plunging as she stared at Aidan Donnelly's channel. His very last video upload showed him walking his mum's dog around his run-down housing estate, thanking his latest subscribers and giving various updates. Clicking around other videos, she was filled with nausea and skin-crawling horror.

But also – relief.

They had a prime suspect.

Rita went back onto Facebook and searched for Caroline McKenzie and the group she was in, Animal Defenders United. Her social media presence had been very active, publicly and privately. Alongside posts about how to be a great manager and get the best out of your staff, Caroline's Facebook was full of angry political rants.

'Look at the state of this absolute sicko! How would he like to be chased through the countryside by hungry dogs and ripped to death!?' Caroline had written on a post about fox hunting, showing a photo of Henry sat on a horse, wearing a red coat.

'Perfect!!! Perfect would be him taking the bull's place, which he'd never do, because he's a coward!' she'd replied to Henry's article about what made 'the perfect corrida'.

'Dixon again 'in defence of grouse shooting'! The last time I said what should happen to this demented animal torturer, Facebook censored my post!' Caroline had written hundreds of such posts about Henry and other politicians. You hated her for that, didn't you, Rita thought. You can't stand to be questioned. You can't stand to be criticised. And you can't stand to be attacked for the things you do.

No way was she getting back to any sleep now.

Her heart pounding, she did a search for the most recently connected victim.

Sure enough, 30-year-old Green Party member Samantha Berger gave an interview to the local paper about her protest, three weeks before she was killed in 2022. 'Henry Dixon has shares in an arms company that supplies weapons to dictatorial regimes, Russian-linked mercenaries, and terrorists. His frequent private jet usage shows total disregard for the environment. Last year, he flew on it 72 times while the pandemic was still raging, including flying to Ecuador for just two nights.'

Of course you did, Rita thought, her breath catching. This guy would have the best lawyers. He was a well-connected politician who possessed unimaginable wealth. There was a good chance he'd walk no matter what she and Heather did.

Then there was Tegan.

'Hi, Rita,' Heather had written in her latest email. 'I have just interviewed Ms Ferry on her exit from prison. She disclosed a sexual assault dating from the early 1990s. Timeline matches HD's years of attendance, as shown by Balliol College records.'

Graham Ferry had given an interview to a local newspaper about a new road he was campaigning against. 'While the government should be investing in green infrastructure, greedy individuals in the Tory Party like Henry Dixon with millions invested into fossil fuels are continuing to give permission for wasteful, damaging projects like this road.'

Three weeks later, he was dead. The 24/7 witness protection programme poor Tegan was under would just be another kind of prison.

Shuddering, Rita searched for articles about the Taurine Club of Kensington, and found one by Robyn Casey. The Club's members were drawn from the rarefied milieu of the privileged British upper classes. Some had government roles and aristocratic titles, and even used taxes to pay for flights round the world, hotels – and bullfighting tickets.

The girl at the kiosk.

She'd seen 'an English guy in posh clothes', arguing with a woman who looked like Caroline. Could that be him? Or one of his accomplices?

The second part of the two-part series hadn't been released. Instead, when she searched for Robyn's name, Rita saw another type of article. Bile rose in her throat. It was like she'd been punched; scrabbling at her desk as all the air was knocked out of her.

'Fears grow for missing Robyn, 25.'

'Police are said to be extremely concerned about the whereabouts of Robyn Casey, a journalist living in Shoreditch, who was last seen last Friday…'

When Rita rang Heather, she didn't pick up. It was 3am; she was obviously asleep with her wife like a normal person.

'Henry Dixon is our killer. He has Robyn Casey, it might not be too late to save them if you act now,' Rita began her email, frantically adding information pointing to his guilt.

She was shaking all over. She'd had almost no sleep and barely noticed Alfonso walking in the study.

'Rita? You OK?'

'I've found the sick fuck who murdered your friend. Henry Dixon. He's the serial killer,' she gasped. Alfonso switched on the light. He wrapped his arms around her, held her tightly and stroked her hair.

The Madrid cops had emailed her with more possible victims. So had someone in the South of France. A detective had even emailed her from Ghana about a suspicious death near a hunting lodge for rich tourists.

'This guy must have killed 10 people at least and someone else is missing. And you – I haven't asked how you were doing after what happened to Caroline. How are you feeling?' She gabbled the words before she even thought, her heart pounding with anxiety, her mind spinning.

'You have asked me. I'm holding up OK. Come get some rest, Rita.' Alfonso held her tight and kissed her, his touch light. She felt calmer.

While he embraced her, she did another search for the Taurine Club of Kensington on her phone, unable to help herself. When she saw the results, she felt like she was going to throw up. Her throat seized up and she couldn't speak. 'Disgraced anti-vaxxer MP takes bull by horns with cruel corrida holiday – with YOUR money!'

Rita dialled the station number, feeling sick and dizzy.

Pick up, pick up, pick up, she thought.

'Dios mio,' she kept saying to herself. 'He's here.'

Chapter 31 – Caught

Silvio's footsteps slowed as he trudged up the track towards the barn. Expecting him to unlock the door, Pepelito stood up.

'Mordedor. Destripadora,' Silvio whispered in a horrified voice, filling him with apprehension. Maribel sensed it too. She hung back rather than trotting towards the entrance in a rush to greet him. Something was terribly wrong.

'My beauties,' Silvio said, fumbling with the barn door. As it swung open, Pepelito saw two members of Silvio's gaggle lying motionless on the dusty path to the field. The goose who had bit him, a huge, white, yellow-beaked bird, sat by Silvio with her eyes half closed, alive but unmoving. Five others hung around near the fence, looking frightened.

Pepelito and Maribel stepped forward, stood over Silvio. The old man lifted the dangerously ill goose onto his lap, cradling her.

'Degolladora,' he whispered, stroking the bird's white feathers and feeding her from his water bottle. 'Please don't go.'

Degolladora managed a hiss and flapped her wings weakly. Pepelito edged forward, rested his head on Silvio's shoulder, knowing what was happening.

'Thanks, my boy.' Silvio rubbed his hand into the fur on his neck. The farmer's fingers shook as he tried to make a call. Pepelito looked at Maribel, sad and helpless.

What could they do?

'Oh! What's up Silvio, how's he doing on the 25% dose?'

'You know him, Alfonso. He's just as good as gold. But I've – I've lost two geese, and… I'm about to lose a third,' Silvio choked out.

'I'm so sorry, I'll try to get there as soon as I can. Did they show any signs of illness before?' Alfonso's voice sounded alarmed over the

203

speaker, turned to its maximum volume due to the old man's poor hearing.

'No. No, they were fine – more than fine, they were healthier than ever.' Silvio sounded broken.

'It'll take me an hour or two to get here, is there anyone else you can call in the village,' Alfonso said. Pepelito thought he could hear Rita's voice in the background. Degolladora flapped her wings weakly and shut her eyes. The other geese looked fearful, grouped by the fence. They were quiet. Two of them moved sluggishly, eyes half closed.

'He's closed on weekends, and he's no good with birds, one of my layers died a few years ago due to that man's foolishness,' Silvio sobbed.

'I'll be there ASAP,' Alfonso said. There was a pause. 'Silvio?'

'Yes?'

'Have you got any glucose syrup, or activated charcoal? You should feed both to all the geese, if you can.'

'Glucose syrup. I do. I know I do. I used to keep it somewhere. I think I still have it. What's the other one. Charcoal?' Silvio lifted Degolladora carefully off his lap and got up shakily. Pepelito and Maribel were left with the goose who had once terrorised them. She gazed at them with difficulty. The formidable bird looked at the two much larger animals, her feathers dull, her once beady eye now with a tired, agonised expression, her long neck stiff and her breathing laboured.

She was trying to tell them something.

Maribel nuzzled Degolladora's soft feathers, her eyes dripping. The white goose didn't react, just turned her head slightly. As Pepelito touched his nose against her wing, the leader of the gang who had saved him closed her eyes for the last time and rested her head on the ground.

Silvio bent down, picked something up from the ground a few paces away, and let out a scream of pain. Pepelito turned towards him. He was holding a small bottle in one hand and his phone in the other; his phone fell from his hand as he howled. It was a gut-wrenching sound. Tears ran from Pepelito's eyes.

Silvio shambled towards the shed, looking like a ruined soldier coming back from a war. He rummaged around desperately, re-emerging after several minutes with the activated charcoal and glucose syrup. Silvio approached the geese but they scattered in different directions, some flew away, some walked, three much slower than the others.

Maybe Pepelito could help.

He looked at Maribel, psyched himself up to approach the remaining geese. Maribel followed a few paces behind as he lumbered towards the fence. Some of the geese scattered from him, a couple flew. The aggression was gone, replaced with fear and horror. A big grey goose with an orange beak, Diablo, hissed at him and backed towards the fence, too sluggish to follow the others. Pepelito stood facing the goose imposingly, snorting at him and backing him against the fence with his horns and much larger size. Diablo managed a weak hiss.

'Thanks, amigo,' Silvio said, patting him. The farmer's hands shook as he grabbed Diablo, who bit him on the nose. Pepelito backed away. Silvio tried to force the medicine down the goose's neck, the bird flapping his wings vigorously.

'My beauties, my warriors,' Silvio muttered through tears. He held the struggling goose, pouring as much of the antidote down his beak as he could. Pepelito and Maribel started towards two others, trying to trap them into a corner between themselves and the gate. He remembered when he'd realised Alfonso was trying to make him better. How could he make the birds see?

'Get it down you, I can't lose you as well. You're a hero, you've got more courage and bravery in one feather than that hijo de puta has ever managed in his entire miserable existence.' Diablo sneezed some of the syrup mixture back out. Silvio held the bird's beak shut for a minute as he struggled and flapped. The fear in his owner's voice alarmed Pepelito.

It told him he should also be frightened.

One of the geese struck his leg with his foot. Pepelito flinched and turned around. As the wind changed direction he smelt the scent of a human he knew only too well.

Had the horse stung him? Blood gushed down his side; he panicked, taking bigger and bigger breaths which didn't give him any air. He felt himself cry out but couldn't hear anything. He galloped towards the other side of the ring. Someone appeared from nowhere, holding a stick in each hand. Could he help?

'Come on, toro. Venga, venga.'

'That's some of the worst offenders taken out. Good thinking with the poison.' The man laughed coldly, too far for Silvio to hear but closer than Pepelito ever wanted to be.

The men's footsteps drew closer, approaching them from the woods five hundred metres away at the top of the hill. He and Maribel both grunted, pounding the track, kicking up soil as Silvio tried to round up another goose.

'What is it, old girl? I know. I know,' Silvio muttered. Maribel pawed the ground, nudging him with her wet nose. He hadn't seen or heard them. She mooed again, prodding him with her foot. It wasn't working, Pepelito thought in panic.

The man leapt away from him. Pain took over everything. He couldn't see. He was frothing at the mouth so much he was choking.

'Let me catch my beauties, Maribel. I can't lose any more.' She shook her tail and stamped. Silvio tried to restrain another goose, who was biting at the air and trying to wriggle free. Neither of them knew what to do. They couldn't make him understand. The handful of healthy geese knew. They flapped their wings and took off, honking as they went.

Leaving everyone else alone.

'No, that stuff's not nice, is it. Good girl,' Silvio said to the goose as she nipped him on the arm. Pepelito scratched a line in the hard, dusty soil. Why didn't Silvio see?

'There he is. That mad bastard.' As Silvio looked up, a man stepped in front of the farmhouse, holding a gun.

'What do you want, son?' he shouted, staggering to his feet. The man did not speak. He lifted up the barrel and squeezed the trigger, firing several times. Maribel gave a horrified cry. Pepelito heard the shots, watched Silvio crumple to the ground. He couldn't see the men now, just hear them and smell them.

Maybe, if he pushed him, he could make him get up. The metallic scent was so strong in his nose, Pepelito knew he couldn't. He walked forward to be near Silvio as he died, to say goodbye to someone who had been so kind to him. As he licked the old man's face, Castella's assistants laughed out of sight. His tail crept between his legs as he heard how they were talking.

'The crazy bastard's treated him like a pet.'

'He won't want to fight. He's been well fed and pampered.'

'Strong, though. I can't stand weak, scrawny bulls. They make me sick.'

As he looked up and growled, pawed the ground in fear, something hit him. They threw a rope around his horns and pulled tightly, swarming and tugging at him from different directions. There was another loud bang and a cry from behind him. One of his legs got tangled in the rope as he kicked out at one of them, he couldn't lift it out from underneath. The rope rubbed the skin where the top of his leg met his belly, scraped it hard and he stumbled.

Maribel was calling out for him. He couldn't turn around properly. Hearing her, he grunted and bellowed in horror. One of them pulled on her tail as she cried for his help. Blood ran down her leg; she couldn't stand.

'That's it, Pepelito, time's up, no escape now,' one of them laughed, as the men pulled on the rope, dragging him towards their truck and tugging at his horns. He dug his feet into the dried mud, knowing it was useless, tried to run back to help Maribel. There were so many of them. They were too strong for him. He was tired and hadn't had much to eat yet. The image of Silvio lying dead was burned into his eyes. The smell of blood and the motionless birds made him want to run. There was nowhere to run to.

'All right, boss?' one of the others said into his phone, stamping on his foot to force him to move. As one of them twisted his tail, he scrambled up the ramp to get away from them, knowing he shouldn't get in, knowing they were taking him somewhere horrible. Maribel bellowed at him in fear, screaming at him to come back. He couldn't.

'Hector! Hopefully you've got a result.' Pepelito's ears flicked; he cringed in fear as he heard Castella's voice.

'Yeah. We've got him.'

Chapter 32 – Hairless Mammals

'That was an excellent shoot, a truly rich diversity of waterfowl,' Lord Owenstoft said as the members of the Taurine Club returned to their villa. While Henry owned a majority share, the property, conveniently placed next to a Spanish hunting range, had been gifted to the club by one of the original patrons.

'Hopefully there are a few left over for the next instalment. We did bag rather a lot,' Henry laughed, striding alongside the other members and eyeing their takings.

'Eloise, you nabbed a pink footed goose. Congratulations, that's a rarity,' he smiled.

'I did, and I'm going to take it to the taxidermist you recommended,' Eloise grinned, clutching the unlucky bird upside down by its feet. She had been quite preoccupied at the previous few afternoons' entertainment, but she seemed to be calmer and back in good spirits this morning. Being out with a gun in the warm weather had done her the world of good.

'Just a pity there was no bigger game to retrieve,' Henry said. It had been a wonderful morning in the field, but the ducks and geese he'd bagged couldn't fully quench his thirst.

It had been weeks since he'd taken anything bigger than a pheasant. Those idiotic birds couldn't stave off the compulsion he neither wanted to control nor could any longer, the urge that now possessed him and occupied his every thought.

He had to kill a human.

He had to do it soon.

Using a large metal key, he unlocked the door to the villa. Like his British properties, it was decorated with animal heads, stuffed birds, pairs of horns and antlers. Controversial exhibits were saved for his favourite English mansion – its true ownership concealed as it was by shell companies. At the bottom of the stairs was a glass case of woodland birds he'd shot one summer's day, frozen in time on fake branches for Henry to gaze at, savouring the memory again and again.

Eloise abruptly excused herself and went upstairs. 'I'm meeting a friend. See you later.'

'Did you see, Pepelito is on his way to Javier Castella,' Lord Owenstoft said once she was out of earshot. A wide smile spread over Henry's face at his friend's words as the two entered an airy drawing room, filled with even more hunting trophies. This news was most welcome after the shock he'd just had.

'Is he?' Henry grinned.

'Yes, so I'm told. There will be a corrida in the next few days at an undisclosed location, as some silly, badly brought up Spanish teenagers have got rather fond of him.'

'Not just teenagers, Rupert.'

'Quite so.' Lord Owenstoft nodded, and the two men exchanged a knowing glance. With disgust, Henry pictured the video of the bull walking beside people who adored him, showing them nothing but innocence, trust and love.

It made him sick.

Animals existed only for the pleasure of humans.

Humans like him.

And since he was packed off to boarding school at age 5, no animal or human had ever, or would ever look at him that way.

'I do like to view the bulls, where possible, before the action happens. What say you, old bean?' Lord Owenstoft said.

Henry enjoyed seeing fighting bulls, observing the impressive, fearsome beasts before they were brought low by the sword. Maybe he'd even get to punish Pepelito again for his insolence.

Would he remember him?

Henry hoped so.

'Let me round up George, and I'll join you with pleasure.' As Henry spoke, Lord Owenstoft looked curiously at his phone, then back to him.

'Dixon? There's a strange message doing the rounds on the Tory WhatsApp chats, and it concerns you.'

What?

Lord Owenstoft's ominous comment rendered Henry on edge. Combined with the news of Valero's arrest and Tegan's release, this 'strange message' filled him with an unfamiliar, unwelcome emotion.

Fear.

Did Rita think he liked living like this? Had she any notion of what he experienced – hunted and pursued, at the mercy of this ravenous hunger and thirst, this beast inside him demanding blood? Did Heather? Did Robyn?

Caroline certainly hadn't; nor any of those trolls and sentimental do-gooders. Did Tegan, with her new-found freedom, and all those well-wishers making a fuss?

Did fucking Pepelito?

As if *he* understood the lot of a predator!

'What sort of strange message?' he stuttered, as Eloise waved a cheerful goodbye, her mind clearly on other things. Henry wished he could be in such a jovial mood.

'This morning, Interpol has issued an arrest warrant for the Tory peer Lord Henry Dixon, wanted in connection with at least 7 murders. The public are warned not to approach him, as he is described as extremely dangerous. What's this about, old chap?'

'It's a misunderstanding, I haven't murdered anyone, the powers that be have just uncovered a series of unfortunate coincidences.' A shiver ran down Henry's spine. Visions of a maximum-security Spanish jail cell came to him unbidden. He laughed in as unforced, natural a way as he could. His shooting companion looked strangely disappointed. The building was registered in Henry's name. He had to leave. Staying would be a fool's errand.

Especially if the police dug up the garden.

'I'm sorry to hear of these troubles,' Lord Owenstoft said quietly, but his voice was anything but light-hearted. Surely a fellow Taurine Club stalwart wouldn't turn him in?

'I do confess to a certain…curiosity on the subject of homicide. I've spent my life shooting game, pheasants, ducks, stags, the odd rhino. And as an 'aficionado practico', I attended that excellent Arruza Institute course in Guadalajara, and learnt to finish off my own bull. I'm sure I speak for many of our friends when I say I hope you could tell me how it feels…pursuing our own species of hairless mammal.'

'You'd like to know what it's *like*, you mean?' Relief and excitement flooded through Henry like a wave.

'Yes,' his friend said, with a knowing look.

'Let's discuss this in the car,' Henry said, hardly able to contain himself.

Caution was paramount. Would-be blabbermouths lurked everywhere, even among those who shared his passion for Spain's finest export. Then again, if things did become dire, he could make himself scarce in Castella's extensive grounds.

In any case, given her bond with Pepelito – and Henry found himself salivating at the thought – Rita would surely turn up. That bull was not only useless and mediocre, but cowardly, a toro manso who deserved the worst. Nevertheless, she would, Henry was sure, make a valiant effort to save the beast.

He'd seldom looked forward this much to anything.

Chapter 33 – Come Back Alive

Driving to Silvio's farm in his van, Alfonso was extremely worried. The old man was very distressed, and he was reluctant to attend the scene alone. Silvio deserved to be told in person rather than by phone, but these deadly symptoms and their rapid onset suggested poisoning.

'Thanks for coming with me, Rita. Really,' he said.

'Any time. Besides, I've been told to take a week off for stress. It's not like I've got anything else to do,' Rita said, sitting beside him in the van.

'How come? Is it anything you can talk about?' Alfonso said gently. Aside from that evening at the restaurant, Rita hardly discussed her work.

'We went to the plaza de toros a few days ago and made an arrest. I can't believe I made it out without screaming at someone. I had a panic attack. I'm not sleeping. We cancelled the corrida and rescued the bulls. I was in a similar state to how they were.' She leaned back in her seat and sighed as the van drove through a pothole. The roads out here had seen better days, Alfonso thought.

'I've been losing it with this case, with this killer,' she said.

'You're not losing it, Rita. If you need to talk, I'm here, yeah?' Alfonso's phone hadn't beeped since he left.

Alfonso nodded. He too felt jittery and anxious. Neither he or Rita had slept after she'd woken up; thoughts of Sonia and Caroline haunted him. Pilar had found Sonia's issues too much to deal with alongside her own battles with physical and mental illness; Alfonso had never known her well. Her murder was horrific, but he and Pilar had been dealing with so much…

'I'll be fine. Just need to get my shit together,' she said.

'Don't be so tough on yourself. I don't know how you stayed calm in that hellhole. And well done for saving those poor creatures.'

'The answer's simple, I didn't, did I,' Rita laughed bitterly. Her phone went. She picked it up and shrugged.

'Nothing, I guess?'

'Just spam. Silvio still hasn't replied to the text I sent him. I'll try to call him,' Rita said.

Moments later she shrugged. 'No. Not answering.'

Alfonso's van approached the farms. He turned onto the dirt track at the bottom of the hill. Knots formed in his stomach. As they climbed the hill, Alfonso glanced across at the beef herd Pepelito adored, clustered at one side of the field for comfort, as far down as they could go.

Looking out the window, the battered van bumping along the gravel, he saw Silvio's field was empty. From the road, the fence looked damaged. The barn looked as though it was open, but Alfonso couldn't see Pepelito or Maribel; he gripped the steering wheel, his knuckles white as the situation hit him. As he stared at the grassy expanse and at what was lying on the path ahead, he felt his face drain of colour.

****

A dead silence hung over Silvio's farm as Rita and Alfonso stepped out of the van. The bodies of several geese lay on the path between the farmhouse and the barn. The remaining birds were huddled against the fence. Some looked sick. They all stared at the pair, frightened, their aggression gone. The livestock truck had moved six metres from its usual spot, with its window smashed. Part of the fence was broken.

Lying a few metres away was the body of Silvio himself, face down on the dried mud in front of his home. The old farmer had been killed mafia execution style with a shot to the head.

'Maribel, cariña, you need to get away from the scene, so forensics can do their job,' Rita said with a lump in her throat. The elderly cow was lying next to his body, crying and panting. Her right front knee was bleeding. The barn door was wide open. Rita already knew Pepelito wasn't there.

At first, Alfonso tried to coax her away from the body. But she couldn't stand up.

'Some sick piece of shit shot her in the leg. Who the fuck would do this to a cow?' Alfonso bent down next to Maribel as she attempted to stand, her legs buckling, horror in her eyes. The scene tore at Rita's heart.

'We'll get you to the animal hospital, Maribel. Just hang in there.' Alfonso dialled the number, and so began the long wait. The cow had been doted on and cared for. Until Castella decided his wounded pride took priority over Silvio's life, and called on his gangland connections.

And now they had Pepelito.

Rita got out her police radio and called for help. She felt strangely detached, as if she was watching herself from above. Far out of range, none of her colleagues from the city responded. Most of them were searching Henry Dixon's villa. Rita was almost grateful Dominguez didn't answer. It felt like her fault Silvio was lying dead.

The village cop who eventually answered sounded far too relaxed. 'We'll send someone in about half an hour.'

'No. We need assistance now! There's one down at the hillside farm in Colmenar. Probable gunshots.' Rita's panic rose. After someone was killed the first hours were always the most critical. With the weather so hot, evidence was already being lost.

Shaking, she called Dominguez, knowing it was irrational but bracing herself for him to blame her. He sounded breathless. 'Rita! You all right? Sanchez said he'd signed you off sick for a week! I've been at Henry Dixon's villa for the last hour. They've dug up three skeletons so far, it's grim, it's like Ted Bundy out here. Guy's gone on the fucking run –'

'Silvio's dead, Jesús, he's been shot,' she said, her voice coming out in a ragged gasp. Everything turned quiet. Dominguez sounded like he had dropped the phone. He made a miserable, choking noise, then swore and muttered something inaudible.

'I'm –' she started to say but he had already hung up. Poor Jesús, she thought. She watched how gentle Alfonso was with Maribel. Suddenly she couldn't stop sobbing. She couldn't blame Dominguez if he held her responsible. He had that right.

'It's my fault,' she said quietly, as she looked helplessly at his poor body, feeling out of control and dizzy. It felt wrong not being on duty, unable to move him or offer any dignity as she usually would. The village cops were approaching from the bottom of the hill in their beaten-up cars, plus a forensics van; some sign of modernity at least.

'Don't blame yourself,' Alfonso said gently, but how could she not?

She'd asked Silvio for help. Castella had just had him killed.

'Silvio wanted to do the right thing, like any normal person would. He didn't hesitate.' Alfonso's voice was reassuring but firm with conviction. Rita was unconvinced.

'Maybe.'

'This is on nobody but Castella, the thugs working for him, and the people who are too cowardly or greedy to bring him to justice.' As Alfonso spoke, Rita's mind was somewhere else. There was nothing more she could do for Silvio but stopping his killers inflicting further harm.

A police car pulled up and two officers got out. A woman approached Rita, short with grey hair. Her card identified her as Juanita Ferrera from the Guardia Civil. She wandered over to Rita, who withdrew her ID from her pocket. Juanita's lip tightened and she drew her gun as she spotted the body.

Slowly, Rita put her hands up, nudging Alfonso to do the same.

'Who are you?' Juanita snapped.

'My name's Rita Silvera, I'm an off duty Policia Nacional officer in Valladolid,' Rita said, taking a shaking breath. Juanita snatched her ID and peered at it.

'What are you doing here?'

'I had a call from this address, regarding a suspected poisoning of geese on this farm,' Alfonso said. Rita marvelled at how he could stay so calm. 'We arrived a few minutes ago and found Silvio dead. We both know Silvio and Rita isn't on duty, so she accompanied me.'

'I see,' Juanita said, as more police cars pulled up and Maribel gave another anguished cry. The man beside her was gabbling into a radio. The old brown cow had been sedated while they waited for more help, her wound was dressed and she was quiet; but she looked at Rita with pleading eyes. A couple of officers were trying to move her from Silvio's body. Alfonso watched them, anxious, ready to step in. Jesús warned you about Castella, Rita wanted to sob. She wanted to scream it to Silvio, too.

'Before we go any further, we'll need prints and DNA samples,' Juanita's partner said. 'And we'll need to take your shoes. Did either of you touch the body or the scene?'

'Just the cow,' Alfonso said, shaking his head. 'She was next to him. We tried to move her, but as you can see, she's hurt.'

'I can see,' the policeman said, glancing dispassionately at Maribel. Rita followed Alfonso, trying not to cry. Both their jobs necessitated carrying around at least one change of clothes, and today, both sets were in bags at the back of his van. She had absolutely no idea how long she would be kept here. She slid into the back seat, shut the door and got changed into tracksuit bottoms while several police officers stood around outside.

'I have to save Pepelito,' she gulped as she forced a clean top over her head. Alfonso turned round from the front seat and looked at her with concern. Images flashed through Rita's mind. Pepelito sprawled on her floor, blood gushing from the gaping wounds in his neck and back. Pepelito letting her hug him when she was upset. The love in his eyes whenever he looked at those who had helped him.

'Castella will break his spirit. He probably doesn't have any water…'

Alfonso took her hand and squeezed it hard. 'He won't kill him now. Castella's a showman. He'll want to perform a beautiful estocada at Las Ventas or somewhere, not do him in with a shovel in his back yard.'

'He's got a private bullring. Or they could just send him somewhere else.' Shaking, she pulled on her tracksuit bottoms and opened the door. She handed over her old clothes and waited for Alfonso. As they followed the policemen she saw another vet's van had parked up. The vets were begging to be allowed through to help Maribel and the geese. Although Rita knew they'd be given permission, the sight and sound was unbearable.

'Did you know the victim?' one of the rural police asked. Rita answered politely, knowing if the rural cops had treated Silvio's reports with the same seriousness, he'd still be alive.

It was an hour and a half of facing the same questions by different people before Rita felt the intensity shift away from her and Alfonso and to forensics. After that, it was a matter of answering remaining queries. Silvio's sweet little driveway was now sealed off as the people in white coveralls did their work. After a further hour of standing around, she decided to see if Juanita was prepared to let her leave.

'Yeah. That's all in order. One of you can go,' she said, then turned towards the crime scene and sighed.

'I know what you're thinking,' Juanita said, her face softening. 'You're asking why things were allowed to come to this. I was on the scene after the last incident. We know who's responsible. We want him behind bars. Certain people see him as useful to keep around. I can only hope even they see he's gone too far this time.'

Rita turned away, not knowing what to say. The guard now stationed at the gate gave her a sympathetic look. She stood by the fence and looked at the village at the bottom of the hill. Alfonso placed an arm around her. Without warning she pictured Pepelito bleeding out alone and uncared for, the sadistic audience applauding as Castella's sword pierced his heart.

'Thanks for being so calm. It's more than I can manage,' she said to Alfonso, turning away from the policeman guarding the gate so he wouldn't see her face. 'The police will need someone to stay. Could you give me the keys to your van and stay here?'

'What? You're not going to look for Pepelito on your own, are you? Castella's a fucking mafia boss. You said so yourself.' Alfonso wrapped his arm around her tighter.

'I know. I don't want to confront him without backup. But he's got so many friends in high places, I have my doubts if they'll even arrest him.' Rita swallowed as he folded her into a hug. She wanted to hold him forever. If only she could.

'I lost someone I loved too young,' Alfonso said, his voice cracking as he handed her the keys. 'Don't let me lose you to these sadistic bastards.'

'You won't.' Rita's voice hardened. 'If he's hurt Pepelito, I'll kill him.'

'I mean, fair enough,' Alfonso said. 'I didn't expect anything else.' He pulled her close to him and ran his fingers through her long hair. For several long moments they kissed, before he broke off to speak.

'Look. If – *when* you find our four-legged friend, call me right away. He'll need lots of love and reassurance. Bulls are very dangerous when they're mistreated. You can be sure that this murderous piece of shit will have done so. I don't want you hurt. You're both too precious to me.' She held him tighter.

'Of course,' Rita said, filled with an overwhelming rush of affection.

'Rita,' Alfonso said. He spoke slowly, running his hands down her back, sending a tingle down her spine. 'You're an amazing woman, you're kind, you're brave, you're funny. I've never told you this, but I need to say it. I love you.'

'I love you too. I've been in love with you since the day I met you,' she said, reaching up to kiss him again.

'Just come back alive,' he said.

Chapter 34 – Nightmares

Pepelito's ears flicked back and forth, his eyes dripping with tears. The rope tying him to the truck roof by his horns just about let him drink. He couldn't lie down or turn around. He hadn't said goodbye to Silvio properly before they dragged him away from him. They hadn't let him show his respect; the old man had been so good to him.

Why was this happening?

Had he been bad? Was it his fault?

'He's got a day or two, give him a last meal,' Pepelito heard Castella laugh down the phone, as the gangsters who worked for him stopped at a service station; one had got out.

'Not too much, though. Don't want him getting comfortable.' Hearing the matador's voice made his whole body tremble with fear. It was boiling hot. He had finished the tiny bucket of water they had given him; he licked the bottom, trying to get more moisture out of it. There wasn't any. He could hardly move; his sides touched the walls of the compartment.

'OK, señor. Be with you shortly.'

'With the others, yeah? One bull isn't fucking good enough.'

'Señor, we're picking another one up now. It's being taken care of as we speak. No security at that place the cops sent him. Fucking hippies, no idea how to handle a brave bull. Treating him like a puppy, I guess…' The banderillero's voice was defensive and anxious.

'Hah. General Franco would have dealt with them properly,' Castella scoffed. The other gangster laughed, relieved, as his boss praised their hero.

Why was nobody helping him, Pepelito thought?

Had something happened to them?

He felt the truck's engine start again and continue on the road; before long, it turned down a dirt track. It was so bumpy and he felt ill. It wasn't Silvio's dirt track; that had been on a hill, it felt different.

The truck stopped. One of the men opened the back. Pepelito tried to smell the grass and fresh air outside. One of the walls slid away from his side and the rope slackened. He heard and smelt another bull nearby, agitated and scared. Straining his head, he saw more men yanking the new bull on a rope.

'Get on with it, Chicero. Why so scared? What did they do to you in Valladolid, eh?' Laughter greeted the gangster's mocking words.

'Everything OK with him, no lameness?'

'Yep. Looks good enough for any arena. Get him in before the dirty hippies notice he's gone. I can still smell them.'

Pepelito's feet clunked on the ground, warning Chicero not to get in. But he needed someone by his side. He felt so scared, away from everyone who loved him, alone in this horrible place.

And maybe two could deal with them better than one.

*

Once Chicero was in the truck, Pepelito tried to calm him down but the grey bull was having none of it. He kept bashing his horns against the panel installed to keep the bulls apart, stopping them from injuring each other and spoiling the show. Maybe they could help each other get out of here, Pepelito thought.

After a while, Chicero stopped struggling so much; the truck reached a smoother piece of road, slowing to a crawl as it hit traffic. At least his arrival had meant more water. The other bull was terrified. Pepelito tried to nuzzle him through the bars, letting him know he meant no harm. Like Maribel had done for him, he told Chicero that whatever had happened to him was not his fault.

Maribel was bleeding. They'd hurt her – or worse.

He retreated into a place in his mind where he was happy, touching Chicero as far as he could through the bars, if he couldn't calm himself down he could at least try to soothe his fellow captive. He pictured himself eating grass, lapping cold water from that stream on the farm he'd grown up on, or cooling down in the pond with the geese. He imagined the splodged cow he liked so much watching him from the neighbouring field.

Did they hurt her too?

Would he ever see her again?

He couldn't see what was in front of him. Not having any clear view frightened him. He bellowed in fear, setting Chicero off too.

The truck accelerated as it bounced over several speed bumps. Pepelito felt nauseous at the sudden jolts as he was thrown around in the truck, hitting the side. His hooves pounded the floor as their water sloshed to the ground. He tried to lick it up, faint from lack of liquid, but couldn't reach it; the rope was too short for his tongue to get near the puddle.

The vehicle turned down another road, slowing down for several hundred metres. Chicero attempted to lick him but he couldn't reach through the bars. Pepelito's eyes welled up; he remembered Ladron groaning, the crowd's deafening whistles and cheers as he stood in the dark, filthy cell. And then, the ring, when the pain kept getting worse, so hot, so hungry, so thirsty, looking round for an exit that wasn't there. He thought of how his rancher and some bullfighters had chased him down on horseback to brand him. Just an 8-month-old calf, he'd cried out for his mum from the pain, but they never gave him back; it was the last time he ever saw her.

He couldn't make any of it go away.

Finally the truck stopped. Pepelito couldn't move as the rope tightened and yanked him forward towards the drivers' part of the truck. A hatch opened from the top and one of them cut the rope tying his horns with a knife. The knife grazed him and he flinched, tossing his head away from it. The divider drew up and the tailgate opened onto a muddy path. Neither got out straight away; the men came towards them with sticks. Chicero looked around, bellowing in fright.

'Get out,' one of the men spat, prodding Pepelito hard with a wooden stick. He stood on the ramp, not wanting to move.

'Just get out! What's the matter with you!' The man struck him harder. Pepelito skidded down the ramp and into the muddy pen at the back of the private bullring, twisting his left front leg. Other than two water troughs and a small pile of grain Pepelito could see nothing. It wouldn't be enough for two of them, let alone whoever else arrived. Soon even that would be taken away; no cowpats could be allowed to pollute Castella's pristine sand.

And *he* was standing by the fence.

Chapter 35 – Death in the Afternoon

'Look at him. I bet he wishes he'd accepted your sword the first time,' one of Castella's assistants simpered to his boss, a shit eating grin on his face. Wearing dark glasses, grey chinos and a crisp white shirt, the matador gave a self-satisfied smirk as he watched his two prisoners.

'Yes. I'm sure he does.' He took his cape and waved it around over the fence. Chicero ran straight at him, and Javier jumped back as the bull's sharp horns went through the wire. He glared at Pepelito, who glanced at him and quickly turned away. The only thing worse than a scared bull was one that showed no reaction at all.

'What the fuck's your problem? Come on, toro. Venga, venga.' He waved the cape and Pepelito half-heartedly walked towards him, then turned back towards his water.

'Don't you dare think *you* can ignore me. Show me some goddamn respect.' He picked up a stone from the ground and threw it at Pepelito; it bounced off his horn. The bull turned around, his sides heaving. Javier picked up another stone and hurled it at him. He waved his cape over the fence again, his Rolex watch glinting in the sunlight. This time Pepelito charged at the material with his head down, slamming into the wire and catching his knees on the fence. He grunted in shock.

'Wow, am I looking forward to killing you,' Javier snarled, grabbing Pepelito's horn over the fence and tugging him around, forcing the animal to look at him. Javier smiled, his ego restored. The bull he'd been so slighted by once again saw him as a dangerous enemy.

Nobody disrespected him.

'That'll do for now,' he said, giving the two bulls a disdainful stare and turning on his heel. More were supposed to be coming later. He used his ring to host private corridas several times a year for wealthy aficionados and 'business associates' of his. Men who, like him, had gained their real wealth, prestige and power through those enterprises the authorities pretended to hate.

The police wanted him locked up. But Javier was never going to jail, not for this, not for anything. Sure the dead man was a policeman's uncle, but his guys on the inside would make sure it went away. Since a three-month prison sentence when he was 19 for supplying controlled substances, he had learned his lesson and never again been stupid enough to get convicted of anything. As with the ring, he always had a cuadrilla on hand to do his work.

People loved him.

If they didn't, they loved his money.

He thanked his attendants and strolled up the shaded path away from the ring until he reached his luscious lawn. The surrounding countryside in this part of Spain was brown, stricken by drought, and fell victim to ever increasing numbers of fires. Javier never paid attention to that; the state-of-the-art sprinklers went 24/7 and the water in his infinity pool was replenished every day. His property here was like an oasis in the desert.

He'd managed to work himself up from nothing, he thought proudly, strolling through his gangster's paradise. A marble statue stood atop a large fountain on his lawn, and he gave it a loving glance. The statue was of Javier with a cape and sword, staring mystically into the distance.

Just inside the house, Javier brandished his cape at a vanquished opponent, a stuffed Miura bull he'd fought in Bogota. Staring ravishingly into a nearby mirror, he recalled the glorious day – Miuras, after all, were 'the Bulls of Death.' Taking place during his first visit since Aguilar was jailed, this corrida was especially memorable. Finally, *he* was the big boss, the man the cartels talked business with. Outrageously, Colombia had just banned bullfighting. He'd need other explanations for his all too frequent trips.

Javier stepped onto one of the soft red rugs covering his marble floor. He admired the intricately designed gold and silver decor, before gazing at himself through yet another mirror. A full-size portrait of himself in his costume hung above the period piece fireplace. He walked upstairs through the hall of mirrors, his eyes lingering on his appearance in each one, making sure he looked as perfect as he told himself he was.

Yet his paranoia was settling in, a frequent occurrence these days. Pepelito's initial lack of interest troubled him; even bulls needed to show him the respect he craved. Maria hadn't spoken to him in over a week. Couldn't someone remind the conservative Catholic politician that not listening to your husband was a sin?

It had been over two hours since he'd used his golden spoon, and his nose itched for another hit. He walked to the dressing table, watched sternly by a large portrait of Franco in military uniform. Opposite Franco was another painting of Javier himself, posing like the one above the fireplace, sticking out his chest with a macho expression on his face – except this time he was naked. Mirrors lined the walls by the bed, and Javier had installed one on the ceiling.

On a bare section of the wall near Franco's picture, were two yellow and red banderillas, plus his first ever sword. He seldom got his own hands dirty, but the sword wasn't just for bulls, and his underlings all knew it.

He put the spoon in his nose and sniffed hard. For all the good it was doing, this shitty batch might as well be sugar. Maybe it was? So many people were out to destroy him! He huffed several more spoonfuls, then pounded the table in rage – there was no difference in how he felt. Exactly the same as two hours ago!

This white gold usually kept him at the top of his game for daring feats of bravery, alert enough to see off rivals for his empire. But this time, the rush he craved didn't materialise. Instead, there was a pain in his nose. He felt a trickle of liquid and then a gush as blood began to pour from his corroded nostrils – which now happened with ever-increasing regularity.

It had to be stress, right?

Or, was Eloise right about vaccines? Could it be that 5G mast down the road?

'*You've got a drug problem,*' Maria had shouted. A drug problem?

As if that bitch knew more about drugs than him!

He staggered to the luxurious en suite bathroom and tipped his head back, sitting on a chair with a warm, wet towel over his nose, but nothing seemed to stop the bleeding. He was in perfect health, he could handle his coke – so it couldn't be that. He wasn't addicted. Today, he'd barely had any!

Maybe it was *poison*?

For a moment, he thought about one of the bulls he'd killed yesterday, the blood pulsing from the tortured animal's mouth and nose as it looked at him with pleading, sad eyes. He forgot the thought in an instant. Its destiny was to die in the ring, by the hands of the greatest matador in history. Nobody could call him cruel; he'd given it the glorious death it deserved. Their endorphins stopped them feeling any pain, and if not, the pain just improved the flavour of the steaks he loved.

As he reflected on this triumph of his, trying to distract himself from his bleeding nose, Javier heard a sound from downstairs. His guests weren't arriving for a while. Was the back entrance closed? Had that useless housekeeper forgot to shut it again?

He didn't have time for that shit, he had people to do it for him. He'd try another vial in a while. No, the bleeding had stopped, he'd do it now. He took another hit, lay down on his bed, gazing up at the gold framed mirror on his ceiling. He shut his eyes, feeling faint and weak. His heart hammered in his chest, but with none of the usual buzzy exhilaration. Something was wrong; he'd make his supplier explain himself, or face the consequences.

There was a noise coming from downstairs. The unmistakable sound of footsteps, growing louder. Probably just one of the servants.

But then the door burst open.

Eloise marched into the room, a look of demented fury on her face and a demonic gleam in her eyes.

****

'Why did you lie to me?' she screamed at Javier. 'Why did you ignore all my texts? How could you?'

'I –' he started, scrambling up. He looked ill. Eloise had a year's supply of Ivermectin at home. It worked for everything – she'd have doted on him, if things were different!

Too late now!

'Did I embarrass you? Is that it? Is that it? And who the fuck is Lola?' She strutted over to the wall opposite and tugged at one of his yellow and red banderillas until it prised off, its huge metal hook catching the sunlight from the open window. It was heavier than she'd expected. A small woman like her had to hold it with both hands. She fumbled, almost dropping the heavy, barbed stick. The papery, brightly coloured material covering it scrunched against her palms.

Wow. This must really hurt the bull, Eloise mused, her knuckles white with rage. Not that she cared about *that* when her own heart had been so cruelly broken!

He'd taken the piss out of her enough. She'd had enough of his lies.

Time to put on a show of her own.

'**WHO. THE FUCK. IS LOLA?**' she screamed at the top of her lungs.

'What are you doing with that? Put that down, you crazy bitch!' Javier shouted. His voice faded to nothing as Eloise strode the full length of the bedroom towards him, thrusting the spiked weapon in front of her with both hands like a gun.

'Crazy, am I? Crazy? I'll show you how fucking crazy I really am!'

'Eloise, NO!'

'You lying bastard! You lying piece of shit! How dare you treat me like this? I was your biggest fan! You told me you loved me!' As Javier tried to shove her away, Eloise launched at him with the banderilla. Again and again she slashed at him, tearing his shirt with the sharp hook, ripping into his chest, deep in a zombified trance, a higher state of consciousness. Doing this felt so good. Men were bastards. She should have done this ages ago.

'Fuck you! Go fuck yourself!' she shrieked, blood spraying in her face.

She didn't notice him stop breathing. She lost count of how many times she stabbed him.

Thirty? Forty? A puddle of blood collected around him. As she slashed and sliced, a sticky film began to cover the bed, the mirrors, the walls. By the time Eloise had finished, the colours on the banderilla formed a gory Spanish flag. Her dress was drenched; the fabric clung to her. After dipping a finger in the deep red pool on the sheets, she climbed off the bed and wrote a message on the mirror – LYING CUNT – before turning her eye to his expensive dressing table. Next to his cocaine paraphernalia lay a green and gold divisa rosette with a small metal dart underneath.

He'd lied to her about the drugs, too. He said he'd only taken them once!

Clutching the divisa with dripping fingers, she set upon General Franco, slashing the dictator's face and stabbing the picture until the canvas broke. Her eyes scanned the room and settled on Javier's full size nude portrait. That couldn't stay intact. Seized by rage, she strode the floor and stabbed the rosette and dart four or five times into the portrait's crowning jewel. She left it there, gave her hands a five second rinse in Javier's en suite bathroom and walked away, footprints drying on the marble floor.

Eloise strolled to the hire car she'd picked up just for this, fingers bruised and throbbing, blood drying in her dyed blonde hair and on her floral outfit. Her rage dissipated. Her sanity felt far more assured. A feeling of peace washed over her. Never before had she attained such a state of blissful calm.

Today was a good day.

Chapter 36 – Audacious Plans

He didn't know what exactly happened after the woman's car pulled up, but Pepelito sensed something had. With no humans tormenting him, he put his head down and drank his water while he still could. Chicero drank greedily from the trough beside his, until it was all finished. Another stood in the far corner, plus one where Castella's minions had dumped a miserable amount of food.

They'd shout at them and hit them for needing it replenished so fast.

They'd do it for any reason they wanted.

Or no reason at all.

But even before whatever happened had happened, all had not been well with his torturer. Pepelito sensed that Castella needed to prove he was still the dominant one in the herd. The matador found his behaviour and recovered strength upsetting, threatening – he was scared. He was ill. Maybe he'd eaten something bad. Weird chemicals permeated his sweat, much stronger than the faint whiff Pepelito had smelt in the enclosure.

The moment he'd seen Castella, *something* had begun replacing his fear.

Once he had drunk enough, he gave Chicero an affectionate lick. What he was learning about the grey bull made him so sad, it hurt him.

Chicero was not from Spain. He was from Italy, born on a farm that bred a handful of fighting bulls for export to the Spanish market, alongside beef and dairy cattle. The journey had been long and difficult, and not everyone had made it. He'd escaped the arena's deadly cruelty, but the corridas he'd had no choice but to hear left him broken.

The day before he was arrested, Valero and the others had goaded two of the bulls trapped alongside Chicero into fighting each other.

The loser was badly injured; they'd driven him into one of the dark cells by the ring. Chicero had heard everything that happened next.

Pepelito was overcome with protectiveness for his new friend, the way first Ladron, then Maribel had cared for him. He knew these people shouldn't have done these things. They'd hurt him and his friends on purpose, and now, they'd killed a human he loved before his eyes.

They enjoyed causing this terrible pain. They did it because they liked it.

Pepelito stood beside Chicero, who was grateful for the loving contact. He sniffed the air. Something had definitely happened. The place was eerily quiet. None of Castella's thugs had come back to torment them; he hadn't even heard them – and he could smell blood.

Then he heard a car pull up in the drive in front of Castella's house. Chicero was trembling with fear. Pepelito tried to reassure him despite his own anxiety. Two men got out and spoke in an unfamiliar language. Did he recognise them? He couldn't tell. They definitely weren't friendly.

'Ah!' Castella's servant said obsequiously. 'Henry!'

****

Javier's choice of exteriors was too vulgar and flashy for a great artist like him, Henry thought with distaste as he got out of Lord Owenstoft's vintage Mercedes, George tailing on behind somewhere. Didn't he realise, these ostentatious fountains, Roman pillars by his door, gold statues of angels and lions – leaving aside the Lamborghinis and limousines in the drive – just made him look like a drug dealer?

The servant said in almost unaccented English, 'I think Javier is preoccupied at the moment with a lady friend. Would you like to see the bulls?'

Henry's relief was tinged with an irrational annoyance. He wanted his achievements recognised. This flunky was clearly a man who hadn't watched the news recently, or checked it as religiously as he now did.

'I would love to,' Henry said, licking his lips at the prospect of the long-awaited corrida. Was that blood he could smell? Perhaps it was simply his imagination – Castella's servant did not seem to notice. Henry and Lord Owenstoft followed the man onto Javier's terrace, then past his infinity pool, tennis courts and luxurious lawn. One side of the lawn had a gate to a wooded path with longer grass on either side, leading to the pen and bullring.

Pepelito and Chicero were standing together in the corner of the pen furthest from them. Chicero was trying to eat a single straggly plant. No grass could be seen anywhere in this patch. Henry was pleased. At the mercy of Man, they couldn't just eat whenever they wanted.

'Let's open the gate for a little danger,' Lord Owenstoft said. A trough of water stood next to the gate, and Chicero approached to drink as they both entered the pen. Feeling like an Eton schoolboy again, Henry gleefully kicked the container off its stand as the bull trudged towards it.

'Nothing like displaying to the beasts that this is man's dominion,' Lord Owenstoft laughed as the water splashed to the ground. Henry smiled at his friend's words as Chicero gave them a miserable stare.

'Indeed, and always will be.'

'Aha! A swift exit is required here, Dixon!'

Henry saw what the fellow aristocrat meant. Pepelito was prowling forward, staring at them hatefully and flicking his tail. He stepped in front of Chicero as if to shield him, lowered his horns and kicked up dust, drawing himself up to look bigger the way they all did, until they couldn't.

Now Pepelito had almost fully recovered, Henry didn't want those horns anywhere near his sensitive regions. The way he was being glared at was unnerving him, although the fence was a robust construction. Shutting the gate behind him, Henry noticed the scars on

Pepelito's back. The agonised bull wouldn't have understood his part in this ancient drama.

He'd have been in so much pain – like Rita would be, soon.

God it was making him hard.

'Would you gentlemen like some refreshments?' Castella's servant asked, startling him from his fantasy.

'Yes, certainly.' Henry stepped back from the fence. Pepelito stood in the centre of the pen, chewing a mouthful of feed. The black bull glared at the men, refusing to go near them. Chicero nuzzled him gently. Enraged, Henry averted his gaze.

'I'll join you in a while,' Lord Owenstoft said.

Henry followed the servant past the long, luscious lawn, the tennis courts, the pool and sprinklers to Castella's terrace, where an imposing statue of the man himself crowned a magnificent fountain. Vulgar and vain, but he'd have to make inquiries; a similar statue of a great torero, Juan Belmonte perhaps, could grace the club's headquarters, or Henry's own drawing room. The man disappeared, returning shortly afterwards to present him with a bottle of Cava.

Yes. He could smell blood.

He wasn't imagining things.

Clearly, the help hadn't noticed, or knew better than to look.

As the attendant went inside the kitchen, using a servant's side entrance, Henry waited until he was out of sight. Then he entered through Castella's back door, strolling past the stuffed Miura bull from Javier's extraordinary Bogota performance. Henry remembered that day well. It wasn't every day one could see six bullfights in a weekend!

He'd let himself relax regarding forensics, with Colombian authorities fighting a losing battle against soaring crime rates and powerful cartels. Those he took out were troublemakers. All things considered, he'd done the police a good turn.

Henry's eyes settled on the dark footprints leading from the stairs out of the front door. Silently he followed them, taking care not to step in any blood himself, a Herculean task made easier by Javier's multitude of mirrors. Once on the landing, he followed the trail into the master bedroom and sharply took in his breath. This was unexpected. He'd imagined a dead prostitute.

The gory profanity daubed on the mirror was in English. As realisation of the likely culprit dawned, Henry smiled in spite of the shocking scene in the bedroom. Javier was a giant among men, who had completely redefined toreo with his exquisite veronicas. The editors of La Salida would no doubt pen a fitting tribute in next month's edition. But he did have to admire the handiwork before him.

Hell really did have no fury.

Without a word he tiptoed back down the stairs and into the garden. He calmly finished his glass and poured himself another one, hoping no servants would check upstairs until he had left. He considered turning on his burner phone and asking Eloise grouse shooting on her own. He decided against risking his whereabouts; besides, if crossed, she was a touch too formidable. Glass in hand, he got up and followed the path back to the enclosure, not wishing to be seen by the police when they inevitably showed up here.

The police.

Rita would surely come here, backup or not.

A few employees from Castella's business ventures had pulled up on the dirt track by his private bullring. Henry hoped none would recognise him; there was no honour among thieves!

One of them had entered the pen. Chicero was chasing him. At the last minute the man dodged out the way. Unable to stop his momentum, the bull skidded and tripped over the dry, grassless soil. He staggered to his feet, grunting. Pepelito, who was stubbornly avoiding any interaction, nudged Chicero away from the man and imposed himself between the two, menacing and defiant.

Henry's chest tightened. His fists clenched.

How he *hated* that bull.

Suddenly, he saw himself in Belmonte's costume, plunging a sword into Pepelito's back to the sound of Rita's horrified screams.

Like many committed aficionados, Henry had attended that two-month course in Mexico. He knew how to dispatch his own bull, on his own terms; he could avoid danger once enough punishment had been inflicted.

'Can I have a word?' he said to Lord Owenstoft, wanting to avoid others overhearing.

'What is it, old chap?'

'Javier's unwell, flu or something. And I need to leave Spain shortly. I cannot possibly stay here,' Henry said, thinking back to their conversation in the car, where he'd told him everything and nothing at once.

'I understand. What a pity about Javier. I wish him better. Am I to understand from that, that the corrida won't take place?' Lord Owenstoft said, his voice concerned.

Henry shook his head, making a sympathetic noise. Lord Owenstoft gave him the same wounded look of disappointment as when Henry denied being a serial killer.

Henry smiled, speaking in an undertone. 'Oh Rupert, but *we're* more than familiar with the art of the Spanish bullfight, are we not?'

The other aristocrat nodded.

'Current circumstances, of course, present an obstacle, but the Taurine Club is no stranger to those. Recall that performance in Scotland with the American chaps and those particularly fine Highland cattle.' A smile crossed Henry's lips. He envisioned Caroline McKenzie's screams of rage on learning the Club had held a bullfight in Scotland with her beloved 'coos'.

'Yes. Such a pity we had to be so secretive, the blasted Cruelty to Animals Act has much to answer for,' Lord Owenstoft spat. But secrecy aside, Henry was safer at home. A few short months ago, he had attended a garden party with the King. The prospect of staying at His Majesty's Pleasure seemed distant and unthinkable. The police wouldn't guess his whereabouts; Scotland Yard's finest didn't know of his cellar. Legally, it didn't even belong to him.

It wouldn't happen.

It couldn't happen.

Not to someone like him.

'It certainly does,' Henry said. 'But, one way or another, we're taking these damned beasts to England to hold our own corrida. With real Spanish fighting bulls, not some worthless imitations.'

All they had to do, with the help of Castella's team, was round them up.

Then he'd wait for Rita.

Chapter 37 – Darkness Catches Up

'This is the BBC news at 5.30pm, with me, Paul Bournville. We return now to our top story. A government in chaos – Interpol name Tory peer and prominent Brexiter Henry Dixon as the prime suspect in one of the world's worst serial killing cases in recent decades. Dixon is wanted in connection with the murders of 10 people in 4 different countries. Police have warned that number might rise again as they continue to link unsolved deaths. Joining me in the studio is our crime correspondent Lucy Peters and our politics correspondent Genevieve Smith. Genevieve. What sort of impact will this story have on the Conservative Party?'

'Oh, it's hard to overstate the impact, Paul. Of course, we must remind listeners that Lord Dixon is innocent until proven guilty. But already, 23 front benchers have resigned. Labour are calling for an immediate general election. The Spanish police say they have made grim discoveries at two properties linked to Dixon, and if found guilty, people will be asking questions as to who protected him over the years – and *why*?'

George Stenton sat alone at a table outside a large cafe. Shaking, he turned his news podcast off, trying to regain enough composure to pay the bill for his unfinished mineral water.

The police hadn't said they were looking for *him*. Had they? Henry had saved George's skin on countless occasions. George probably owed him his freedom, if not his life.

They both knew what happened to people like him in prison.

Without Henry ever having to spell it out, George knew that failing to carry out his instructions meant his patronage of countless children's charities, his honorary position on the local school boards, would disappear immediately. Thus, Henry's requests were a price worth paying. George seldom had to clean up. Henry had other people for that. He just had to drive him around and help with the hunting when required – sometimes as little as once a year. It wasn't that bad, compared to what his life without Henry would be.

George hadn't left any of his things in Henry's villa, thank heavens. He always travelled light in case airport security wanted to inspect his devices, a risk he was not willing to take.

After paying, he walked out in search of his car. Henry wanted to meet him at Javier Castella's property. George didn't want his friend to think he'd left him in the lurch; he'd let him down of late rather too often for comfort. He pressed the button on his car key. It wouldn't unlock. Something was wrong with the door. It had been having trouble recently, so George walked over to the door, trying to pull. Nothing happened. He looked around for something to open it with.

'Qué crees que estás haciendo con mi coche?' a burly, thickset man in a white vest and tracksuit bottoms snarled, appearing from nowhere at the top of the road. A cigarette was hanging out of his mouth and he was walking a fierce-looking Doberman, which growled at George.

'Estás tratando de robarlo, bastardo?' the man spat. George stepped away from the vehicle. As he did so, a young policeman, thin, with a light beard, walked past. George had never had any reason to fear the police. But now, the sight sent chills all over his body.

'I – I wasn't doing anything,' George gulped, stumbling as he walked away. But the man grabbed him by the shoulder and shoved him against the whitewashed wall. He smelt of strong deodorant.

'Habla español, cabrón! Por qué estabas tratando de entrar en mi coche?' he spat.

'Es *mi* coche! Por que? Huh?' The policeman walked towards them as the angry driver pinned him against the wall. George couldn't understand Spanish, but the context was obvious. As the man restrained him, the glimpse of a courtroom flashed into his mind. Henry had rescued him from innumerable legal issues, yet of all the possibilities, this rough looking Spaniard believed him a car thief?

'Policia! Este imbécil estaba tratando de entrar en mi vehículo!' the man snarled, finally letting go of his shirt. Mansouri looked unconvinced as George looked imploringly for help, but then stared at him curiously.

'I'm sure it's a misunderstanding. This gentleman –' but Mansouri cut him off.

'Passport, please,' he said in a cold tone. George put his hand in his pocket, shaking. What should he do? Ask for a lawyer? Would that look worse? This didn't happen to respectable people with his kind of background. It happened to other people. Refugees. Scroungers. He wasn't either of those.

It's only Henry they want, he thought, handing it over. Some young Spanish beat bobby would have no idea he'd paid for *those* websites. Mansouri leafed through every page of the booklet, his expression inscrutable, and then looked at him without handing the passport back.

'George Stenton,' he said.

'Yes?'

'George Stenton who lives in Richmond, in Great Britain?' His voice was stern and emotionless. George scrambled for something to say. The furious motorist watched in triumph.

'I'd like to speak to you regarding an ongoing investigation. You're not under arrest, but I'd like you to clear some things up. Is now a convenient time?' George's stomach plunged. Mansouri's tone didn't indicate he could say no.

****

The traffic on the motorway was almost stationary. She'd never been there but Rita knew exactly where Castella lived. She turned the van's engine off. This was crazy. *She* was crazy. Someone was calling her work phone and she answered because it felt normal, despite knowing she so badly needed a break.

'It's Laurentia,' said the young officer, sounding out of breath and dazed. 'Rita, you aren't gonna believe this. Abdul told me to leave it till you were back, but Jesús said, given everything that's happened with Castella, he said you should know…'

'What?'

'So, like, I'm on my way home from work. We got a call about an hour ago. They don't want me at the big crime scene yet, so they sent me with that new woman from Madrid, Catalina. Some British woman walked in an ice cream shop, absolutely covered in blood from head to toe. We got there, and straight away she said to me, 'I've killed Javier Castella, and it was the best thing I've ever done,' with a great big smile on her face.' Rita's breath caught in her throat. Had she heard right?

'*Killed* him?' she gasped, feeling dizzy.

'She's friends with Henry Dixon – they met because Henry introduced them! Look, I know Castella's a horrible, horrible guy, but I got so much blood on me when I put the cuffs on her. I'm actually a bit traumatised…' Laurentia was laughing in a distressed, frantic way. Rita sat stunned in the middle of the tailback. The sky was darkening; dusk was starting to fall.

'Killed? Castella's *dead*?'

'Well, I seriously doubt he's alive. She was *soaked*.' The traffic cleared. Rita turned towards the road to the private bullring as if on autopilot, then pulled over on the side of the road to continue the call. Rather than dissipating her anger towards him, the news of Castella's murder intensified it. All the lives he'd destroyed, his terrible cruelty, the costs his actions exacted on her – all for nothing.

Rita wanted to ask about Castella's gang – had any of them been picked up – was anyone at the house? Instead, she stumbled for words, tearing up as her thoughts went to the animal. 'What about Pepelito?'

'Oh, is that the bull?'

'Yeah. Castella had Silvio murdered so he could steal him. If something happens, I don't know…' Rita's lip trembled, remembering how he'd become relaxed around her, playful even, as he learnt some humans could be trusted.

Approaching Castella's mansion filled her with foreboding.

Was Pepelito still there? What if she found him hurt, or worse?

'Maybe you think that's stupid, but I love that bull,' Rita said, tearing up.

'No, of course not. You know how I am with my dog. He's my baby.' Laurentia took a deep breath. The young woman was the baby of the team, just 21, and in that moment sounded even younger.

'Are you OK after that shock? Take some time for yourself.' Should she go in the house and make sure he was really dead?

'Yeah. I just need to – I don't know what. Have a long bath. Forensics are sending a team to the house now. I don't know about your bull. We had a call about another bull being stolen – I'll see what's going on with that…and I'll – I'll let Abdul know he's got to make sure someone finds them both.' Rita wished she knew for a fact that would happen. She trusted her colleagues, especially given the history with Castella. But some law enforcement officers saw themselves as defending Spain's traditions. They'd be proud to say they'd been the ones to kill the bull.

If anyone looked for him at all.

'How's Lucia?' Rita said. With the horror of Silvio's murder, she'd hardly given the teenager a thought.

'Staying at her older brother's. Took a bit of persuasion to let someone monitor the house, but she's OK.'

'Thanks, Laurentia.' She should tell her where she was, she thought. On ending the call she drove past the immaculately tarmacked track to the main entrance, with its gold statues, ostentatious fountains and Lamborghinis in the drive. Instead, Rita drove onto a track far more bumpy, full of potholes, leading directly to Castella's private ring – the track where Pepelito would have been taken.

She drove closer, over a row of thick high speed bumps, past long dry grass and thickets of trees. Rita's stomach tightened at the stress Pepelito would have felt. As she looked out of the window she noticed the skeleton of an animal, probably a deer. Eventually, she reached a set of farm style gates that swung open when she drove the car forward. They were unlocked, but she couldn't see anyone, making her nervous.

The gates opened onto an untidy area obscured by trees. Rita could see the pool and perpetually watered lawn beyond. This area suffered constant droughts. How could her sister have been OK with any of this – or her mother? What was Maria going to do, now Castella was dead? She'd long given up wanting any sort of relationship with her, but wondered for a second whether to call her and try to salvage something.

Rita stopped the van. She could hear sirens, becoming louder as the first police cars approached Castella's mansion. They would not know she was here; the long, winding path to the ring led to the side and was hidden by trees. She texted Alfonso, Laurentia and Mansouri her location, before stopping the car on the grass by the bullring. Castella used it to entertain wealthy guests and host tientas – where young cows got harassed by men with capes, then speared by men on horseback. If they charged, they were 'brave' enough to breed.

Nobody was there.

And the pen was empty.

Seeing it empty filled her with dread and worry for her four-legged friend. Had the thugs made off with Pepelito and sold him on? She clutched her gun inside her pocket, nausea rising inside her throat. A gate stood at the end of the pen with a narrower path, a series of stiles and a metal door at the end, leading into Castella's ring.

She walked along the side of the fence, taking a sip from a bottle of water and feeling the gun in her pocket. As she approached the wall, an anguished rumble sounded from the direction of the ring. Was that Pepelito? Or another poor animal Castella'd had stolen to order?

Mansouri had replied. She ignored the notification.

Helping the bull was more important.

On the other side of the fence was a metal bar with a hook at the end. She picked it up and followed the fence until she could see the door the bulls were driven through. A tree overhung the path, its branches low. Its shadow lengthened. Once they were inside, the real nightmare would begin. He'd be so frightened.

The bull bellowed again. It was a gut-wrenching sound. How long had he been trapped there? Would Castella's thugs come back? A narrow metal staircase snaked from the fence, to the ledge from where they opened and closed the different compartments in the passages leading to the ring. Rita put the crowbar down the back of her shirt and clambered up.

She followed the ledge round; the platform, though not as convoluted as some of the others she'd seen, passed under a row of seats and out by the stands, overlooking one of the gates. As her feet clanked on the metal she could hear increasing sounds of distress. Was that Pepelito? Then a second bull bellowed somewhere else.

'It's me, pobrecito,' she whispered, as something heavy bashed against the metal. She looked down at a steel hatch below her feet, sparsely dotted with tiny holes. 'Don't be scared. Please. You know I'm not like *him*.'

She slipped the hook into the hatch and slid it open. A bull looked up at her. Not Pepelito, the grey one they had rescued from Valero. Her heart was filled with pity at his short-lived respite.

What was wrong with Castella, Rita thought? His pathological obsession had meant he couldn't let any of 'his' bulls live in peace – even ones he'd rejected as 'opponents'. Chicero stared at her about a metre below her with terrified eyes, flinching at the light after being kept in total darkness.

'I'll never hurt you, I promise,' she whispered. The bull tried to shrink away, but was too big for the tiny compartment. She took out one of her bottles of water from her bag; she was too far up, the gap between his nose and the door too narrow to let him drink from her bottle. She crouched down and poured the water in front of him, getting much of it on the wall. The sun was slipping from the sky but the heat remained. Somewhere, she could smell smoke.

She wrote a text to Alfonso. 'I think he's here. I found another one. ♡'

'It's so cruel to keep you here, Dios mio,' Rita whispered as the bull lapped up the liquid. She would use the crowbar to open the door to the ring, and keep it open so Chicero could turn around and go back out into the ring. Once Alfonso got cleared to leave, she'd call him and they'd sort out picking them up.

As Rita carried the implement above his head the bull shook with terror; whatever had led to this response made her sick. She crouched down, attempting to drag the door open from above; it would not budge. As she struggled to force it open she heard a noise from the opposite side of the ring; something bashing against metal, then a miserable grunt.

'Hold on, Pepelito, I'm coming for you too,' she said under her breath, yanking at the sliding door once more. This time it came up. Chicero pelted into the ring; she collapsed onto her back, exhausted from the effort. The door slammed down with a thud. She scrambled up, tried to pull it open again so Chicero could get out of the arena. It didn't move. Her phone was vibrating; she put the pole down for a second to answer.

'Rita! Why the fuck are you at Castella's? Don't be fucking stupid, get the fuck out of there,' Dominguez yelled, with real panic in his voice. As she opened her mouth, a shadow fell across her, too big and in the wrong place.

'Henry Dixon's there, Rita! Get the fuck out now! Now!' As she spun around, trying to stand up, she felt Henry's hands around her waist, grabbing her from behind. Her phone clattered onto the metal platform.

'So nice to meet you at last, Rita. I knew you'd help a bull in need,' he said softly, forcing the damp cloth over her mouth until she was out cold.

Chapter 38 – Whatever Doesn't Kill You

Even as Pepelito felt the effects of missing his final doses of painkillers, faint from lack of food and water, he worried for his beloved rescuer. Trapped in yet another hot, hard, dark, moving container with Chicero, he could still detect her scent. He couldn't see Rita, she hadn't spoken since he'd heard her in the ring, but he knew she was close. But then, that new horrible guy had hurt her, and they'd forced him and Chicero in here.

He knew she was alive.

But she was sick.

He panted, taking a breath of filthy air. Despite the holes at the top it was getting harder to breathe, and it stank. While sunset had cooled the air, the heat was stifling, with nothing to drink. They'd finished everything half an hour into their journey; whatever was in it had made him throw up twice. The thick rope tying his horns to the ceiling dug into his skin.

He pawed at the front of the box with a low growl; the side clanked and rattled but it was locked, too heavy to move. Flicking his tail just hit it on the metal behind him. Chicero's horn poked him in the side of his neck when he tried to nuzzle him. There was no light. Despite the panel dividing them, the squeeze was so tight that the other bull couldn't help occupying his personal space. Pepelito tossed his head and snorted. Chicero tried to lick his fur to say sorry.

It didn't help.

Sniffing the air, he realised someone had died violently in here; a human or one of his own kind, he didn't know. The blood had dried long ago but the metallic scent lingered in the air.

Were they going to kill Rita?

He pounded the metal floor with his hooves, stubbed one of them and bellowed in pain, fear and rage. He threw himself at the box, bashing the iron door with his horns. It didn't open. Why? Chicero nudged him, licking his scarred back as far as he could, horns just shy of touching him. This time he let himself be comforted, grateful for the gesture. Pepelito felt cooler and marginally calmer.

It gave him strength.

He thought about Silvio's field where he felt so happy and loved, where he and Maribel could chew grass and sleep and chase each other around and play with beach balls and old tyres. Remembering the good times made his terror less overwhelming. Pepelito knew Chicero liked to swim; he'd swum in the river running through his field. Maybe his friend would like their little lake.

Some humans were good, Pepelito thought. Chicero didn't understand that, and maybe never would; humans terrified him. He couldn't imagine feeling anything like the affection Pepelito now did for Rita and Silvio. Ladron too had lived and died not knowing or believing any humans cared; as far as he'd been concerned they were all monsters.

Rita had gone out of her way to protect him. She had helped him get better. She'd shown him endless amounts of love and patience, played with him, given him food, water and shelter. She'd protected him from his torturers. Men she, for reasons he found impossible to understand, *hated* in a way alien to him, Chicero, Maribel, Ladron and even Degolladora.

The way only humans could.

Her tone of voice alone had told him everything. Rather than calling Castella 'boss', 'señor' or 'maestro' in a sycophantic tone, Rita had spat out other words in pure and absolute despisement.

'Maldito cobarde.'

'Escoria.'

'Hijo de puta.'

He had to help her, like she'd helped him.

He only really knew one way.

His horns and feet were the only weapons he had. The only weapons he knew how to use. His abusers had tried so hard to cripple him, making even thinking of fighting back unbearable. The twinges he got when he raised his head too quickly were painful reminders of their brutality. His awkwardness and clumsiness, the way he so frequently misjudged his surroundings, meant he could never forget what they had done. Only now was he starting to understand everything they'd stolen from him, the life they hadn't let him live.

At the farm he'd grown up on, when he'd had tussles with other young bulls, the sparring matches ended amicably and they made up without either getting seriously injured. He'd had fights, sure, he'd been irritated, but never set about to hurt anyone, not like they did; even when he'd charged at that horse, he was trying to make it all stop. He'd never tortured anyone or starved them or locked them up. Such things were beyond him in every way.

His only crime was being a bull.

He was bigger than them. He still had his horns, and the strength the bullfighters had literally tried to bleed away. He had the caring nature their warped ideas of 'bravery' encouraged them to beat out of him.

Pepelito knew he scared these people. Behind their cruelty hid weakness and fear.

But he was a long way from overcoming his own terror. The vehicle sped up towards its unknown destination, flinging him around and bruising his sides. His eyes and mouth were dripping. He was so hungry. Chicero put the tip of his nose against his back. Pepelito relaxed, glad he was not alone, that he and Chicero were looking out for each other.

He'd do the same for Rita. She needed him too.

He had to make it stop.

And he would.

Chapter 39 – What Friends are For

'He's a sadistic serial killer who's abducted one of our officers, we don't have time for this fucking shit, don't you know how serious this is?' Mansouri shouted at George in English, his usually calm demeanour shattered. Dominguez sat beside him in silence. He'd heard Henry Dixon's voice as he abducted her. He'd been crying moments before, though he wasn't going to let that on in front of this creep.

What made it so much worse was that part of him had blamed Rita for Silvio's death. A very small part but a part nonetheless; that bull was cursed, he'd thought, much as he loved him to bits. And that inevitably led onto blaming himself for what Castella had done.

'In the name of God, why do you protect him, what's wrong with you? You think he'd do the same for you? You think he'd not throw you under a bus if he thought it would benefit him?' Mansouri demanded, desperation in his voice; George wasn't giving anything up. Dominguez knew the younger man's recent work with Rita made her abduction hit all the harder.

'He's murdered 10 people at least, and we have evidence you're an accessory to many of those murders. You don't need to protect him. We know he's the killer. If you tell us where she is, you could be out in 10 or 11 years! Consider that, at least.' George sat in silence, saying nothing to Mansouri's furious pleading.

'We know he went to Castella's. Where did he go after that? Where has he taken her?' Mansouri looked at George in despair. There was an interpreter sat with George's lawyer, but the four years spent working behind a bar in Wellingborough before Dominguez came back and followed in his dad's footsteps would have their use now.

'Henry Dixon's got a hold over you.' After not trusting himself to speak the entire interrogation, Dominguez finally spoke, ignoring his pounding headache; his voice dripping with contempt, his fists clenching under the table. George again said nothing.

'Why's that, George?' George took a glass of water and drank it in silence.

'You're trying to stretch this out. I get it. Not a good feeling, not being in control,' Dominguez said, reaching into his bag and getting out a plastic folder.

'Shall I tell you what I think,' he said in a whisper.

'I think you've got a secret. A secret only he knows, a secret he uses to get you to do things for him.' As Dominguez took out a printout from the folder, George clutched the edge of the table and gaped at him in horror, like he was about to be sick.

He went on, 'Except, it wasn't just him. The UK police had you in their sights before anyone even suspected him.' He passed the page of photos to George as if it was contaminated.

It was.

George stared at the paper open-mouthed, his skin turning grey.

'Thought your secret was safe with him, didn't you?'

'I've never seen…' George's voice trailed off. Mansouri clenched his fists and stared at the photos in revulsion and horror. Dominguez couldn't blame the guy. His wife had just had a kid.

'That's interesting, because the site's owner got arrested three weeks ago. You made seven separate payments in six months.' Dominguez leafed through the vile images, until he found the card receipts the London Met had provided. The silence seemed to go on forever.

'He's not going to protect you now. And you know what? I don't think he wants to, he's got what he needed from you, that's why he's not getting you out of trouble. I think he got fed up,' Dominguez said coldly, hoping, praying something would break.

George looked like he was going to cry.

'Everything you've done for him, and he couldn't keep his side of the bargain. Everyone knows. It's over. He's not coming to save you.' George stared down at the table.

'I heard that sick bastard kidnapping my best friend. Tell me where he's gone. You think things are bad now? If something happens, if he hurts Rita, then, trust me, I'll make your life worse than you can even imagine.' Dominguez's voice dropped, thick with the barely concealed threat.

'He's gone,' George's voice was a barely audible whisper.

'Gone where?' Mansouri regained some of his composure. He looked visibly ill from seeing the pictures. When George did not reply, he shouted, 'Gone where, where's he taking her you fucking –'

'He's left. He's leaving Spain, he's going back to England. Are you happy now,' George said miserably, tears pooling in his eyes. The nonce just wanted to save his own skin. Could anyone believe a word he said?

'How's he getting there, driving, what?' Dominguez said, sending out an alert on the national police app with his phone.

'He took Lord Owenstoft's car,' George gulped.

'So he's driving, through France I guess?'

'Heavens, no, he's flying! He'd never take the channel, that's for peasants!' George snapped, then stopped himself, looking mortified. He clapped a hand over his face, his eyes wide with terror. These fucking guys, Dominguez thought.

'*Peasants?* Are you fucking serious?' Mansouri laughed in disbelief.

'I can't say any more, I can't, I've said too much, he'll kill me,' George sobbed, holding the table to keep himself steady.

'Oh, will he? Really? Because rest assured –' Dominguez started saying, then stopped himself, standing up abruptly. The lawyer began to protest. He didn't want to hear it.

'I can't carry on, Abdul, if I spend another minute I'll do something I regret – interview paused at 20:52,' he swallowed, walking out the door and slamming it hard behind him.

'Laurentia, good to see you,' he said as the young woman wrapped her arms around him. Her shell-shocked, wired look showed that long bath he'd ordered her to have had never happened.

'I came back to work as soon as I heard,' she said, looking dazed and shocked. Standing beside her was the woman newly transferred from Madrid, he couldn't remember her name, Carmen or something. She was Black, about a foot taller than him, with glasses and long braided hair.

'I can take over from here, it's OK,' she said, hugging him. Her name badge said Catalina, not Carmen. Oh. Dominguez nodded dumbly and blinked back tears.

Moments later, Mansouri emerged too.

'Don't you think you should get some rest, you two, there's several teams of officers on this. Dixon's presumably got her weapon, he's a dangerous psychopath –' Catalina said, concerned. It was the last thing Dominguez felt like doing.

'I'll rest when she's back safe,' he said, as he and Mansouri headed out.

****

'What's going in the hold? What's in the container, if you've got animals in there, you know they need their certificates…' a woman asked, alarmed, as the metal box was lifted off the truck, with Pepelito and Chicero inside it.

'You don't need to know, 'Clarissa'. This aircraft doesn't belong to you. Your job is to serve us tea and coffee and shut up.' Pepelito felt nauseous as the metal container bumped along the tarmac. It was now as dark outside as it was inside, giving the bulls some relief from the heat. Pepelito could just about lick the condensation on the wall, but it wasn't enough.

'It's a legal requirement but suit yourself! I'm out, fuck this for a game of soldiers!'

He couldn't recognise the voice or understand any of the language. As Chicero tried forcing his way out, Pepelito listened to the handful of people outside, chortling unpleasantly as Clarissa's voice faded.

'That bull gave me a most peculiar look when he sauntered out earlier,' he heard Henry say in hateful tones.

'They're certainly in need of correction.' Someone else kicked the side of the box Chicero was on. Pepelito's back and shoulders tensed up, thwacking his tail hard on the wall as the other bull shrank away.

It made him so sad when they hurt Chicero.

But the fear had left him.

'I wouldn't take any chances with those horns,' someone else said, laughing nervously as Chicero bashed at the locked box. They were being wheeled somewhere. Maybe they'd make him run into the street and chase him, like what happened to the bull who'd attacked him in the enclosure. Then he'd have a chance to get loose. Maybe someone in the crowd would help him.

Maybe he could find Rita.

Someone climbed up the side of the box and it shook, tilting upwards. He could feel Chicero shivering in the dark; this situation usually meant pain. The rope slackened and Pepelito licked his friend's back as much as he could. Let them beat me, he thought. He didn't care any more. Then it tightened again. They both cried out as they slammed into the door; the resin dislodged from one of Pepelito's horns and he felt a sting at the tip.

Then the metal container slid open and the rope tugged them towards whatever was on the other side. Whoever was up there hit him hard on his neck. He couldn't see anything. The metal was cold on his feet as he skidded, one of his hooves sliding into the other. It didn't lead to the street or another pen, let alone a field. It led to another, bigger container.

Unable to rid himself of the rope, he skidded on the floor, knocking his leg on the metal bars between him and the other bull. He pulled himself back. Chicero reached his head between the bars and licked him. He could just about turn round and the rope was now much longer, tied to the wall in front of him, but Pepelito stayed as close as he could to his friend.

Was Chicero less scared? He hoped so.

The door to the second container slammed shut. There were four cameras and a row of spotlights on a very low ceiling. A bull's head loomed above him on a wooden board, attached to a light-coloured plastic wall slotted with small holes. Its scent was gone, replaced with an unnatural chemical aroma. The wall above was stamped with 'Taurine Club of Kensington – Founded 1959' and the association's stylised T symbol.

Pepelito sniffed again, walking close to the side of the container. His water trough was empty, but there was a steel bucket of water near the divider. He began to drink but despite his thirst, could only finish half; it was foamy and tasted like cleaning products, like Rita's bath except worse.

Then he saw who was lying in front of him.

Rita had a chain round her waist, attached to a hook in the wall. Her hands were tied behind her back with a cable tie. He sniffed her and nudged her with his snout, trying to make her wake up, but she didn't move. Making a low noise in his throat, his desperation increased as he pawed at her side with his feet. She was alive, and breathing.

Pepelito lay down beside her and licked the back of her top, the fabric rough against his tongue. Despite his sore horn he shut his eyes and breathed out, resting his nose on her back. He thought of green fields with nice cows, far calmer than the situation warranted.

After several minutes, Rita startled him as she wriggled around, trying and failing to sit up. He shifted back from her. The cable tie scratched him as she tried to get free of it. Sometimes he forgot his rescuers weren't as big or heavy as he was.

'Hola, dulcito. Where am I,' she gasped, trying to lean against him as he shifted around. She looked at the ceiling, at Chicero, who was watching her fearfully, and around the container.

'Where am I?' she said again, her voice more insistent.

Then she screamed.

Chapter 40 – Leaving on a Jetplane

Rita sobbed, curled up on the floor, as Pepelito licked her face and arms in an effort to calm her. Lying with her hands tied behind her back, she was unable to do anything about his kind, well meant but thoroughly unwanted show of bovine affection. His long black tongue was rough like a cat's. He'd been startled by her screams, but otherwise seemed unnervingly chilled – much more so than her.

Chicero was as far away as he could get, shivering, drooling, giving her frightened looks and horning the floor. What kind of life had this poor animal had? Seeing his terror, her heart broke for the bull – but she was glad not to be anywhere near him.

She remembered turning down Castella's track – and nothing after that.

How long had she been here? Hours? Days?

Managing to sit up against the side of the container with her knees against her stomach, Rita rubbed her restraints against the wall, trying to sever them. But she couldn't undo the zip ties. The chain was about two metres long, but tied tightly around her waist and secured by a padlock. Metal bars ran down the side of the container, separating her and Pepelito from Chicero.

'He knows I'm a cop, dulcito. This man is completely insane.'

While she stared at one of the cameras in the corner of the plastic box, Pepelito licked her shoulder. She froze, feeling vulnerable on the floor as he lumbered around. He would never hurt her on purpose, but he was horned, often clumsy, and a hefty size.

'Yeah, you're going to want to stop him climbing on your bed again, let alone lying down, especially if you're in it,' Alfonso laughed. Rita had taken to wearing steel capped police issue boots in the house in case the bull stood on her feet.

'How much do you reckon he weighs?'

'Um, the toros bravos are bred to be athletic, so lighter than some of the beef breeds, but 'lighter' is relative. I'd say he's average for the breed, maybe about 600 kilos? The bigger ones can get up to 800. Resting his head is fine but you'd be in trouble if he sat on you.'

Where was Alfonso?

He would be going out of his mind with worry. She swallowed, listening to the footsteps above her, as the cable tie cut into her wrists. With a lurch of nausea, she realised exactly what was happening.

Henry was leaving – and taking them with him.

Rita blinked back tears, self-conscious, as if the bulls were an audience requiring she compose herself before them. Pepelito blithely got up, walked several paces away from her and then peed on the orange mat covering the floor, before grunting loudly, walking back and licking the back of her top. Suddenly, the tears gave way to laughter, especially when the black bull turned away, seeming embarrassed. Despite the worry of Pepelito's horns, the two bulls lightened an unbearable situation. They took her mind off whatever Henry had planned.

With them, she wasn't alone.

'Thanks for being here,' she said to both animals, and meant it.

'Right, you two. The subject of today's talk is serial homicide. There are two types of serial killers, organised and disorganised,' she said to the bulls as if she was giving a presentation. Chicero looked at her through the bars, confused but maybe less frightened.

Pepelito lay down beside her again. The tip of one of his horns had been trickling blood. Rita's stomach tightened. She could now see the 2 or 3cm they'd filed down to disorientate him and make the matador's job easier.

At least *he* was dead.

'The FBI say organised serial killers like Henry Dixon often devolve into disorganised ones. Disorganised killers leave a chaotic crime scene, they act recklessly and make bigger and bigger mistakes, don't they, Pepelito?' The bull nuzzled her hard in the side, giving her a fright, then licked her nose with his rough sandpaper tongue. Could she get him to use his horns to break the cable ties?

Probably not.

Chicero stared at Rita without blinking and she started laughing again. This time, she could not stop. 'Think we'll agree, Chicero. There aren't many bigger mistakes you can make than *this*.'

As Rita spoke, a roar started beneath them and a fan powered up past the holes in the container, out of sight. The floor began to vibrate as the plane's wheels scraped along the tarmac. Pepelito heaved himself up and trotted the few steps to the opposite wall, knocking over the bucket of soapy water. The lukewarm water sloshed all over the floor. The 600-kg bull put both his front feet on the side of the bucket. As he slipped it landed on its side, clattering towards her.

The rim was damaged; it wasn't the first time this had happened.

Rita lay on her front on the sodden mat, clenching her fists and trying to angle her hands over the sharp edge of the bucket to cut the tie. Pepelito pushed the bucket back towards her. Now she could hold it in place. She rammed her hands against the rusted edge, tightened her fists and pushed them one on each side, pressing down. The tie dug into her wrists. Biting her lip, she tried again, unable to see where it was as she rubbed it back and forth; loosened, but not broken. She lifted her aching arms from behind and thrashed them down again. The tie snapped in two and she lay on the floor, panting from the effort, hands cut and scratched, relieved she'd just renewed her tetanus jab.

'Thanks, dulcito,' Rita gasped, pulling herself up against the wall again. She patted the bull and hugged him gently around his neck. It was so cold in here, and her clothing was drenched with soapy, dirty water. The chain was secured in place with a padlock.

'Let me see what I can do for you.' Rita noticed blood on the rope tied round Pepelito's head. As he lay beside her, head between his feet, she loosened it, nervous about untying it completely. As she undid the knots, the plane picked up ever more rapid speed. She slipped forward, landing awkwardly on her knee against the wet mat. The chain dug against her stomach; she almost threw up.

'It's going to be OK,' she whispered, sitting up, knowing it was anything but. The plane lost contact with the ground; both bulls opened their mouths and bellowed, but Rita was unable to hear anything except the engine, her ears splitting from the pressure. Which bastard was enabling him – and where?

Was Henry himself flying the plane, or an accomplice? Had he coerced someone? These prospects were all equally horrific.

Pepelito rested his head on her knee. Rita stroked his nose gently and scratched behind his ears, staring at the bucket and the snapped cable ties. She couldn't slide them towards herself simply by using her foot. The bull's horn was too close to her stomach for any sudden movements.

When she'd first become a cop, there was a suspect in an armed robbery who escaped from the cells by picking a lock with a bit of plastic. Maybe she could use the cable tie on the padlock. The chain was too tight for her to slip through. Pepelito's rope, too, was tied far too tight for her to undo quickly with her hands.

Pepelito began to lick her trousers, slurping at the fabric with his huge tongue. She dragged at the bucket with her other foot. Pepelito looked up and snorted. He stretched, got up and walked back across the wet mat until he was standing by the bars alongside Chicero. The grey bull seemed much calmer with his friend beside him.

That was her chance, Rita thought, leaning forward and grabbing one of the broken cable ties lying beside the bucket.

The padlock was one of the newer ones with a thick blue button and a key combination; she slid the broken end under the button and scraped around underneath until she could twist it off. Then she dug the sharp, pointed end into the hole, pressing it up and down, feeling where the pins were. It didn't come off.

Pepelito and Chicero stood close together, nuzzling each other between the metal bars as she fiddled with the lock, her attempts becoming more frantic the longer she stared. She jiggled the cable tie around in the hole more slowly, biting back tears. If one of them escaped the container and stamped around in the hold, it could be disastrous. Could be?

It already was.

Gritting her teeth, she dug the broken tie hard into the hole, not expecting anything as she manoeuvred it around. Something clicked. The padlock was stiff; she removed it after three or four pulls, then lifted the heavy chain off herself, feeling completely out of control.

Rita looked up at the cameras, ill and hungry. Henry would be watching. What were he and his friends going to do to them when they landed?

If they landed.

She'd only been on a plane once since she was 20, during that awful Turkish holiday with her ex-husband. She told people she didn't fly 'because of the environment'; that wasn't the real reason.

Once it took off, there was nothing you could do if things went wrong.

'You sick bastard, Henry,' she shouted, leaning against the bars, her face hot with fear and anger. Pepelito turned around and approached her. She stroked his scarred, disfigured back, pressing her face against his side as she cried.

****

Dazed and weak with shock, Robyn pictured a family with a distraught child, missing a beloved member; a retired person without their walking companion. They hadn't cried in a long time – if anything did it, this would.

'That dog up there, that was someone's pet, wasn't it?'

'This, here is my canine collection. Myself and George found this one tethered outside Lidl. Look at the jawline. Such a fine example of the breed, utterly wasted on its master.' Henry pointed out the head of the Red Setter gazing mournfully from his wall as if he was showing Robyn the decor of a stately home. To its left was a wolf, to its right an endangered Indian dhole.

'I don't suppose you've ever been hunting, Robyn. Few things in life are more satisfying.'

All the canned food and drink Henry had left was gone. There wasn't much; cold soup and tins of sweetcorn. They had no idea of the day; the light was constantly on and the door was locked. At first Robyn had tried to reason with Henry on why he should let them go, or at least not kill them. But nothing had worked. One day he'd suddenly announced he was going to Spain for several weeks.

Now they lay, too weak to move, in a tiny, locked room adjacent to Henry's secret bullring.

So thirsty and hungry, they'd almost stopped feeling the ache once they'd got every scrap of food from the tins. When they sat up they felt faint, so they lay down, tried to sleep, and stayed in the corner or on the ground, slowly fading away.

Henry must be back, they thought, from the noises upstairs. Maybe he'd brought them food or water. That was all they could think about, too dehydrated even to cry properly. Someone was banging and crashing around upstairs. Henry liked a drink; maybe he'd got drunk and hurt himself. They'd be stuck there forever, Robyn dimly thought, too tired to assemble the right emotions.

Loud footsteps were descending the steps to the cellar. People were shouting. They hadn't seen anyone, but Henry's posh friends frequently visited to discuss hunting.

Maybe he'd brought back another victim.

Was he going to kill them?

The thought no longer seemed so bad. It no longer seemed…anything.

'Jesús,' Robyn heard a woman's muffled voice saying.

'I've never seen anything like this Subeera, let's get the explosives dogs to make sure the place isn't booby trapped,' a man said. Dogs… Maybe they were dreaming.

'Possible human remains found, this needs to be bagged up and taken as evidence,' a second woman said as Robyn tried to sleep again. The footsteps drew closer and it was a good idea to open their eyes but they couldn't keep awake any more.

*

'Robyn? Robyn? Stay with me. The ambulance is on its way. You're going to hospital. You're safe now. Can you hear me?' a man's voice said urgently. Robyn's eyelids were stuck together and they could only see him as a blur.

'The victim's breathing. Seems like they've not eaten in several days and they're suffering severe dehydration.' The policeman's voice was grim.

'Can you hear me?' he asked again, desperation in his tone.

'Yeah,' Robyn whispered, about a minute later.

Chapter 41 – Disclosure

Henry was a cunning bastard, Dominguez thought as he and Mansouri crossed the station car park towards the other man's car. Maybe he hadn't left. Maybe he only wanted them to think so. The sounds of people in the distance, happy diners and drinkers, only made the night more eerie.

For the last hour, Dominguez had been sat in the canteen, sending emails and writing reports, doubting the words made any sense, his mind not on work but unable to face anything else.

'You're in no state to look for Rita, you should go home. I'll drive you,' Mansouri said, but Dominguez didn't want to go home.

He wanted to find Rita.

His phone vibrated. Stupidly, he wondered if it was her. The memory of his last phone call to her played over and over again in his head. She was crazy but she was his best friend and he knew he'd do anything to have her craziness back.

It wasn't.

'Hello, is that Jesús Dominguez? I'm calling from the animal hospital. Do you have a moment to talk?' A middle-aged woman's voice. He grunted a response.

'Señor Dominguez, I understand that under the circumstances it's hard for you, but it's my opinion that the kindest thing to do at this point is to put Maribel to sleep. So I wanted to have your consent before we go ahead with this.'

'You don't have my consent. She's my uncle's favourite cow. You're going to do everything you can to save her,' Dominguez snarled, an instinctive reflex reaction before he'd even thought about the words. At the intake of breath on the other end, he yelled, 'Everything you can. If I agreed to this, my uncle's ghost would haunt me until the end of time.'

'We'll try,' the woman said. 'But I hope you'll consider it. Otherwise, we'll have to amputate her leg. And that's expensive…'

'Fine. I don't care. Do it. Save her. It's what Silvio would have wanted. Don't give that murdering fuck Castella one last kill,' Dominguez snapped. He hung up. It wasn't fine. He'd hardly begun to process his uncle's murder. All he could think about was that phone call, that moment when Henry took Rita.

He looked, disorientated, around the small car park. A heavily built blonde woman with a ponytail was staggering across the tarmac, unsteady in heels. She was tottering away from the direction of the police station.

'Excuse me?' Mansouri said after a second, looking as lost as the woman did. 'Can I help you?'

Helping anyone except Rita was the last thing Dominguez felt like doing.

'Do you speak English?' she said. Her voice was brittle. 'I can't think in Spanish right now. I need to speak to someone that speaks English.'

'Go to the front desk and someone will see you there,' Mansouri said tersely. 'We don't have time right now.'

'They're all busy, I tried, and I tried phoning 112 and couldn't get through,' the woman said, much more businesslike than Dominguez felt. He looked at the dark blue flight attendant's uniform the woman was wearing, and his stomach turned inside him.

She took a deep breath. 'Right. So about half hour to an hour ago I saw Henry Dixon get on a plane leaving for the UK.'

*

In every high profile case, and many low profile ones, there were people who claimed to have knowledge about the crime. Sometimes they made false confessions. Dominguez reminded himself of this as he stared at the woman across the table in the interrogation room, the sound recorder on with its flashing light. He sipped at a glass of water. If only it was something stronger.

'What happened?' he asked in as gentle a voice as he could manage, sounding as together and balanced as he could make himself.

'My name's Clarissa,' the woman said in an official tone, taking a big sip of water. 'I work for a company that provides cabin crew for private jets. We had a booking tonight from an…organisation. To put it politely, these guys are my least favourite customers. They changed the date of the booking. Said something had come up, and they had to go back today.'

Spit it out, Dominguez thought, his hands clenching under the table. Mansouri kept his face impassive. Clarissa kept the same calm demeanour. 'So, that client. Any work I do with them is covered by an NDA. But as I've lost my job that probably doesn't matter now.'

'What client?' Mansouri said.

'The Taurine Club of Kensington. That's the name the booking was under. I didn't know. So now – I'm freaking out. I could have been on that plane, but I walked off the job. It was really sketchy and I didn't want to be involved.' Clarissa took several deep breaths. Dominguez felt his heart lurch in his chest.

'So – I'm pretty sure they were smuggling bulls, you know – for a bullfight. They made us go to a tiny little airstrip in the middle of nowhere. There was a massive truck they wouldn't let us help with. I heard them mooing and stamping about. They wouldn't show us any documentation. When I questioned it, he – Henry – said my job was to serve him drinks and shut up.' Her voice didn't change but she was visibly angry. Dominguez put his head in his hands.

'Interpol have put out an international arrest warrant for Henry Dixon,' Mansouri said in a stiff tone that failed to cover his obvious shock. 'And this plane was allowed to take off with him on board?'

Clarissa blinked, a tremor in her voice. 'Yeah. That client do all their security online, so they don't go through any checks. They don't even show us their passports. I didn't know about the arrest warrant. If I did…'

'That's illegal,' Mansouri said, his voice shocked. 'Nobody did any checks at all? Anything could have been on that plane.'

'Well, yeah. Damn right it's illegal, isn't it, but you try telling them that. They've got enough money they don't have to worry about the law. If you have a problem the agency just says there's no more work. Nothing I or anyone can do.' Clarissa gave a long sigh.

'Anyway. I just lost my job. I don't want to be part of it any more. I said I wasn't going to help them do something so blatantly dodgy, in much less polite terms than that. Anyway, as I was driving back home I put on a true crime podcast. Talking about this exact same group. The first thing it said was about the Interpol thing and how Henry's on the run for killing 12 people. I've worked on their flights before. Henry's arrogant as fuck, they're all weird and disgusting. But this, this, I didn't imagine…' Clarissa said, her knuckles white as she gripped the glass of water. 12 is a low estimate, Dominguez thought, his mind filling with the grim scenes at the villa.

'You did the right thing coming to us,' he said slowly.

'I had to. My workmates are up there, aren't they. With him,' she said, her voice cracking.

*

Dominguez stared out of the passenger window, feeling numb, as Mansouri started his car. Henry Dixon had been one step ahead of them, the entire time. He'd used his wealth and privilege to plan for something like this, like he used them to gain access to his victims and stay above the law.

'It's a pity we can't pursue this sick bastard ourselves,' Mansouri said.

Dominguez felt his stomach tighten. He snapped, 'Of course we can pursue him. What are you talking about?'

'He's crossed an international boundary. We can't go to another country off our own bat and arrest him ourselves. I wish we could but that's the law.' Mansouri spoke through gritted teeth. His voice was full of a bitterness Dominguez had never heard before.

'I think we can pursue him where the fuck we deem fit at this point, Abdul. He doesn't give a shit about crossing an international boundary, or any sort of boundary. He definitely doesn't care about the law. Does he? Right now, stopping him is more important.' He gave a dismissive snort. Mansouri nodded miserably as he prepared to turn off for Dominguez's flat.

'No, I'm not going home. Drop me at the station. You should go. Help Halima with the baby. I'll go on alone. I'll ask Heather to pick me up.'

'Heather?' Mansouri said, his eyes widening. 'I'm not letting you get a plane to England on your own, man. I'm coming with you. It's pointless trying to talk you out of it.'

'Guess it is,' he said. 'But Halima needs you.'

Mansouri's voice softened. 'Halima's got her mum over from Morocco for a few nights. And she's a cop too. She gets it.'

Dominguez opened WhatsApp to write to Heather and stared at his inbox. The vet had tried to call him again. They had amputated Maribel's leg; according to them, it had gone 'well'. There was a message from a guy on a dating app he'd joined after his breakup, and one from Alfonso.

'Hey man. Are you holding up OK?' it said. How could he even begin to answer that?

He began to type out an approximation of a response before his phone pinged again. Mansouri said, 'Forget the station. Let's go direct to the airport.'

It didn't register. Dominguez stared, unhearing, at the text.

It was from Rita's number.

Henry had sent him a video.

The video showed Chicero trapped in some sort of cage, looking up at the camera, pressing himself into a corner and shaking with fear. The view switched; the camera zoomed in on Rita's terrified, tear-stained face as she hugged Pepelito. Dominguez couldn't breathe; his best friend's indescribable distress tore through his chest.

Then a text appeared, alongside a photo. 'A disgraceful, unworthy display of cowardice. I await your verdict, Inspector – does the situation require these?'

The photo showed several pairs of black banderillas with double spikes.

Dominguez rolled down the window and threw up.

Chapter 42 – Descent into Hell

Henry reclined in his leather seat, a glass of port in his hand, watching the screen embedded in the seat in front of him. The private live feed he'd been watching for two and a half hours was more gripping than any trashy Hollywood movie. He wasn't remotely surprised Rita had broken from her restraints.

He'd expected that.

The Gulfstream was mostly empty. On it, along with some of Castella's assistants and the young, fresh-faced and almost entirely British hired cabin crew, were the handful of trusted souls who hadn't been arrested, gone home early, absconded, or fled. Where was George, anyway? He'd told Henry he'd be late, then never arrived. Probably got lost wandering past a school.

What fine entertainment this live feed was. The marvels of technology! From Henry's vantage point in the corner of the plastic lid, he watched, both amused and sickened as Chicero stood shaking.

The bull hailed from the ancient, prestigious Saltillo bloodline, but insulted his purebred lineage with an utter lack of bravery. Before their final glorious drama played out on the sands, these beasts lived like kings. Henry expected better than this ignoble comportment.

What other animal got to do that? Better than being a battery chicken!

A member of the cabin crew walked past. Henry quickly turned the screen off, checked WhatsApp on Rita's phone, then his own. The Spanish police had read his messages, and he smiled, enjoying this hitherto undiscovered thrill.

But his social standing seemed a collapsing edifice. He'd been unceremoniously kicked from many Tory group chats, though several had renamed themselves and quietly added him back. His erstwhile

Oxford chum had shunned him, replying to his emails about Tegan with a terse 'I'm in enough hot water. Never contact me again'.

The comments in his remaining WhatsApp chats incensed him further. 'This Henry Dixon saga keeps getting worse. Serious damage control needed I think. I'm getting so many letters from angry constituents asking me if I knew he was a serial killer.'

'Yeah, it's pretty much nailed on I've lost my seat with the latest polls.' Two MPs reacted to this with crying emojis.

Someone posted a Mirror article saying, 'KILLER TORY LATEST: Missing journo found ALIVE in demented Dixon's house of horrors – along with heads of stolen cats, horses and dogs.'

The first text underneath read, 'Jesus. We are fucked.'

So they'd found his cellar.

Henry had whiled away endless hours perfecting the space. All that work – gone in an instant. The police would be poring over his exhibits with their grubby hands. A lump rose in his throat as he recalled the thousands – nay, millions! – he'd spent on the project.

For the first time in his life, he felt like one of the homeless people who blighted his view of London. He stepped over them daily on the way to the Houses of Parliament. He'd see them kicked out from the doorways of the sumptuous hotels where the aficionados had their lunches and dinners.

Just where was he supposed to go?

This didn't happen to people like him.

But he'd been added to a secret Telegram chat, called 'Henry Dixon is innocent', run by a group of Tory MPs. While he detested the idea of his achievements going unrecognised, he would have to take the help. A smile came over his face as he scrolled through his messages.

The panic was over.

In that Telegram group, already ready with an offer of help, was the proprietor of his favourite five-star Cotswolds hotel, Sir Jolyon Richmond. There, he could figure out his next step – and the location was wonderful for deer stalking and pheasant shooting.

And there, he could perform his masterpiece.

The Taurine Club had organised top secret corridas there before, with tickets selling for thousands on Telegram and the dark web. Jolyon had scheduled one for tomorrow. Despite Henry's distaste for these illegal ticket-buyers, there for the violence rather than artistic passes, excellent capework and skilled swordsmanship, Pepelito's last dance demanded an audience. The entire mundillo wanted that bull dead – now.

True, he was taking a risk.

But what did Papa Hemingway once say? Ah yes. 'The corrida is the only art in which the artist is in danger of death.'

Henry turned his attention back to the screen, wishing he could hear sound. Rita was saying something to the bulls. He knew it was about him.

'Good evening, sir, would you like any snacks or drinks?' a flight attendant asked.

'Get me some Cava, would you. And after that, let the pilot know there's been a change of plan, we're landing at the Armitage Hotel, near Burton on the Water,' Henry said without looking. The young man did not respond. Henry had forgotten to turn the camera feed he was watching off. The flight attendant stared at the screen, his eyes wide with absolute terror. Turning pale, he abandoned his drinks trolley.

After turning the camera feed off in case another nosy little scrote came by with a trolley, Henry got up and followed the young man as he half walked, half ran through the aisle, past the other passengers. The handful of club members who turned around merely gawked as if they were sat in the stands, watching their – and his – favourite spectacle.

'He's the k –' the flight attendant started to yell, but Henry grabbed him and clamped a hand over his mouth. If this pleb was expecting help, he wouldn't get any from those on board, Henry thought, pushing him away from the aisle, through the door of one of the toilets.

He needed this.

He'd waited long enough.

Henry stood behind the steward and pulled out a knife, pressing it against the man's throat as the anticipation built inside him. Rita's gun was in his suitcase, so he'd use this tried and tested British method. No tedious, bureaucratic security procedures on a private jet purchased with his own money, thank you very much. He whispered in the man's ear. 'Do you want to say what you were going to say again?'

The man shook his head, trembling with fright. 'No. Please. I'll tell the pilot.'

'Don't be silly,' Henry said, drawing the blade across the flight attendant's neck. The blessed release flooded through him as the man took his last breath, as it only did when he took a life.

Henry shut the door, pushing the man's feet into the cramped space, then locking it with an app on his phone. Then he calmly walked back to his seat and waited for someone who would actually do their job.

****

'Hey, Chicero,' Rita said, looking at the grey bull through the bars. He was a bit bigger than Pepelito; his rough fur was slightly curly on his back. While still timid and frightened, he seemed calmer, standing beside Pepelito on the adjacent section of the compartment. The rope round Chicero's horns was tight and clearly hurting him. If only she could cut it off as she had done with Pepelito. Seeing the friendship between the two bulls and their mutual care and affection made her smile.

Maybe these emotional, curious, sensitive creatures could one day forget what humans had done to them.

Then she saw the door.

It was camouflaged, sealed shut and marked 'Only for emergency use.' Chicero had already bashed at it. As he had failed, she was unlikely to break it through force alone. Beside it was a keypad. The bottom rung of the metal barrier was high enough for someone to fit under. Chicero was unpredictable, maybe aggressive.

But she had to take the risk.

'Help him see I won't hurt him. Can you do that, dulcito,' she said, as Pepelito licked her arm. Chicero lay staring at her, so Rita edged away as far as she could before attempting to get under the bars, not making eye contact. Her heart pounded. Until recently, he'd known nothing but cruelty from humans.

That made him dangerous.

'Help me out. I'll be back,' she said to Pepelito, sliding her legs under the bars, as painstakingly as she could with the wet floor and trousers. As Chicero's huge wet nose sniffed her ankle, she froze.

'I promise I'll never hurt you,' she whispered, and pressed herself against the ground and held her breath, hoping he wouldn't step on her. Eventually he turned around. She continued trying to wriggle under the bars, taking care not to startle him. She was too old for this shit, once you got past 40 the backaches just got worse. Once underneath, Rita lay there, watching the bull until she was sure getting up was safe. Then, she got to her feet and tiptoed towards the door, creeping as close to the compartment wall as she could.

Chicero got up, turning to face her as Rita pressed the emergency exit button. It emitted one loud beep, but absolutely nothing happened. He growled, his posture threatening, pacing towards her as Pepelito watched from behind the metal bars. She tried not to make any sudden movements.

'I'm not like them. I won't hurt you,' she kept repeating. Chicero watched her warily, taking another step towards her. With one eye on the bull, she took the broken cable tie and slid it down the door. There was no handle. It didn't move. The blue LED display on the keypad said she had 3 attempts and needed an 8-digit number.

'What? You've gotta be *fucking* joking.'

Chicero scraped the ground with his hooves and bellowed. He took several steps backwards, his tail twitching. Rita's heart pounded in her chest, trying to say something. She couldn't. She had to get out. Now. Her wet clothes made it so cold. Chicero stamped threateningly on the ground with his head lowered, then bounded towards her, his sharp horn slamming into the side of the container inches from her face. He walked back, but neither of them had anywhere to go.

There was a metal bar on the ground. Maybe she could open the door with that. Deter him –

She dove towards it as Chicero prepared to charge again, slamming to the ground and snatching it up, yelling out in pain as she fell with her weight on her knees. As Rita pulled herself to her feet, the pole slipped from her hands and struck Chicero's foot. Before she realised what happened he was cowering in terror, pacing back into the corner, shaking his tail and crying.

'Oh no. Oh, I'm sorry.'

'I'm so sorry, pobrecito, I never meant to hurt you,' she whispered, feeling herself well up. She rammed the door with the bar and kicked the door hard. It just wouldn't open. Putting the pole by the door, Rita looked back at Chicero, whose aggression had receded. He gazed at her miserably, like when she'd first seen him in that horrible pen. Hurting the bull was the last thing she'd wanted; she'd just wanted him to stay away from her.

Taking the long rope tying him to the wall in her shaking hands, she cut a small notch with the tie, wishing the cord was thin enough to sever. It couldn't stop him goring her anyway. As she watched, shaking all over, he turned to Pepelito for reassurance. She felt even worse at Pepelito's miserable, reproachful look.

'Founded 1959', the logo of the Taurine Club declared from above the stuffed bull's head. Didn't the website say it was founded on the 5th of July 1959, during the Pamplona bull-run? Rita entered the date. It did nothing. Maybe it was Juan Belmonte's birthday – when was that? Maybe Manolete's – or that of some other famous matador, like Castella?

Sometimes, matadors got gored. Nowhere near enough in Rita's opinion. Aficionados viewed their dramatic deaths like martyrdom in a holy war. Some animal rights activists also marked these gruesome occasions in their mental calendars. Perhaps Alfonso could name a date. He'd definitely know someone who could. Instinctively she reached for her phone. Its absence provoked more nausea. She imagined the killer looking at her pictures, reading her texts, searching through her contacts. It made her feel violated.

He'd have her police phone too.

And her gun.

As she stood facing the keypad, feeling dizzy, sick and faint, Chicero snorted from behind her. Rita's legs shook as the large bull approached her.

'How am I supposed to guess, eh, torito,' she gulped. As she spoke, the angle of the ground shifted beneath her feet as the plane began its descent.

'What the…' Chicero's feet skidded on the mat; he grunted, staring into the empty trough. When was the last time the bulls drank? It was freezing in this part of the plane, but today had been hot. Had she dreamt giving Chicero a bottle of water?

Centimetres from the door, Rita noticed a label stuck on the wall with a barcode and an 8-digit number. Maybe it was that? Not a date at all. Keeping an eye firmly on Chicero, Rita entered the code, but again nothing happened. The plane lost more height and she felt herself well up again as she peered to see if the bull was limping.

She had one more attempt left, and decided to try a different tack – Henry's birthday. She'd seen it on Wikipedia. Biting her lip, she entered the date she recalled carefully – 17th September 1978 – as Chicero edged forward, sniffing the air around her. His horn grazed her back and his throat rumbled. Come on, she thought. Please.

The code was incorrect.

Chapter 43 – Done with All The Bullshit

'No attempts for two hours! It's landing. Fuck. Fuck.' Rita kicked and punched the door, her rage and frustration palpable.

Pepelito thumped his tail on the mat, grunting in discomfort as the pressure in his ears increased. He lay with his head between his hooves and his nose on the bare floor. Chicero, who was in less physical discomfort, having experienced long journeys before, reached through the bars and licked his back. It took away most of Pepelito's tension, but not the pain in his ears, the hunger and thirst rising inside him.

He watched Rita with his eyes half closed and wedged his front legs under the bars. In one hand, she clutched the metal pole in front of her. Even understanding the differences between humans, *knowing* she wasn't a threat, just after food, water or a way out, her stance made him wary. Chicero made to get up, and Pepelito lifted his head to nuzzle him through the bars, warning him off. Rita and Chicero were scared of each other. The thought of them fighting worried him.

Pepelito wanted to convince Chicero that Rita was more like a small cow who walked on two legs. What happened with the pole had upset him. It hadn't helped. But it had to be an accident, or because she was scared; far smaller than they were, she had no horns and could not defend herself.

'He can't get away with this. The police will be waiting on the ground. Won't they?' Rita gulped, pulling herself underneath the barrier and crawled close to him. Her hand was that bit too tense and hard as it rested against his back; he sat up on his front feet, wishing for once he could lie on his own. She really was frightened, he thought.

The ride became bumpier; the air felt hotter. The wheels slammed into the runway. Rita tripped and fell forwards, scraping her hands on the plastic wall. On the other side of the bars, Chicero's feet squeaked against the mat, thudding against the barrier as the plane came to a sudden stop. Worried and sad, Pepelito glanced at him, and back to Rita.

He was now the dominant bull in this 'herd', the one they both turned to for support and protection. He'd never been at the bottom but he'd never been anywhere near the top.

But there he was.

It was a strange feeling.

'Fuck you, Henry,' Rita spat, giving the camera the finger. He couldn't see, hear or smell anyone. Who was she talking to? The container jerked up and the plastic wall slid away, revealing a tunnel lined with cats' eye LEDs and a dim light at the bottom, illuminating a space he couldn't really see.

Chicero took a frightened glance at Rita through the bars, before bounding down the tunnel, his feet skittering on the metal ramp. Pepelito told him to hesitate, but his friend just wanted out of these cramped, wet, miserable surroundings. The rope tying the bull to the wall soon hung by a thread, before snapping where Rita had attempted to cut it. Pepelito tensed up, feeling ill, hungry and thirsty, as slamming metal doors muffled the sound of Chicero running. The soapy taste of the water in the bucket lingered on his tongue.

Pepelito took a few halting steps down the metal ramp after his friend. Divided by more metal bars, the ramp was too narrow for Rita to walk alongside him. She stood in the entrance to the plane. The passage was too narrow for him to turn around; he edged forward one or two paces with his head down, anxious. He made a low noise in his throat. No reply came from Chicero; he scraped the ground hard, kicking up non-existent soil to scare predators he couldn't see.

Bad things happened here.

Rita took a step forward, clutching the metal pole, and the door to the aircraft slammed shut behind her. She jumped; the vibration reverberated around the tunnel. Disorientated by the sudden noise, Pepelito bolted to the bottom of the ramp, his feet tearing the thin carpet at the end of the tunnel. He winced in shock as his horns collided with the wall, ripping a hole and exposing the cavity insulation inside. Looking back, he saw Rita no longer had the pole in her hands. Pieces of plaster settled in his nose and ears. He sneezed, turning away to follow Chicero's scent. He couldn't see Rita when he looked back, but he could hear her behind him.

As he took a definitive step off the metal ramp, he was plunged into darkness. A grid slammed behind him. Rita's footsteps faded. He could smell a packet of crisps and a half-eaten roll on the ground, but no water and nothing he liked to eat. He picked up the crisp packet in his mouth and chewed it, swallowing most of it before eating the roll. It was better than nothing.

'Don't just stand there. Move. Bad bull.' Something poked him hard on one of the scars Castella's assistant had inflicted from the safety of his half-dead horse. They knew how to stay out of the way. They'd had hiding places around the edges of the ring where he couldn't reach or see them. He'd had no help and nowhere to hide. There had been only one of him and so many of them.

They still couldn't do what the crowd had screamed for.

And where was that guy now? He was dead. Maribel had killed him.

'Bad bull,' the unseen, unfamiliar man snarled, prodding him again.

He trotted towards the light at the end of the passage, and another grille slammed behind him from above. This is all they know how to do, he thought. And they couldn't even do that. They didn't want to face him.

The horrible one who hurt Rita was scared to even look at him.

The tunnel opened out into a pen like the one he'd been in that first time with Ladron and the others, but empty. Hard soil and a sprinkling of straw covered the concrete underneath. There were a set of strip lights on the ceiling, and on the walls hung stags' heads, antique rifles and paintings depicting hunting scenes. The pain in his right horn had lessened since he'd bashed it, but everything was dark and cold. He walked around a few times and then lay down to sleep, tired and disorientated from the flight.

*

He could tell something was wrong when Chicero bounded into the pen from a door on the opposite side. As the two bulls greeted and groomed one another, Pepelito realised his friend's long, sharp horns had been 'touched up'. They'd also dropped something heavy on his back. Filled with sadness at his friend's pain, at how he'd failed to help him, Pepelito licked behind Chicero's ears and lay down with him near a brick wall, his hooves touching his friend's back.

He could still use his horns to hurt them, given enough force.

He'd done it before, on Silvio's farm.

Bleeding on the ground, Castella's assistant had shrieked in agony, screaming for an ambulance and crying for his mum.

Chicero was silent, crying with shock and pain. Don't be scared of them, Pepelito told him. He nuzzled his head on Chicero's back, licking him again and again, and snuggled as close as he could against the cold air in the basement.

Something hit the ground with a thud. The noise of shouting and clapping was deafening. Something bad was happening. He couldn't move or see anything; all he could smell was blood. It was hot and the sides of the cell touched his skin. Ladron always stood up for him. He seemed so strong. But he was bleeding, alone and scared.

And Pepelito couldn't help his friend.

You won't die like that, he told Chicero, I won't let you. But as he comforted his sensitive, shy friend, the terrible scenes playing in his mind on repeat no longer filled Pepelito with fear and sadness. Instead, a new, unfamiliar emotion overwhelmed him with its all-consuming intensity.

Hate.

Eventually the other bull sat up, licking Pepelito's nose gratefully. While Chicero brushed his ear, Pepelito tensed, hearing an unpleasant voice from behind the smooth stone wall opposite him. Henry was there with a group of Taurine Club aficionados.

He was the one who hurt Rita.

'When do you want to get them into the torils?' the hotel owner's son was asking.

'We'll start at 7.30, so possibly noon. Whenever the other bulls arrive, or once the stable hands bring over those old nags of yours, Rupert. Certainly after breakfast. What is it again?' Henry said.

'Did Father not give you a menu? You've had our classic full English breakfast. You could enjoy eggs Benedict, or our champagne breakfast selection – the smoked salmon is quite delicious. Alternatively, we do have a Spanish-seeming option, given the occasion…'

'Oh yes, I remember. I'll choose shortly. As I was saying, Edwin, the design of your father's bullring is truly spectacular. What I particularly appreciate is that the doors and ceilings are big enough, a man on horseback can enter this complex without difficulty and have a good go at the bull,' Henry gloated. Chicero was crying again, cringing in fear, bigger and stronger but so much more vulnerable. Pepelito laid his head on his back, letting him know how much he was loved.

And where was Rita?

At least he couldn't smell any blood.

'These two will be a piece of cake to dispatch, compared to those at the Arruza Institute a few years ago. Look at them,' Henry laughed.

Lord Owenstoft nodded. 'Yes. They were Miuras as I recall, whereas I *think* Pepelito is a Domecq. A McDomecq as it were. They're all the same, are they not? Docile and witless.'

'According to Revista Taurina, Pepelito is Domecq crossed with Jandilla. Bred for combat, yet failing to embody their purpose,' Edwin sneered, to more pompous laughs. Something hard hit Pepelito in the side; he felt the momentary shock, then the impact. A golf ball bounced onto the ground beside him. Someone had hit him with a catapult. He got to his feet, breathing hard, making sure he stayed between the aficionados and Chicero, blocking their view with his body. He pounded towards the wall with his head lowered, feeling nothing but hate.

'I say! Perhaps there's a fighting spirit in there after all!' Henry laughed but his voice was high pitched and alarmed. He took several rapid steps back. Pepelito flung himself at the wall. He scrabbled at it with his hooves, struggling to scale it, wanting to hurt them the way they'd hurt him, to kill them the way they'd killed so many.

It was that bit too high to jump. Pepelito paced backwards, kicking up dust so hard it scratched his feet, staring them down, before bounding back again. This time he landed his front feet on the edge, poised to leap over the high, smooth wall. But his left leg slipped, squashed between the wall and his belly. Pepelito gave up and slunk back to where Chicero was lying. Don't be scared, he told him, not of *them*.

'This calls for some champagne breakfast, I rather think!' Henry's voice was full of fake bravado, as the club members disappeared out of sight, giggling like the overgrown public schoolchildren they still were.

Pepelito wasn't scared. He knew without any doubt what was coming. This time, he was ready.

He knew what he had to do.

Chapter 44 – Sand and Blood

'…everything is wonderful, yes. Just wonderful,' Henry simpered to the hotel owner and his son. Their shoes clunked on a metal platform. The group stood metres, possibly centimetres away from Rita; the first time she'd heard Henry's voice since he kidnapped her. Her cell was the length and width of a bull slightly bigger than Pepelito. The ceiling was too high for her to reach, even when she jumped. The tiny holes at the top let in no light.

Rita had tried to follow Pepelito after the plane doors banged shut, when he'd run into the darkness; fright and shock had caused her to drop the pole. Unable to see where she was going, she had stumbled down the lightless corridors after the bulls and blundered through a labyrinth of narrow passages. Several doors had slammed behind her; she'd taken a wrong turn into the tiny compartment. She'd screamed at first, banged on the door to be let out, before the thought of Henry getting himself off to her screams repulsed her so much she'd stopped.

Nobody seemed to have heard anyway.

'It's my great pleasure, Henry. As long-standing, wholehearted supporters of yours, we will most certainly assist you in whatever you require. Won't we, Edwin?'

'I do have a slight quibble about the sand, given my bulls are from authentic Spanish encastes, and their gait will be of some import,' Henry said. Rita punched her mouth with her fist to stop herself laughing. This sadistic serial killer, who presumably planned to kill her, was complaining about *sand*?

'The sand?' the hotel owner said.

'Yes, Jolyon. Why have you filled the arena with builder's sand from an industrial estate, rather than authentic Spanish albero? Will it not be rather dense? I'm risking my life with two raging bulls.' Henry's voice was ice cold. Rita could not believe what she was hearing.

They have all lost it, she thought. Not just him.

'As am I, Henry. One of mine is even authentically Spanish. It is my 25th birthday, after all. I see no problem with the sand, it's from a British source, better than some EU import. Carlos Lopez, who will face Bulls 2 and 4, has informed me he prefers it to the traditional variety,' Jolyon's son Edwin said in a haughty, aggrieved tone.

Rita held her breath incredulously.

Bulls 2 and 4?

'I see,' Henry said with a slight sneer. Rita wanted to laugh at his folly and scream in horror. Like Castella, he'd put himself above the law – where he probably still remained – with wealth, power and connections.

'I am sure it shall be suitably different. Perhaps, when taurine activities are once again legal in our land, this uniquely British sand will be part of our own tradition.' Henry's voice was mocking and sardonic.

'Rest assured, Henry, there is nothing to worry about, old sport,' Jolyon said. Maybe he didn't know she was there? If Henry pissed these people off enough, would they grass him up themselves?

'I'm sure not. Forgive me.'

They were obviously part of some illegal British bullfighting network, so they'd probably keep their mouths shut, but Henry's case was all over the news. Maybe one would be tempted to claim the reward; these men treated each other as terribly as they did the poor animals. And planes were noisy. Someone would have heard it landing.

Surely?

Rita tensed up. From the way their steps vibrated, she knew they were directly above her. Early that morning – she assumed it was morning – she'd heard a bull whimpering in distress as a group of men laughed, a terrible sound made worse by the silence of the place. Please, don't let that be Pepelito, she'd thought. She had tried forcing her fingers under the door, but she'd only scraped her hands underneath the metal and cut her finger.

'So the opening bull, and your first, to confirm, Henry, is the grey Saltillo. Chicero. Is that correct?' Jolyon said.

'Yes, although he seems very cowardly. Quite a lack of nobility there. How much of a show I can wrangle out of him remains to be seen. One can try to be optimistic.' Feeling ill, Rita pictured Chicero shaking with fear after she dropped the pole on his foot, clearly expecting worse to come.

'Very cowardly. You should see what a fuss he made when we fixed his horns. Pathetic,' Edwin scoffed. Rita's heart went out to the animal as she felt along the walls, searching in vain for a way out in the dark. These men despised the bull's vulnerability. If they got what they wanted, Chicero would die never knowing humans could be kind.

She missed both of them.

'And, of course, Henry, you'll take number 6. Something of a special occasion for our mundillo, is it not?' Jolyon, Edwin and Henry all laughed, their voices full of excited bloodlust. It was obvious which bull they meant.

The one who got away.

'Number 6, yes. Pepelito. The very last bull of the evening.' Henry sounded delighted.

'Shall we make a move? Let's get them out of the pen and into the torils.' Panic filled Rita at Jolyon's words. Were they going to drive a bull into her cell? Any bull entering the tiny space could kill or injure her, let alone one driven crazy with pain and fear.

'Yes. I'm sure you won't mind, Jolyon, but I've taken the liberty to store a traje de luces and espada in one of them, in preparation for the final bull of the evening. They belonged to Juan Belmonte, so they're exceptionally valuable, and as we can all appreciate, tickets sold on the dark web attract some disreputable characters.' Henry used a completely incorrect pronunciation for the Spanish words for matador's costume and sword. Rita stifled a laugh, in spite of her terror.

She held her breath. They didn't know.

Killing her in front of an audience corrida style could be too much, even for people willing to host Henry. They'd be in enough trouble once the police discovered they were harbouring him. Illegally murdered animals were OK, but a dead cop – maybe too much jail time for them to risk.

'You do realise there are only six torils, right?' Edwin said.

'Of course I realise, I've been to enough corridas,' Henry said irritably. 'I don't wish to attract the attention of your housekeeping staff, masters of discretion as I'm sure they are. I'm a wanted man. And in any case, I'm sure the police would have something to say regarding this breach of the Cruelty to Animals Act.'

'You'll have to move them, so we can fit another bull in.' *What?*

'I realise. Myself and Rupert will do that,' Henry snapped.

'Very well. I do understand how particular many of the greatest toreros are about their suits. Though what a pity you do not trust us, I must say.' Sick with fear, Rita thought she heard Edwin mutter something under his breath as two – or was it three? pairs of footsteps retreated.

How was Pepelito holding up? He'd been so calm on the plane. After a few minutes, she heard a miserable sounding cry and a man shouting. Her heart broke for the poor creatures. Being unable to see made it worse, as her imagination filled in the gaps. Whatever they did to the animals, they could do to her.

*

'Hello, Rita.' Henry's sudden voice made her jump and her stomach twist with nausea.

'Fuck you, Henry,' she said quietly, determined not to show fear. He laughed, sliding back the lid. She winced, blinded by the unexpected light above her. She couldn't see his face; just his shiny loafers as he stared down at her.

'Since you like bulls so much, I thought I'd let you share this experience. But don't worry, I'll bring you out in time for you to see Pepelito running across the sand, tossing his great crown for his final moment of glory.' Rita stared up. He was breathing heavily. The thought of her watching the bull die was clearly getting him off.

'That 'moment of glory' won't happen. You're insane. He'll gore you!' Spitting out the words, she made herself believe it.

'He's manso. Have you seen him? He won't gore me. What wishful thinking. Relying on a cowardly bull to save you.'

'Manso?' Rita sneered.

'Such an aficionado, throwing around these words. I guess you know how many years my brother-in-law had to train to become a matador. The training isn't easy. It's not some course you do on holiday with your friends.' She mocked him, remembering an email from Heather that morning about the Taurine Club and their Mexican adventures. Praising Castella truly stuck in her throat, but she had to speak Henry's language.

Betraying no fear, she continued, 'This isn't some underweight 3-year-old novillo. He's a full-sized bull who's already survived a corrida. He's tame with me, so you think it'll be easy, I get it. But that's *me*. You have no idea what you're doing.'

Henry was silent.

'He knows his enemy. He gored one of Castella's assistants. Almost killed him.' Rita kept her voice calm. Unnerve him enough, and maybe Chicero would have a chance if the cops hadn't shown up by evening.

'I'll be in good company, then! Juan Belmonte was gored 50 times in one season!' Henry spluttered at last. Rita's lip curled as she stared dumbfounded, unable to hold back the giggles.

'50 times? Are you sure?'

'Shut up, you bitch, don't fucking laugh at me. Will you just fucking shut up! Shut up! Shut up!' Henry snarled, stamping his foot. He thrusted the metal pole for spearing on the divisas at Rita, scratching her in the face with its sharp steel point, then her arm, breaking the skin so it bled. He poked her hard in the stomach, again and again. The pain registered; a small spot of blood showed through her top. She grabbed at the end. He was too fast –

'Pardon? Fine, yes, I'll fetch Lord Owenstoft and we'll move the damn thing just before it starts.' He withdrew his arm, flustered, tossing the pole away from him.

'You really want to kill him? Good luck with that,' Rita said under her breath. Henry slammed the lid down and she was enveloped in darkness again.

In his fury, he didn't shut it properly.

*

After Henry left, Rita had tried to reach the hatch, taken off her clothes and stood on the pile to gain height. It hadn't worked. Freezing from the air conditioning, she'd dressed herself again in the dark, but the wet, dirty clothes made her shiver and she was feeling the lack of food.

Now, she covered her ears against the sounds of doors slamming, men shouting and bulls grunting and bellowing as they were driven into the cells. How had they got hold of another *four*? Sitting in the darkness, Rita felt as alone and frightened as the bulls did. Was anyone coming? Did anyone know where she was? Had her colleagues abandoned her?

Footsteps lightly trod on the metal platform above and Rita held her breath; a shadow blocked out what little light came from the slightly open hatch.

'Costume my foot. So the allegations are true. Stupid fool didn't close it properly.' Edwin looked inside and glowered, propping open the hatch and lowering his legs into the hole.

'You better get me out,' Rita spat, hating him, as he swung down into the cell, pulling the hatch shut after him. All the light disappeared.

'No such luck, Señora,' he laughed, breathing hard. 'After everything Father and I have done for the ungrateful blighter, why should Henry get all the pleasure? Probably my last opportunity, after all.'

Rita sprang up. She couldn't see him in the dark. He pinned her against the wall and pressed a sharp object to her throat. She pushed him away and tried to knee him in the groin. It didn't work. His warm, sweaty hand reached under her top. She stamped on his foot, shoved him in the stomach and bit the air in front of his face. Somewhere nearby, a bull knocked against its own metal door, snorting.

'Fight all you want. I don't take no for an answer.' Edwin pushed her against the cold stone wall, fumbled with the buckle on his trousers. Fuck this. She elbowed him hard. He gasped; she did it again. The knife clattered to the floor, and she kicked in the direction she thought it had landed. The box was so narrow her foot hit the wall. She struck out again with her knee and he grunted in pain. His fist collided with her stomach, knocking out the air.

Dizzy, she slumped to the floor over his foot, her hands aching, her stomach stinging from where Henry attacked her. Unsuccessfully, she reached for the knife. Was that it? No. He kicked her hard. She couldn't think from the pain. She had to do something, fast. She couldn't see the knife, but. But. That was his foot. Gripping his trousers, she sat up, and sank her teeth into his bony leg, clamping hard until she drew blood. The bull bellowed somewhere. As Edwin screeched in agony, she headbutted him in the groin, scrabbled to her feet and punched him hard in the face.

At the punch Edwin slipped and toppled backwards. There was a sickening thud as his head knocked against the wall, and again on the metal door. The knife's handle clacked on the ground as he fell. Rita crawled around the floor, running her hand over the concrete. She found it. Good. He sat up and gripped her arm – while her other hand clenched the cold wooden handle.

'You bitch,' he gasped, gagging, falling back onto the cold floor as Rita buried the knife deep in his chest. What she'd done sank in as she sat shaking beside him. She'd fired her weapon before but this was the first time she had ever killed anyone. The court would accept self defence, wouldn't they?

She put her hands in his pockets and found his phone and a key card for the cells. With the torchlight, she saw it had expired a month ago. How did he imagine he would get out?

Wait for his dad? Or Henry?

Stupid.

His phone was locked, and the bar of signal for emergency calls disappeared as quickly as it appeared.

'No network,' the screen said as Rita waved the phone around to try and make a call.

Still, she had light now, and a knife.

And, if only for a second, the signal bar had displayed.

Chapter 45 – Pack of Sickos

'The bastards might have switched off the transponder but someone, quite a lot of people, must know where the fucking thing has landed, planes don't just get lost over the UK.' Dominguez nursed a cup of strong coffee in his hand. A chicken wrap lay in a bag under his chair, but he had no appetite for it. Heather and Mansouri sat on folding chairs just inside the forensic tent now on Henry's lawn, in stark contrast to the grandeur of the residence.

Heather had picked the two up from the airport and driven straight to the killer's Surrey mansion.

They were prepared for his arrival. It hadn't come.

Heather sighed, fanning herself in the afternoon heat. 'We're at a dead end. Trying to find individuals convicted for animal cruelty with their own private airstrips. This stuff doesn't even get reported. They're in a different world to the likes of us. These networks are very tight. They don't speak to coppers at all.'

'Unless it's to buy them off,' Dominguez mumbled. Mansouri looked uncomfortable. He was a good lad but he didn't want to believe police anywhere could do anything wrong. But Dominguez hated himself for the wrong he was doing, not being out now, searching for Rita. She'd sacrificed everything for that bull; she'd do the same for him in a heartbeat.

Henry had sent worse since the banderilla photo. Bloodstained walls. Crime scene photos, audio recordings from his murders. All burned into his head to keep popping up and make Dominguez flinch when he got a text.

He had one now. Laurentia. Thank God. 'Any update????'

Dominguez stared. His fingers wouldn't type. How could they not know where the plane landed? Why couldn't they disable that fucking app? Our time's running out, he thought, nauseous and wired from lack of sleep. At first he didn't register someone was calling him. As he stared at the screen with itching eyes, he saw the caller's British ID.

Acid rose in his throat.

'That's gotta be him, or someone in that club.' The phone continued ringing. Why couldn't he make himself answer?

'If she's still alive, we need to keep him talking as long as possible,' Subeera, one of the Met Police officers who'd found Robyn, said kindly. Dominguez hadn't noticed her enter. She was short, about 5"1, with a hijab and a stud in her nose.

'I'll take this, if you aren't up to it,' Heather said gently.

Dominguez handed her the phone. She put it on speaker. The caller didn't speak. The line kept breaking up; there were strange noises in the background. It disconnected within seconds. Heather shrugged.

Then it rung again. The team held their breath.

'Can you hear me, Jesús?' a woman's voice said in Spanish on the other end, crackly but clear enough. 'Jesús?'

'Who am I speaking to?' Heather said to the caller. Dominguez breathed through gritted teeth, bracing himself for the worst, thinking about what he'd do to Henry and his pet nonce. If he'd put her on for them to listen while he –

'It's me, Heather,' Rita said in English, her voice urgent.

The line went dead. Heather took a breath.

'No GPS disguiser on that call.'

Dominguez gulped more coffee, digesting the news, shaking with relief. He reached over and hugged Heather tightly, unable to speak.

'15 minutes mate, we'll have the location.'

****

While he stays with us in France, I would like to introduce the boy to my passion for the bulls. There is no better place than the arena of Ceret for an introduction to the exquisite dance between man and beast.' With curiosity, Henry listened from behind the door. Whatever could Uncle Herbert be talking about?

'Herbert. Are you sure that is wise?' Henry's aunt sounded anxious. His mother often complained that her brother had married below his station. Until recently, Henry hadn't been sure what that meant. Now, the day before his 9th birthday, he was starting to understand.

'How could it not be, Constance! This is art, as I keep telling you!'

'Herbert, I'm not sure this is sensible at all.' What was Constance so afraid of, and why, wondered Henry as he hid outside?

'You've never appreciated good art. You'd rather go to church, wouldn't you! You'd rather hear Père Baudret droning on with his sentimental claptrap about love and kindness. But let me tell you something – the oldest Indo-European myths involve the sacrifice of a bull!' Sacrifice? Henry thought excitedly.

Like the Aztecs?

Henry's history textbook said the Aztecs did human sacrifices by cutting people's hearts out.

'Have you forgotten why he's been sent for summer with us, instead of staying with his parents?' Constance whispered. He didn't like her one little bit. She was such a goody-goody; making him pray before mealtimes and constantly dragging him to church. This last didn't interest Henry in the slightest, especially since the service was in French.

This sounded much more exciting.

'Oh, Constance. Control yourself, dear. It wasn't that bad.'

'Herbert! He gouged another child's eye out with a pencil!' What? Why did the grown ups still care about that? Cecil started the whole thing, stealing Henry's fountain pen!

Herbert scoffed. 'All the more reason to go! Let him learn to channel these tendencies of his in a more aesthetic direction!'

Fortunately, common sense had prevailed. The very next day, Henry's birthday, Herbert had overridden his wife's wishes and brought him along for the highlight of the Ceret feria. It couldn't have proved a more perfect introduction, with astonishing performances by the greatest matadors of the day and the triumphant win of 4 ears. So much had Henry enjoyed the experience, he had begged his uncle to attend another one.

Herbert was delighted.

'That boy of mine must have slunk off to the village pub after his birthday pheasant shoot,' Jolyon said, interrupting Henry's nostalgia. The small group stood in a lobby between the lifts and the stands, enjoying a cigar and a drink courtesy of the hotel's bar.

'I'd be delighted to take his place, if he's late. I can't imagine my part in the Saltillo's demise will be altogether taxing,' Lord Owenstoft smiled, glancing at the ancient, blindfolded horses by the fire exit, tethered behind portable metal barriers and swathed in dirty yellow coverings.

'Indeed not. Sending Chicero heavenwards shouldn't be a trial.' Henry sipped a glass of champagne. He'd insisted Pepelito be the final bull, as both the triumph of the evening – his triumph – and to ensure the spectacle proceeded without incident.

'Chicero reminds me of that bull we saw, Henry. Where was it now? Denia. A fine tradition they have – that spectacular chase to the sea,' Lord Owenstoft said with a wistful expression.

'Oh, yes. What a marvellous few days. I remember that bull. Blasted thing was cowardly. Drowned itself rather than fight,' Henry scoffed.

The dark web ticket buyers were now trickling in. Jolyon's bullring could seat 800 people, and tonight it was a full house. And why not? Legality aside, there was something magical about an evening of bulls in the relaxing surrounds of the Home Counties. The Victorian-era lamps, shiny flooring and gold detail on the walls created an atmospheric, elegant ambiance, without any dinginess.

'I've always wanted to see this for real, not just watch it on YouTube,' one customer said joyfully, dressed in a t-shirt emblazoned with a swastika.

'Covid took a most dreadful toll on our earnings. Fewer corporate conferences, so we've shifted our focus to events which are more…*under the counter*. Although the crowds do tend to be somewhat vulgar,' Jolyon lowered his voice as the Nazi walked past; the others nodded in sympathy. Then, a young woman passed, dressed in tastefully chosen designer clothes worth several thousand.

Perhaps they weren't so vulgar after all.

Jolyon added quickly, 'Not that a man of my status has to worry overly about financial matters. Lest you think I'm poised to join the proletariat.'

Henry squirmed inside, self-conscious about his own finances. Even his bank in the Cayman Islands now refused him access. He had succeeded in anonymously paying Jolyon for two months' stay with all meals included, but no further funds were available. He had almost placed his card in the hotel's ATM earlier, before Jolyon's blasted son had reminded him, in his mocking, supercilious way, of the foolishness of this idea.

Despite his high regard for his father, Henry disliked Edwin intensely.

'You have customers and staff, do you not, who have absolutely no idea.' A shiver of excitement passed through Henry as he changed the subject, picturing their horrified revulsion.

Like that Labour Party bitch who'd stolen his seat last election, and her hysterics on Radio 4. *'These people claim to be cultured, but they're just a pack of sickos…'*

'Yes,' Jolyon grinned. 'My head receptionist. Worked here twenty years. Never shuts up about her grandchildren and some bloody dog. About as observant as a sack of potatoes. Looks like one, too.'

'Anyway, chaps, my son will be here soon, inebriated no doubt! He wouldn't miss a corrida for anything,' he continued jovially, puffing on one of Hemingway's favourite cigars.

'You've brought him up well,' Lord Owenstoft said.

'Yes. I'm so relieved he shares our passion for a proper art form, rather than, I don't know. Grand Theft Auto or whatever it's called.'

'Fuerza, torero!' one happy customer yelled at Henry. He smiled at the word 'torero' with its connotations of sex appeal, bravery and machismo. By the look she gave, she recognised him, as did the people behind her.

'Shit! Is that – is that *him*? If it is, I want his autograph,' said one.

'I love serial killers,' said another.

'Do you think I could…you know, risk *it*,' he muttered to Lord Owenstoft, imagining his most tantalising fantasy come alive before 800 people, a fantasy which had remained just that until now.

'Rita?' Lord Owenstoft whispered. Henry nodded.

'Hmm. Looking at this audience? Yes. I think so.'

Only a few seats now remained in the arena. Henry was glad for Lord Owenstoft's forthcoming assistance; the inevitable confrontation with Rita unsettled him. Her mocking words rung painfully in his ears. Dreading telling Jolyon the truth, he hoped Lord Owenstoft's judgement was correct.

How dare Rita laugh at him?

Who did she think she was?

And at the back of his mind lurked Pepelito. How he despised the very thought of that loathsome bull, sickened by the animal's hateful stare. The way he'd not only ignored the goading of Castella's attendants, but stepped in to halt their baiting of Chicero. The way he now carried his head high, not just unafraid, but, in Henry's perception, contemptuous of the corrida and its devotees – disdainful even of *him*. Worst of all, the way he'd vacated the arena of his own accord – alive.

The sand bothered him, too; dense, heavy, the odd stone – ideal for Pepelito's feet, not his.

Still, in the ring, that bull was a cowardly opponent.

Wasn't he?

'We have half an hour. Rupert, I fear you must take charge of Bull No. 3,' Henry said. Jolyon rolled his eyes in despair. Edwin wasn't back from the pub. What a disrespectful, lazy young man. Alas, as his host's son, Henry had to tolerate him.

'With pleasure,' Lord Owenstoft smiled.

'Chatting up some girl, no doubt. Sexual harassment, these days, if you're woke about it,' Jolyon laughed.

'We must hurry, so the opening procession can start on time. Come on, Rupert,' Henry said. The two men left the group for the changing rooms, where Juan Belmonte's costume awaited him.

*

Half an hour later, Henry waited by the gate, impatient, holding the stiff pink and yellow cape with which they'd play with the bull while it was still fresh. He didn't have great hopes for Chicero. Even after the door slid open, the Saltillo remained behind it, a quivering wreck.

Utterly unacceptable.

'Get out,' someone spat, sitting over the hatch and trying to kick him. Chicero looked up, unmoving, as Henry waved the pink cape around in front of him. The bull hadn't always been this bad. Had Pepelito or Rita exerted some dread influence? What had that ludicrous woman said on the plane? His anger rising, Henry threw his cape on the ground with a flourish as Chicero looked around miserably.

What a shitty bull,' someone said.

'Useless.'

His anger at a boiling point, Henry left the ring and walked up the steps, snatching up a metal pole standing near the gate. Stuck on the end of the pole was a divisa rosette in the green and black colours of Chicero's breeder. In his current position, the bull's thick neck muscles were unreachable; even worse, the hatch door was jammed.

'Allow me,' he said. On the flight, Chicero's phobia of poles had provided welcome amusement. The bull would bolt senselessly at the mere sight. No compassion entered Henry's mind when he considered the likely reason. He dangled the pole in front of the bull's face. The effect was immediate. As Chicero scrambled to escape the cell, Henry plunged the sharp end into his neck until the colourful rosette was firmly in place.

Planting it took skill – and practice. This was art, as his uncle had said. The crowd agreed; as Chicero fled into the ring, cheers and applause echoed throughout.

A pack of sickos, they said. If that was so, Henry was proud to lead this pack.

Now, at last, the show could begin.

Chapter 46 – Lex Talionis

'Now we're getting started!'

'Yep, here we go! 2 and a half hours of bullfighting – best thing is, there's none of that bloody hassle with passport control in Madrid!'

As the spectators chatted, Chicero's feet skittered across the sand, running round and round. The metallic scent of the other bull's blood reached Pepelito's nostrils as he stood in his cell, unable to move. In the dark, cramped space, bombarded with awful sounds, he could smell his friend's fear and almost feel his pain.

Pepelito had expected to be first, tried to prepare as best he could.

This was much, much worse.

He had to stop them. But trapped here, what could he do?

'They've even managed to get horses down here – the horseback matadors are always my favourites!' The spectators' happy voices filled Pepelito with loathing. He shifted around desperately, scraped the floor with his feet. A slight depression lay in the ground in front of him, under the door; he could wedge the very tip of his right foot into the opening, when he pushed hard. When he rammed his foot in harder, it gave way a little.

He took a step backwards and slammed his hind leg against the back wall. He paced forwards and pressed his foot to the narrow gap. The rough metal scraped his hoof hard but he could jam the end in a bit further. He kicked the ground with his other foot, but it did nothing.

They were going to do to Chicero what they'd done to Ladron.

Rita was sobbing somewhere, almost inaudible above the baying audience. Pepelito had smelt her scent earlier; she was so sad and hungry. He'd heard her in a fight; a bad one. He kicked at the tiny depression until a speck of light appeared, jolted it until he could get his right foot all the way underneath, and part of his left. He shoved one hind foot, then the other, against the back wall, forcing the gap wider with his whole body.

'This bull's not charged once. I didn't pay £1500 to see it running away.'

'Bet he wishes he'd tried harder to stay inside,' one aficionado laughed above him. Some spectators were smoking cigars. Most were drinking heavily. Indoors, all these smells overpowered his nose, making him sneeze. A Highland bull, stolen from a farm in Scotland, gave a pitiful cry from a nearby cell.

'Now, what's the matter? This won't cause any harm,' Lord Owenstoft's soft voice mocked Chicero. Pepelito didn't like horses. But as he wiggled his foot around in the gap, he sensed *this* horse was ancient. He smelt its terror; like him, it didn't want to be there. The crowd booed timid, gentle Chicero as he bellowed for help, all alone.

Don't go near that horse, Pepelito told him.

'Too bad they can't use the old-style fire banderillas on this coward. Doesn't anywhere still sell them?'

'Oh, Chicero, I know you're scared. But if you won't come to the horse,' Lord Owenstoft's voice was full of fake kindness. The crowd fell silent with expectation. Panting, Pepelito jammed both his feet the whole way into the gap between the door and the arena, the urge to stop them hurting his friend overriding his every instinct.

'Then, I'm afraid, we'll have to punish you.'

Pepelito pushed his hooves further forward. They now touched the sand. Don't be afraid, he told Chicero. His friend was in no place to hear him. With a horrendous shriek, Chicero leapt high into the air, landing with a sickening thud. Pepelito's tail thrashed in rage. He kicked the back door hard, unable to bear the torture they inflicted.

Oh no. Was this his fault?

He kept both his feet wedged underneath the door and pushed up with his lower legs, ignoring everything but this, not noticing his bleeding hooves and cut ankles. The heavy door slammed into his feet and he snorted, crying in fury at himself. Maybe he wasn't strong enough.

Chicero grunted in the terrible pain Pepelito knew so well. How could he make it up to him? Eyes dripping with tears, he forced his right foot under the metal, driving it twenty centimetres above the ground, then pushed and kicked with his left, the skin on his legs grazed. Now the bottom edge was level with his ankles. Pepelito lowered his head, trying to force the door upwards with his horns, create space that didn't exist. The stabbing sensations in his neck he thought had gone returned.

'The querencia, eh? Come on now, out your comfort zone,' a spectator laughed. Chicero pressed himself against a wooden board near the one obscuring Pepelito's door, his agonised cries almost drowned out by excited shrieks, applause and laughter. With the scent of blood overwhelming him, Pepelito tried to sit, scraping his horns and ramming his bleeding, bruised knees under the door, panting as he heaved it higher.

What if he couldn't stop them?

'Go on. Get him out his little corner, make him fight,' a woman snarled, her voice full of hate.

'Hah. That'll teach him to run. Pathetic.' The door was now high enough that Pepelito could lower his head and push with it. Clenching the teeth in the back of his mouth until his eyes rolled back, he pushed upwards with his forehead and horns, then his nose. The resin plug on his other horn came off, stinging him. He pushed until he could fit his whole head underneath, his neck squeezed so tight his throat constricted. As he sniffed the air in horror, a bullfighter stabbed a fourth pair of black 'punishment' darts into Chicero's back.

Jolyon waved his white handkerchief. To the sound of a trumpet, Henry re-entered the ring alone. The crowd screamed its delight. Hold on, Pepelito begged his friend, forcing the rusted barrier up with all the strength he had.

'This is it,' a man said, breathless. 'The suerte suprema. Just watch.'

His entire body was sore from the effort but he couldn't give up, not now. Out of breath, Pepelito watched, unable to intervene, as Henry led the exhausted, bleeding bull around in the sand with his matador's cape. Sand and dirt stung his eyes. His friend's pain was breaking him with rage and sadness. The door weighed heavily as he nudged it upwards with his neck, his spine about to crack.

He paced back, put his head underneath the metal door and heaved up with everything he had, until he could fit his shoulders underneath. He pressed at the depression with his feet, drawing his aching muscles upwards until the door clicked and the lock mechanism snapped.

'Convention dictates that I must dedicate this bull to someone,' Henry grinned, waving around Belmonte's sword as Chicero panted for breath. He took his hat off, placed it between the bull's horns, leaned forward and screeched, inches from his face. Then, flourishing his cape, he theatrically spun round, turning his back on Chicero. The crowd cheered, enraptured with barbaric excitement. Someone yelled, 'Henry is Innocent', another spectator shouted 'Bravo'.

Pepelito edged forward cautiously, the door heavy against his scarred and tender back.

He took a step, then another one.

Time to fight.

'Allow me, then, to dedicate this first bull of ours to the esteemed proprietor of this most magnificent of establishments, the great aficionado, our wonderful friend, Sir Jolyon Richmond. Who could fail to appreciate his excellent hospitality?' Before Henry had finished speaking, the heavy door answered him with a metallic crash.

Pepelito leapt at the barrier, knocking over a wooden burladero, shattering the gate in front of him. Digging his feet hard into the sand, he sent stuck together clumps flying. Everyone stared. Rather than cheers and clapping, Henry's dedication was met by total silence.

'Oh. Fuck.'

'What the hell's it doing?'

'I'm scared!'

Then the screaming started.

Shrieks of shock, disbelief and unholy terror filled the air. Those who had found beauty in Chicero's suffering now gasped before the horror they knew had come for them.

Pepelito locked eyes with Chicero for a few seconds. Then, to a background of screams, he filled his lungs with a deep breath and stormed towards Henry, faster than he'd ever run in his life, his mind only on one thing. His feet felt surer on the dense builder's sand, knowing these people saw in him the retribution they'd thought would never and could never touch them.

He would never let them kill Chicero.

He couldn't lose another friend.

'Get back in there, you stupid animal!' Henry's shocked face turned red, then white as his nemesis tore towards him across the arena, head down, horns forward.

Pepelito knew what he had to do.

'No! Stay away from me!'

Launching himself at Henry, Pepelito thrust his horns into his stomach. Hard spikes ripped Juan Belmonte's gaudy £350,000 costume, tearing a hole in the soft flesh beneath. Bright red blood gushed from the serial killer's stomach as he flailed at his attacker in a fruitless struggle. The liquid seeped into the bull's fur, dripped into his eyes. The great matador's precious sword slipped from Henry's hand as Pepelito's hooves pounded him into the rough construction sand. Howling in agony, he rolled around clutching his stomach, blood spurting from the wound.

Pepelito raised his head to see Lord Owenstoft struggling to tether his horse just behind the ring. The horse reared up, screaming in fright, dislodging its blindfold and the stained yellow covering over its back. The sound of its hooves clopping as it ran for the elevators unnerved Pepelito; he shuffled backwards, leaving Henry sprawled in front of him.

The guy in the swastika t-shirt sprang out of his seat, sobbing. He sprinted towards the lifts, tripped and fell on the shiny floor as the huge horse sidled with menacing steps. The man tried to stand up, whacking the keypad again and again, pummelling the door with his fists. Through a gap in the barricade, Pepelito watched, astonished, as the carthorse kicked the man in the head, then stood on him as he lay motionless.

Perhaps horses weren't so evil.

Sounds of cracking wood and clanging metal echoed from the other side of the arena as Chicero shot into the stands. Cries of terror reverberated as he gored and trod on spectators in their seats. Tears streaming down their faces, terrified aficionados rushed for the doors, trampling each other in blind, petrified panic.

Pepelito knew his friend had found his courage.

'That's the exit! Let me through, you pricks!'

One man shoved several people out of his way, flinging open the door to a tiny, dark room. Four others ran inside, blundered into and broke several shelves full of bullfighting equipment, knocking down a box of daggers and darts. Lances, banderillas and swords crashed onto the floor and rolled into the stands. Fleeing spectators tripped and tumbled over the weapons clattering down the steps. One landed on a dart. 'Fuck!' he screamed, slicing his hand on its sharp metal blade.

Multiple pairs of flailing legs knocked one of the long picador's lances as it fell, sending it sailing through the air. It struck a diamond and crystal encrusted chandelier in the ceiling, shattering it on impact and showering the sand with glass. With the remains of the chandelier scattered around, the spear landed, pointed end upwards, in a dense mound of builder's sand. Jolyon gazed at his broken light with a tear-stained face.

'How dare you do this to me?' Henry screeched at Pepelito, his furious yells tearing through the bull's ears. He staggered to his feet, clutching Belmonte's sword like a walking stick, his other hand pressed to the dripping wound in his stomach.

'How could you?' Henry shouted. Pepelito turned his head in his direction, heart pounding, and scraped a line deep into the sand.

'Leave me alone! Just go!'

Powering towards him, Pepelito rammed Henry with his horns and leapt, hurling him and his sword across the arena. Screaming like a banshee, Henry soared through the air and landed right on the lance's sharp point. He struggled and waved his arms, but his shouts of rage became a gurgling noise as the tip of the spear emerged from his back. His lifeless corpse slid down the lance's handle before reaching the bottom, like a vampire with a stake through his heart.

Somewhere, Rita was shouting. In the chaos, Pepelito couldn't tell where. She was scared. So was he. He needed human help. He sniffed the air and listened for the sound. There. Behind him. Pepelito turned around, his bleeding legs stinging, and half ran, half walked towards where he thought he heard it. He trotted around the ring, much more slowly on his aching feet, his tongue hanging out.

Pepelito steeled himself to approach the metal door behind the gate Chicero had smashed in his rampage. He walked forward and pressed his horns underneath Rita's door, but couldn't find the strength to lift it. Breathing was harder. The gap between the metal and the floor was too small, the tips of his horns too wide. He stood on a nail with his back foot. Someone grabbed his tail from behind, twisting it hard.

'Only one thing to do with such a dangerous bull!' A group of aficionados and bullfighters in costumes were surrounding him, shrieking in rage. He was so hot, so thirsty. Everything hurt. The woman in designer clothes had a dagger. Someone punched him. He was ready to collapse. He had to protect Chicero. Where was he? Pepelito tossed his head and caught one of his assailants in the stomach, wanting to drop.

That meant death.

He had to fight.

But Pepelito heard another noise above the crashes and rage filled screeching, as he stood precariously on the broken board, exhausted, dazed and panting. A high-pitched wail the soundproofing at the Armitage Hotel couldn't eliminate, starting faint and growing louder.

The noise of sirens.

With every last bit of strength he could summon up, Pepelito threw himself at his attackers. His hooves knocked the air out of the woman's stomach. Her dagger fell from her hand and she lay sobbing, sand all over her Balenciaga handbag.

'Armed police! Drop your weapons and place your hands on your head!'

Pepelito watched, exhausted, as fifty officers with guns and riot shields stormed into the room from the lifts and stairs. The officers grabbed the fleeing spectators, shoving them against the walls. The carthorse reared up, neighed and brought its hooves down on someone. As the woman in designer clothes dug around for her dagger in the sand, Chicero bounded towards her. He delivered a ferocious kick, trampling her as she slipped. The grey bull stepped forward two paces, then collapsed front legs first, exhausted and bleeding.

'What the fuck happened *here*?'

'Another fucking bullfighting stadium! With actual bulls!'

Pepelito approached Chicero, needing his company, anxious about these strange people and worried about Rita. He didn't have the strength to free her. Breaking himself loose had taken everything he had. The horrific black banderillas meant Chicero could barely move his head, but he lifted it for a few seconds to give Pepelito a big, grateful lick on the nose.

'Rita?' Dominguez shouted.

Pepelito's spirits lifted as he heard his friend's voice. He edged a tiny step towards the sound. The police dragged Lord Owenstoft past him in handcuffs, shouting, 'Politically motivated witch hunt!'

The Scottish bull who'd called to Pepelito earlier had forced himself out of his cell too, and was wandering around the ring, confused.

'I'm here,' Rita sobbed, struggling to make herself heard. Pepelito wanted to help her but his legs wouldn't move.

'Coming.' Dominguez walked towards Rita's metal door with a few people he didn't recognise. Good. Humans were helping her. Maybe he could even let himself lie down.

He needed water.

Heather ascended the steps above Rita's door and used Henry's metal pole to yank it open. Moments later Rita emerged, her shirt stained with blood, her hair messed up. She stood, dazed, hugging them all in tears.

Pepelito was crying too.

'Um, well done.' Mansouri reached out a hand and touched his nose awkwardly, gaping at Henry's impaled body.

'You brave boy,' Rita sobbed, putting her arm around Pepelito's back. He loved his friend so much. But his back and neck were too bruised to be petted. He backed away, sinking to the ground next to Chicero, unable to stay on his feet or cope with everyone swarming around, feeling dizzy, feeling sick. He wanted to sleep on a bed of soft grass.

Maybe he could soon.

'There's 3 more bulls locked up. And Chicero needs a vet, or he'll die!' Rita yelled at the armed British officers.

'Of course, ma'am.'

Pepelito licked Chicero's back. He slashed his tongue on the vicious metal spikes, let out a grunt, but didn't leave his side. Heather gently laid a blanket over the wounded bull. We're safe now, Pepelito told his friend, knowing Chicero believed it.

'Nice work, amigos, have some water, both of you. My uncle would be proud of you.' Dominguez knelt beside Pepelito with a huge bucket, kissing the top of his head and rubbing behind his ears. His nose and tongue were dry, he felt so hot and he was struggling to breathe.

But he'd saved his friends.

Soon, he could go home.

He took several gulps of water, then collapsed.

Chapter 47 – Too Much

No longer trying to keep himself awake, Pepelito opened his eyes and glanced briefly at the people helping his friend. The two bulls lay side by side in the sand, with his head just touching Chicero's bloody side, one front leg sprawled over his foot.

'…poor thing's so scared of humans. Try to keep him still while I sedate him, every time he moves those darts lacerate his back even more. They're stuck so deep. It could take hours,' a woman urged in a gravelly voice. The spectators' screams and shouts of abuse faded as crime scene officers and medics invaded the arena.

The woman replied to Chicero's bellows of pain with soothing, comforting words. 'Aw, darling. I know. You're so brave. It'll be over soon.'

'Isn't Peps loyal? He's done for, bless him. Look how tired he is,' Heather said. She seemed kind but Pepelito wished they would all go, feeling ill and utterly finished. After another few gulps of water, he shut his eyes tightly, his legs too stiff and tired to move.

When Heather spoke next she was on the edge of tears. 'I was one of the first on the scene when we found Aidan. To think people paid money to watch *him* hurt a bull like *that*. It's…it's…'

'Evil,' Rita said.

'Yeah. Make sure you save Chicero. Please,' Heather begged the vets, her voice choked up with emotion.

'Peps needs some help too, his nose is very dry, his breathing's quite laboured. Shit, he's very hot.' A young guy pressed Pepelito's nose a bit too hard with a sandy finger. Confused, he opened his eyes, then shut them again. While uncomfortable, he didn't have the energy to protest. His throat felt tight; his sides ached.

'Yeah. He's not well, he needs to be treated. Let's get them in the truck,' the guy said. 'And Rita? We'll get you to A and E.'

*

After what Pepelito thought was a few minutes, voices woke him up again. The woman who'd helped before said, 'Well, Chicero survived the night. He even stood up and had a little walk around. We'll see, but I think he has a good chance.'

Why were these people dressed in weird uniforms? Surely he wouldn't have to fight again? Was he back with Maribel in his field? Or was he *there*? Confused, ill, sleepy and boiling hot, he half realised someone was stroking his back; a lot of humans were talking about him.

'How's our legend doing today?' one of the nurses said brightly. She had blonde hair and a ponytail. Pepelito thought she might have led him out of the hotel.

'Better than last night. We were worried, weren't we, Peps?' said the young man who had touched his nose.

A drip led from his leg to the ceiling. His legs wobbled when he stood up; tight bandages restricted his movement. Looking over, he saw Chicero lying in a pen adjacent to his, swaddled in a thick blue coat. Were they hurting him? Would he have to save him again?

Maybe not.

A bed of thick straw covered the floor. They both had plenty of food and water. He took a gulp, lay back down and buried his face in the straw. His muscles had given up after yesterday, or today or whenever it was.

'…well, his temperature was 42.5 last night. It's still over 40. He needs lots of fluids and medication. This action hero stuff is all a bit too much. He's got a bacterial infection,' Pepelito dimly heard one of the vets say.

'…yeah, probably from the original injury. He had a few days of antibiotics left to go, just needs another course. And yeah, he's meant to spend his days grazing in a field, not fighting serial killers. Aren't you?' Looking up, he saw Alfonso standing in front of him, holding hands with Rita. Both OK. He licked Alfonso's hand and tried to settle back to sleep, knowing these humans were here to help.

He could drop his guard.

'When do you think these two can go home?' Rita's voice sounded exhausted, shellshocked, but relaxed.

'Well, his temperature's come down loads, his breathing's better. With Chicero, difficult to say, but with him? A few weeks, probably,' the English vet said.

'I'm sure Maribel is missing him,' Rita said. Pepelito's ears swivelled around at his friend's name.

He'd see her again soon.

Some time later, he pushed himself up on his unsteady feet, helped himself to a carrot and wandered over to the barrier separating his and Chicero's pen, feeling hot, nauseous and dizzy as he chewed. Shivering, Pepelito rubbed noses with his friend through the bars, tormented with guilt for warning him away from Lord Owenstoft's horse. He could still hear Chicero's scream as he leapt into the air, the heartbreaking thud as the bull skidded and fell in the rough sand.

But Chicero had once lived in a field for a few months with some horses. These horses, he insisted to his shocked friend, had never tried to sting or hurt him. This horse was the same; terrified like the bulls, it was just another victim. Pepelito's pleas had made no difference. Chicero wouldn't have charged anyway. The bullfighters had punished him for his kind, gentle nature.

Not Pepelito's fault.

He was still sceptical about horses, though. Maybe one day his friend could convince him of their merits.

He popped his nose back, snuggled into the straw with his head between his hooves and fell back to sleep, thinking of fresh grass and his favourite cow.

****

'How are you doing, Rita?' Alfonso said as they sat on the budget Ryanair plane, waiting to take off back to Spain. She squeezed his hand. He'd come to the UK as soon as they told him where she was. At such short notice, that couldn't have been cheap.

She'd spent a night in hospital and then the following 2 nights with him in a cheap hotel. She'd needed the wound on her stomach dressed with one or two stitches, but the main injuries were psychological. Alfonso had sat by her bed and picked her up when she was discharged – after which, of course, they visited Pepelito and Chicero.

Hopefully, she wouldn't be hit with a medical bill, not being a UK citizen. Once they'd got to the hotel, Rita had cried at the thought of the hospital, flight and hotel bills – and the builders' quotes to redo her ruined flat. She'd had a panic attack, worried her department wouldn't let her claim the flight and hotel money. She'd almost blocked out the kidnapping; the kind of displaced reaction she often had.

'This is kind of my worst nightmare. To tell the truth, I've always been scared of flying,' she finally said, reaching for his hand. The flight was full. Someone was eating a packet of crisps loudly; a baby was crying somewhere.

'I feel a lot more able to deal with it now, though. Plus, this time is safer, and I know that in the hold, it's just suitcases,' she laughed. He leaned towards her and kissed her hard. She relaxed, gripping his hand tightly. Being with him, she realised she hadn't given her fear of flying a second's thought until he asked about it.

'I didn't want to tell you, Rita, but I probably ought to. I had some messages from Henry Dixon the night you got kidnapped,' Alfonso said. Rita tensed up at the mention of his name. Knowing this was a poor way of dealing with it, she was attempting to dissociate, imagining it happened to someone else. Although he was dead, the thought of the perpetrator – as she now tried to think of him – contacting those she loved made her want to vomit. Her skin crawled. She felt exposed to something repulsive.

'I don't want to ask what it said,' she said.

'But you have to know?'

'Yeah. I think if I don't, I'll just torture myself wondering what it was.'

Alfonso found the text and passed her his phone. Rita winced at the sight of Chicero's green and black divisa with its sharp double spike. The caption said, 'Your girlfriend loves bulls. She'll look good wearing one of these.'

'Bastard! I'm sorry he sent that to you,' she managed, imagining his horror.

'You don't have to be sorry. It's on him.' Alfonso took a breath, stroking her hair.

'He tried to call me, as well.'

'Call you?' Her fists clenched. It was a shame the scumbag was dead…

'Yeah. I got a call around 5pm from a British number. He didn't say anything, he just kind of breathed heavily. There was a bull in the background, mooing really loudly. Henry hung up after about 6 seconds. Thank God.' Alfonso looked tormented as he remembered the call; despite herself, it filled Rita with guilt. She'd wanted to hear his voice, didn't know if she had the right number, but only succeeded in sickening him.

She couldn't blame him, but a tiny part of her was devastated. 'That wasn't the killer. That was me.'

'What?'

Her voice cracked. 'Yeah. I unlocked Edwin's phone by pressing on the sensor with – with his dead finger. I called 112, I called Jesús, I called Flavia – I know their numbers by heart. And then – I called you – I knew you likely wouldn't hear me but I wanted to tell you … I just wanted you to know I was hanging in there. I couldn't hear anything you said. I just wanted to hear your voice…'

Alfonso squeezed her hand in both of his. He was so comfortable to lean on. She shut her eyes, wishing she hadn't taken this so personally.

'I'm sorry, Rita, it wasn't your fault I got scared,' he whispered, holding her gently.

As Rita spoke, the plane began to move and the seatbelt light came on. 'It wasn't yours either. I told you I loved you. But it didn't connect long. The signal wasn't strong enough.'

'It's OK, I know. I love you too,' Alfonso said, kissing her hair.

As the plane's wheels rolled faster against the ground, she glanced at her latest WhatsApp message. She didn't recognise the number, but that only confirmed who'd sent it.

'Hi Rita. I know you don't want to speak to me, but I saw on the news you were kidnapped – and Javier's bull saved you!!!? Wtf? I hope you're OK now! Javier and I actually saw a lot of Henry, it feels so weird, thinking I knew someone who murdered so many people. Once you're feeling better, there's a lot of things I need to get off my chest about what Javier was like as a husband. Mum says you might be the best person? He brainwashed me. He cut me off from everyone. I don't have any friends any more or anyone else who might understand. Maria.'

As expected, no apology – this was probably the best she'd get. Maria had been a very enthusiastic aficionado. Probably still was. But Castella was an abuser. He would have isolated her from anyone who could have cared; Rita could sense the loneliness, emptiness and misery. She wrote, 'Thanks for the message, Maria. Yes, I'm OK. Let me think about it.'

Resting her head on Alfonso's shoulder, Rita watched him take out his iPad for the flight. This plane wasn't fancy enough to have WiFi. Just before putting her phone into airplane mode, she texted Maria as an afterthought. 'The bull's name is Pepelito.'

'Right, Rita, we've got a choice queued up for the flight. A Scandinavian murder series on Netflix or a documentary about lions,' Alfonso said, doing up his seat belt, and then hers. They both knew what they were going to pick.

'These detective series never get anything right. Let's go with the lions,' Rita grinned.

Chapter 48 – The Nicest Treat of All

Several months later

Pepelito was having a nice happy day. Rita and Dominguez were sitting on the bench Silvio used to sit on. The gate was open, and they were feeding him treats from a paper bag of vegetables they'd picked up on the village market, stuffed between them on the bench.

'I thought you'd blame me,' Rita said. The bull took a huge courgette in his mouth from the paper bag and chewed messily as Dominguez patted him. I've taken a bit too much here, Pepelito thought, trying to eat the enormous courgette and dropping it on the ground.

'Yeah. I was angry, Rita, I admit that, I did blame you a bit.' Dominguez sighed. Pepelito swallowed most of the courgette.

'But, look. I went into this job knowing people like Castella could target those close to me. Everyone knows that. That's part of being a police officer. But I carried on. And sometimes the right thing isn't the most sensible or safest option. Is it, amigo?' Dominguez seemed relaxed enough, leaning forward to kiss him on the nose. If his friends were happy, so was he.

He had worried Maribel would be upset with him for leaving her alone so long, and that she wouldn't get on with Chicero. But the old girl had been accepting and kind. They still played together, but she spent a lot more time lying down than she used to on her prosthetic leg. It made him sad.

'You agree, don't you, dulcito,' Rita said. Pepelito pulled a carrot away from the bag of vegetables, enjoying all the love and affection. Recently, he hadn't seen his favourite humans as much as normal. He missed them. When they spent lots of time with him, they were less tense and stressed.

The feeling was mutual.

'No! I'm not a cow,' Dominguez yelled, holding his arms in front of him as Pepelito stretched out his long, black tongue. Humans never wanted to be licked. He couldn't work out why.

'What are your family going to do about the farm?'

'You interested, Rita? You're a bit late. We've got a buyer, we're selling the farm to an animal rescue charity. In the meantime, someone's always here keeping an eye on this lot, my brother or the neighbours,' Dominguez said. Pepelito turned his head towards the oval-shaped lake down the bottom of the hill where Chicero was swimming, his favourite thing to do. Pepelito loved seeing his friend so happy.

Scratching him under the chin, Dominguez laughed, 'The attention my family is getting from all sorts of farmers wanting to introduce such 'well-bred bulls' to their cows. It's got well out of hand. The fucking stories I could tell you.'

'Look at Chicero, he's like a water buffalo in there,' Rita smiled.

'Yeah, that one loves it, he's always in there. We made them an obstacle course too, me and my brother, out of some old pallets and tyres. He can't get enough of that either.' Dominguez laughed. Chicero had lost so much fear, but he was still nervous of humans.

Maybe he always would be.

And that was OK.

Nobody kicked or beat the bulls here for not meeting their 'standards', and nobody ever would. They'd never be punished for the lack of bravery they showed before the twisted, baying audience, fighting for their lives in an unwinnable contest. They weren't alone here; they never had to be afraid. Here, they saw nothing but kindness and love.

They were safe.

'How are you feeling about being back at work, Rita?' Dominguez asked.

'Oh, all right. Alfonso's been really supportive, which made it easier,' she replied, feeding Pepelito a carrot. He was thinking about getting in the water himself. Chicero had told him it helped with the pain in his back. To his surprise, it had worked, although that now rarely bothered him. Pepelito had made some interesting discoveries of his own lately, like a bush of nice tasting berries the other two hadn't found.

And the weakness in the fence separating them from the neighbour's cows. They had so much space it seemed empty sometimes; Silvio once had a whole herd, and there were girls Pepelito wanted to introduce himself to. He and Chicero had set themselves the task of knocking it down altogether. They'd made progress, especially after recruiting some of the ladies to their cause.

He'd get there. He'd done something far more gruelling.

'You know, I had an email from Robyn Casey, that journalist who got kidnapped,' Rita said.

'Yeah?'

'Yeah, they're making…like, a 12-part podcast about the case, say it's helping them heal. They asked me on for an interview. I told them not right now,' Rita said, holding out another carrot.

'Here. Give us their address. Maybe I'll write to them, dunno. That profiler's report was something else,' Dominguez said quietly.

'Yeah. Money and power got him impunity.'

'That piece of shit killed 22 people. 22! If that expensive school he was at had paid any attention to what that psychiatrist told them, instead of covering it up and pocketing the parents' money, I reckon some of them would still be alive,' Dominguez sighed.

'Yeah, those relatives of his, wanting to 'channel his violent impulses' into killing animals, thinking that would, I don't know, dampen his cravings.' Rita rubbed under Pepelito's chin. The distress in her voice told him what they were talking about. Sometimes, the thoughts wouldn't stop; the trucks, the pens, the spectators crying out for blood and pain. Don't be sad, he told Rita, the first human he'd ever trusted.

It didn't matter that she didn't understand, because she was here.

'Most serial killers start with killing animals, right? But that lot don't think one of their own could do wrong. In their world only poor people are criminals. Eh, Pepelito? You agree.' Dominguez offered the bull a pepper. It was sweet and juicy.

He growled, 'If that was a working-class kid, I doubt anyone would have bent over backwards to spare him the consequences of gouging out that kid's eye, let alone anything else.'

'Yeah, and if someone had taken Tegan's accusations seriously, instead of branding her an attention seeker and a slut.' Rita spoke through gritted teeth.

'Yep, then her ex-husband would be alive, and she wouldn't have spent 8 years in jail. That really got to me.' Dominguez sighed. Both he and Rita had visited on their own and told Pepelito these things; he didn't understand the words, but he sensed the sadness behind them.

'It wasn't just him. He always had people who would cover for him or downright assist in his murders, and saw his victims as lesser, like he did.' Rita spoke bitterly. Pepelito came close enough for her to put her arms round him without catching herself on his horns.

'Yeah, just 'peasants' as his noncey sidekick put it. They were people whose lives didn't matter, didn't usually matter to us either. Look at Sonia Gutiérrez, her mother will rinse the Policia Nacional in her court case, and she's right to,' Dominguez remarked, patting him. A butterfly flitted past. Ladron told him he liked chasing butterflies. He would have liked it here.

Rita nodded. 'And animals mattered even less. That hijo de puta thought they were put there by God to be tortured by humans, and if you look around, plenty of people agree with him.'

Dominguez took a deep breath. 'You won't like this, Rita. Yesterday I had a call from a girl. Turned out to be the daughter of the fighting bull rancher who bred him.'

Rita was unimpressed. 'After a stud service? Hope you told them where to go.'

Dominguez shook his head. 'She was very apologetic. Told me the day he escaped from Castella, her dad sent this one's mum to the slaughterhouse. Usually, that only happens when the bull kills the matador. But our Pepelito was *so* disgraceful…'

'Just makes me want to hug him even more, doesn't it, dulcito,' Rita said, stroking his nose gently as he blinked away flies. Seeing her sad made him sad. They'd all lost so much. His friends understood everything. It still hurt to imagine life without them.

'Exactly. After this one took out Europe's worst serial killer in decades, he now regrets it, apparently, like all the other farmers think, he was 'well bred' after all. The daughter's disgusted, she's stopped speaking to him. Can't say I blame her.' As Dominguez spoke, Pepelito sniffed at the remaining vegetables. Maybe later.

'It doesn't surprise me, this behaviour. They're making out they have nothing to do with Henry, or Castella, now he's dead and everyone knows he was a drug dealer. Or, saying this proves the spirit of the fighting bull. They're so brave, so different to other breeds,' Rita laughed without humour, scratching the bull behind the ears. Sometimes he found it hard to believe he was safe. Did she feel that way too?

'That's why only a brave matador can honour him with the finale he deserves. I know just the coked-up egomaniac, too bad he's dead,' Dominguez said. Rita flinched, a protective hand on Pepelito's neck.

'Jesús! Don't even joke about this.'

'Sorry. I don't like thinking of it either. See the nonsense that prick from the Association of Picadors was spouting off? Castella wasn't a real matador apparently, just an impostor. Henry – just some psycho with nothing to do with anything. We condemn crime, blah, blah…then you see this guy's own trial for selling drugs and beating up his wife starts next week,' Dominguez scoffed. Rita gave a contemptuous snort. Pepelito guessed this was something he didn't need to worry about.

Chicero had traipsed up to the fence. He was eating a tuft of long grass and staring curiously at a tiny bird scratching on the ground. He didn't walk through the gate towards the humans. But Pepelito knew his friend wasn't scared. Slowly, things were getting easier for them all.

'Hola,' Rita smiled.

'Wow, that's the closest that one's ever got to me,' Dominguez said.

'Talking of Sonia, Lucia Gutiérrez called me again yesterday, that girl's serious about joining the police, wants to arrange a work experience placement next year. Thinks her grandmother might be a bit more amenable,' Rita said.

'How old is that kid?'

'Just turned 15,' Rita said.

'Not starting next week, then. Good for Lucia, although no idea why she'd want to join.' Dominguez leant back on the bench, took a cigarette out of his packet and offered one to Rita.

'Go on then. Do you need a lift back to Valladolid?' Disliking the smell, Pepelito turned away and trotted out through the gate to join Chicero. Maribel was approaching from the grassy bank by the lake. For a moment the only sounds Pepelito heard were bees buzzing and grass being torn out of the ground as he ate with the two friends he loved so much.

'Thanks, Rita, but my new boyfriend is coming over in a sec, remember.'

'Oh, yeah! Tell me about this guy, Jesús. I thought you said you'd only date cops,' Pepelito heard Rita saying.

'I did yeah, but me and Roberto just…happened.'

And then, the sound of a truck approaching. Both bulls looked up, then put their heads down, relaxed. Chicero sniffed at a daisy, then ate it.

'Don't laugh at me, Rita.'

'Why would I do that?'

'He owns the cows down the bottom,' Dominguez chuckled. The noise of tyres against gravel grew louder. He took the buzzer out of the pocket of his now crisply ironed shirt and let Roberto in through the farm's new steel entrance gate. Pepelito sniffed deeply, inhaling the scent that drove him crazy every time he sensed it. Thinking of that scent had comforted him when he was broken.

'I don't want to cramp your style, so I'll go shortly,' Rita said.

'Oh, come on, woman, stay for half an hour,' Dominguez laughed. The truck stopped on the gravel. Roberto got out, a tall, slim man with sunglasses and jeans. In the long grass, Pepelito and Chicero looked at each other and sniffed the air, enthralled. Chicero gave a loud, excitable cry as Roberto kissed Dominguez on the lips. From inside the truck, someone responded.

'Roberto, meet Rita, she's my best friend.' Pepelito heard Dominguez making the introduction. But Pepelito wasn't interested in humans' greetings as he looked past the fence where the butterfly rested.

'I've heard so much about you. All of it good, don't worry.' The dapperly dressed farmer shook Rita's hand effusively and laughed. For a second, Pepelito wondered what he should do; he wandered close to the fence, bellowing, then, suddenly self-conscious, he took a step back, as Roberto walked round to the back of the truck.

'Before we sit down for a drink, there's someone I want these guys to meet,' Roberto said, gesturing into the field. He liked to talk a lot, but Dominguez was always happy when Pepelito saw them together.

And when Roberto came to check on the bulls, he always brought a nice treat.

Today, he'd brought the nicest treat of all.

'…so, I've been having a bit of a crisis, honestly. I'm not cut out for farming, and I don't want to stay in this village. It was my dad's farm, he died two years ago. I never expected to still be here. By training, I'm a hairdresser. I want to open my own salon.'

'So what does this mean?' Rita said, strolling over to the gate.

'I couldn't bear to send these five to the abattoir – any of the girls, but especially not these five,' Roberto said, as the truck door came down and a ramp slid onto the ground, just beyond the grass.

'I want these ladies, especially, to go to the people buying Silvio's farm. I mean, this one – look. I see her staring at Pepelito every day,' Roberto said in a loud, charismatic voice, as the brown and white splodged cow and four of her equally gorgeous friends trotted down the ramp into his field.

She made her way straight towards Pepelito, licking his face and neck, mooing happily. A little smaller than him, her horns were thinner and curved upwards. He didn't look at Chicero, or the humans, or the cows trotting to greet Maribel – his focus was only on her.

'He stopped a serial killer. He's a hero. Doesn't he deserve to get the girl?' Roberto laughed, holding hands with Dominguez, who looked faintly horrified.

'Oh, that's a pretty one – she clearly likes him. What's her name?' Rita said, shutting the gate.

'Tulipan,' Roberto said. She turned around and mooed. 'She was so tiny when she was born, I had to bottle feed her. She's beautiful, right?'

'Pepelito clearly thinks so.' Rita and the others laughed.

Chicero stood beside a black cow with no horns. They tenderly brushed noses together, bees landing on the flowers around them.

Happy and free.

Pepelito shut his eyes, enjoying Tulipan's gentle licks. They had all the time in the world to get to know each other. This was all he wanted to do; enjoy fresh grass and clean water, play with his friends, meet nice cows and have a relaxing sleep. He didn't have to be brave. He didn't have to be especially friendly. He didn't have to be anything special at all.

He could just be a bull.

That was all he'd ever wanted anyway.

THE END

Author's note

I was 'inspired' to write this book after researching an article for the Ungagged Collective about politicians involved with bullfighting. Some details were so distressing that telling this story through fiction, with a happier outcome for the bulls, was a catharsis. Some of the quotes by villains are things bullfighting aficionados have said in their own literature.

While researching the book, I read an article by an aficionado which stated, 'if a story about bullfighting was written today, it would be extremely negative and judgemental'. However, I did not manage to find any stories like this, so I thought I would write one myself.

Unfortunately, as far as possible, I based this book on facts. The horrifying details of the drowning bull at Denia and the 'black banderillas' used to torture 'cowardly' bulls that won't charge, are unfortunately true. They are also deprived of water and food, kept in tiny dark boxes and mistreated before the fight. In many cases, bulls also have their horns filed down, which causes pain and affects their ability to judge distance.

CAS International is a charity that not only campaigns against bullfighting and other cruel festivals with bulls, but has helped to ban these activities in some parts of the world. They also rescue these animals from abuse. Some of the proceeds from this book will be going to this cause.

It felt important to me to put Pepelito's story front and centre. I always wanted to write this book as a battle between good and evil rather than a conventional murder mystery. I hope that it worked, and I truly hope you enjoyed this book as much as I enjoyed writing it.

Thank you so much for reading.

Acknowledgements

Writing and editing this book has been a huge task and I am grateful to everyone who helped me along the way. Thanks so much to all the people who read and offered constructive feedback on the book on Wattpad, especially Joe, Deejay, Paul Jennings, -T-, John Shirey, AJ, Ellis, Marrion Wayne, EY Huff, s00gifted, Sarah Nana, Ron Sewell, Gary Jarvis, Maia, Tonya, Jon, Volana, Klara, Dennis, Amore O Diamanti, Gideon Easton, Julie Dove, Rebecca Batteur and Katrina Blackwood.

Plus, of course, Nisha who designed the cover, and Vann for editing it and providing valuable feedback.

Several friends read this book or extracts from it, or just offered moral support, especially Anne Berkeley, Jesse Sprague, CT Remchin, Buddy Hell, Natalie, Charlotte, Jim Jepps, V, Dalya, Wasim, Paul Cresswell, Emma Rock, John Attiwell, Emma Bickford, Amy, Debra, Akira and the members of the Oxford Writers' Circle. Thanks also to Jason Cohen for his advice on publishing and covers, and Gytha Lodge for her writing retreat and advice on marketing.

Estefania from CAS and the admin of the International Anti-Bullfighting Movement also read early drafts of this book and offered their support. Dominique Arizmendi from No Corrida helped with my research. The Ungagged Collective (https://www.leftungagged.org) who published my original piece on politicians and bullfighting also deserve a mention. I know I must have left several people out but please know I appreciate you all enormously.

Lastly, my family, Mum, Dad, Jess, Charlie and Rory have been a great support this year. Love you all lots.

Printed in Great Britain
by Amazon